# The Highway West

*A Journey into the Magical Heart of America*

Written By Jason Andrew

# Copyrights and Credits

ISBN: 978-0-9794221-2-6

Cover by Mark Henry

Editor: Jen "Loopy" Smith

Copy Editors: Lisa Andrew, Emilynn Henderson

# Acknowledgements

This novel is dedicated to the father I never knew, but inspired me throughout my life. You deserved better than to die in a robbery at a Zip n Go.

The genesis of this story was born on a family vacation with my Uncle Fred and Cousin Lisa to New Mexico, when I was nine years old or so. We traveled the back highways in the desert, seeking out every possible tourist trap in an old brown corvette. I remember the day we reached the Grand Canyon. I didn't see much of Uncle Fred after that vacation, but his kindness imprinted on me and there's a lot of him (along with my actual Uncle Marty) in the character of Martin Carver.

I stand on the shoulders of giants, and I want to thank those that helped or inspired me along the way; those special people that believed in me, and helped support me over the years: (listed in chronological order) Jan and Wayne Messer, Doug Houston, Michael Dyer, Chris Beron, Mario Medina, Lisa Andrew, Stephanie Williams, Lenza McBride, Robert Bennett, Jason Carl, Sean Mooney, Kerry Beckett, Evonne Traffanstedt, Jen "Loopy" Smith, Philip Jones, Ally Foxworthy, and Emilynn Henderson.

# Table of Contents

# *Chapter One: Never Going Back*

The blackbirds were always watching him. Nathan listened to their agitated caws under the warm shade of the citrus tree. It felt as though they were encouraging him to action, but it was way too hot for such nonsense. Cruel bright blue skies offered no clouds for shade or shelter from the sweltering sun.

He rested his bare feet in the irrigation trench that lined the farm allowing the cool ditch-water to cool him down. Pulling out a fat orange from his pocket, Nathan jabbed his pocket knife into the peel. Thin fingers peeled back the skin. The boy pulled the fruit in half and greedily gobbled each piece until sweet-sour juice dripped down his lips. The wash of relief was brief, but welcomed.

The power had gone out in the bunkhouse, and with it the refrigerator and the washing machine. He washed his hands, soaked his worn t-shirt in the water, and then slipped it on over his head, simultaneously shivering and aching from the heat, and then stood to return to the grape fields. Nathan kept himself from staring at the long winding dirt road that led to the main road. *She'll come back for me*, he told himself silently. He believed it less and less each time it came to his mind.

He walked back to the house and then emptied the dog's water bucket into the irrigation trenches, and washed out the film of slimy green-black algae that collected around the edges in the Fresno heat. The large, bulbous brown head of a droopy-eyed bulldog timidly peeked around the oak tree. She stepped away from the tree, dragging the rusty chain that bound her to the yard. It had wrapped so often around the trunk that the metal had slowly scraped away the bark.

"Don't be that way, Gertie." He refilled the bucket and hefted it back under the shade. She huffed lightly, keeping her head and ears down low. He knelt down and cradled her head. "I'm sorry, Gertie. I won't do it again. The whispers just scared me, you know?"

She gingerly licked his hand. He tried not to imagine tears in her eyes. The boy hugged her close. You have to forgive the ones you love no matter how terrible they treat you. "I don't know what I would do without you."

Gertie wiggled her stub-tail fervently. The rhythm of her heavy breathing and occasional snorts were soothing to the boy. He unlocked the chain and Gertie galloped into the field. Nathan gripped tightly on the chain, jogging double-time to keep up with her. She leapt joyfully into the murky ditchwater and rolled onto her side. He scratched behind her head. "Let's get you fed."

Nathan opened the door to the porch and found the sealed fifty-pound bag of gourmet dog food. *Your pooch will love our real steak flavor!* Smirking, he scooped several cups of the dry bits, and then mixed it with a can of moist food that smelled of beans and mushroom. "At least she thought about you before she left."

Holding the bowl like a French waiter, the boy bowed to Gertie presenting her meal. "Only zee best for you, Madame Gertie!"

She nearly choked trying to gobble the meal. The boy quietly went to the shed and pulled out his shovel. He dug a small hole outside the field to bury the gopher. The blackbirds cawed above his head, perhaps angry they were denied a meal.

When he finally returned to the bunkhouse, he noticed the familiar and comfortable buzz of the fluorescent bulbs and the motor of the old refrigerator. "We have power, Gertie!"

He washed his hands and feet at the outside faucet, and then carefully stepped onto the porch. Nathan opened the freezer door and enjoyed the wash of cold air over his face. The first order of business was to refill the water jug. Cold water eased the summer days. Next, he needed to inventory his food. The power had been out for over a day, so he wasn't sure what he could trust in the refrigerator.

He had kept some of the cans and jars in the trench to keep them cool. The canned jelly looked good, but the TV Dinners felt warm. The milk smelled a bit funny, but he figured he could thin it out a bit with water and he only had enough for two, maybe three, bowls of cereal.

Wistfully, Nathan tossed two empty pizza boxes into the garbage pile. Did she know that she would be gone so long? Was that why she bought the two extra-larges for just the two of them? It wasn't uncommon for him to sleep alone in the bunkhouse. His mother often took extended trips overnight, but she always returned sometime the next day.

Nathan ate a bowl of cereal, and then visited the woodpile. Selecting a few sturdy planks, he prepared the tool shed. He had never cut anything with the saw before, but he had seen his grandfather use similar tools to cut pipes many times. It took several tries before he learned the proper way to shape the wood. It wasn't until after his short lunch break and half-eaten peanut butter and grape-jelly sandwich that he finally succeeded at building a passable sword.

"Come on, Gertie! We have to defend the house."

Together, they fought the evil twin of Errol Flynn, battled massive robots from the year 3000 and resisted living shadows from the Land of Dread. The day passed quickly, and it wasn't until the skies began to darken that Nathan remembered he was still waiting for his mother.

He took hold of Gertie's leash and paced up and down the rows of grapevines. He told himself that his mother would return once he finished his circuit, and that everything else was just his imagination.

A pair of lights flashed on the road far, far from the ranch. He darted down to the dirt driveway, heart racing. The lights turned down the street and faded into black. A soft rustling of long grass and leaves put Gertie on alert. She barked at the darkness. "Something there?"

Gertie yelped fearfully. Nathan had seen the dog attack a small truck just because she felt ornery that day. What could scare her so easily? He swallowed nervously, but knew he had to look. A fearsome shape, seen only as a brief flicker, slowly crept toward him in the black of the night. It reached out with what Nathan could only assume to be vicious talons towards him seeking to touch him.

His skin prickled as the shadow caressed his arm. It felt like ice cutting his skin. Somehow Nathan yanked his body away stepping back wildly, trying to drive it back with his wooden sword. The shadow merely watched and waited patiently like a spider for him to run.

The wind picked up, rustling the trees around them, sounding like a chorus of voices singing in a language Nathan had never imagined. He had never heard them so clearly before. Nathan gripped his sword, stepping back. It might only be made from broken plywood, but it was all that he had.

His stomach twitched and burned as though his very blood had been mystically transmuted into acid. Rapid heart palpitations banged deeply against his chest. He had to force himself to remember to breathe.

They backed away slowly, then raced to the safety of the light. The yellow moon illuminated the sky by the time he returned to the bunkhouse. If something was still out there, it stayed beyond the reach of the light. Nathan promised himself that he'd keep the light on until morning. He silently prayed that the power wouldn't go out again, and locked the doors.

What if something happened to his mother? What would happen to him? Where would he live? He tried to imagine staying with any of his relatives. Papa Ray was getting older, but would he appreciate the company again? Uncle Marty hadn't been heard from in months.

He resolved to give her one more day.

If only his father were still alive. He found his father's lighter and held it close to his chest. Nathan knew a special trick had been taught to him the day they put his father into the ground and it was the first sacred promise that he had ever made.

*     *     *     *

Scenery passed by the windshield in a series of colors; dark green changed to yellow and then brightened to orange. A sweet breeze that smelled of leaves and rain blew through the old brown 1977 Dodge Tradesman van. The details of the funeral flashed through his mind. Uncle Marty flashed a small grin. His mustache seemed to magnify any expression. "You hungry, Nate?" He didn't answer. Nathan let the hum of the engine and the base of the stereo wash over him in silence. "I imagine you haven't eaten anything since breakfast. I tell you what. There's a little greasy spoon around the bend a bit called Ruby's. It was your dad's favorite place in the entire world."

"His favorite place?"

Marty winked. "We must have stopped there a hundred times since we were kids. Best avocado burger in the state."

"Where are we?"

"We're pulling into Lemon Cove. Near Sequoia." He leaned a bit closer and stage-whispered. "We're gonna spread a bit of his ashes there."

"Why?"

"Some of the oldest trees in the entire world are there. That's where we found out the truth about everything."

"What truth?" Nathan asked.

"Your dad and I made a promise. One of these days when you're a bit older, I'm gonna bring you back here and teach you the way he taught me."

"And this promise is why we're taking some of his ashes here?"

"It's a good way of letting go and saying good-bye."

Marty turned the steering wheel and pulled the old van onto the gravel driveway. The old majestic sign that read *Ruby's* had burned out long ago, but there was something majestic about the sign. He imagined his father eating here.

His uncle fished out a lighter from his vest pocket and presented it to Nathan in the palm of his hand. "This lighter belonged to your father, son. Don't tell your mother, but it's yours now."

Nathan cautiously plucked the lighter from his Uncle's palm and examined it. "Why does he have a dog's head?"

"That's Saint Christopher. Patron saint of travelers and pilgrims. Bill and I bought a matching set on our first road trip." Marty rolled up his sleeve and showed off the tattoo on his right underarm. "When you live on the road, you take every bit of magic you can."

"Magic is just in stories."

Marty guffawed. "There's magic in the world, son."

Nathan frowned, skeptical. "Didn't do Dad any good."

"Sure it did. Did him a world of good. The bad doesn't take away from any of the good things we did. Those days are still there in our hearts."

"Then what good is magic?"

"Magic doesn't fix the world's problems. It makes it worth living in it." Marty leaned closer to Nathan to whisper a secret. "If I show you a trick, do you promise not to tell anyone? Not your mother? Especially not your grandparents?"

Nathan nodded. He liked magic tricks and somehow he sensed that this was important. "Will you teach me?"

"If you're clever like I think you are, you'll figure it out on your own."

Marty took back the lighter, opened it, and winked. He took a deep breath and Nathan felt a strange series of goose bumps along his arms and neck. Something was changing and Nathan could feel it all over his skin as goosebumps spread from his arms to his neck and all over his back. His uncle blew forth a spark of flame that connected to the lighter producing a small flame.

"You just spit fire!"

"There's magic in the world, Nate. You know it in your bones. Listen and the world can teach you great wonders."

"I don't hear anything."

"Give it time, kiddo. You'll be wanting a bit of peace before you know it. Let's have that burger."

*　　*　　*　　*

The bunkhouse only had one picture of Nathan's father. It was a candid Polaroid shot in front of an old Pit Stop convenience store taken a few years before the robbery featuring smiling group of proud looking men.

His father stood in the center, grinning wildly, with his arms wrapped around his Uncle Marty. Nathan tried very hard to remember his father, to like the unknowable man in the picture, with friends and a life he knew nothing about. He only recalled a kind voice reading stories and a pair of loving green eyes. It could have been anyone, he knew, but he needed it to be his father. He studied the picture for anything familiar. Was that his nose? His toothy grin? It might have been a dream, but it was one he needed.

He wondered where Marty was at that moment. He traveled the world with rock bands and experienced a number of amusing adventures according to his tall tales. His favorite was the wicked tale of the ghost of Mamie Thurman on 22 Mountain Road.

That night he drank the last of the colas, ate the last of the bread, and finished off the jelly. Gertie paced the house uneasily, and then often sniffed the wind and ran to one of the windows. She crouched low and growled. Nathan checked the yard. A shadow flickered on the edge of the porch light, then nothing but the unnatural silence that had swept over the fields.

He cuddled next to the dog and read until his thoughts were heavy and too tiring to process. Sleep did not come easy to him that night, and when it did, he woke easily. Gertie jumped often at what Nathan thought was the wind, until he heard minute scratching along the outside of the house. It moved from window to window across the house, bringing the strange sound closer and closer. Hushed whispers speaking gibbering inhuman languages surrounded the house. Gertie whimpered and then backed away from the window. Pulling the blanket over his head, Nathan closed his eyes.

The sharp scratching sound grew louder and more desperate. Trembling hands and clattering teeth overtook Nathan. He tried to keep quiet, despite his panic-filled breaths. "Go away. Please go away."

Silence.

He waited for several minutes in the dark. It felt like an hour. Slowly, he pulled off the blanket and peeked out the window. The yard was clear. He feverishly dragged his bedding to the large closet in his mother's room, and then beckoned Gertie to him.

One of Uncle Marty's stories had been about a ghost that he had banished using a circle of salt. They hunkered down for the rest of the night behind a protective line of table salt across the entrance. Nathan slept lightly, waking up often, hearing Gertie's snorts and appreciating the safety of the walls on all sides.

He woke early the next day, with Gertie licking his face. Curious, he dragged the dog around the house, looking for any sign of a coyote. Whatever had been outside of his window the night before had not left any tracks.

Nathan checked the phone for a dial tone, completed his routine, and then waited near the dirty road that led off the farm. Could he leave? He had three dollars in quarters and he remembered his grandparents' number. They lived two counties away, but that wasn't more than a couple hours drive. What would happen to Gertie? She would starve if he left her alone. How long was the walk? He hadn't left the farm much since the end of school, and even then, he had only recently moved there. How many miles away was the nearest phone?

He needed water. Nathan scrounged through the garbage until he found an empty two-liter cola bottle, washed it out, filled it with clean water, and left it in the refrigerator. Gertie and Nathan took one last pilgrimage around the farm. While the dog rested next to the swamp cooler, he gathered all of his favorite belongings. He collected his action figures, his comics, his father's old lighter that Uncle Marty had secretly given him, and the faded photograph, and carefully pressed them all into his pack.

That night, he listened to *Fleetwood Mac* before attempting to sleep in the closet. It was his mother's favorite album, and somehow he found it important to feel close to her. The shadow did not venture close to the house, but it made itself known on occasion via the whispers. Small fragments from the whispers slowly became intelligible. *Leave, boy.*

The flickering light did not instill Nathan with confidence. He didn't sleep until very late in the evening.

The next morning, Nathan fed Gertie as usual, and then prepared for his trip. He ate dry cereal, then locked the shed. With the chilled bottle of water in hand, and the wooden sword tucked under his belt, he unlocked Gertie's leash and started down the dirt road. He thought of the characters in the book he was reading. They were headed on a journey, as well, across an entire continent. If little people without shoes could throw a ring in a volcano, he could walk a couple of miles.

The pavement cooked the underside of his tennis shoes. Nathan made an effort to stick to the dirt on the side of the road. Gertie panted feverishly, but wagged her stubby tail apparently to raise attempt to Nathan's spirits high. He dreamed of crossing the misty mountains with grumbling friends and wondered if his father had been afraid in the end — alone at that store.

Trucks occasionally passed them. Nathan and Gertie hid wherever they could find a spot. He wasn't exactly sure why, but it seemed like the thing to do.

The sun has risen to its zenith when he spotted the bright red sign for the Pit Stop. There were dozens of these stores spread throughout Fresno. The store where his father died was a long way away, but that didn't stop Nathan from worrying.

He reached the Pit Stop, and was surprised by his reflection in the windows. His face was dirty, his hair wild, uncombed for a week. He hadn't thought of such things when alone. He fumbled through his pockets, found the quarters. He dialed his grandparents. "Hello?"

"Papa Ray, it's me. Mom left and didn't come back."

"Left? Left when?" His voice was angry.

Nathan, worried about his mother. "Friday."

"Son, its Thursday. Where are you now?"

"At the Pit Stop. There's an address here."

"Read me the address and wait there."

The clerk eventually came outside and offered Nathan a sandwich and a bowl of water for Gertie. "I don't have any money."

"Your grandfather will pay when he gets here. You want to come inside for a while. I can give you some quarters to play Space Invaders."

He looked young, Nathan thought. "Can I bring in Gertie?"

The clerk smiled uneasy. "She can stay right there. We'll give her plenty of water. Don't want to get in trouble with the boss."

Nathan ate the sandwich, but secretly gave half to the dog. He later took the clerk up on his offer to play Space Invaders. It felt good to shoot down the pixel aliens. He tried to lose his thoughts in the game.

Papa Ray arrived much sooner than Nathan expected. He wore a forced smile on his dark, gentle face. The old man had spent countless hours in the sun and if Nathan had to describe him, he'd use the word swarthy. He found the word in one of his old adventure paperbacks, describing men from a far away desert land. Somehow, it reminded Nathan of his grandfather and the stories of his time in the army.

Nathan climbed into the old truck quietly. Gertie jumped in the back. "We'll get the rest of your things, and then go back to the ranch. We'll figure out what's what then." Nathan resisted the urge to cry. "Don't you worry, Nate. I'm sure she's fine."

He didn't reply. Miles went by in silence. Had he imagined everything at the farm just to build up enough courage to leave? Would the shadow follow him?

"Your mother is sick, son. She can't help the things she does. That's not on you."

Nathan looked out the window in silence. He understood what the old man was trying to tell him. You have to forgive the ones you love, no matter how terrible they treat you.

# Chapter Two: The Terror of Knowing

Nathan Carver hefted the fifty-pound bag and poured the kibble into the trough. It was his job to feed the dogs every morning, but ever since Gertie died a few years back, he lost his patience for it. The hollow sound of food poured into their bowls brought forth all of the dogs on the ranch. It was strange to see her features echoed in her puppies that had long grown into adulthood.

He carefully looked both ways before reaching into his jeans' pocket and produced a silver-plated oil lighter that had been engraved with a man with a sad dog's head carrying a blessed child with a halo. It belonged to his father and the only reason that his grandmother allowed him to keep it as a boy was that it carried the mark of Saint Christopher.

He reached under the trough and found the creased pack of Pall Malls just where Papa Ray stashed it. Nathan didn't normally smoke, but he had felt an itching along his skin all night. Graduation was only a few days away and then if he was lucky he could leave the farmland ghetto of Sanger forever. This ranch might have been paradise on earth to a farmer or a hippy wanting to get back to nature. To Nathan, it was just a reminder of the years of isolation away from the city and everything else he wanted to see in the world. He was more than ready for college and a chance to start his real life. Of course, that depended on if he could withstand the stress of finals and avoid getting caught smoking. Eighteen or not, Nathan was fairly convinced that his sixty-year old grandmother could and would take him with a kitchen knife if she caught a whiff of smoke on him.

He flicked the lighter three times, frustrated. The morning wind quickly extinguished any spark or flame. Nathan snuck a last look around him, before attempting the unthinkable. The main house was a beautiful old-world style house with a large porch and two pillars supporting the second floor. There had been many repairs over the years that didn't quite blend together. This house would never grace the cover of a magazine, but it had been well loved by those that lived there. Seemingly endless rows of citrus trees surrounded the house on three sides delineated by irrigation ditches. The front yard doubled as a fenced-in pasture for the small herd of cattle.

He was positioned between the house, the old willow tree, and the barn. The willow was crowded with a watchful flock of blackbirds. His presence was blocked from the line of sight of the kitchen windows, but that left him vulnerable to the morning wind and the very rare summer rain storm. Checking the sides of the house once more, he placed a cigarette behind his ear.

Nathan Carver knew a trick that he had never shared with anyone due to a promise. He held his breath and concentrated imagining that the very air in his mouth had changed. When he couldn't stand it any longer and his lungs hurt from the effort, Nathan blew over the lighter and flicked it once more producing a prodigious flame. He quickly popped the cigarette into his mouth, lit the end, and then puffed until the soothing buzz of nicotine hit his lungs.

The blackbirds cawed excitedly. He had never told his grandparents about his magic trick or what happened the week that his mother abandoned him. It was too close to an unreal nightmare and to speak of it aloud would give it a reality he wasn't prepared to accept. Besides, his grandmother clearly wouldn't approve of such nonsense.

It was early enough that he could almost see the faint outline of the moon and stars, but the bright rays of the dawn lit the horizon. The air was brisk, but invigorating when combined with the warm smoke coursing through his lungs. It had been years since he had seen his uncle. He yawned sleepily until he noticed the soft rumbling in the distance.

Twin lights shined in the distance towards the house. The gravel road turned sharply to avoid a ditch and two tree trunks. The vehicle was taking the curves on the dirt road tightly. Who would be visiting the ranch this early? Was that a van? Was it possible?

The old brown 1977 Dodge Tradesman van slid to a stop just short of the old willow tree. A familiar face with a wry grin greeted him through the dirty windshield and when he spoke it was with a voice that suffered years of abuse from cigarettes and whiskey. "You ok, kid? You look like you've seen a ghost."

Nathan blinked surprised by the arrival of his Uncle Marty. His skin was tanned and hardened like a leather jacket worn in the rain, but the familiar smile remained. Marty's long dirty brown hair had turned grey and now he kept it tied back into a neat ponytail. He had a large, thick mustache, which had always been a point of pride to his uncle. "That's funny." Nathan folded his arms. "You look like you died."

Marty Carver slid out of the van and stretched a bit. Nathan noticed there were a number of new tattoos on his uncle's arms.

Strange symbols written in a squiggly script and circles overlapped the old familiar Saint Christopher. He seemed to have aged decades since last they had been together. "Not yet, but give me enough time and anything can happen. How are you doing? You're just about the graduate right?"

"In just a couple of days," Nathan replied tersely.

"How have you been? Do you have a girlfriend? I bet you do. Just like your old man!"

"Her name is Phoebe." That wasn't strictly true. They had broken-up a couple weeks previous, but he wasn't quite ready to admit it. Marty hadn't earned that sort of familiarity. After the last time he visited, Grandma Loni almost cried for what seemed to be a month. It was a week before she changed out of her robes and left her bedroom. "What are you doing here, Marty?"

His uncle shrugged his shoulders slyly and tilted his head in a gesture that seemed to suggest contrition and also to playfully ask if Nathan could blame him for trying. "Can't a man see his brother's only son?"

"After five years? Seems a bit odd." Nathan turned away from his uncle and put out the cigarette in the dirt with his shoe. He picked up the smashed butt and slipped it into the cigarette package and then put it in his pocket. "They can't give you any money. Money is tight around here."

"I'm not here for money, son," Marty stated, waving away any concern with a flick of his wrist as though he were a barker on a sideshow.

Nathan grit his teeth. "My father died on Halloween chasing pumpkin thieves." There was a lot more anger in his voice than he intended. His cheeks felt like they burned with rage. Why did it still hurt after all of this time? "You are not my father."

"That's right. I'm your father's brother. His best friend." Marty opened his arms wide, hoping for a hug, and smiled. "Speaking of which, since when do you meet your favorite uncle and not give him a hug."

How did he always manage to sucker them into letting him back into their hearts? Nathan shook his head and then reluctantly embraced the old man. "For the record, Wayne's my favorite uncle."

"Since when?"

"Well, he gave me a job at the gas station. And he hasn't disappeared the last few years without a word."

"Grandma let you work there?"

"Money is tight right now," Nathan said and then added almost as an afterthought. Would Marty try to scam money off him? How low would he go? "And I'm saving money for school."

"Well there is that I suppose. Just surprised she lets you out of her sight." Marty pulled his nephew closer and sniffed. "Ugh! When did you start smoking? And Pall Malls? Can't you afford something decent at least?"

Nathan blushed and dropped the hug. "Use to have to steal them from Papa. And only every once in a while. Helps calm me down."

The blackbirds cawed and then took flight circling the ranch in a pattern known only to them. "Jeez, there are a lot of them around these days?"

Nathan shrugged, scratching his forearms. "All my life. No big deal."

"Skin itching? Hearing things? That used to happen to Bill back in the day. Drink root beer." Marty caught the skeptical look in his nephew's eyes. "No really, I'm serious. Something about the carbonation helps. Not as good as smoking, but then you aren't killing yourself."

Somehow Marty managed to do everything wrong and still look distinguished. "Never seemed to hurt you," Nathan complained.

Marty lifted his arm, rolled up the sleeve and pointed to the round grey patch near his shoulder. "Let's just say it never helped my singing voice."

"Just don't tell Grandma about my smoking," Nathan pleaded. "I want to live to see my next birthday."

"I doubt she'll give me the chance. I'm expecting a beating with a frying pan if I'm lucky."

Nathan nodded, showing the first signs of sympathy for his uncle. Grandma Loni had a natural Italian temper that could match an active volcano. "I'll speak kindly at your funeral."

"I'd expect at least that much after all I've done for ya," Marty said with a faux-offended expression.

Nathan scratched his head, confused. "I haven't seen you in five years. I love you and all, but what have you done for me?"

Marty grinned like a snake-oil salesman and placed his hands inside of his vest's pockets. "Well, I've been a bit busy ensuring your inheritance, son."

Nathan groaned. There was a bit of unease in his stomach as he prepared his sales resistance to whatever con his uncle planned to pedal. "Look, I've been through hell this week. I've been working nights plus pulling a full school schedule. I'm tired and I don't have time for a con."

The old man scoffed gently, but his mustache twitched just a bit. Did he really feel regret for the past? "You've been listening to the folks a bit too much. You think I'm here to con you, boy? I went through a lot of trouble to get here. I left a big tittied woman in Tallahassee to make it here. I did it because I made a promise to Bill."

Nathan resisted the urge to shake his uncle. He hated that undeserved smug I know better than you expression. "So you've said. You've never bothered to actually tell me what that promise was."

"I told you the day we buried your father." There was a strange tint of somber sorrow in Marty's voice, something that rarely happened. "There's magic in the world and now I'm going to show you the truth of it."

"Marty, I graduate in three days. I have three months to make enough money for school in the fall." All of the frustration and the waiting seemed to flush straight to his face. He felt like his head could explode from the stress. "I don't have time for stories."

Marty tugged on his vest and smirked. "I suppose if you'd rather work, that's fair enough. But I'd think you'd want to use the money Bill set aside for ya to go to school."

The mention of his father and the money wasted by his mother during her benders set his teeth on edge. "Marty, you know my mom put everything my dad saved up her nose."

"Not every thing of value can be measured in terms of the o' mighty dollar." Marty waved all around the ranch. "This bit of paradise could bring the folks a pretty penny, but they love this place. Brings them more peace than money can buy."

"That doesn't get me to school. And we're not selling their dream to buy mine." A bit of bravado returned to Nathan's voice. The idea of living without a net in another state scared the shit out of him, but somehow he knew he would make it happen. "I'll make my own way through school. I don't care if I have to scrub toilets or dig ditches."

"There's plenty of money for school, Nate. Bill left his mark in the world. We just need to collect the inheritance." He leaned close and then whispered as though sharing an important secret. "And if you are smart enough, we could pay off a fair share of the mortgage on this old place."

"How's that?" Nathan asked

"First, we eat breakfast." Marty rubbed his stomach and licked his lips. "Grandma makes the best pancakes in the world. Believe me, I've been to a good share of it and nothing has ever come close."

He followed his uncle around to the front porch of the house. Marty stopped for a moment to glance up at the house he had shared during his childhood. Knocking twice awkwardly, he opened the door and stepped inside only to be confronted with the hall of honor. Photographs of the Carver family from the past century lined the walls in colors ranging from crisp and new to faded browns and reds, to stark black and white. Nathan wasn't quite sure how many generations the walls covered. Many of the older photographs had only a name and a date on the back to mark their place in history.

Nathan had studied many of the pictures on that wall over the years. His favorite was a picture of Papa Ray as a young man in the army with his friends in London. It was difficult to imagine his grandfather as a young man, just a little older than he was now, fighting in a terrible war and watching his friends die. Papa Ray rarely spoke about his experiences in the war. For his senior project, Nathan scanned all of the photographs and newspaper articles that Grandma Loni had saved over the years and created a memory book.

He remembered the day he presented a copy to Papa Ray and the afternoon they shared on the couch. It was the only time that his grandfather discussed the war and after that he would only say that he missed the friends that he had endured such terror with.

Marty's eyes stopped at the photo of Bill and Marty together as young men. Nathan waited understanding that his uncle's eyes watered due to being lost in old memories. He had never thought to consider what losing a brother might feel like. "Mom?"

Nathan turned into the kitchen surprised Grandma Loni was already busy cooking. She had already prepared a skillet of scrambled eggs, a plate of bacon, a stack of pancakes. "Is he here?"

Marty knocked on the door to the kitchen and let himself in. "Mom! Dad!"

The lack of surprise on his grandmother's face concerned Nathan. Papa Ray put down the paper and sipped his coffee. "Good to see you, Martin."

Grandma Loni was a short Italian woman with sparkling blue eyes that still dyed her hair blond well into her fifties. She had the rare bit of class and sass that made the perfect lady and a terrifying parental figure. Marty bent down to accept her hug and kiss on his cheek. "Five years!"

"I know, Mom. But it's been important."

She leaned up on her toes and cuffed him on the back of the head. Her voice turned angry like one of those mobsters in the old movies before they whacked one of their best friends. "Nothing is more important than a phone call to your mother."

"At least she didn't use the frying pan," Nathan added wryly.

Grandma Loni held up two fingers and gestured towards her grandson. "Don't think you won't be next!"

Nathan resisted the urge to smile, knowing that if he did that Grandma Loni wouldn't hesitate to make good on her threat. "Yes, ma'am."

"You two sit. Breakfast will be ready soon enough."

Nathan numbly followed Marty to sit at the table. How did they know he was coming to breakfast? Last time Marty visited, there had been a huge fight and he had left in the middle of the night. He hated being the only person in the room not in on the joke. Did someone die? "Can someone tell me what's going on?"

Papa Ray took another sip of his coffee. "We found a way to pay for school, Nathan."

Images of his grandparents moving from this place that they had lived most of their lives made Nathan want to puke. "We're not selling the ranch!"

Marty poured himself a cup of coffee and nodded. "There's no need, Nate. Bill socked away enough scratch to pay your way for a couple of years at the least."

Nathan looked to his grandparents hopefully. Would college be easier than he had dreaded? "I thought Mom blew it all before you guys took me in?"

Grandma Loni opened her mouth to comment, but Papa Ray coughed cutting her off. "It turns out Bill managed to save some money. Marty's been adding to the fund over the years."

He turned towards his uncle in surprise and found it difficult to believe that he could have been so fiscally responsible. Marty winked. "Who's your favorite uncle now?"

"I don't understand. Why?"

"I told you, son. I made a promise. But there's a catch."

Would his school be paid for? Nathan looked to his grandparents? They had looked after him for the last six years better than any parents could have. Did they believe Marty? "What's the catch?"

"You have to take a trip with Martin to get the money." Grandma Loni answered. It was clear this was not a situation that met with her approval. "If Marty's not satisfied, you won't get the money."

"What? That's crazy." Nathan scowled. This had to be some sort of trick. "Why didn't we get the money before? Why would Dad do something like that?"

Grandma Loni brought breakfast to the table and returned to the kitchen. Her face was flushed and he knew that she was resisting the urge to cry. Nathan hated it when Grandma cried. On occasion, she would have one too many beers and cry over her dead son. His father's death affected so many people that it was like hearing a bunch of people discuss a movie he had never seen, but now he knew everything by heart. Nathan heard the same stories so often that it felt like he was there.

Marty took a strip of bacon and gobbled it. "That's delicious, Mom." He gulped his coffee and then turned to his nephew. "I made a promise to Bill. A blood promise between brothers. We're family and we take care of each other."

There was a certain appeal to a guilt-free summer vacation with Marty. "But I promised Papa Ray I'd help out around the ranch this summer."

"Sounds like someone has a girlfriend they don't want to leave," Marty muttered playfully under his breath.

Grandma Loni nodded approvingly. "A very nice girl."

"Grandma, I broke-up with Phoebe weeks ago," Nathan protested. "I'm just worried about you guys."

"Nathan, we'll manage. You getting the money for school is more important to your grandmother and me than anything else."

"And that's all I have to do? Take a road trip with you?" Nathan asked suspiciously.

"Same route your dad and I took twenty years ago. You want to be a writer, don't ya?" Marty smirked a bit. It was one of those big shit-eating grins that made Nathan want to punch him in the nose. "How are you gonna learn to tell stories if you don't live a little?"

"And this is legit?" Nathan asked his grandparents.

Papa Ray nodded, uncomfortably. "We talked to a lawyer yesterday by the name of Remington Borri from Seattle. Looks like there's enough there for your schooling and a little extra to get you started."

"How long is the trip?"

"As long as it takes. Afterwards, you'll have enough scratch to go wherever you want. If you still want to go to school."

"You don't have to go, Nathan. We can find another way." There was fear in Grandma Loni's voice and it set him on edge. She knew something that she wasn't sharing. "Community college for a year and then we can get loans."

Marty shrugged. "Or you can come with me once you graduate and learn about the old man."

"You have three days to decide, Nathan. Finish breakfast and I'll drive you to school."

Marty gulped down a swallow of his pancakes. "I can take him, Dad. We have a bit to discuss."

Nathan looked uneasily at his grandparents. "I don't mind, Grandma."

Grandma Loni muttered quietly in the kitchen and then returned to the living room with a pitcher of orange juice. "You best finish here and then get to it. Don't want to be late the last week of school."

They finished breakfast listening to Marty spin tales of strange cities and interesting places in far-away lands. Grandma Loni reminded them again of the time. Nathan rushed to collect his backpack and kissed her on the cheek goodbye. He hugged Papa Ray and then met Marty outside at the van. "You know, this is my last trip, Nate. My passing of the torch as it were. If you come with me, this van will be yours. I won't need it anymore."

Nathan resisted the urge to laugh. The old van looked as though it had seen far better days. He imagined trying to impress any girl while driving this old piece of crap. "Thanks for the thought."

"This old van has seen a lot of road." Marty's face flushed with pride. "She has heart and won't let you down."

"Things can't have a heart." Nathan opened the side door and climbed into the passenger's seat. "I know you've been on the road a long time, but you have to be actually alive to have a heart."

"We leave a piece of ourselves every place we go, kid." Marty rubbed the leather dashboard. "This old girl has a lot of me and your old man inside her. I'm getting on in years. With any luck, you'll see a few miles in it."

"You aren't that old, Marty."

"It's not my age. It's where I've been. What I've seen."

Nathan laughed nervously. "Are you trying to scare me again with one of your ghost stories?"

Marty reached behind the front seats, opened a large seat compartment, and produced a small wooden box inscribed with a number of strange runes and exotic letters in a foreign-looking script. Papa Ray spent a lot of time working wood with Nathan. He never had the talent, but he enjoyed watching him and appreciated craftsmanship. Someone had spent a lot of time and effort on this box. "What's this?"

Marty smiled. It was a smile honed to perfection and used to beguile many. Nathan imagined him conning people all over the country with that smile. He had heard a lot of stories about Marty while growing up on the ranch. "Magic."

"Right here in this box? Real magic?"

Marty looked at the box and then glanced over at Nathan. "You think so? There's no real magic? You learned the trick, didn't you? I can smell it on you."

"That's just a trick. Not real magic. The only magic we have is what we make."

Marty nodded, approvingly. Nathan hated being lectured to and he felt like he was stuck in a class he never agreed to take. "I think you know a lot more than you realize, Nate. Took me years to figure that out."

"So what's in the box?"

Marty winked, mischievously. "Magic."

"Are you going to pull a rabbit out of it or what? This trip is going to have a lot of head games, isn't it?"

Marty put the wooden box back into the trunk. "Of a heroic and epic nature, I assure you. But you don't seem ready for what's in the box just yet. Maybe you will be later."

The numerous cautionary tales often told about Marty came to mind as Nathan blurted out, "I'm not into weed. I've seen too many burnouts to feel comfortable."

"You think we're going to be running drugs?" Marty looked hurt like Nathan had just kicked him. "Really? I risked a frying pan to the noggin for that?"

"I've heard enough stories about you. You're a legend on the ranch."

"Yeah, I bet you've heard some stories." Marty visibly flinched and Nathan felt horrible. "I could tell you even worse ones. You don't trust me. And you don't have to. I'm here because of a promise. I'm here to present you with a question. It's up to you to find the answer."

Nathan took a deep breath. His head hurt. He imagined eating out of dumpsters the entire summer. "Look, I'm not trying to be rude. You popped back into my life after who knows how long and ask me to trust you and then to drive around for some unexplained reason. You won't tell me where we're going or why. This is crazy!"

Marty stopped him short with a single question. "Don't you think they are worth it? I know I put them through Hell and I'd do anything for a chance to pay them back."

Nathan thought of the sacrifices that his grandparents had made to raise him. It couldn't have been easy to be responsible for him into their golden years. What would he have done on that horrible day at the Pit-Stop without them? What would his life had been like if they hadn't rescued him from abandonment? "Can we really pay off the mortgage?"

"Enough that the folks can take it easy for their last couple of years. Not that they will mind you." Marty laughed ruefully. "You're handling this better than I expected. It's difficult for someone to surrender themselves to the wind. Especially someone like you. You like to be in control. But life's not about control."

"It's also not about jumping blindly without knowing what you are doing," Nathan added.

"That's your grandfather talking. And, as much as I hate to say it, he's rarely wrong. You want to know what's going on and why your dad set all of this up, don't you?"

Nathan nodded. "I'm willing to play along, but you have to be straight with me if you want me to trust you."

Marty dropped his smile. There was a hint of danger in his eyes. Nathan wondered what dark things his uncle had seen to have such a look and for the first time Nathan realized that Marty was a dangerous man. "We're going to take the Highway West." He started up the van and it made a soft growl like a lion calling his pride.

"What's the Highway West?" Nathan asked, curious.

His uncle's voice quivered just a bit as though he were about to tell the most important secret in the entire world. "It's a bit of a metaphor. A spiritual walkabout. When your father was nineteen, he and I took a trip. It was after his first year of college and he wanted a chance to see the world. I just wanted an excuse to spend some time with my big brother and maybe score some dope."

Most of what Nathan knew about his father came from stories from Grandma Loni and Papa Ray. Most of that involved cautionary tales about the dangers of sex, drugs, and booze. Both of them loved Nathan as much as they loved their own children. He couldn't imagine growing up anyplace with more love or guidance. There was also grief. Each year, he looked more and more like the son that had died. They grieved more over his death than Nathan. He rarely liked to talk about his father with them. "So what happened?"

"We found magic, terror, and wonder. We found things that changed us forever."

"There's not an actual Highway West, is there? I've never heard of it."

"Don't you listen to the classics?" Marty asked, a bit annoyed. "The Highway West is from a song called *The End* by the Doors. Besides, just because you haven't heard of something before now doesn't mean that it doesn't exist."

"I recall the song. Lots of weird shit in it." Nathan shook his head and then added wryly. "I don't want to kill my father or sleep with my mother, I promise."

"We named the route the Highway West," Marty explained. "There's a lot you don't realize about our family. Our family crossed the Atlantic on the Mayflower. The Carver family has this land in our blood. We have magic in our blood going back generations and generations. That's what we have between us. Blood."

"And Papa Ray doesn't know?" Nathan asked skeptically.

"He knows more than you think. You ever heard the story about his grandmother and how she married his grandfather?"

Nathan smiled a bit remembering the familiar romantic family story. "That was my favorite story growing up! I used to make Papa Ray tell me that story all the time. His grandmother was an Indian

Princess named Eurias, the pride of the Cherokee tribe until Douglass Carver wooed her away and they moved alone to California with nothing but the clothes on their backs."

Marty nodded, hearing the summary of the familiar family story. "There's a funny bit that Papa Ray doesn't tell, but Grandma Loni knows. Indians don't have princesses, Nate. That's only in the movies."

"I don't understand."

"Papa Ray's grandparents moved to California from back east. Back then, if your skin was too dark, it worked against you," Marty explained. "Hard to get a job or a loan for the house."

"What do you mean?" Nathan asked.

"When you get home, look at the pictures on the wall. 'Indian Princess' was a polite way of saying mulatto." Marty grinned a bit. "What I'm saying is that the Carver family ain't so lily white. Look at Pappa Ray and think about that. That's not all tan, Nathan."

"Grandma Loni knows?"

"She's from back east and Italian. She knows. Some stories are just agreed-upon lies. Just like they ignored some of the things that happened when Bill and I were growing up. You were smarter and hid things from them, didn't you?"

"I didn't want to worry them," Nathan admitted.

"We made a promise that we'd take our children on the same trip and teach them. I never had any and your father died way too early."

"So my dad decided to hide his money?"

"Some of that money your dad stashed away years ago. Some is compounded interest collected over nineteen years. Some of it I added when I was flush." Marty smiled again. Nathan was learning to distrust that smile. "He loved your mother but he knew that she was lousy with money. He wanted you to live a little on your own. He wanted you to become your own man. Think of it as a rite of passage."

"A rite of passage? Aren't I a little old for a rite of passage?"

"The journey is important. Way back in the day, a father would take his son on a trip. The son would learn the lessons of manhood there and the father would pass along whatever wisdom he had. You have potential."

The dreaded word used by teachers and councilors and grandparents his entire life. "I hate that word."

"I imagine that you've heard it all your life. You were smart, even as a baby. It's possible you have the touch, like your father."

Nathan groaned. "If you call me the chosen one, I'm leaving right now."

Marty laughed. It was hollow and bitter. "No one is ever chosen. All we have is potential."

"Potential for what?" Nathan asked.

The old van pulled into the Sanger High School parking lot and stopped at the front steps. Marty answered the question with a single word as though it would answer any questions that Nathan might conceive of asking. "Magic.

# Chapter Three: Children of Tomorrow

Raisins were always a portent of dark times for Nathan Carver. He had popped into the cafeteria early during his lunch period for cereal hoping for a quick sugar boost before the rest of his finals of the day. Grandma Loni never approved of store-bought cereal and so he often ate it for lunch. He was quite horrified to discover that the only cereal left was generic raisin bran cereal. As a young boy, Nathan had loved raisins. Grandma Loni considered them a healthy snack and so he ate them in his cereal, his muffins, cookies, and sometimes sprinkled into peanut butter and jelly sandwiches. His love for them ended on a scorching summer day just a few weeks after Nathan started living with them.

He was napping in Papa Ray's red pickup truck while on the way home from dropping off the newspapers at the recycling center. It was a long, hot trip and the soft vibrations of the truck had lulled him to sleep. The truck slowed to a stop and the hypnotic rumble died. Nathan woke to find his head slick with sweat and stuck to the plastic seat.

Dazzled, he sat up and rubbed his eyes. He spotted several police cars, a fire truck, and a black hearse with the state of California symbol decaled on the side. The various vehicles were parked haphazardly alongside of the road. "What's going on, Papa?"

"Well hello, Sleepyhead," Papa Ray said warmly. "You have a good nap?"

Nathan peered over the side of the door with his nose pressed against the glass. His heart beat very fast, like Christmas morning, to see dozens of men in uniform scrabble through the field looking for clues. There were cops, firemen, ambulance drivers, and worried men in dark suits. It was like watching an action movie only he couldn't hear the men talk. "Was there some sort of fire?"

"Don't know yet, Nate." Papa Ray patted his grandson on the head with a comforting smile. "I'm sure it's nothing. We might be here a while so try to sleep."

Papa Ray rolled down the window, popped a cigarette into his mouth and then lit it with the truck lighter. He wasn't supposed to smoke, so he only indulged on trips when Grandma couldn't catch him. "They look upset, Papa."

A shrill whistle caught their attention and a friendly-faced man in a dark sheriff's uniform waved them to the side of the road. He had a shaggy brown monk's crown of hair around his head and a thick mustache. The sheriff walked around the front of the truck to the driver's window. "Hi there, Ray. Who is this young man?"

"Hullo John. This is my grandson." Papa Ray beamed with pride and couldn't help but pull him closer. "Nathan, this is Sheriff Messer."

"Hello, Sheriff," Nathan said, trying to put his best foot forward.

"What's the problem, John?"

The sheriff scoffed and his face soured. "One of the pickers found another severed hand. We figure it's just another Wetback that couldn't afford a funeral plot. We're gonna go plant him in the potter's field when we're done."

Nathan returned his gaze to the field. Dark-skinned Mexicans in orange jumpsuits with bandanas covering their mouths like banditos shoveled through the dry dirt of the fields over some old and tangled grape vines while a number of Caucasian cops watched lazily. A group of faceless men in strange gas-masks clad in bright green plastic protective suits gently lifted a short, bloated body into a black bag.

He had never seen a real dead body. There were hundreds of little details that the spooky, weekly Creature Feature movies glossed over. The leg had turned gray and the flesh seemed to be liquefying before his eyes. Was that a child? Nathan was very glad when the two men zipped the bag closed and removed the chance to know for certain.

Papa Ray pulled Nathan close, blocking his view. "Is there anything we can do, John?"

The cop grunted, understanding. "Nah. I'll signal the boys to let you through. The Wetbacks get so scared that we're going to deport them that sometimes they won't come to county services.

Papa Ray was fond of saying that it was quantity of a man's sweat not the color of his skin that mattered. He didn't tolerate such talk on his ranch, but Papa Ray didn't react as Nathan expected. He just nodded thoughtfully. "That's the third time this year, isn't it?"

"The fourth, actually."

Their words faded together into a numbing dissidence. All he could think about was that the raisins that he had been eating all of his life could have been grown from dead people.

He thought of that day every time he had to eat a raisin. Staring at the large plastic container filled to the brim with generic raisin bran,

Nathan wondered if this was going to be a sign for the rest of the day.

He walked from class to class in a haze. The halls seemed strange to him, disconnected and elongated, as though he had never belonged in this school. Nathan looked at the confused and distracted faces of his schoolmates and wondered if he had made proper connections with them. Were they his friends? Would he remember them in twenty years? He tried to imagine their futures and what would it mean if he went on the Highway West.

Nathan sat down in a daze, almost by routine, at his desk for the US history final. It was one of his favorite classes in no small part due to the teacher, Mr. Barrett. He glanced over the test very glad that he had managed to cram in a few extra hours of study. A small groan slipped out of a tall, gangly curly brown-haired boy as he banged his head against the desk.

Nathan snickered. "It's not that bad, Doug. We covered this. You can do it."

"Eyes front, Mr. Carver!" Mr. Barrett had long been a legend amongst the students due to his acerbic wit, amazing humor, and one unusual physical characteristic; he was missing his left hand. Nathan had heard he lost it during a war. The teacher often told wild tales explaining the absence of his hand. Naturally, he was a very popular teacher with the students. "I highly doubt that the test will take the full two hours to complete, and you and I have one last game. Honor is at stake Mr. Carver!"

The words and arguments came easily. He knew the concepts well enough, even if he occasionally forgot the exact dates. He was the first to finish, but the rest of the small class turned in their tests quickly and the real games began.

Mr. Barrett dazzled the class with his spectacular one-handed shuffling trick. "How did you do Mr. Houston?"

Doug grimaced. "I think I passed. I just don't think I got the point of the League of Nations question."

The old teacher raised an eyebrow with half-mocking concern. "Really? Perhaps then my duties are not quite yet over for the semester as I had thought. Do tell, Mr. Houston."

"It didn't work, did it?"

"Astute observation. I presume you can tell me why?"

"The countries weren't really willing to work together. They just wanted to punish Germany and get their own way. Right?" Doug answered.

"A limited, but essentially correct answer, Mr. Houston. Why the confusion then?" the teacher asked.

"You make it sound like a great achievement. It didn't stop anything. Just screwed things up even more."

Mr. Barrett pointed his stump directly at Nathan's face. "Mr. Carver, I'm in danger of drowning myself in the pond if I can't feel like I've made some sort of difference here. Can you enlighten us?"

He thought about the Highway West and the risks of the journey. "It's important to try, even if you fail, to build communities."

"Correct!" Mr. Barrett stood over the table and placed his hand on Doug. "Mr. Houston, there is a slim chance in this world that in a few scant weeks you'll have completed Boot Camp and will be serving this country. Do you think you'll win every battle?"

"I hope so. But probably not."

"You can learn from a defeat if you are wise enough to pay attention. And just because something fails, doesn't mean that it wasn't worth it to try."

Nathan felt like somehow Mr. Barrett could see into his very skull and read the conflict about his uncle. He accepted the cards from Mr. Barrett and dealt them half-heartedly. "Mr. Carver, do you realize what just happened?"

Nathan blinked, realizing that his teacher had been addressing him. "Sorry? What?"

Doug laughed. "He's been like that since Phoebe dumped him!"

Mr. Barrett ignored the side comment. "Do you see the hand you drew?" He gestured to the cards with his stump. "You drew the infamous aces and eight!"

"I don't understand," Nathan muttered.

"Aces and eights! The dead man's hand. Wild Bill Hickok's famous last hand at poker before he was killed in Deadwood by Jack McCall." Mr. Barrett lifted his stump to make his point. "History is more than dates to remember. History is really His Story. Little stories of men and woman that lived. That's where the magic really is. Remember that and you will go far."

Nathan blocked out the rest of the conversation and thought of the trip. Was this a sign? Was he going to die? He thought of all of his friends and people he barely knew and wondered if they worried about such things. He waited until the bell and then slowly meandered to his last class.

He had spent four years every day in this class surrounded by the words of the classics and inspiration in the form of the delightful Mrs. Strandberg. She was not beautiful by any magazine standard, but there was something about the way she carried herself and her smiling cheekbones he had always found appealing. Nathan could look at her face and believe in a world beyond the ranch; an exciting universe of beauty and possibility.

"Don't fret Nathan. Only one last test together."

He had almost forgotten about tests and graduation. "Looking forward to it."

"This should be a breeze then since you wrote a paper on it." She pulled her hair back over her shoulders and then started passing out the tests. "*Death of a Salesman.*"

He remembered sitting in this very classroom a year ago listening to the subtle words of Steinbeck when Nathan realized he wanted to be a writer. He studied harder than ever before to polish his words and learn how to craft a story. Mrs. Strandberg helped ignite that love and more importantly give him hope that it might be a future for him.

Nathan walked past his fellow students for the last time and handed in the test. Mrs. Strandberg leaned forward and whispered. "Are you feeling alright? You normally smile during writing tests."

"I have a bit on my mind," Nathan admitted.

"Do you want to talk about it after class? I have time." She smiled with the excitement of a young girl. "I'm already packed for my trip."

He felt silly standing there surprised as though he had completely forgotten that his teachers were real people with lives away from this school. "What trip?"

"Barcelona. I've always wanted to go."

"Why did you wait so long?" Nathan regretted the question almost as soon as he asked. "I mean why wait until now?"

"I was too afraid to go when I was your age. I wanted to tackle the world. Afraid I'd waste the time." She leaned close and whispered conspiratorially. "We writers take ourselves too seriously at that age. I wanted to be serious."

"My Uncle wants to take me on a trip." Nathan swallowed trying to figure out how much to tell her. "I'm trying to decide if I should go."

"Are you afraid?" Mrs. Strandberg asked.

He nodded dumbly. "More than I can say."

"Then do it." She adjusted a strand of her blond hair and grinned wryly. "We fall in love with the words and the stories and then it burns us when we try to force them to come out. A little adventure now and then is good for the soul and the muse. There's magic in the world, if we just know how to look for it."

*    *    *    *

Rays of light reflected through the dirty windows and trophy cases blinding him. Nathan slowly took the steps down through the main doors with a bit of trepidation as he finally admitted to himself that he felt something odd. There was a reason for the sleepless nights of worry and a small part of him had always known it. Conflicted between relief and anxiety, he scanned the parking lot.

Marty greeted him wearing a pair of old-fashioned aviator glasses and leaning against the old Tradesman van, which was noticeably parked in a teacher's parking space. He pulled down the shades and winked. "Have a good day?"

He walked around his uncle, opened the passenger's door and slung his backpack inside. Silently, Nathan climbed in and slammed the door. His uncle followed suit, turned on the stereo, and drove onto the open road. Many miles passed before either of them spoke. "Everything you said was true. There's magic in the world. This isn't a con."

His uncle kindly dropped the smug smile. "Yep."

Rows of trees and fields whizzed past them. He felt that if he said everything he was thinking, it would somehow make it come true. "Something really bad is gonna happen at school, isn't it?"

"Yep." Marty tapped his nose. "I can smell it in the air."

"People are going to die, aren't they?" Nathan swallowed. He felt like a pocket of air was going to explode in his chest. "People I know from school. My friends. That's why you came now, isn't it?"

"The French have a saying. Plus ça change, plus c'est la même chose." There was subtle shift in Marty's shoulders; they drooped with worry and guilt just like Papa Ray. "The more things change, the more they stay the same."

"What's that mean?"

"You graduate in two days, right? Where's the party?"

"What party?" Nathan felt uncomfortable discussing this with his uncle. "Why does it matter?"

"It used to be on Channel Road. A little road between a couple of farms and the river. Plenty of parking and a bit of off-site camping." Marty grinned lecherously. "Quiet places to enjoy the night with a few friends. Anything sound familiar?"

"We call it Snake Road now. What's going on, Marty?"

Marty flinched at the question. It was sometimes hard to remember he was mortal. "Grandma Loni told you about the accident, didn't she?"

Nathan shook his head and waved away his uncle's concern. "Ugh! Not that! You should have seen her on Prom Night. We'll be careful. I'm not a drinker anyway. Is someone gonna die in a car accident?"

"She only told you the story that we told her. It was a lie. We couldn't tell the truth. She'd lock us away. She'd beat us with a frying pan and then lock us away." He cleared his throat and Nathan wondered if he was wearing that pair of sunglasses on purpose. "The truth is how we got started on the Highway West."

Was there ever going to be a time when there weren't more secrets? "What truth?"

"A couple of kids died that night. There was drinking. And there was an accident. That much was true." Marty pulled the van over to the side of the road along a patch of dirt that reminded Nathan of the dreaded day he first saw a dead body. "We saw something. A lady in white that wept blood. She killed those kids."

"La Llorona? Seriously? I wrote an essay on her." Nathan held up his hands frustrated. "A poor woman that lost her children and now she's condemned to walk the earth until she finds them, now she punishes bad kids. That's just a story brought over by the immigrants."

"The universe is made of stories," Marty said grimly. "And some of them aren't so nice."

"I've been there before." Nathan bushed. He didn't want to discuss what he did there with an older family member. "Nothing happened."

"There is something that lives near the river." Marty slid out of his seat and went to the back of the van. He flipped over one of the side seats and pulled out a scrapbook and flung it over. "It takes on the form of La Llorona or it's some sort of tulpa. And every twenty years or so it wakes up and feeds."

Marty's sudden confidence and knowledge took Nathan back a bit. Could his uncle actually be telling the truth for once? Was there magic in the world? Did that mean that what happened on the farm actually happened? "What's a tulpa? And what do you mean feeds?"

"It's a Tibetan concept. The idea is that you can create an entity entirely by your imagination. They come from the energy all around us." He waved his hands about as though to say the entire universe. "And our will gives them shape and purpose. Kind of like a character in a novel, except you don't write tulpas down."

The concept sounded intriguing, Nathan had to admit. "Are they dangerous?"

"Some stories have them being dangerous creatures that try to trick you out of your life-force. Others have them as protectors of children. There are things out there in the universe so large and terrifying that we can't understand them. They're too complex for our brains to process and perceive so we replace them with images from our memories." Marty scooted out of the driver's seat and opened the secret nook under the side passenger's seat, sorted through the compartment, and produced the wooden box. "It took me two years but I finally found this little baby."

Now that he opened his mind to the possibility of magic, Nathan could sense the power within that wood. There was power trapped inside shaped by the curves of the symbols engraved on it like a glass shaping the water. It felt like being next to a giant speaker at a rock concert. The sheer mystical energy tickled his skin with vibrations of power. The power of his hunger for knowledge surprised him. "What is that? No secrets."

Marty lifted the box and presented on his hand as though it were a silver platter and beamed with the confidence of a used car salesman. "This, my friend, is a bona fide, genuine Dybbuk Box. A pocket dimensional prison for malignant spirits and demons. Wood blessed by Rabbis centuries ago and bound with the word of God."

"Seriously?"

"Kabbalah isn't just a joke washed-up celebrities use to stay relevant." Marty gestured to one of the glyphs inked on his arm. It was placed perfectly into a star surrounded by a snake consuming its own tail. It looked like a squiggle deformed from a question mark.

"Those Rabbis don't take any shit from tulpas, and when it comes time for a spiritual throw down, you don't wanna fuck with them. They know how to use the ancient Enochian language to great effect."

He was new to all of this, but this sounded way too pat, too easy to be true. There had to be a catch of some kind. "So we wait until graduation and then put this thing in the box? There's gotta be a catch, right?"

His uncle winked and Nathan felt it in his bones that he had already been trapped by the con. "That's the trick. You have to put the tulpa in the box. And I assure you that walking up to it and politely asking it to hop inside won't go over well. This is going to take a powerful binding ritual. That takes will and skill in equal measure."

"And you can do that?" Nathan asked hopeful, but already dreading the answer.

"I have the knowhow, but not the juice. To make this work, I'm gonna need a partner that has potential."

He wiped his head, surprised at the amount of sweat. The heat sweltered in the van giving him a resounding headache. "I don't know magic. I can't fight a monster before the first lesson. Isn't there some trick you can teach me involving brooms and buckets? That'd be comedy gold."

Perspiration beaded along Marty's slightly receded hairline. If he felt the pain of the heat, he said nothing. Marty held up his hand to stop Nathan. "How did you know?"

"Know what?"

"You knew something was wrong." Marty wiped his head with a

handkerchief and grinned. "How?"

How did he know? Nathan tried to put it into words. "There were raisins and the dead man's hand. Signs. Everything pointed to it. And then I just knew something was wrong. Does that sound crazy?"

"Synchronicity."

Nathan shook his head. "I don't get it."

"Synchronicity is when you see a pattern in the chaotic unrelated events in the universe." He lifted a single finger as though he were teaching the lost secrets of the universe. "Also, it's the name of one of the greatest rock albums of all time."

"So it was all random and meaningless?" The windows in the van stared to fog as though they were sitting inside of a sauna. "I thought I felt something."

"You did. A feeling is always real. You saw something and found meaning in it. A part of you knew that you and your friends were in danger." Marty mopped the back of his neck. The heat inside of the van was turning oppressive. "Carl Jung believed that we learned things about ourselves from seeing reflections in the random actions of the universe. Oracles once saw such things in the entrails of a dove. Fortune tellers see the future in cards. That shows you have the gift."

"How's that gonna help me fight a monster?"

He grinned and wiped the side window of the van with his handkerchief. Streaks of fog cleared in a large streak. "Getting hot, isn't it?"

"Please tell me you have air conditioning."

Marty grinned and opened the side door letting in a quick

refreshing breeze. "Wouldn't help in the long run. Pardon the expression, but you are hot, kid. That heat is your body processing your magical energy being magnified by the steel in the frame."

"What? Couldn't be. I'd know it, wouldn't I?"

He carefully placed the Dybbuk Box back into the compartment and then slammed the seat back into place. "The ancient greeks believed that all living things that could speak had a divine spark inside them. The logos. A lucky few have the ability to access that spark of fire via their blood. They've been known by many names over the years. Gods. Wizards. Witches. Seers. Only for you that talent seems to manifest literally as fire."

"Fire? Really?" Nathan held out his hands as though they were going to burst into flame. "How do you know?"

"You learned the trick. It took me fifteen years to master that and you learned it in fifteen minutes on a whim. With a bit of time, you'll be able to start fires with your mind and control them." Marty fanned himself. "And, if nothing else, maybe you can keep the temperature down."

Nathan felt the back of his neck and then wiped the sweat and the grime on his jeans. Was he generating the heat? "How? I didn't even realize that I was doing it!"

"Calm now, Nate. You're opening your energy too quickly. Gonna burn yourself out if you don't pace yourself." He reached into his vest, fished out a tiny white oval-shaped stone that was perfectly smooth, and passed it to Nathan. "This is a meditation stone. Keep it in your palm and it can help you balance your temperature."

The stone felt cool in his hand. "How do I use it?"

"Concentrate on the texture of it inside of your hand. Feel the smooth finish and imagine how your body might feel just like that." Marty nodded warmly, beaming with pride. "Just let it go."

Skeptical, Nathan closed his eyes and tried to listen to the words. Letting go had never been easy. He focused on the smooth feel of the stone and imagined his entire body feeling the same way. "That feels a bit better."

"That's the ticket!" Marty patted him on the back. He reached into his ice chest and dug around until he found a cold bottle of root beer. "I'm starting to feel the breeze. Drink a bit of this and you'll feel better."

Nathan gladly accepted the bottle of root beer and held it to his forehead. He wrapped the top of the bottle with a bit of his t-shirt then twisted off the cap and gulped down a bit. "That does feel better."

Marty found a beer for himself, opened it, and then toasted his nephew. "Bill and I fought this thing alone without warning. Almost died. This time around, we'll do one better. We have time to plan and the Dybbuk Box."

"I don't know how to use this power yet."

"That's going to take a lot of time, Nate. And we have months ahead to practice." He took a long swig of his beer. "But if you trust me, really trust me, I can help direct you. We can set this trap real nice."

"And no one has to die?"

"That's the goal.  And hopefully bury a few ghosts in the process."
Marty finished his beer and flashed a wicked grin.  Now listen up,
because I have a doozy of a plan."

# Chapter Four: We Laugh Like Soft, Mad Children

Nathan Carver waited on stage wrapped in a bright purple gown and cap staring at the rows of friends, parents, distant relatives, and teachers. Each of them brought to mind a memory of the joys and sorrows of his adolescence. He saw the reflection of their hopes and genuine affection then felt an uncomfortable ache in his stomach. A myriad of memories bubbled randomly into his thoughts.

A brutal fist fight in the bathroom with best friend Doug Houston during freshman year suddenly didn't seem so epic. He couldn't even remember the cause of the fight. All he remembered now was the countless excited whispers about comic books, the all-night Monty Python sessions, and exploring Snake Road after curfew. He found it difficult to imagine Doug being deployed to Afghanistan or carrying an assault rifle. Would they ever see each other again?

An awkward adult kiss shared with Robin Dooley on a rare rainy day seemed more special now three years later. They had kissed for hours until their lips were chapped and sore, and it felt like mere seconds. It was the first time that Nathan truly understood the theory of relativity. She had seemed so wise, worldly, and beautiful to Nathan as a sophomore. With her short blond hair and greyish blue eyes, he imagined that she was an angel. Robin graduated two years previous and had written the first few months, but they drifted apart. The embarrassment of his braces catching onto her wool sweater only now seemed laughable.

Paging through his yearbook, Nathan wondered what he did with his life at school. The ink scribbling in the margins represented the last message about high school his friends would ever send him. So many of his fellow students wished that they could have gotten to know him better. How often did he merely exist in this world rather than let it touch him? Was he really that weird?

Sweat dripped down from his forehead. The truth was that one of the notes surprised him. He flipped casually to the spot. The pages of the yearbook were already well worn and easily opened to the exact page with the candid snapshot of Phoebe Lomlei hugging Nathan. Her black hair covered a bit of her face, but her eyes were locked onto his. It was the first time that anyone looked at him with such love and devotion. He remembered the day they took that picture. It had been sweltering, but both of them couldn't stop holding hands. Their skin itched to be in contact with each other.

*Thank you for the best year of my life. Good luck in school. I hope you find what you're looking for.*

*Love ya, Phoebe*

The thought of not seeing her daily felt wrong, like he was missing a hand and still needed to scratch a phantom itch. Phoebe had been his first serious girlfriend. They spent the majority of senior year together. He thought of all that they had experienced. She introduced him to their shared love of John Lennon and the Beatles, the stories of Ray Bradbury, and old horror movies. On a magical spring night that seemed to be imbued with every known dream teen cliché, they went to Prom together. They embraced before the starry background and posed for a picture that would define their youth. That night they camped by the river along Snake Road. Where had the time gone? And what did she think he was looking for?

Sometime during the during the commencement speech, Nathan scanned the crowd to find his family. It took several minutes, but finally he spotted Marty comforting Grandma Loni in the stands. Papa Ray quietly snoozed in the sunlight. He grinned wildly and stifled a laugh until he realized who was missing. It had been almost a year since he had last heard from his mother, but somehow he expected that she would make it. When it was Nathan's turn to stand at the podium, Grandma Loni jabbed Papa Ray in the ribs and together they stood and cheered. Nathan accepted his diploma and nodded to the couple that had been his real parents.

The next few hours were a blur. Friends and family congratulated him and swarmed around him like an angry ant hill. Phoebe somehow snuck through them and gave Nathan a warm kiss on the cheek. Her soft lips made his entire body ache with the want of her. She had bright almond eyes that seemed to dance with excitement. "Will I see you at the party tonight?"

"I thought you didn't want things to get weird." Nathan remembered what she wrote in his book. "Not that I'd complain."

She leaned close, standing on the tips of her toes. He remembered the look of adoration in her eyes the night of the Prom. That night he was her entire world. Was his desperation to leave Sanger so strong that he was oblivious to the things that he would have to give up? "Saying good-bye isn't weird, Nathan. And we still have the summer to bump into each other on occasion," Phoebe said with a bit more enthusiasm than maybe Nathan had wanted.

"I have to leave in a few days with my uncle." He felt the keen disappointment of wasting the last month of school. "I don't really have much choice."

She smiled in that wry, sexy way that he found irresistible. "Well then, we'll have to make sure the party is good enough to remember all summer."

"You won't forget me?"

"Silly boy." She pushed his shoulder playfully. "You never forget your first love, no matter how much it might suck."

"Ouch!"

"I did stress the word *might* in that sentence." She kissed his cheek once more and then pivoted on her feet to face away from Nathan. She looked meaningfully over her shoulder. "I suppose that depends on how well tonight goes."

Nathan felt a bit warm in his cheeks like he was in a comfortable fog. Grandma Loni grabbed him by the ear and pulled him down to hug her. "I'm so proud of you, Nathan." She gestured over to Marty. "This one didn't graduate."

A wince flashed over his uncle's face, but he said nothing and forced a smile. "You did good, kiddo!"

"You still going to dinner with us?" Papa Ray checked his watch.

He hated to be late for anything. A trait he shared with Nathan. "We only have twenty minutes to make it to the steak house in time for my discount."

"Steak house? That's kind of pricy." Nathan blushed at the thought of his grandparents overspending. "Can we afford that?"

"I'm helping out there, Nate." Marty winked. "I figure I owe the folks that much for all of the headaches."

Poppy Ray nodded thoughtfully. Nathan wasn't quite sure of the expression. "It'll have to be a very large steak, son." He grinned and slapped his son on the shoulder. "I should have brought my sweatpants. I'll bust my belt for sure."

Marty opened his mouth to speak, but words failed him. Nathan elbowed him. "That looks like a bit of pride."

"Listen, the sun will shine even on a dog's ass on occasion." Papa Ray put his arms around both his son and grandson and pushed them towards the parking lot. "I'm very hungry."

"Just you watch your language at the restaurant," Grandma Loni warned holding up two fingers with false menace. "We're not hill folk! You weren't raised in a barn!"

"You always say that! Who exactly are the hill folk?"

Grandma Loni reached up and clipped her grandson behind the ears. "Never you mind, Mr. Graduate!"

It felt oddly charming to be the youngest, not quite an adult, for one last time. As he sat in the backseat of the old Monte Carlo, he wondered if this would be the last time he was taken to dinner by the grandparents and felt a bit sad. Would staying around town for a few years really make that much of a difference?

Dinner at the steak house seemed to melt away all of the previous tensions and anxiety in the family. Nathan chewed the delicious steak slowly, letting the juices run over his tongue. Marty and Papa Ray exchanged stories about the road and various family members spread throughout the county peppered with warnings from Grandma Loni to avoid unscrupulous behavior. Afterwards, he felt himself drifting to sleep in the old Ford comfortably surrounded by the voices of his loved ones.

A soft hand rubbed his belly gently. It was his grandma's favorite way of waking him as a boy. There were nights that it was the only thing that would calm him after a nightmare. "Nate, you don't want to sleep away graduation night!"

He blinked and stretched feeling glad that he rested a bit before the party and Marty's plan. It might be the last time that he would be able to do so and feel totally safe for a long time. "I just needed to close my eyes a bit, Grandma." Nathan noted the lack of light in the sky and started to worry. "How long did you let me sleep?"

"Just an hour. You looked so comfortable, we just let you sleep. Marty said you needed it."

Nathan glanced around the yard. The old van was parked in its spot. "Where'd he go?"

"He borrowed the truck. Don't worry, he left me the keys. You go out and have fun." She kissed his forehead and then hastily added. "Not too much fun."

"Grandma, I'm the designated driver. That's why Marty lent me his van." Nathan thought of Marty's plan and resisted the urge to frown. He didn't want to worry Grandma Loni and if she knew the truth of what was planned she'd never let it happen. "How much trouble can I get into?"

"Were you drinking when you tipped Mrs. Higgins?" She ruffled his blond curly hair, stifling a laugh. "Or when you drove the tractor into that sink hole?"

"Woah! Woah!" Nathan held up his hands defensively in protest and then gestured to the pasture. "Mrs. Higgins is just fine. That was a complete accident. Doug never slept on a farm before and didn't know they were so jumpy."

Grandma Loni scoffed skeptically and folded her arms. "And the tractor?"

"How was I supposed to know there was a sink hole there?" Nathan stretched a bit. "Besides, the insurance said that it was an accident. Gophers."

"Don't be a smart ass!" She held out her hand and helped Nathan out of the Monte Carlo. Nathan wrapped his arms around his grandmother always surprised that he towered over her. She had seemed so large all of his life, but now she barely reached his shoulders. "Now get out there and do some good in the world."

That had been the question he'd been contemplating. He often imagined as a boy that she could read his mind. "Think I will?"

She leaned up on the tip of her toes and cuffed him on the back of the head. "You'd better or I'll haunt your scrawny ass. Don't you think I won't!"

"Before or after you kick the devil out of hell?"

Two fingers were lifted into the air. Nathan wasn't sure if it was a curse or a rude gesture. "And you best be on the side of angels this summer." She handed him the keys to the van. "I'll know."

\*     \*     \*     \*

Nathan Carver took a sip of his frosted, bottled root beer while he waited for the antiquated gas pump to fill the old brown 1977 Dodge Tradesman van under the flickering florescent street lamp. This might be the last time he ever bought gas at Sun Maid's, he thought wistfully. The old wooden storefront wouldn't have looked out of place in an old black and white movie. It had the rustic sort of charm that caused tourists to pose for pictures. He thought of the secret trips here with Papa Ray to buy cases of Coors Light and Pall Malls, and long discussions with the kindly owner of the store, Mr. Winn, who was almost a distant uncle to him.

The roar of a powerful engine echoed around the station as a lone headlight lit the street. A sleek, classic Harley Shadow rolled through the gravel into the covered station, circled the van, and skid to a stop near an empty gas pump. The rider kicked open the stand, placed the motorcycle into a parked position, and pulled off her black-tinted helmet. She shook her wild curly black hair and turned her neck slowly like a lioness. There was a feral beauty about her face like it had been carved from marble like the Venus de Milo. "Hi, there!"

He nodded dumbly to this strange beautiful woman with grey eyes and a perky nose. "Hi."

The rider unzipped her leather jacket and hung it on the bike. She dismounted the motorcycle and sauntered towards Nathan. Her combat boots ground into the gravel. "Nice van. A real classic. Where'd ya get it, cutie?"

Nathan furrowed his brow confused, and glanced from the van to this enchanting woman. She had the perfect face with high cheekbones of a classic actress. "This thing? It belongs to my Uncle Marty. I'm just borrowing it for the night."

The rider tugged almost unconsciously at the leather choker around her neck. Nathan found himself drawn to her neckline down to the luscious curve of her full bosom. He blinked, stopped himself, and returned to the choker. It failed to conceal the single blemish on her skin; a ring of dark lesions, scabs, and scars that circled her neck just above her collar bone.

She noted his attention and her grin turned to a full, open smile showing off rows of white teeth. "Would that be Marty Carver?"

How would Marty possibly know this glamorous lady? He tried to guess her age, but she had that magical quality about her skin that could have placed her anywhere in her early twenties to her late thirties. "You know Marty?"

"You must be Bill Carver's boy." She ignored his questions and continued to pace around him with her head tilted as though she were studying him. "How old are you?"

Nathan couldn't help but answer. "Eighteen."

Her voice turned sickly sweet. "You must be about ready to graduate."

"I just graduated today actually."

"Did you?" Her low sensual voice caused his skin to tingle. Her smile teased the possibility that she knew every way to pleasure him and just a bare hint of all of the ways that she'd punish him for the enjoyment of it. "How sweet! A last night of childhood with the budding power of being a man. Your first summer of real freedom."

He blushed a bit. What was it about this woman that turned every thought dirty? "Did you know my father?"

"I am a very old friend of your family, Nathan Carver." She sniffed the air around them, stepping closer to him. Her wild eyes stared unblinking, almost pulsing with excitement. "I bet your Uncle Marty is about to take you on a trip! A road trip?"

"How do you know about that?" Was this woman dangerous? Nathan stepped back, a little afraid.

"My friends and I have waited a long time to meet you. We've been waiting for you for almost twenty years." She sniffed the air cautiously. "The Highway West is beset by all manner of dangers. I'll be looking forward to seeing how you handle them."

"Marty never mentioned you."

"Really?" She stepped closer to Nathan and leaned close studying him. "And where is your Uncle Marty?"

Nathan felt the heat rise from the back of his neck. "He's out for the weekend. Said he'd be back on Monday."

She laughed madly. "You're a terrible liar, Nathan Carver. I think that's sweet."

He swallowed, uncomfortably. "You kind of have me at a disadvantage. Who are you?"

"My name was Joy." There was a bit of bitter irony in her voice, with an undeniable undercurrent of anger. "That is until I met the Carver brothers."

"Your name was Joy? What's it now?"

The lady that had once been Joy laughed. "You are everything promised. It must be kismet to find you while chasing a runner. Acrimony was right. Gods below I hate saying that."

The gas pump automatically clicked off. Nathan tapped the nozzle twice and then out of the van and hung it on the latch. "Do you have a message for Marty? For when he gets back?"

She extended her hand as though to stroke Nathan's cheek, and then seemed to think better of it. "Tell him that Cenotaph does not forgive welchers."

"Who's Cenotaph?"

"You'll find out." She winked and blew Nathan a kiss. She sauntered around the gas pumps and then mounted the Harley. She slipped into her black leather jacket and kicked started the Harley in a solid, fluid motion. "By the way, since you asked so politely Nathan, I figured you deserved to know my name. Agony."

She tipped her fingers to her forehead in a mock salute and then pulled the helmet over her hair and onto her head. Agony mounted the motorcycle, revved the engine, and wildly spun out of the gravel parking lot pelting Nathan and the van with tiny rocks.

What sort of woman would have the name Agony? Nathan Carver had the sickening feeling that one day he would find out.

*     *     *     *

Blue-black skies above Snake Road were pocked with bundles of full grey clouds around the yellow moon. The gentle flow of water rushing over the rocks and pebbles of the King's River could be heard just under the bustle and roar of the party on the encampment. Nathan Carver wished that Marty carried a phone with him. The strange woman and what she might want with them concerned him, but there was nothing to do about it. He unloaded a case of root beer and a box of oranges from the van and dropped them on one of the wooden benches that lined the camp. Fellow graduates, underclassmen, and various hangers-on swayed to the music.

"Hey, Nate, you got a lighter?" Doug Houston waved from the fire pit. The stones had been arranged and the wood collected. He dug around in the pit, trying to arrange the driftwood into a loose pyramid configuration to start a fire. "The wood's wet or something. You always have the magic touch."

"Sure thing." Nathan needed to use his gift to attract the beast, and this seemed like a perfect opportunity, but he needed to distract his friend. "I can handle it. You get the sleeping bags, OK?"

Nathan fished out his lighter from his jeans pocket and flashed a grin. The others had turned to other tasks including unloading the rest of the supplies from the van. He crouched down near the pit and slowly sucked in his breath. Nathan concentrated on the mental picture of changing the content of the oxygen in his mouth. When he felt ready, he slowly blew it under the pyramid of wood. Flicking the lighter ignited a prodigious flame.

Doug cheered from the van. "How do you always do that?"

A smile appeared on Nathan's lips mirroring the smug, knowing smile that Marty always flashed. It was infuriating, but Nathan had to admit that being on the other side of the smile was simply awesome. His answer was simple. "Magic."

\*     \*     \*     \*

Nathan Carver had the dubious honor of serving as the Key Master. One by one, he accepted the keys of his friends and former classmates and secured them in the van. He circled the party as an outsider peeking into intimate conversations, lost moments, and emotional farewells.

Marty once explained that a proper party always starts like a a battle and now Nathan understood why. Squadrons of friends positioned themselves upon the field ready to claim territory with the occasional soldier left trapped behind enemy lines. Discarded bottles, empty plastic cups, and vomit littered the ground like fallen comrades as the party raged and towards the end of the night, the so-called survivors looked like the walking dead.

He eventually spotted Doug flashing a wide shit-eating grin and his arm wrapped around a smiling blonde girl with a cute nose.

They spent an hour near the fire, talking about the future in vaguely optimistic terms. Nathan bit his tongue and mostly listen, feeling morose that he couldn't share the strange new world of magic that he had discovered.

Phoebe arrived to party late. Her sisters, cousins, and friends scattered into the various conversatons, yet kept a close eye upon her. She tilted her head searching through the crowd until she spotted Nathan and greeted him with a warm smile. She wore a long white strapless summer dress that accentuated her curves.

A strong elbow cut to his ribs. Nathan blinked and turned to Doug. "Ouch!"

"Nathan, I've known you ever since you moved to Sanger. Remember?"

He remembered the first day when that scraggly brown-haired kid with big expressive eyes dared to talk to the new boy. "Hard to forget. No matter how hard I try."

"Have I ever steered you in the wrong direction?"

"Early and often. Mrs. Higgins still walks with a limp." Nathan shrugged his shoulders without an ounce of regret for their years of friendship. "What's your point?"

"I've only really learned one important thing over the years. This is very important." His friend smiled content with a pretty girl under his arm. He nodded suggestively towards Phoebe. "Don't be a dumbass, Nate."

It felt like the most sincere and best advice that he had ever heard. They laughed together and at that moment Nathan imagined that he could forget any worries about a monster and that the future would always take care of itself. He tried to summon the courage to go to there, but Phoebe took the first steps towards him instead. He quickly followed suit and took her hand. They walked together along the path to the river and she pulled his arm around her. "Your skin is warm like a blanket."

"Is it?" Nathan hadn't noticed it until that moment, but his body temperature did feel like it was running hot. "Careful, I might burn you."

She placed her head gently on his chest, covering her face with her dark hair. They watched the ripples on the water and time seemed to distort and fade from their consciousness. When Nathan checked his phone for the time only an hour had passed, but it felt like he had spent the entire night holding her. "Are you OK, Nathan? You're starting to sweat."

White flashes out of the corner of his eye distracted him. Something was close. He felt the vibrations of power against his skin. This time the sensation crept along the surface of his flesh, giving him chills like slime sliding down a wall. "Can you get me one of the bottles of water? I'm not feeling too well."

Phoebe eyed him suspiciously, but kissed his cheek and started up the trail. She wasn't going to argue with him on a night like this. He turned to the river, searching for the light. The monster was near. The vibration from her power was so close that he now felt it in his teeth like a dull ache. This night she would reveal herself to him. He muttered to himself in order to steel his courage. "Ok, Marty, she's caught my scent. Let's hope you're half as smart as you think you are."

He turned back to the trail and hurried before Phoebe could return. Marty promised that it wouldn't attack until there were less people around, but he didn't want to take the chance that Phoebe might get caught in the crossfire. Nathan caught up to her on the trail. Confused, she handed him the bottle. "If there's something wrong, tell me."

He unscrewed the lid and gulped several swallows of water trying to think of a good excuse to get her to leave. "I just think its better that we don't start something tonight that I can't finish."

Phoebe blinked quickly, clearly held back tears in an attempt to remain strong. "Saying good-bye doesn't have to be like that."

"You make me want to stay."

"Would that be so bad?"

He thought about the thing that waited in the river and wondered if she really did suck the marrow from the bones of her prey. "I don't have a choice now. I have to leave. At least for a while."

She said nothing further and turned her back upon him. Her sisters quickly separated from their own conversations. Dozens of angry eyes cast dirty looks his direction from the feminine revenge squad. He returned to his spot near Doug. "I am such a dumbass."

"So it has been said." Doug patted him on the back. "And it will be said again before we're done."

"Doug, you are always such a comfort."

"That's what I am here for."

Near the end of the battle, the soldiers departed in small groups.

Each of them checked with Nathan and he verified at least one of them was sober enough to drive. It was close to four in the morning before he released the last of the keys and helped clean up the huge mess. "Do you need me to stick round, Nate?" Doug nodded expectantly towards the very attractive blonde with wide eyes. "I mean I can if you really need me."

"I think I'm good. I'm almost ready to go." Nathan was much relieved he didn't need to convince his friend to leave. They bumped fists last time. "Be good."

"Not if I can help it."

Nathan watched the last car drive away and then poured the last of the water over the embers of the bonfire. The sizzling smoke wafted towards the sky. His teeth ached once more and he felt her leave the water. If Marty's plan was going to work, he needed to hurry. "Here we go."

Quickly, he slid into the van and started the engine. Marty had promised that the creature couldn't enter the van due to the magical wards burned into the steel frame, but Nathan wasn't about to take any chances. Shifting into gear, he slammed his foot down onto the pedal. The wheels screeched loudly trying to gain traction as it accelerated up the long winding road.

The old brown 1977 Dodge Tradesman narrowly made the winding turns up Snake Road. Nathan turned onto the base of the hill that led straight through to the wetlands. He revved the van, but it slowed in speed. The roar of the engine faded to a puttering whimper until it stalled. The ache started to freeze his jaw. He opened the door and slid out of the van. Nathan tried to look around, but the blackness was impenetrable and he went with the only option available to him. Running up the hill, his sides cramped, but the cold followed him until mid-way up the trail, she appeared to him.

Nathan instinctively knew her face was a mask and the eyes were pools of shimmering black blood filled a lifetime of sorrows weighted like stones. Wild black hair like the night in a tempest storm from the center of creation blew wildly in the wind. A ragged, white dress — yellowed from age — clung to her thin frame. Upon further inspection he realized that it was not made from cotton or any other earthly cloth. It writhed with thousands of faces within it and all of them screamed in a malicious cacophony chorus. She held a bony finger towards Nathan as a challenge or perhaps even a gesture of kindness.

This creature had lived between the stories eon after ego. She had worn so many faces, so many roles, so many stories, that all of them began to blur into one. He loved her. How dare he not drop to his knees then and there to worship this beast deigning to cling to flesh and lore? He loved her and despaired and therein lay her power.

In the dark city of Tenochtitlan, made of bones and blessed with fertile blood, the goddess Cihuacoatl stalked the night in white. In the posh safety of the suburban houses, children whispered her name at midnight peeking into the mirror. The children of a dying land choking in its own poison and waste tell of her mask with a different story and a different name; La Llorona. The crying lady forever searching for her drowned children, always weeping and never grieving, for in grieving you admit that it is lost and sundered forever.

The cry came from across the sea keening at the moment of death and the burning regret of all that still live. Wearing the mask of the banshee, she appeared as an ugly, frightening hag that would steal the last breath of the dishonorable and the lost. "On this night, your soul will be mine."

She wept tears to rage against all life that dared to live outside of the shadow; the ancient urge to surrender; to allow the sorrow to lull him into the primordial abyss hidden in the soul of man. It was tempting, but Nathan Carver felt the fire, the logos, and the divine spark burn. He knew well this feeling. It had haunted him as he walked the endless trail along the dead grape vines waiting for his mother. He felt it creep into his bones waiting and wondering if she would ever come for him. The fear of all children, lost and alone, to never have a mother, to never feel the warmth of an embrace.

How dare she use this on him? He needed the anger and nurtured it like a proper hatred that blew sweet air into the furnace to fuel the fire. How dare she use this diseased boil on his soul against him? Was that all she was in the end? Was she just a parasite?

Bitterly frozen fingers slithered up his arms. She was pulling him closer to the gentle cold. Nathan Carver stared into those shimmer pools of rotted blood. "Is that all you got?"

Her fingers sizzled at the touch. The flame danced in his eyes. Waves of heat cut through the air. His hair became drenched with sweat and grime. He twisted and wrenched wildly to get free. She could not hold him; the fire was too strong. She scratched with the

73

full fury of her power. None had escaped her grasp in memory; none had burned her flesh.

Nathan tried to remember the plan, but Marty's words failed him. He only knew in his terror that he had to run to the crossroads. It was still almost a half a mile away, up the winding road, but there at the edge of nowhere he knew there would be sanctuary. The hill was steep, but the creature provided the proper incentive, and he quickly ascended towards the peak. It followed, stalking him, keeping its distance until his flame no longer had the fire.

Heaving and huffing, he climbed the hill until it flattened. Stumbling, he righted himself and kept running forward. One foot in front of the other until the crossroads was in sight. Where was Marty?

She did not tire. The wind carried her gently towards him as she savored the moment. She spoke with the voice of broken dreams and shattered glass. "You will not find shelter here in this place between the worlds; neither here nor there; betwixt and between. I have consecrated this place with blood."

Covering his ears, Nathan pressed forward until he stepped into the center of the crossroads. The world shifted all around him. It was though the angle of the road had been twisted against the rest of the world and suddenly everything turned into focus. There sat Marty in a lotus position cradling the Dybbuk Box. She followed Nathan and roared with anger. Marty grinned and opened the box. "Bet you never saw this coming, did ya bitch?"

Once inside of the protection of the Heptagram, the lesser seal of Solomon, Nathan was able to concentrate on the memory of Marty's plan. The Heptagram was a seven-pointed star drawn into the earth with in seven straight strokes. They had worked together to gather enough iron shavings, ground snakeskin, graveyard dirt, and sulfur to create enough goofer dust to hold almost any monster that could pass through the Great Barrier.

This was the heart of chaos magic. The elements and the symbols were lenses that would focus soul energy. Long ago, innocent blood had been spilled here. A virgin sacrifice to the blood god. Here, she had fed and murdered and feasted. Places have a memory, a soul, and this one had been blessed and tainted by her deeds with a magic resonance that could be accessed and trapped. What was once a place to gain power was now a subtle trap.

The vortex of the void swirled within the wooden box bound by the name of God. Nathan tried to slow his breathing like Marty had taught him. The creature had come from another place, another world and could only manifest in the form of a legend. Marty held on tightly to the Dybbuk Box. "Nate, I don't have the power to hold it."

Together, they clutched the sides of the box. Nathan pushed the flame, the logos, from his chest into his arms, into his fingers and willed it to power the box. The tempest erupted with power; the primeval forces swirled and raged. She could not resist that which came before her bound by the will of a higher power. Fingers and hands and arms dissolved into her true form. It was an amorphous wave of flesh and teeth gnawing at the edges of the world; feasting on the bones of the living.

"Mercy!" it cried. "Let me serve you. Much there is that I can teach you."

It frightened Nathan exactly how tempting the offer had been. There was so much he needed to learn and he began to understand the concept of actual power. Marty said something to him, but with the wind and the screams, everything was muted. This was the last temptation and it failed. He closed the Dybbuk Box and sealed it away forever.

# Chapter Five: Black Magic Woman

The 1977 Dodge Tradesman skid to a sudden stop at the edge of the dirt road. Blackbirds cried in the distance as the bright summer sun shined over the Carver Ranch. Nathan Carver hung his arms out the open passenger window and gazed at the seemingly endless rows of orange trees and breathed in the citrus scent. The engine hummed ready and almost eager to take on the open road, but Marty shifted to park and turned the key. He leaned back into his seat and nodded solemnly to his nephew. "You know there's still time to back out. This life's not for everyone and I shouldn't have tricked you into it."

The entire ranch seemed to be waving good-bye to the favored son from Grandma Loni to Papa Ray to the barking dogs and finally a single sad moo from Mrs. Higgins. When Nathan finally spoke, his voice cracked with worry. "If I stay here, will they be safe? You have people looking for you. Won't they eventually come for me?"

"If you decide this life isn't for you, there's a ritual to bind the magic inside of you forever." Marty waved to his parents. His uncle felt like a big brother that occasionally dragged him into trouble. "You'll be like them. Blind to the mystical in the world, but free to make your own choices. Just like your old man and the old battle axe up there. Bill could hear the spirits of the land when he was just a boy. Like you. Most of the rest of us can't hear something like that unless there's some sort of event crisis, or we receive a lot of training."

"Agony and her friends won't come for me? Won't they find me eventually and take their revenge?" Nathan paused to remember their gang's name, but flashes of Agony's eyes were all that he could recall. "What did you call them, again?"

"The New Flesh. They might eventually try to come for you, but only if I don't make amends first." Marty shrugged and his mustache twitched uncomfortably. "If you do decide to go that route, I promise to make sure that business doesn't blow back here."

"I saw that monster. I felt it in my teeth, my bones. I can't just forget that." Nathan rubbed his temple. The tension and stress felt like they had teamed together to escape his head by knocking through his skull. "It hit me where it hurts, Marty. I couldn't sleep. I don't even know that I could look Grandma Loni or Papa Ray in the eyes if I stayed."

Marty pulled out a stick of his nicotine gum, unwrapped it, and popped it into his mouth. "I saw it too when I was just a little older than you. Nearly had to change my shorts. Afterwards, it made me hungry to see what's out there. I had to know that it wasn't all bad. That there was good magic in the world."

"Why did my dad give it up? Do you know?"

Marty clapped him on the shoulder. The subject of his father always cheered the both of them. "He fell in love and had a son. Lucky bastard."

It never occurred to him that his uncle might have missed out on having a family. "Didn't you ever fall in love?"

"Of course I did. A beautiful woman. But we couldn't be together. It wasn't meant to be. Your dad found something special. That's part of why he gave it all up. He wanted to be there for you,

Nate."

"And look how well that turned out for us all," Nathan replied bitterly. "I just wish I could talk to him."

His uncle grinned wildly. "There's a way you can, in a manner of speaking. That's one of our stops."

"I can talk to my dad? You aren't shitting me?"

"It only works just the once, but yeah." Marty gestured to the open road away from the ranch. He reached down into his plastic crate filled with old cassette tapes. "If you can stand taking the trip with me and my music."

The first few bars of an old Journey song warbled through the ancient speakers. Nathan sighed and shook his head. "Just drive."

Marty honked the horn twice, shifted into gear, and the old van finally hit the road. They rode miles in silence except for the sound of the road and the songs that came to define their journey. Nathan watched as the scenery through the window gradually turned from farmland to less and less familiar barren roads until the cassette tape started to flip back to the first song for the third time. "You know I brought my music with me. I bet we could connect my MP3 player through your deck."

A scowl peeled across Marty's face as though he had sucked a barrel filled with lemons. "Hell no! If you want a change of tunes, look through the collection." He shook his head with disgust and Nathan found it difficult to resist a smile. "Geez, you don't know how lucky you have it. The world is at your feet and you don't appreciate it."

"If you start ranting about the younger generation, I'm going to start making fun of your grey hairs." Nathan started rifling through the box of mix-tapes. Most of them were arranged and categorized by theme, such as the worn tape with the faded label *Love Songs* or arranged by bands. "How many Led Zeppelin tapes do you really need?"

"Listen, that is an ancient and unknowable question akin to how many angels can dance upon the head of a pin."

Nathan found one tape sealed in plastic. "What is Bill's Battle Music?"

His uncle snatched the tape from his hand and tossed it back into the box. "That's only for emergencies."

"Dad made a mix-tape only for emergencies?"

"He spent three months working on a tape that he dreamed about playing when going into battle." Marty laughed as though he realized exactly how ridiculous he sounded. "It might be silly, Nate, but your dad and I promised that if we were ever going to be heroes and ride into a hopeless battle, we'd play this tape."

"It's wrapped in plastic," Nathan observed.

He laughed a bit embarrassed. "I'm not a hero, Nate. I've always subscribed to the theory that discretion is the better part of valor."

"But we fought against that monster."

"A man will do strange things as he ages and sees the end of the road." Traffic slowed to a crawl on Highway 99 as they passed Kingsburg. Marty groaned and honked the horn angrily. "I earned these grey hairs and wrinkles Nate. Very few men at the end of their lives say that they wished they could have played it safe more or loved less."

Nathan shrugged, not understanding the need for the speed. "I'm not insulting your lifestyle."

"My lifestyle? Shit. Half of you kids want to drink yourself silly and get laid. The other half is too busy looking down on me to notice."

"That's not what I meant." Nathan shook his head. "Look, I'm a little scared here. A week ago, if you told me I was going on a quest to learn about magic, I would have laughed. I think I'm handling this entire situation pretty well and if I offend you with a wrong word choice, I'm sorry."

"Aw...crud! I'm not trying to pick a fight with you. This trip isn't easy for me either. I look into your eyes and I see the ghosts of the past." Marty slipped on his sunglasses and leaned back in his seat as though trying to relax while the traffic came to a standstill. "I wish I could explain how much all of this meant to me."

"Why don't you? We have another hour or two until we get even close to Sequoia in this traffic. Hell, we could just drive all night and take turns."

"We need to hunker down before nightfall in a room." His voice was solemn and revealed far too much worry. "We'll be safe at the campground. There's a cabin and the grove has been considered sacred for centuries."

"Why bother?" Nathan gestured to the slow traffic and the hikers passing them. One of them smiled and waved. She was an older hippie chick with braided grey hair. "If someone was following us, they could catch us on foot."

"Not during the daylight."

Nathan turned to his uncle. "Wait a minute. The New Flesh aren't vampires, are they?" He switched to a faux-eurotrash accent and held his fingers to his mouth to mimic fangs. "One, two, three, I want to suck your blood!"

"There's nothing funny about the New Flesh. They're vampires that believe in the de-evolution of their humanity to get back that which they lost. Mercenaries that work for whatever dark overlord that can properly pay them."

"Agony was a vampire?" Nathan rubbed his neck, imaging her biting him. It was not a totally unpleasant prospect. "Why didn't she grab me? What did she want?"

"I imagine that they were sent for the Dybbuk Box. There's not many of them in the world and this one is special." Marty shrugged his shoulders. "They would have found me eventually. Agony has a score to settle."

"The burn marks around her neck, right?"

"Good eye, kid. Those marks were given courtesy of your old man the night she tried to make a snack out of yours truly. He had the touch of fire, just like you."

"That sounds like a good story to share."

Marty coughed. "There will come a time on this trip for stories. We'll be around a campfire or maybe playing pool drinking a couple of beers. This is just as hard for me as it is for you. We need to bond a bit before we start getting into the deep shit."

"Is this the part where we go to a sweat lodge and beat a drum? Or maybe go into the woods and do some man yelling?"

"You look a bit fresh to be taken to a bar. We'll have to pull a whammy to get you in." Marty laughed at the suggestion. "Stay near me the whole time. I don't know that you can handle yourself yet."

"Handle myself?"

"Well, this would typically be the part in the road trip where a bar fight would occur. You look kind of untested as it were. You ever been in a fight? Not talking about last night, but an actual fist fight where you have to punch someone?"

Nathan saw his own face in the mirrored lenses. "Marty, I wrestled for three years in high school. Got quite a few medals as I recall."

"Yeah, I know that Nate. Every time you did there was a news flash. Hell, I even knew about it. I don't think you appreciate how much hope the family has for you, but still that's not real experience," Marty said.

"If that was the case, how come you guys left me with my mom? Or bounced me around so much?" Nathan asked bitterly.

Marty sighed, releasing a long stream of pent-up energy. "Hell, I couldn't take care of me, much less anyone else. As for your mother, who knew? It took a while to figure out what was going on inside her head. You didn't tell anyone until you ran away and there wasn't anything that could be done. She was your legal guardian as it were. The law said we couldn't do anything. It wasn't until you ran away that

Papa was able to get a lawyer."

"What do you mean wrestling's not real experience?" Nathan asked, annoyed. "And I fought the monster. Or at least, I ran away very well."

"Well, yeah, you did better against it than me and your old man put together." Marty tried to keep from smirking. He was glad the conversation had changed. "Wrestling is fine. I did it, so did Bill. It's a civilized way of competing. There's nothing civilized about fighting. You ever been socked in the jaw? There's a stinging sensation and there's also a disjointed surprise. You ever hit anyone close-up? It's not the most pleasing feeling in the world. It goes against most of what we've been taught."

Nathan rolled his eyes and held up his arm where the fingers of the creature burned him with frostbite. "So you're saying I'm a big fat wuss and you need to protect me."

"No, I'm saying you haven't been tested yet. There's no shame in not wanting to hurt anyone. There's going to be a time when we might both be tested."

Nathan took in a deep breath. "You think the New Flesh is coming after us? Seriously."

Marty nodded grimly. "Maybe not right now at this moment. When the sun sets, who knows? Sooner or later, the word will get out. When it does, you'll be a marketable commodity with untold fortunes."

The thought that he could be sought after as a prize didn't make Nathan feel comfortable. He was very glad when the pace of traffic picked up to a comfortable speed and they could place more distance between themselves and Sanger. "Who would want me? I don't have any training and like you said, I'm untested. I should be worthless."

Marty groaned, spat his gum out the window, and then reached over to open the glove box. He fished around inside until he found a silver box filled with cigars. Flashing his best shit-eating grin, he slipped one into his mouth and lit it. "Any number of creatures with black hearts would love to capture an untrained mystic. They could mold you in their own image or just use you for spare parts. Some demons find your type a bit tasty. And speaking of which, I don't suppose you're a virgin?"

"What the hell does that have to do with anything?" Nathan pointed at the cigar. "And I thought you quit smoking!"

"It's been a stressful couple of days. And, it's not like it will kill me any faster." Marty took a long drag from the cigar and then blew floating smoke rings. "And as for the other thing, some creatures find that particular status very attractive. Good enough to eat as it were."

"What? You telling me some of them are going to try to eat me?"

Marty waved away his nephew's concern. "If you are lucky. There are far worse things in heaven and earth, I assure you. And speaking of which, I'm going to have to teach you to shoot a bit."

"That I can do. Papa Ray took me hunting a couple of times," Nathan said defensively.

"Not quite the same, but at least you've shot something. Nine times out of ten if you get into a fight, it's your fault. I'm just looking out for the random element. I think you'll do OK, don't worry."

"Yeah, creatures from beyond want to taste my flesh."

"And some of them will want a little more from you." He flashed a smile and leaned closer. "And they won't be taking you to dinner and movie first."

"What?"

"Well, yeah, some of the creatures will want your essence in their progeny. But, we're not exactly talking about attractive creatures here. You'd be better off as dinner. Just be glad that the monster didn't take you to her lair under the river."

"If you tell me there are monsters waiting to anal probe me, we're turning around right now," Nathan warned.

"Well, if you hear banjos, then you should run like a bat out of hell. Just in case."

They both laughed and it felt like the future had infinite possibilities as words died to the gentle feel of the open road, hot wind rustling through their hair, and the loud roar of classic rock. The first few chords of Aerosmith's *Dream On* raged through the speakers and Marty started to sing along. Much to Marty's surprise, Nathan followed suit and actually knew the words. They sang together, slightly off key alone, but a serviceable harmony when blended together.

Miles of faded black pavement flew past as the hours passed and the highway hypnosis gradually took over until traffic once again began to slow to a leisurely crawl. It was then that they noticed a figure walking along the highway, a hitchhiker. None of the cars or trucks stopped for this person. Marty slowed the van down and started to turn to the side of the road.

Nathan blinked, surprised that they were stopping. "You in the habit of picking up hitchhikers?"

"You ever been lost, alone, no money, and need a bit of help?" Marty shook his head fervently. "I've been out on the road alone. No help. Won't ever pass someone in need if I can help it. If it feels dangerous, we'll know. Besides, it's still daylight so we should be plenty safe."

As they drove closer the indistinct form focused into a slouching feminine shape with a long curve from the shoulders down to a slender waist and back to the delightful thighs of a powerful set of legs. Nathan wondered if his uncle had some sort of mystical power that could sense a pretty woman in need. Marty wiped his mustache with a bit of excitement and winked. "It used to be common to pick up strangers in need. I once traveled across California with just a back pack and a good pair of boots. Now, it's a crime. Meh!"

As the van slowed, Marty rolled down his window and stuck his head out like a dog panting. Nathan felt something odd, but didn't want to alarm his uncle right away as it didn't feel malicious. It was a strange, disquieting sensation in his stomach, but it didn't seem dangerous. She was standing between the shadows of nearby trees and the flashing reflected sunlight from passing cars.

She instinctively pulled back a rogue strand of her walnut brown hair behind her ears. Nathan thought she looked almost his age, but her large, expressive hazel eyes seemed to burst with innocence and the natural shape of her face straddled the border between girl and woman. The delectable curve of her thin body was highlighted by her height and long hair. She might have been a model in a painting if it weren't for the random mismatch of torn clothing that she wore. It looked as though a hyperactive, blind five-year-old had dressed her in rainbow of colors, ignorant of sizes, and then forgot to add shoes to the mix.

They had stopped in an area of the country without many signs of civilization. It seemed a bit odd that she would be out here in the wild without shoes. Marty beckoned her to the van. "Hello there."

"Hullo," she hesitantly replied. Her voice seemed broken and unused, like she had not spoken in years.

"Are you having trouble?"

She tilted her head as though she were struggling with language. "Trouble is having me."

Marty glanced over at Nathan. He shrugged his shoulders, confused. "Are you lost?"

"I'm right here." Her lower lip quivered and then pouted in a very appealing way. "I just don't know where I am at present."

Something about this girl troubled Nathan. He leaned over, trying to look past Marty. "Where are you going?"

"Home." She titled her head as though looking at something far away on the horizon. "That's where I'm supposed to find out who I am, isn't it?"

"I never really put much stock into that line of thought. We grow and evolve each day. And then I went home. Put the last twenty years into perspective and taught me everything about who I want to be." Marty chucked a bit under his breath and then glanced back to Nathan with a confused look on his face as though he was completely surprised he had shared that. "Do you need a ride? We can at the least get you someplace you can call your friends or family."

"I've tried to call them, but they can't hear me so far away," she said sadly.

"Where's your home?" Nathan asked. It felt wrong leaving her on the side of the road. She clearly had some sort of condition. Her eyes dilated and constricted. She rubbed her arms as though she had been hurt. Was that a spot of blood on her shirt? "If it's nearby, maybe we can just take you there."

"The nurse said home is where the heart is, but then I'd never leave home since my heart is here." She tapped her chest and then blinked as though trying to remember the exact words. "I'm going to the Emerald City, like the girl in the ruby slippers, to find my home."

Marty blinked twice, doing a double-take of what she said. "That sounds like Seattle, I guess. Or maybe Oz. You can't walk to either one from here. Don't you have someone that can help you?"

"The doctor asked that as well. I'm afraid I'm not myself today. Of course, I don't really know who I am so I can't really tell at present"

Nathan groaned just like Papa Ray did that time he brought home a box of kittens. He knew he was going to give in and would regret it. He sighed and then nodded to Marty. "We're going up to Sequoia for a bit. There's bound to be a bus station around or maybe we can find someone to help. Do you want a ride?"

She looked at the both of them and nodded innocently like a child. Marty got out of the car and opened the side door. She stepped gingerly into the backseat. "Did you have an accident?" Nathan asked.

"I don't remember." She rubbed her arms. There were dozens of scratches and faded bite marks that had long scabbed over with black, bubbling puss. "The days and hours have faded together into a white haze."

"Like snow blindness. You can't see anything for all of the light," Marty said in a soft voice, almost as though he were far away in a memory. "Happens sometimes with infections."

"I can't remember anything of the time before the hospital." She stifled a sob. Her eyes twitched. "What must I have been to not have anyone waiting for me? They wouldn't let me leave."

"I'm Nathan, this is Marty." Nathan said softly. "Right now you have us. We'll try to help you."

She tilted her head to examine Nathan. The tears stopped. Her eyes dilated as she seemed to peer straight through him. "The nurse named me Eve."

"Should we take you back to the hospital?" Marty asked, a bit concerned. "Honey, you don't look well."

"They couldn't keep me there. I want to go home." It was like listening to a child explaining why the sky was blue. Her voice was strong and absolute. "They couldn't make me better."

"We're going to stop at a hotel in an hour or so. You want to stay with us until we figure out how to help you?" Marty asked.

She paused a moment as though trying to solve a complex mathematical equation. "I am unwhole."

"We can see that," Nathan replied, a bit sharply.

"Nathan," Marty said carefully. "Remember what we were talking about before. I think this sort of applies, although not in the way we expected."

There was a major understatement. "That was my impression too. Not sure what we should do about it."

"You should drive. I'm going to see if I can put something on those cuts." Marty climbed inside of the van and pulled the door closed. "Let me know if you see anything weird."

Nathan hopped over to the driver's seat and started the van. He turned on the stereo and the first few cords of *Black Magic Woman* by Santana played. Marty had taught him to pay attention to the details and look for signs of synchronicity and commonality. Was this a sign? This girl didn't seem to be a threat. Shaking his head, he shifted the van into drive and took off down the road.

Marty turned around in his seat to face her. "Eve, can I look at your scratches? I can see if there is anything I can do for ya. I have a medicine bag back here."

"Yeah, Marty is good at examinations," Nathan quipped.

"I have wounds you can't see." Fear cracked her voice and her hands trembled. "Needles inside my eyes blocking thought and memory. But you can look."

There was an aura of innocence about Eve that was very attractive; there was also an undercurrent of menace. Nathan half expected for her to sprout fangs, except there was something tragic about her. And, of course, it was daylight. Marty opened a hidden compartment under one of the backseats and pulled out an old leather medicine bag that a doctor might have carried around in the fifties and sat down next to Eve. He groaned and rubbed his back muscles; it sounded like a dying animal.

"You OK there Marty?" Nathan asked.

His uncle ignored him. "Can I look at your wounds, Eve?"

She nodded sharply, clearly terrified. Nathan glanced back at them via the mirror. He expected her to roll her sleeves back. She blinked at him as though she was examining him and then slipped her frayed and torn ill-fitting shirt over her head. He had expected an undershirt, or maybe a bra, but instead was surprised by pale-naked flesh. "Whoa there!"

"What do you see, Doctor Martin?"

"Knock it off, Nate. She doesn't seem to know any better."

Eve seemed surprised. "You wanted to examine me, Doctor?"

Marty took a deep breath. "I'm not a doctor, Eve. Just a guy that knows a bit of medicine and other tricks. Please hand me that bag."

She obeyed without question. The scratches looked like they were caused by a savage animal and now were turning infectious. "If it's OK, I'm going to touch you on the arms."

He placed two fingers on her forearm, on top of the infected scratches and then sniffed. "A regular doctor wouldn't have given these marks a second look and assumed you were attacked by a wild animal. I've seen them before."

"What is it?" Nathan asked.

"The wounds smell like decay and death. Those scratches will never heal unless properly treated." Marty had her raise her arms and then checked her body closely. "Two more sets on her shoulders and one across her stomach. That explains her delirium and her fever."

Without so much as looking at him she exclaimed, "Nathan is worried that I'm a monster. Am I?"

"I don't think you're a monster."

"You don't think I'm human either. I'm not like you. You can sense it."

"Honey, it doesn't matter what you are. You are hurting. Do you know what caused these scratches?" Marty asked.

"Dead things, but the doctors told me not to tell. Can't look outside the lines."

Nathan and Marty made eye contact through the mirror. Nathan shrugged as if to say he had no idea what to do. Her skin was uniformly pale as though she had not seen the sun in years, but it had a certain appeal. Her flesh was perfectly toned from her exquisite neck down to her shoulders, a perfect chest and stomach muscles, and torso. Clearly she had been eating well and exercised regularly or had been blessed with the perfect score of genetics.

The van jarred slightly. "Eyes on the road, Nate!"

"Sorry!"

"Eve, I have a paste that will ease the pain and cure the infection. My brother and I developed it the last time we were out here. Can I apply it?"

Her eyebrows twisted with concern, but Eve nodded gingerly. Marty began to mix the ingredients, concentrating to make sure he had the right technique. "I need to concentrate here. If it's not mixed properly, the paste would be useless. Nate, I'll show you how to make this salve when we hit camp."

Eve sniffed and turned her face away. "It smells of knotweed and burdock."

"It is. It will suck out the poison, I promise." Marty continued his work. "I'm surprised that you can identify it by smell. Do you have experience with this sort of thing?"

"I don't remember." She extended her arm to Marty and he gingerly applied the salve. She winced from the stinging at first, but it cooled her skin. Marty applied it to her forearms and shoulders and allowed her to finish the job. Eve wrapped her arms around her body and shivered. "I'm cold."

"Put your sweater back on. I'll try to dig out a blanket," Marty ordered.

He pulled back the seat and reached into the trunk. He took out an old army blanket and wrapped it around her. "I feel sleepy," she said.

"You're safe for now. Your body needs sleep to heal. Go ahead and rest. We're going to pull over in a half an hour. You can share our room there," Marty promised, as he slipped into the front seat.

"Now she's staying in the same room?" Nathan asked.

"Looks like you and I are gonna have to share a bed, Nate."

Nathan looked back at Eve and she was already sleeping like a kitten. He felt a sense of peace hiding a swell of trouble. Aside from the wounds, there was something that wasn't quite right. It was like having a sore on the tip of your tongue. She was human and young and innocent; but he sensed an ancient, tragic soul. "You trust her?" Nathan asked.

"Oddly, I do. It's like she's generating good feelings, know what I mean?"

He smirked. "I feel it too. What is she?"

"I don't know."

"That's not too comforting."

"But there's a touch of fate with her too. Like we were meant to pick her up," Marty explained.

"Synchronicity. Like she's at the right time, and in the right place."

"It is unsettling that we both feel it. Could be nothing, but it could be important." He plucked his cigar from the tray and took a long drag. "We need to keep our eyes open and see what happens."

"Won't that screw the schedule?"

"There's no schedule on the Highway West. We learn what we learn in the time it takes to process. Trouble is bound to find us along the way. And I suspect this is trouble we were going to run into on the journey."

"How's that?"

"Agony let you go. There's no way she would have done that unless the New Flesh were hunting for someone else." Marty glanced back at the sleeping girl. "That girl survived a fight with vampires. She took some solid hits and kept on fighting."

"You think the New Flesh are after Eve?"

"I've never seen them separate before. Whatever the New Flesh is hunting for must be really important. And maybe we were meant to find this girl and help her along."

Nathan grinned. "Do some good in the world. That's what Grandma Loni told me."

"Well then, never let it be said that the old battle-axe didn't know her shit." Marty rolled down the window to take in the breeze. "Tell you what, we have a bit of a drive. I'll tell you the story of when Bill and I went for a joyride when he turned sixteen."

Somehow the drive seemed easier and the traffic not quite so slow.

# Chapter Six: Bound by Wild Desire

A hotel room, Marty Carver once explained in a hushed and reverent tone, is a place in search of meaning and definition. It can be the heart of a party, a refuge, or a place to lay a weary head after a long day's travel. It is a room that has no purpose until filled with people and imbued with meaning. To Nathan it was just a dingy place to sleep.

The dusty Tradesman pulled into the parking lot of the hotel, and Marty quickly arranged for a room. The sour-faced lady behind the counter frowned at the thought of renting a room without a valid credit card and forced him to pay a $300 deposit.

Nathan carried Eve into the small, grimy hotel room and tucked her into one of the beds. He wrapped the sheets around her. "She's a bit warm still."

It was a small space with the simple amenities expected in such a low-rent room: a swamp cooler, a small refrigerator, and a television on the dresser positioned opposite of the two beds. Marty nodded and flipped on the swamp cooler. It whirled like a small lawnmower and quickly pumped cool air into the room, which helped the circulation a great deal. "That should help her a bit. If the infection doesn't heal, we'll fill the tub with ice and dip her in there."

"I'm surprised she's still sleeping." Nathan dipped one of the wash rags from the bathroom in water and then placed it on her forehead. "We're not exactly being quiet here."

"Sleep is the natural way to cure most ills. The salve is a soporific

97

that helps that along." Marty peered through the blinds out the window. Dusk had arrived and the last rays of the sun shined across the land. "We have a bit of work to do, and not a lot of time to do it."

Nathan followed his uncle to the Tradesman and then watched as he opened the back hatch. He was quite surprised by the organized nature of the arrangement. There were tools, plastic containers, duffle bags, and even an old, ratty black guitar case. Marty lifted one of two heavy army duffle bags and gestured to the other one with his head. "That's not gonna move itself, you know."

"We're only staying one night. Why unpack everything?"

"We're not unpacking, kid," Marty said with a grim smile. "This is our armory. "

They dumped the duffle bags on the second bed. Nathan noted with some regret that he'd be sleeping very closely next to his uncle. "I hope you don't snore."

"Horribly so." Marty unzipped the duffle bag and started pulling out ingredients and strange items. He lifted two containers of purified salt and tossed them to his nephew. Nathan quickly dropped to his knees to catch them clumsily. "Draw lines around all of the windows and the door."

"Why does salt hurt the bad guys? Doesn't really make sense if you think about it." Nathan started clearing off the windowsill and poured lines of salt along the cleared space. "I mean vampires aren't slugs right?"

"Demons and vampires and some other creatures that go bump in the night hate the purifying element." Marty removed several large, sealed plastic containers of the greyish ash-like goofer dust from the bag. "In Morocco, they hang rock salt from leather straps and use them as amulets to ward off evil spirits. Some Catholic baptism rituals require that priests anoint salt on the lips of babies as a symbol of wisdom. Some chaos magic traditions claim that semen is a symbol of life."

"How do you know what's right?"

"What do you mean?"

"How do you know which traditions work and which ones don't?" Nathan started pouring the rock salt in a semi-circle around the door. "You've quoted Kabbalah, Catholic dogma, Tibetan philosophy, Aleister Crowley, Motley Crue, and everything in-between. How do you tell the truth from the thousand and one different of crocks of shit out there?"

"Well, truthfully, I'm more of a student of hoodoo than anything else." Marty continued to pull items out from the bags: A pickled severed human hand in a sealed jar, several sharpened stakes, a small leather pouch, a ring of iron skeleton keys, a large metal flask, a griss-griss bag made from an old red bandana, two swords that seemed more like giant daggers, and long strips of a dark brown wood. "Some of the scholars try to give it fancy names like chaos magic, but that's what it all boils down to. Use what works. We take bits from Indians, Creole, the Brits, the Celts, or anything else that can be used by the common man."

"What the Hell is this?" Nathan picked up one of the swords. It was much heavier than he imagined. "What is this thing made of?"

"Kid, that is a bonfide gladius. Latin for sword. The Romans conquered the known world with those bad boys. Good for slicing and dicing." Marty grabbed the other sword and pulled it out of its sheath. The short, but potent blade gleamed under the halogen lights. "Most swords have a crucifix shape that keeps a vampire's form from completely dissipating when you slice into it. This little bad boy can cut through almost anything made of flesh."

"I don't know how to use this. Never really had a sword. Grandma Loni would have flipped out."

"We'll practice for a bit when we make camp. I'll make you better than Flynn in no time."

Nathan pulled out his sword and held the blade close to examine it. "I see little glyphs. Are they magic?"

"The swords have bits of iron in the blade. Sometimes that's better than magic." Marty pointed to the glyphs. "Don't think of the symbols as two-dimensional objects. These runes have three-dimensional shapes that can't be seen with the naked eye until you're trained to see it."

"I don't understand."

Marty slid the sword back into the sheath and pulled out a large stick of chalk from one of the bags. "We perceive things as a matter of perspective from our location to the observed." He drew a square on the table. "From our perspective, that's a square. If we were able to change our location, we might see that square as a cube.

He added additional lines to create the illusion of a cube. Nathan shook his head. "No matter where I stand here, I'm always gonna see a square."

"In this dimension. Those eggheads studying string theory have it right. There are many dimensions on top of each other and we'd need infinite regress in order to see it all." He drew the seven-pointed star. "This is the heptagram. We used it for protection last night."

"That shape meant that it couldn't cross the lines, right?"

"Sort of. Nate, we're creatures of this world. We only see the two-dimensional lines because we lack perspective. If we had necromantic energy and existed in other dimensions, we might see that sigil as something like this." Marty added additional lines to create the illusion of a star-shaped column. "Those lines collect, store, and magnify certain types of energy like gnosis or Chi. You were able to power those lines because of those exercises I taught you."

"And that was why we were able to power the Dybbuk Box?"

Marty grinned and clapped his nephew on the shoulder. "Right as rain, kid. And it kept the Dybbuk Box from going crazy and forced it to trap all that energy. I'm good. I'm not entirely unwilling to use the word brilliant."

"There's a lot to learn."

"Don't worry, kid. I didn't learn all of this overnight. You've just started. My job is just to teach you enough to survive." Marty arranged the materials around the room until he was satisfied that a weapon would always be in reach. "And now, I think I need a drink."

"Great, leave me alone with her. What am I supposed to do here if she gets sick?"

His uncle winked in that special way that always led to trouble. "I just happened to notice that there is a small, but illustrious tavern just a few minutes walk from here and I think that might just be the next best lesson for you."

"You want to leave her here alone?"

"Why not? She's out. Her pulse is good. Breathing normal. Sleeping off the poison." Marty checked her temperature on her forehead using the back of his hand. He shrugged and looked around the room. "Her skin is already cooler. Let's leave her a note and step out for a few. Worse comes to worse, she'll join us across the street. We've protected the room as best we could. There's not a vampire in the world that could get in here unless she invites him inside."

"What about us? You said the New Flesh might be after us. Won't it be dangerous?" Nathan asked.

"The van has a number of runes and sigils burned into the frame. Took me and your old man two years and a lot of hoodoo to trick it out. They'd have a hell of a time tracking us mystically." Marty smoothed over his mustache with his finger. "And even if they could track us, that's a lot of distance to cover in a short amount of time and it just turned dark. They'd have to fly to get here in time. And, after the shit from last night, I could use a drink. Besides, it'll be an educational experience."

"You think I'll learn something from eastern California rednecks?" Nathan asked.

"Well sure, you've got to learn how to fuck goats sometime, son," Marty retorted. He opened the door, careful to avoid the circle of salt, and gestured for Nathan to follow him. Afterwards, he closed the door and locked it.

"Why can't a vampire just break down the door and then scrub away the dust?" Nathan asked.

"Vampires can't break into a house that's occupied by a human. Our soul imbues places with a residence. If a single family has lived in a house for a long time, they don't even need to be present to block a vampire." Marty checked the door to make sure it had been locked properly. "She'll be safe as houses in there. "And now, Nate, if we're lucky you'll find yourself in the middle of an ancient Carver tradition."

"What's that?"

"A bar fight."

The illustrious tavern was a rickety building with bits of side panels falling off and a flickering neon sign that burned the standard *Oasis* into the darkness. It was a single beacon of civilization surrounded by mountains, valleys, rivers, and empty winding roads. The hotel was already dark with the single exception of the dimly lit *No Vacancy* sign. Nathan Carver's experiences with actual bars were fairly limited. Most of what he knew was from movies and television. Somehow he imagined a lonely place surrounded by dark paneling.

There were a number of motorcycles, trucks, giant diesel haulers, and cars in the surrounding parking lot. He wondered why there were so many people here on a Sunday night. The bar was a lot louder than he expected, almost like a concert. People shoved and pushed past him like snakes in a bucket trying to find a comfortable place to rest. Smoke hung over the bar like a mist. They wormed their way through the crowd. Marty held up two fingers as they saddled up to the bar. "Two beers!"

The bartender was hairy and a bit weathered. He pointed to Nathan and shook his head. "No way."

"Show him your ID, kid." Marty bumped shoulders with his nephew and winked. "Trust me."

Nathan found his wallet and flipped it open. He pulled out his driver's license and slapped it onto the bar. Marty kept his eyes locked on the bartender with a surprising amount of concentration. The large man picked it up, studied the license for a few moments, and nodded. "You look fresh-faced for these parts, Mr. Carver."

The bartender returned the license and then poured the beers. Nathan gingerly glanced at the license to make sure that nothing had changed. Marty just grinned knowingly. He politely accepted his beer and quickly started swilling it. "How'd you do that?" Nathan asked once the bartender left.

"I glamoured him. Doesn't always work, especially if your target is aware. I changed how he perceived your license." Marty passed a beer to his nephew. "I figure if you are old enough to face down a creature from the beginning of time, you can have a beer. Remember, confidence is ninety percent of any game."

"You'll have to teach me that one." He sipped the beer and tried to hide the sour expression on his face. Nathan recalled sneaking a taste of Papa Ray's beer years before and thinking that it tasted horrible. His taste buds had not changed over time. At the occasional high school party, Nathan had always quietly gone for the fruity drinks, but figured this wasn't the place to ask for that sort of thing. "Smooth."

Marty laughed joyfully and patted him on the back. "I can't believe I'm finally here with you! This feels great!"

An old man sang *Ring of Fire* at the Karaoke station and the entire crowd cheered. Nathan imagined for a few moments that farmer or trucker felt like Johnny Cash and suddenly, he felt a strange kinship with this place and quickly joined the crowd. He often felt uncomfortable in a group, like he was always the one that didn't belong. It might have been the music or the beer, but Nathan felt completely at ease.

Several of the crowd took turns singing their favorite songs and sharing their dreams. Marty sang a rousing rendition of *On the Road Again* and managed a very passable Willie Nelson. By the time that he returned to his seat, there was another drink waiting on the bar from a smiling lady with a blond beehive, red lips, and an ample bosom. He took the drink, toasted the lady, and then smiled lecherously. "The things I do for you, Nate. Or rather don't do. Meaning that lovely lady over there."

"I can watch over Eve, if you'd like. I mean she'll be OK right?"

Marty took a big swig of his beer. "Sleeping like a baby, I expect. The salve I put on her will knock her out for a while to get the poison out. When she wakes up, she might be more herself."

"Might?"

"Something is really wrong with her. I don't know what it is. Didn't you feel it?" Marty asked.

"What do you think she is?"

"She's alive. I felt her heart beat. That rules out vampires, zombies, and any of the standard creatures of the night. She's not a mystic, or you'd know it."

"How so?" Nathan asked.

"The longer you are around one of them, the more your energies will sync. It's like being around two radios dialing into the same station. You'll feel the energy from the other person. It's not an immediate thing, but you were in the van with her for an hour. You would have felt it by now."

"What was the real reason you wanted to come in here?" Nathan asked.

The noise of the crowd made it a bit difficult to hear everything Marty said. He shrugged his shoulders. "I could lie, but why bother? I wanted a beer."

Nathan opened his mouth to attempt a biting comment suggesting that Marty should engage in few acts of bestiality, when he was cut off by a cold chill that started in the back of his head and slowly crept down his entire back. He looked around and the other residents of the bar were drinking, laughing, and making Polack jokes. In the back of his mind, he could hear music – dark, frightening music. "What the hell was that?"

"Don't know." Marty said, looking around worried. "I'm not as sensitive as you are."

Nathan glanced around, but couldn't see anything out of place, still he had the oddest feeling that there was something at the edge of his vision that he couldn't quite see. "What's it feel like to be glamoured?"

"I think you already know, kid." Marty gestured towards the door. "Something's here. I can feel it now."

They slowly stood from their stools and Marty casually led Nathan to the back exit. A large man in a black leather trench coat and a fedora blocked the hallway. He wore dark round sunglasses, a scarf that covered his lower face, and black boots that seemed made to stomp heads. Nathan had the sense that this man would kill him without a moments thought or hesitation. The local rednecks didn't seem to notice him.

"Son of a bitch!" Marty took a step back and held up his hands in a pleading position as if to announce that he was not a threat; a submission gesture to a greater predator. "Acrimony! I'm surprised to see you here."

When the man spoke, his voice was cold like shattering ice and deep as the deepest hole in the earth; a voice that delighted in suffering and laughed at death. It was as though someone shoveled a pound of gravel down a gentleman's throat. "Delightful to run into you, Martin! What do you say? Shall we go outside for a bite?"

"I don't think we look at the same menu." Marty stepped to ensure that his body shielded Nathan. Marty looked around the room hopefully, but was clearly disappointed. "Besides, we're far too valuable to you alive."

"We? Who is we?" Acrimony loomed over Marty and sniffed towards Nathan. His voice dripped with mocking faux-jealousy. "Who is this you invited to our special rendezvous? Have you been cheating on me?"

"This is Nathan Carver." Marty said in the only tone that is possible when faced with a rattlesnake. "Nate, this is Acrimony."

The large man bowed politely and then held up a single black-gloved finger as though he were addressing a class. "Acrimony: defined as the following. Bitter, sharp animosity, especially as exhibited in speech or behavior." Nathan unconsciously extended his hand. Acrimony waved away the offer. "Touching makes the hurting start. And we don't want that in public, do we? That would be impolite."

"Why are you here, Acrimony?" Marty asked.

"We're on the hunt. Looking for that which was lost and happy fortune smiles upon us that we find you. Luck runs out for all of us in time, does it not?"

"Maybe we could help you? Pay off a bit of the debt." Marty stepped back again, pushing Nathan into the crowd. He gestured behind his back for Nathan to run. "Everything changes and evolves, doesn't it?"

"Everything devolves. Everything decays." He followed Marty menacingly. Acrimony seemed supremely confident as though he had little doubt in his mind that he could slaughter everything in the room and fill it with blood to his knees should he find it necessary. He gestured to Nathan with a black-gloved hand. "The son of William Carver shall become part of the flesh as it has been prophesied."

"What did I do?" Nathan asked over Marty's shoulder.

"The sins of the father shall be paid in full by the son. That which the Carvers have taken from us shall be redeemed with their flesh. So it has been written in the Book of All Flesh and thus shall come to pass," Acrimony declared. "Sorrow was taken from us. You will replace him."

"You guys killed a bunch of vampires?" Nathan asked, impressed.

"We were young and immortal and really, really stupid." Marty pushed back into the crowd until he reached the bar. The natural sway of the crowd filled in many of the spaces between them, except for Acrimony. The people instinctively knew to avoid his reach. "But now, I'm older, smarter, and a hell of lot sneakier."

Slowly, Acrimony followed them and a wicked shark-grin pressed against the scarf. Nathan shivered at the thought of what that mouth might look like uncovered. Marty somehow managed to maneuver a crowd of loud men between them and Acrimony. The leader seemed to be a giant, fat man dressed in a bright bowling shirt swilling bottle after bottle of beer. He was the only one that stood taller than Acrimony. "How do you have sex 'cowboy style'? You fuck your wife from behind and then tell her 'this is how my girlfriend likes it' and see how long you can stay in her!" The fat man joined his buddies in roaring with laughter.

"That is so funny Chet!"

Martin tapped Chet on the shoulder. The Neanderthal-sized man turned to him and grinned derisively with a chipped toothy grim. "That's pretty funny. And speaking of which, that is one beautiful shirt," Marty said coyly. Chet laughed again and his friends nodded because that seemed the smart thing to do. Martin paused a moment to let his words sink in and then delivered the punch line. "Did your husband buy it for you?"

There was a pregnant pause that seemed to overtake the room all at once. The other rednecks stopped laughing and looked at each other dumbfounded. The music died stillborn as a murmur washed over the crowd. The bartender took a step back quickly pulling bottles away from bar and making a note to look the other way. Chet loomed over them, leaning far too close for comfort. "What did you say?" the fat man asked.

"I said 'did your husband buy that shirt for you?'" Marty repeated himself.

Acrimony chuckled and then tipped his fedora. Chet's buddies were moving to surround them like a pack of wolves trained through thousands of years of evolution to support their alpha. "Marty! What are you doing?" Nathan asked, worried.

"Family tradition." He leaned back and whispered to Nathan. "Acrimony won't get involved if there's a public brawl. Too high profile."

"I hope the ass beating is worth it." Nathan balled his hands into a fist and readied for the fight. "For the both of us."

The fat man cracked his knuckles and his buddies cackled. There were four of them and their laughter and jibes were feeding each other and building to a wild crescendo. "You saying something about my character?"

"Not at all," Marty said confidently. Chet laughed again like he won a victory. It was a hollow laugh that seemed to magnify with sheer malice. He turned to Nathan and then shrugged. "I'm just saying that with your big man titties that you look like the sort of guy that would crawl on his belly through a whore house to get sodomized by a large black man named Leroy."

Chet nodded towards Nathan and then grunted. "Sammy, Jethro, hold the boy. This little piss pot is mine."

The fat man swung his fist and it swished through the air like a jackhammer. Marty barely dodged under the blow and started rabbit punching into his side. Time seemed to slow for Nathan while everyone else sped up around him. Chet brought his elbow down upon Marty's back knocking him to the floor. Nathan leapt to defend his uncle, but the others blocked him and pushed him against the bar. The tall skinny redneck with the bandana stepped up and then donkey-punched Marty in the back of the head. "Take that!"

Dazed, but determined, Marty grabbed hold of one of Chet's legs and swept the other into the air. Chet lumbered back onto the hardwood floor with a loud thud, knocking against his friends. He didn't get a chance to press any advantage as the rednecks quickly set upon Marty and helped Chet to his feet.

Nathan tried to stop the fight, but Sammy and Jethro caught him by surprise. They hammered his sides with blows. The acids in his stomach burned and seemed to travel up to his heart and throat. His legs buckled and the room seemed to spin wildly. Each of them grabbed one of his arms and forced Nathan to watch his uncle get curb-stomped by the giant.

Acid in his stomach seemed to transmute to fire. It expanded into his arms and his legs giving him strength. Frustrated, Nathan screamed and extended his arms wildly with a single burst of energy. Catching them by surprise, he wormed his way free and knocked his attackers to the side. He pushed Chet away from Marty. The fat man flew forward as though catapulted.

Sammy picked up an empty beer bottle and cracked it over Nathan's head. It failed to shatter upon impact, but did provide a solid blow with a loud CLUNK sound. Strangely, it did not stagger him. He stood dumbfounded that he wasn't in pain and tilted his head surprised. The energy he felt when facing the creature the night before returned. His skin burned and ached with fire. He turned to Sammy confused.

Sammy cracked the bottle on the edge of the bar and then used the jagged remainder of the bottle to stab Nathan in the stomach. The glass crumbled; melted bits and shards scattered over the ground. Nathan looked at where the gash in his stomach should be and then grabbed Sammy by the neck. Feeling very powerful, he flipped Sammy on the bar and rolled him through the various glasses and bottles until he fell off the other end.

Jethro hit Nathan with a bar stool. The force of the blow somehow was blunted. It was as though Nathan reached out with his magic and stopped it before it could hurt him. Jethro pulled back the bar stool and then lifted it to use as a shield. Angry, Nathan grabbed the bar stool as though it were a toy and yanked it from him. Jethro and Sammy decided that Chet wasn't worth the grief and ran.

He realized that he had forgotten about Marty. Nathan scanned the room and discovered Marty was standing over Chet returning the favor by kicking him. The other redneck was on the floor knocked out. "Marty! Don't you think that's enough?"

Marty shrugged and fished in his pocket for his pack of cigarettes. He pulled one out of the package, lit it, and glanced around the room looking for their enemy. "I lost Acrimony during the fight, but he might still be around. Thankfully, he won't dare attack with so many eyes about."

He rubbed his knuckles, surprised that he had been that strong and could move that fast. Marty was limping and there were multiple bruises and bits of blood on his face, and yet he grinned like a Cheshire cat. "What the hell are you grinning about?" Nathan yelled.

"I knew you had the stuff, kid. I knew it!"

Other customers were whispering. Marty pulled out a small wad of twenties and dropped it on the bar. "That's for any damages and paying their tab. There's not going to be any problems, is there?"

The bartender seemed happy to have such a large tip so he didn't question it. "Well, normally, we have the fights on Friday nights, but no one was hurt too badly."

Nathan decided not to argue the point. He wouldn't know how to explain what happened anyway. Marty nodded enthusiastically. "We should be getting back anyway."

They decided to head back to the room and quickly left the bar and started crossing the parking lot. "Why'd you start that fight? Nine of ten times you can avoid a fight."

Marty took a drag off his cigarette. "Acrimony was gonna bite off my arm and worse. I owe their boss Cenotaph. I owe him a lot. They want to collect before I die."

"What do you owe them?" Nathan asked.

"My eyes."

"What? What the hell could you have gotten that was worth that?" Nathan asked.

"Time," he said quietly.

"What the hell are you talking about? What have you gotten me into?"

"Nate, I told you that this was my last trip. I didn't tell you that I'm dying. Lung cancer, if you can believe it?" he said, savoring another long drag from his cigarette.

"Jesus Christ! You didn't think that was important enough to tell me?"

"Nate, listen to me. I was in the hospital. Alone. I had the chance to look at my life. I made a promise to your father. The trip we made was the happiest time in my life. If I can put you on the right road, I've made my own amends."

Nathan didn't know what to say. "That's a lot to put on me."

"That would be why I didn't say anything before," he replied.

"What about Acrimony?" Nathan asked, worried. "Does that mean he wants to make me a vampire like them?"

"Doesn't matter, I settled it all. There's enough power in the Dybbux Box that I can pay off Cenotaph to make them leave you alone." He took a last drag off the cigarette. "And they'll deal to make sure I give up my eyes."

"Don't you need your eyes?" Nathan asked, horrified.

"Only for a while," Marty explained. "They gave me enough life to find you and get you through this summer. There's a little blind girl that needs my eyes. That girl's a decent sort, even if her family is a bunch of crazies that mix with vampires."

"OK, so we can't stay here with Acrimony knowing where we are, what's our next move?" Nathan asked.

"We press on to the camp in the morning. We should be protected in the hotel. Vampires can't enter a room without being invited inside. Tomorrow morning, we take Eve with us, for now we..." Marty's reply was cut off by the sight of the hotel door to their room ripped in half. "Son of a bitch!"

The hair on the back of Nathan's neck tingled. Startled, they rushed into the old hotel. Their bags had been thrown around the room. The cheap, dusty television had been tossed to the side. The goofer dust and salt had been washed away and replaced with giant puddles on the floor.

Acrimony sat on the bed smoking a cigarette with a big shit- eating monster grin that went beyond any possibility that Nathan could have imagined. It was although some mad god had cut a shark's jaw and magically merged it onto the face of a cruel man. "I made myself at home, boys. Hope you don't mind."

"Where is she?" Nathan asked, balling his hands into fists. "What did you do to her?"

Acrimony laughed and took a long drag on the cigarette. "Whoa! Ease up there, Trigger. She's fine. I didn't molester her or anything.

What do you think I'm gay?"

"Gay? She's a girl. What are you talking about?" Nathan asked, anything to keep the monster talking until he could reach a weapon.

"A soft girl. Feminine. The primal woman you might say. Why would I waste myself on her flesh? You are what you eat, after all? Why would I want to be soft and weak?" Acrimony explained. The vampire started thrusting his pelvis. "That's why I only consume men and force them to accept my special love. Only a real man fucks other men."

Nathan didn't have an answer to that. He looked over at the gladius on the bed and wondered if it would cut through this monster's flesh. Acrimony laughed and snatched the weapon quicker than human eyes could track. "You think this little toy could hurt me? That's almost as funny as that stunt at the bar Martin pulled."

"Figured you were trying to lay low," Marty replied. His voice was surprisingly calm. "It made sense. How did you get past the wards?"

"Easy once I got the door open. I just filled an old bucket with water and washed them away." He laughed, a metaphorical grinder consuming any joy or mirth around them. "Like you could stop me from going where I will."

"How did you get the door open?" Marty asked.

"I kicked it open."

"How did you cross the threshold? You can't do that when there is a soul occupying the residence unless you are invited in."

"Wouldn't you like to know?" Acrimony laughed and then put out the cigarette on the bed sheets. "Alas, that is not important to this discussion."

"Where is Eve?" Nathan asked.

Acrimony paused a moment while smirking as though waiting for something. A flush from the bathroom startled them. Eve opened the door and walked out of the bathroom. Her face seemed less flushed than before, but it was clear she was very concerned. "Nathan! Marty! I was so worried you were gone. Mr. Acrimony was keeping me company."

Acrimony adjusted his fedora. "Here's the thing. I was all set to kill her. I had a plan and I must admit that it was spectacular. It would have been a masterpiece. The angels would have wept my name for centuries. And then something strange stopped me. Magical even. You know she's not human right?" Acrimony asked.

"Yeah, sorry to disappoint you." Marty tried to edge closer to his weapons.

The vampire shook his head, disappointed, and waved his finger in front of them. "Quite alright. Turns out I can't harm her anymore. Called the boss. He found it delightfully amusing that you would be the one to find his little lost girl. You see he's glad you're back. Apparently you made a real impression when you met before."

"Who the hell are you talking about?" Nathan asked, frustrated.

Acrimony scoffed, ignoring Nathan. "He said to tell you two things. First, you can't trick him twice. Try again at the cost of your soul."

"And the second?" Marty asked.

Acrimony pulled off his sunglasses revealing twin holes of

blackness and then cleaned them on his shirt. "Bring him the girl and the box and all of the debts of the Carver family are settled."

"I don't wanna see the boss," Eve protested.

"What about Nathan?" Marty asked.

"The New Flesh has eternity. Not a one of Zeal's prophecies has ever failed." Acrimony laughed. His shark teeth clattered together. "We are patient. He will come to us in the end. Pack up the girl and go to Seattle. I'm supposed to give you a head start."

"And if we say no?" Nathan asked.

"Well, I can't seem to harm this girl. I can, however, kill you. There are such delights we can share. Think of it Martin, you end it all here and now."

Nathan felt energized from his fight. Why was Marty cowering from this vampire? "There's two of us. We can take him."

"No!" Marty held up his hand. "You're not trained yet. And he can kill me pretty quick."

"Take the deal Martin. Or when next we meet, I'll be taking both an arm and a leg. Literally. Cenotaph said I could have everything but the eyes." Acrimony carefully counted the remainder of his pack of cigarettes. "Know this. I am going to take in the night air and find Chet. This plan is simply too good to be denied for very long. And then I am going to smoke each and every one of my seventeen cigarettes. When I am finished, I am coming for you. Run, Martin Carver. Run!"

Acrimony blew Marty a kiss and then pulled up his scarf. He tipped his hat to Eve. The vampire slowly sauntered out of the hotel room, and politely lifted the door just enough to close it. There was a silent pause, the kind that happens after a natural disaster or a massacre. Marty coughed a bit and then turned to Nathan and Eve. "Pack everything as fast as we can. If he can catch us in the time limit, he'll do as he promised."

The three of them worked quickly at a frenzied pace. Nathan made certain that he kept one of the bags up front in case there was trouble. Now that there was an emergency, Eve was very quick on the draw and seemed to have a natural affinity for packing and putting everything in the proper place. It was only once they had packed the van and been on the road for several minutes that Marty realized the final insult. "Damn it. Now, I won't get the deposit back."

# Chapter Seven: Whispered Words of Wisdom

Marty kept the Tradesman running at a steady pace throughout the night, fearful that Acrimony might break his word on a whim and start chasing them down. The wide paths of Highway 99 narrowed into rural Highway 198 and then eventually faded into the winding roads that led past Red Hill and the three rivers. Once they crossed onto the General's highway, he released a sigh of relief. "Son of a bitch! I think we're in the safe zone. The New Flesh won't follow any farther into Sequoia."

"Why not?" Nathan asked. "Is there something nastier in here?"

"I feel warmth and calm. Life." Eve poked her head into the driver's cabin. "The water runs pure here."

"She's right. This land is sacred. There's pure energy untouched by man or beast here. We're going to a healing place." Marty kept his eyes on the road. Even with the high-beams, it was clearly dangerous taking these turns at night without slowing down. "We should be safe here until we leave."

"Great, can you tell me what happened?" Nathan asked. "I swear to God one of those rednecks cut me with a broken beer bottle and it didn't hurt. No blood at all. Just made me stronger."

"I need to concentrate on the road to make sure we get there in one piece. Tomorrow, I'll tell you anything you want."

Gradually, the light from the moon dimmed in the shadow of the rocks and later the giant sequoia trees grew larger the farther they drove into the mountain range. The radio produced only static, so they shuffled through several cassettes until finally, at dawn, they turned onto a winding dirt road that led to a rustic one-room log cabin with faded red shingles covered with moss and leaves.

By then Nathan could barely keep his eyes open. The three of them dragged the bare essentials from the van into the cabin. There were only two beds, but Marty had extra sleeping bags stashed away in the van and so he made a cozy bed for himself in the corner. A jug of water was all that they had until they could make a run to the store for supplies. Nathan took the top bunk, afraid that Eve would fall off in her sleep. He kept a gladius cradled next to him and his back firmly against the wall. When he finally slept, he dreamed of hideous, chattering shark teeth.

Sweat slowly dripped from his drenched head as he hid from the light under the flannel blanket. He wiped his drenched hair and kicked off the covers only to discover rays of sunlight beaming over him. Pulling the thin pillow over his face, he tried to stay in sleep's soft embrace. His poor muscles ached as though he had run a marathon. His feet felt like they had swollen to twice their natural size and his mouth tasted as though he had cleaned out an ash tray with his tongue. "Man, I feel like burnt shit on a shingle."

He waited for the natural typical sardonic comeback and rubbed his eyes when there was no response. Nathan peered over the bed to discover that Marty's sleeping bag had been rolled up, tied, and placed comfortably in the corner. Hanging upside down like a bat, he peeked under his bed to check on Eve, only to discover that her bed was not only empty, but it had been made as well. Did they leave? He looked out the window to find that the van was gone. How had he not heard the van leave?

Tucking the gladius under his arm, he climbed down the steps to the hardwood floor and stretched. Where did they go? Where did they leave the water? Rummaging through the boxes on the table, he found the water jug, filled the canteen, and gulped down several swallows. He couldn't remember the last time he had drank so much water without getting sick. What time was it? He checked his phone. No signal, which was hardly a surprise in the mountains. The time however was a complete surprise. *5:23?* Just a couple hours to sunset. Did he really sleep that long?

The breeze on the front porch was cool and refreshing. Nathan changed into a pair of shorts and sat barefoot on the steps sipping water and feeling the sand between his toes. He scratched his head through his unruly mop of curly hair. It felt surprisingly good to simply breathe and feel the sunlight on his face.

A short time later, the hum of the Tradesman rattled through the trees and the old van quickly rolled up the hill and onto the yard. Sporting his sunglasses, Marty waved from the driver's seat. Eve mimicked his greeting from the passenger's seat wearing a pair of cheap, side of the road "bargain" sunglasses. "Marty took me to the store! It was wondrous!"

Nathan stood to greet them and stretched his back. "You sound like you've never been inside a store before."

"It's difficult to say. It felt like a new experience. Marty asked if I was born in a barn," Eve answered and then added sadly. "I wish I knew. If I was born in a barn that is."

Marty exited the driver's seat, walked around to the side door, slid it open, and gestured to the cardboard boxes filled with groceries, bottled water, and sundry items. He grumbled a bit. "It's been a trying experience. Let's just unload the van. I'm starved!"

"Shopping that bad?" Nathan asked.

Eve jumped out of the van and then twirled excitedly, showing off her new white cotton sundress. Her hair whipped around her neck. "Marty bought me clothing. And flip-flops and feminine hygiene products."

Nathan looked over to his uncle and tilted his head. "Really?

"Don't ask, don't tell." Marty grabbed a couple of the boxes and hauled them inside. Nathan and Eve followed suit. "This should keep us solid for at least a week."

"How long do you figure we're going to stay?" Nathan asked.

"The plan was three weeks, but now I just don't know." Marty started unloading the groceries. "I stopped by the manager's cabin. We should have water and power now."

"What do you mean, you don't know?" Nathan asked, irritated. "I thought you were the man with the plan."

"I don't plan anything on an empty stomach. That just leads down bad roads. You like omelets, right?" Marty started gathering onions, mushrooms, and tomatoes onto a large cutting board and started dicing and slicing ingredients with a large knife. "Nothing better than a good meal to make things look better."

"I want to feel the sun on my face. Smell the trees." Eve poked her head through the door. "I want to know this place."

Marty quit chopping and thought about it. "You should be safe here, Eve, but will you promise to keep the cabin in sight? It isn't hard to get lost around here and until you remember things I think it would be better that you don't stray too far. OK?"

Eve smiled thoughtfully and tilted her head. "I'm already lost. Can't be more lost."

"Just so I don't worry, OK?"

"Yeah, Marty is old. His heart can't take the stress," Nathan added.

She stepped outside the cabin and leaned her head back. Strands of her hair covered her face. "I will stay close," she promised.

Through the window, they watched Eve start to explore her new world. She stopped at a sequoia tree and examined it closely as though it was completely alien to her. "There's something not right about that girl," Marty declared. "She's not just suffering through a memory problem. Amnesia doesn't take all of your experience. Memory doesn't work like that. You can forget events, but not knowledge. Everything is new and fresh like she's been formed out of nothing."

"Could she be faking?" Nathan asked. "I hate to ask, but it was strange that we found her when we did."

"How would that benefit her? It might earn sympathy, but I think she had that covered in spades." He looked up from the cutting board to check on Eve briefly and then returned to his work. "Acrimony couldn't hurt her. That's something rare and worth commenting on."

"I felt it when I first saw her." Nathan took another gulp of water and tried to process the experience. "You know how when a cat sits in your lap and purrs. You keep petting it because it feels good and relaxing. That's what being around her is like."

"I suppose that's possible. There's something about her that makes you want to protect her. Some sort of defense mechanism, maybe? I don't know," Marty admitted.

"What about what Acrimony said? Is she human?" Nathan asked.

"She looks human, but that can be deceiving. She's not a vampire. I tested her with the goofer dust and splashed a bit of holy water on her. Today, I tried every possible test I could think of. I ran her through the dairy section and none of the milk curdled."

"What does that prove?" Nathan asked.

"Curdled milk can be a sign of demonic possession or bonds with the infernal. Or a number of other known demonic curses." Marty shook his head. "She has a pulse. We checked her blood pressure at the machine at the pharmacy. If she isn't human, I don't know what she is. But it would explain one thing."

"What's that?"

"Acrimony was able to break into the hotel room. He shouldn't have been able to cross the threshold without a direct invitation from Eve."

"How exactly does that work?" Nathan asked. "It doesn't make sense. Aren't there magic laws? Isn't there an order to how the universe works?"

"Nate, the world, the universe, is vast on a scale our brains can't conceive. If we had the ability to know everything, we'd be gods." Marty grabbed a beer from the box, popped off the cap and took a swig. "That said, there are a couple of theories. Here's the one I tend to believe. Plato believed that the soul had three parts. Logos is the divine spirit that gives you the ability to reason. Thymos is that element that allows you to love and feel empathy. Eros is the hunger and desire that burns you."

"What does that have to do with vampires?" Nathan asked.

"The process that transforms a human into a vampire destroys the thymos part of the soul. It burns it away. That leaves a gap in the soul. Eros expands to fill that space. That's the nature of the vampire. To consume without regret. To take without guilt. Everlasting hunger."

"And that missing part of the soul is their weakness?" Nathan asked.

"Exactly. That's why vampires shy away from crosses when presented with faith. They lack the ability to withstand that sort of spirituality because they lack a full soul." Marty poured a bit of water to the egg mixture and then started adding ingredients. "A vampire can't enter into a home where a soul has created a resonance without an invitation. That invitation forms a tacit permission that provides a bit of spiritual shielding."

"Maybe the New Flesh found a way around that?" Nathan asked.

Marty shook his head. "Nah. If vampires found a way to do that,

I'd have heard about it. The New Flesh seek to break down their weaknesses. There'd be a rash of murders the likes of which this world hasn't seen in years. I think for some reason Acrimony was right and that because Eve isn't human that the threshold curse didn't apply to her."

"Is she dangerous?"

"Anything that the New Flesh would be interested in should be considered dangerous."

"Am I dangerous?" Nathan asked.

"Only if I train you properly." Marty winked and then started cracking eggs and pouring them into a large metal bowl. "And if you get a chance to grow on your own."

"You said that you would answer questions."

Marty nodded, adding a bit of ground black pepper and a pinch of cayenne pepper into the bowl. "That I did. Limited time offer. Ask your questions. Just start dicing those potatoes while we're talking. I haven't eaten solid since yesterday."

"Fair enough." Nathan washed several potatoes and stared dicing them. The first question was the most important question. It had weighed on his mind since they had run from the hotel. "How long do you have?"

He nodded as though he expected this. "Hard to say really. I know I have this summer. Maybe a bit longer. My lungs are too far gone for most magic and I'm not willing to deal with necromancy or bargain with the creatures that wait beyond the Great Barrier."

The bitterness in Nathan's voice was not disguised in any way.

"Why didn't you tell me? Or the family? We could have taken care of you."

"Nate, you've never looked into the eyes of your parents and seen nothing but disappointment and regret and then wondered if they would have preferred you had died instead of your brother." Marty took a long deep breath to stabilize himself. "I had to make things right. I couldn't come back until I had a plan and made things good. I'm doing this just as much for me as I am for you."

Nathan was eager to change the subject. He wasn't quite ready to accept that his uncle would die. "What are the New Flesh? What do they want? Why do they want me?"

"The New Flesh is just a modern nickname. I think Acrimony picked it from some old movie. I've learned about some of their names. The Cult of Scorpio. The Scions of Kali. The Sindici." He covered his mouth with a napkin and coughed. It was a wet, nasty cough. It lasted several seconds, but the weight of the worry seemed to stretch it out for hours. "I doubt they even remember where they came from. History isn't a big priority of theirs."

"What do they want? Why do they want me?"

"They want to overcome all vampire weaknesses. They believe that if they can overcome the flaws in the black pits that remain in their souls they can become invincible."

"How does that work?"

"They believe as per ancient Hindi beliefs that all human emotions can be divided into four aspects. The New Flesh think that vampires don't have enough of the thymos to break free of the vampire curse, but there is just enough spark that they can do it together. They combined bits of pagan and Hindu traditions to create four roles that they believe encompass all human emotions coming from the thymos: sympathy, anger, gratitude, and guilt. They each take a role and take on that emotion for the group."

"So then Acrimony represents anger right?" Nathan asked.

"Yes, he hates. It burns him. He channels it all into a laser-like focus." Marty poured the eggs into a sauce pan and held it over the butane oven. The eggs sizzled as they cooked. "And when they feel that they have mastered said condition they evolve in the circle. Agony was once Joy."

"And why do they want me?"

"They are missing a part of the circle. The most advanced level."

Nathan washed a couple more potatoes and then started slicing them. "I don't understand."

"The most advanced level of their system is Grief. To feel grief you must have empathy and a sense of morality. You must feel the pain of loss. I bet they haven't had someone to fill the role of guilt since Bill and I killed him," Marty explained. He stirred the eggs until they bubbled from a liquid mass into a yellow solid. "Just needs to cook a bit more. Start on the potatoes."

He salted the potatoes and added bits of pepper and onions into the mix and then threw it into a pan and started cooking next to Marty. "What does that have to do with me?"

"We met them on the road near Seattle years ago. They were friendly and kind at first. We didn't understand their nature until in the middle of a party one of them named Zeal had a vision. He prophesied that the son of Bill would be their new Grief. That started a fight. We killed several of them including their leader, named Chagrin."

"So I'm going to be turned into a vampire?" Nathan asked horrified.

"Seers glimpse a thread of a possible future. That's in the name augury. They fish for the future. The future is always in flux until it isn't." Marty laughed a bit. "We aren't that lucky and the universe isn't that ordered."

"And they work for a boss?"

"He is called Cenotaph. I don't think he is human enough any more to know his real name." The mere mention of his name seemed to darken the room. "He was once just like you, hundreds of years ago. Only he learned to use his power to hurt, to corrupt. And then at the end of his life, he learned to live through consuming the essence of others."

"That's what you meant about the cost, isn't it?" Nathan asked, horrified.

"The things we do leave a mark, kid. Believe me some things are better left undone." Marty flipped the eggs, took a long whiff, and turned down the flame. "These are almost done."

"I started a bit too late."

Marty bumped Nathan and took control of the skillet. "You have to move the potatoes around a bit." He used the spatula to rotate the potatoes to even the exposure to the heat. "This really helps with the taste."

"Why not be a vampire? Isn't that a form of life for you?"

He stirred the potatoes and shook his head. "I wouldn't want to live a life where I had to kill to survive. I might be a bastard, but even I have limits."

"You couldn't feed without killing?" Nathan asked.

"Maybe at first. I'd lose that part of myself that cares and who knows what I'd do. My soul is bad off as it is." He salted the potatoes a bit more and then grinned. "Death's not the end of the world. Maybe that's not the right way to phrase it. If you lived your life right without regret, then I think it all works out."

"You mean heaven? You know if there is a heaven and God? Angels and saints? All that?"

"If there is a heaven, really a heaven, I just hope they serve beer. In the meantime, we just do the best that we can down here and hope it pays off somewhere down the line." Marty checked the potatoes and nodded. "Call for Eve. I think we're finally ready."


They ate the meal between quiet bits of conversation. Eve fervently described everything she had seen outside. When she bit into her meal, she chewed slowly as though savoring the taste for the first time. "Make sure you drink some water with that," Marty suggested.

Eve nodded her head, mimicking Nathan, and then drank a bit from her water bottle. Nathan took another bite and then asked, "So the big question is what do we do next? We can't stay here forever."

"I like it here. I feel myself here, even if I don't know who that is,"

Eve protested.

Marty finished chewing his food, swallowed, and then wiped his mustache clean. "The plan was to stay here a couple of weeks to bond and then introduce you to Papo."

"Papo?"

"Papi means father in Spanish," Eve added.

"You know Spanish?" Nathan asked flabbergasted.

Eve nodded gingerly as though just now realizing it. "Papo is a slang term for affection between two men."

"That's right, Eve. The special love between men." Marty's eyes were as wide as saucers. "Only not so gay. It translates better in Spanish. Something akin to the feeling of brotherhood. Anyway, Papo is a mystic. A traveler. Twenty years ago, Bill and I saved his life, and he taught us a bit about the world and promised he'd help us anytime."

"And he's still around?" Nathan asked skeptically.

"If you live right and have the power running through your veins, you can live a long while. He agreed to stop by here in a few weeks and spend a few days giving you a push where it's needed."

"What do we do until then?" Nathan asked.

"We live. We breathe. Enjoy the summer."

*     *     *     *

Nathan, Marty, and Eve settled into a relaxing routine at the cabin. Time seemed to flow together. Sleep came easy at night after hours of laughter, discussion, and occasional music. Eve convinced Marty to open the old, ragged black guitar case and play the guitar around the fire. Much to Nathan's visible surprise, Marty was simply brilliant and could play virtually any song that Nathan called at random. Eve sat lotus position in the dirt swaying like a charmed snake. He plucked the chords with such precision and delight that Nathan couldn't help but feel a bit jealous. "I never imagined you were that awesome!"

Marty waved away the complement. "Bah! I just have a good ear for mimicking others. Nothing original."

"You could play professionally. Did you ever try?" Nathan asked.

His uncle shook his head. "I failed the test, kid. I have a bit of the talent for it, but not that spark of greatness."

"How do you know unless you really try?"

Blood flushed through Marty's cheeks. Nathan realized that it was a touchy subject. "I failed the test, kid. There's nothing else to say."

"It is hard?" Eve asked, her eyes wide open with enthusiasm.

"Playing guitar? Just takes practice."

"Will you teach me?" Eve placed her hand on Marty's shoulder. Her fingers seemed to buzz like a low-level purr from a favorite, spoiled cat. He turned to Nathan not certain what to say. "I want to make music with my fingers."

He swallowed and shrugged his shoulders. "I don't know that we'll be together for that long, and I don't want to make you any promises, but I can get you started, Sweetie."

During the mornings, Nathan and Eve hiked along a new trail discussing the world and trying to think of something in the world that she remembered. He tried to stump her with new words, but that was the one bit of information she still remembered from what they started referring to as the time before. Marty spent that time reading or tinkering around under the van.

Around noon, they all returned to the cabin for lunch followed a couple of hours of lessons with Marty. They started with the gladius and then progressed to stakes, knives, and guns. "During a fight, if you practice, you can access the power you have inside of you. It can make you stronger, faster, tougher, but it's dangerous to do it for too long. You aren't immortal. Your body wasn't designed to run that hot."

"What happens if I run too long?"

"I've never seen it mind you, but I did hear a story about a man setting his own blood ablaze." Marty shrugged, as though to hide his fear. "It could happen, but I'd rather not find out. As it was, you burned a lot of energy at the bar."

"Is that why I slept so long?" Nathan asked.

"And it looks like you lost a couple of pounds." Marty slapped Nathan's stomach. "You were dangerously close."

"That redneck was gonna stab me with a broken bottle," Nathan complained. "It's not like I had a choice."

By early evening, they put away the tools of training and prepared dinner together. Most nights, they ate under the stars and shared stories. The first couple of nights Nathan felt strange not having access to his messages, television, or the world. He checked his phone a dozen times that first night before he just gave up on the hope that he would eventually connect with a signal. The next couple of nights he felt a strange pang, but that faded as he felt recharged.

Once the stars shone overhead, Nathan took out the meditation stone, closed his eyes, and tried to feel the flow of the magic inside of his veins. It came slowly, but he learned to trace the energy inside of his body. Marty described the exercise as a runner following the route for a race. As Nathan learned to mediate upon the magic, he became able to draw forth the power.

Once a week, they rode into town to buy supplies and Nathan called Grandma Loni to give a weekly progress report. He skipped the more deadly details about the New Flesh, but told her of the cabin and everything he learned. "I've never heard you so happy Nathan. I think this trip was a good thing for the both of you. Tell Martin that we're proud of him."

When he told Martin that night, he studied his uncle's face for the complex blend of emotions. That night, they played songs until very early in the morning. Before coming to the cabin, it was as though there were so many distractions and demands on Nathan's spiritual battery that he had always felt drained, too tired to sleep, but now he was feeling stronger. Each morning, he awoke refreshed and eager to meet the day.

Nathan almost forgot about the rest of the world as the weeks passed. He led Eve up one of the trails that led back to the cabin. She stopped mid-step, confused and tilted her head as though listening to a distant sound. "I feel something."

He had learned to listen to her feelings. Once it stopped them from walking blind onto a path where a giant brown momma bear was protecting a wounded cub. "Where?"

Eve pointed towards the direction of the road. "The Laughing Man comes. Always dancing and laughing at the edge of it all."

"Maybe one of the bad guys got through? Let's run back."

They quickly climbed the last bit of the hill and ran back to the cabin. A murder of blackbirds surrounded the cabin and seemed to watch their every move. If he hadn't known better, he would have thought that these were the blackbirds that followed him around at the ranch. Marty climbed out from under the van and started wiping his hands clean with an oil rag. "Eve felt something."

"As she should." Marty gestured to the lone figure walking down the gravel road. "We have a guest. I'm going to start lunch. You guys should go greet him."

"Do you know who it is?" Nathan asked.

"It is the Laughing Man," Eve added confidently.

"She's right. That's one of the names for our guest in some parts of the world. I know him as Papo. He's everyone's friend, not on any side," Marty explained. "But he owes us one last favor."

"A last favor? When did he ever do me a first favor?" Nathan asked.

Eve pointed at the birds. "They watch for him. Whisper secrets into his ears."

"There's always birds around here in California." Nathan gestured to the birds. "Those little bastards are all over the place."

"I know it seems that way to you." Marty shrugged and his face twisted uncomfortably. "They watch over you. For Papo."

"This guy's been watching over me my entire life? Really?" Nathan swallowed and wondered how much this guy had seen. Did he know him? "That's just creepy. And why is he walking?"

"He travels through the dreamlands, stepping in and out of reality in the quiet, soft places. It's a hell of way to travel." Marty smiled. "It is said that he has a skeleton key made from the bone of an angel so no place is ever barred from him."

"Why don't you travel this way?" Nathan asked.

"I don't have the power to breech the wall of sleep. But, if you listen and learn, you might one day." He pointed to the advancing figure. "Go ahead and say hello. I'll start on the chicken. I bet he's tired and hungry."

Surprised by the trust shown by his uncle towards this strange man, Nathan did as he was asked and walked towards the approaching figure. As they walked closer to each other, the incoming form focused into a mountain of man wearing an old straw cowboy hat, sunglasses, blue jeans, thick combat boots, and a vest. He had a wide smile with a salt and pepper beard and short dark, curly hair. On his hands, he wore a number of silver rings and his left arm rattled when he moved due to the bone charm he wore.

They stopped just short of each other and it was then that Nathan realized that he knew this man's face. He had studied it for years in the single photo he possessed of his father. This was the large smiling man that stood to the left of his father. He had not aged in the twenty or so years since the picture had been taken. "I've waited many years to see you in the flesh, Nathan Carver."

He wasn't entirely certain he liked that turn of phrase anymore. "I've known about you for two and half weeks or so, but I've known your face all my life." Nathan offered his hand. "Sorry, you were in a picture I had of my dad. Nice to meet you, Papo."

"I am very beautiful. I hope I did not stunt your growth as a child by seeing perfection too early." Papo accepted the hand and pulled Nathan close, and hugging him like a brother. "This is how men of worth greet each other."

Nathan coughed, a bit surprised, and then wrapped his arms around Papo. There was a slight buzz in his skin where they touched. An echo, a reflection, of the energy in his skin. "You really are like me, aren't you?"

"We spring from the same place, if that's what you mean. That doesn't mean we're alike." Papo smiled and laughed. "You have some choices to make, Nathan Carver."

"Well, Marty's making the chicken. We have water, soda, and beer." He gestured towards the cabin and Eve. "You can rest a bit and then hopefully you can help us out."

They walked up the road to the cabin. Eve waited for them on the front porch. Papo stopped mid-stride. "That is the girl you found."

"We call her Eve. She doesn't know her real name," Nathan explained.

"I sense something strange about her." Papo pulled off his glasses to get a good look at her. He tilted his head as though trying to peer straight through her. "I can't place my finger on it, but there is something horribly wrong with her."

"She doesn't remember anything. Could that have something to do with it?"

"Hard to say, but I'll keep it in mind. We'll find out everything we need to know in due course." Papo picked up the pace towards the cabin. "For now, I could use a drink and a bite. You'd be surprised how well you can feel after a good meal between new friends."

By the time they reached the front porch, Marty had prepared a solid meal of barbequed chicken, chips, and green beans. They sat around the wooden picnic table and ate together in fellowship. After Papo drank a bottle of water followed by two bottles of beer, he wiped his mouth and stretched back. "That was mighty tasty. You've gotten a lot better, Marty. You didn't burn the chicken this time."

Marty flashed a half-assed grin. "I did manage to drop yours on the dirt for the extra flavoring."

"Worth the effort." Papo laughed and wiped his hands on a napkin. He gestured towards the cabin. "I can sense the wards, sigils, and guardian runes. Don't you think that's a bit paranoid for these pure lands?"

"We ran into the New Flesh and they caught a bit of our scent." He ruffled Eve's hair. "And then we found this one on the road. We fed her, now we're responsible for her."

"I can check your work, if you are not offended. You mentioned that a vampire managed to pass through your defenses once before."

"And that vampire wasn't invited into the room." Marty shook his head, frustrated. "I've tried everything I could think of, but I don't have the gift. Not like you. Now's not the time for egos. Do what you can."

Papo stood and wiped the dust from his jeans. He took off his hat, handed it to Nathan, and walked around the cabin as though to soak in everything about the place. Taking a long, exaggerated breath, he popped his neck and found the center of the cabin. "I can feel many layers of protection here." He stretched out one hand, palm up, and called forth a mighty crackle of magical energy from his hands. A globe of frightening blue eldritch flame rested in his palms. The light illuminated several hidden sigils and runes inscribed into the walls with magic.

"What did you do?" Nathan asked.

"This is a simple strobe spell. I can teach it to you later. It illuminates and reveals magic in the vicinity." Papo waved to the arcane symbols emblazoned on the walls. They glowed with potent energy. "The symbology is quaint and inelegant, but the shields are quite effective. Very few creatures that walk this world would be able to breech it without a great struggle."

Marty scoffed. "Thanks. I wasn't going for *War and Peace* here."

He had held his tongue as best that he could during the meal, but now the thought of his future burned in his brain. "Will you guys tell me why Papo is here now? Why do I have a picture of him with my father? What's going on? Do you know what Eve is?"

"I am an old family friend, bonded by fellowship and struggle. You never have anything to fear from me, Nathan Carver." He turned to Eve. "Do you wish me to look into your destiny? I can gaze into the universe."

She nodded eagerly. "Please, sir, if you know who I am, tell us? It vexes me. Am I am good person? Do I have a family? A mother? A father?"

"That I do not know yet, but there is a way to discern the truth." Papo pulled an ancient leather pouch out of from a side pocket, unlaced it, and emptied it onto the wooden table. Dozens of clay chits inscribed with strange symbols fell about the table haphazardly. Papo looked closely, his eyes darting back and forth seeking a pattern. "I have never known these runes to reveal anything but the truth. Strange."

"What is it?" Eve asked.

Papo turned to her. "May I touch you?"

"You won't hurt her, will you?" Nathan asked.

"Not if it can be helped. Not if she lets me inside," Papo explained.

"I want to know." Eve scooted closer to Papo and leaned forward. "Is there someone out there looking for me?"

The large man reached out with his hands and cupped her innocent face. He stared deep into her hazel eyes. "How is this possible?" He let her go and then reached into his pocket and pulled out a pocket knife. "Might I cut a strand of your hair?"

Eve looked to Nathan, confused. "Will it hurt? I don't think my hair has ever been cut before."

"You might be correct in that, but no it shall not hurt." Papo promised. He gently separated a strand of chestnut hair from Eve's gorgeous, long mane. "There! And now we shall see."

He wrapped the hair around the blade of his knife and poured a bit of salt upon it from the table. "Do either of you have a lighter?" Nathan fished his father's lighter out from his pocket and handed it over. Papo grinned. "Saint Christopher. Good choice."

Papo flicked the lighter and held the blade under the flame. The hair shimmered for a moment and then caught fire in a high intensity blue flame. "What does that mean?"

"It means that Eve has no family. No mother waiting for her. And I know why the New Flesh and Cenotaph search for her." He turned to Eve. "You are a miracle. A spirit made flesh. A life created from nothing. A homunculus."

Marty scoffed. "Bah! That's nonsense. Every two-bit wizard for the last thousand years has tried working that mojo."

"And yet, it is true. A woman born of the universe. They captured her essence from the cosmos and trapped it in flesh." Papo studied every feature of her face. "A true marvel."

"You can't magick a soul, Papo. It can't be done," Marty argued.

"I know." There was no joy in Papo's voice. Nathan had an eerie feeling in his heart. "She has no soul."

"A hollow!" Marty unconsciously seemed to look for a weapon. "Jesus! No wonder they want her!"

"I don't understand. What do you mean by a hollow?" Nathan suddenly felt very protective of her. "Eve wouldn't hurt anyone."

"She's a sweet girl, Nate. But, she's very dangerous. Not just to us, but the whole world. Without a soul, she can be possessed freely by any higher power." Marty looked to Eve with heavy sadness. "Eve, bad things are out there and they can take over your body and hurt people."

"Can't we just protect her?" Nathan asked. He waved at all of the mystical symbols around them. "There has to be something we can do, right?"

Papo shook his head. "There are great and terrible beasts out in the black of the universe and they want to breach the Great Barrier to access the power on this world."

"What's the Great Barrier?" Nathan asked.

"What does that have to do with me?" Eve added

"The Great Barrier is an unseen energy field that blocks most mystical access to the Earth. Look at it this way." Papo drew a large circle on the table with a bit of Marty's chalk and then a net over the circle. "Think of it like a giant net that works on a large scale. The large fish are captured, but tiny plankton have free movement through the net. And so, there is evil in the world, but it's rarely dangerous on a large scale."

"So what does this have to do with Eve?" Nathan asked.

"Wrapped in her flesh, one of the great beasts can slip through the Great Barrier and enter our world." Papo explained. He wiped away his sketch as though to mimic Armageddon. "And then on that day, the world ends."

Nathan shook his head. "Can't we strengthen the Great Barrier instead?"

"This Great Barrier is powered by ley lines; alignments and

patterns of powerful, invisible earth energy that connect various sacred sites, such as churches, temples, stone circles, megaliths, holy wells, burial sites, and other locations of spiritual or magical importance." Papo shook his head. "It takes many years to prepare such things. We do not have the time."

Eve sniffed. Tears welled in her eyes. "I don't want to hurt anyone. Everything could die. All the trees, the people in the stores, the birds, the cats, Marty, the Beach Boys. All gone."

"We need to remove the threat," Papo said calmly.

Nathan felt the fever return. Waves of heat washed over him. "You mean kill her. And the answer is no."

"Do not be childish, Nate. The danger is terrible. If one of the Old Ones possesses her, the world suffers and perhaps ends the age of man." Papo shook his head sadly. "No single person is worth that risk.

"How do you get a soul?" Nathan asked. Neither Papo or Marty had an answer. "We don't know, do we? What if you get it by experience? The New Flesh are trying to grow a new part of their soul by playing a role. What if living with us is helping Eve?"

"You can't know that, Nate," Marty argued.

"I know she offered her life to you because of a theory. How many people without a soul would do that?" Nathan pointed to Marty. "How many people do you know that selfless?"

"You have a point, kid. I hate to admit it," Marty replied. "Metaphysics aside, she's a danger to us."

"So we protect her. Do some good in the world."

Papo turned from Nathan to Marty and nodded, satisfied.

"Perhaps, you will in time."

"That's the answer you wanted, isn't it?" Nathan asked.

Papo merely grinned and slipped his glasses back on. "Perhaps."

Nathan's eyes narrowed. "You aren't going to tell us why, are you?"

"Some things you must learn on your own." Papo scooped his runes back into the pouch. "I am not here to provide easy answers."

"Why are you here?"

A coyote's smile crossed Papo's lips. "I'm here to take you to the Highway West."

# Chapter Eight: Lived and Learned
# From Fools and Sages

Thirteen empty beer bottles lined the old wooden fence from post to post like soldiers bravely awaiting the firing squad. Sunlight reflected brilliantly through the brown bottles into a prism, creating a dozen diminutive rainbows. A gust of wind whistled through the Sequoia trees, making a deep, empty sound as it grazed along the tops of the bottles. Nathan Carver stood a solid twenty paces away from the post glaring at the bottles with intense concentration. Blackbirds surrounded them, peering down curiously from branches squawking as though to cheer him on. He craned his neck up to the birds and tried to shoo them away. "Ah, come on! I'm working here."

"Again." Papo adjusted his cowboy hat and nodded to Nathan. "Shatter the bottles."

"I might have a better shot at it if you let me use the meditation stone," he complained.

"Such things are proper tools to learn. To get started upon the path," Papo explained, shaking his head. "There comes a time when you have to take off the training wheels and stand on your own. You cannot use a meditation stone in the Dreamlands."

Nathan Carver narrowed his eyes and concentrated on the targets. He tried to invoke the energy that he had felt during the fight, but without the fear motivating him, it was quickly washed over by frustration and doubt. The bottles at the end of the row began to tremble, vibrating side to side, as though the posts shook with a furious wind. "Damn!"

"Nathan, you're thinking yourself outside of the process." Papo clapped him on the back. "You know what to do inside. When you get out of your own way, nothing can stop you. Just try to do it without thinking too much about it."

"That doesn't even make sense," Nathan complained.

"Imagine you are at the free-throw line, trying to sink the ball through the basket." He waved at the blackbirds and the trees. "You are surrounded by the crowd, and you feel pressure. You've made many such shots in the past but you start to concentrate until the basket blurs in your mind's eye and you forget that you ever knew how to throw the ball."

"But, I've never done this before. I'm trying to feel my way there. Give me a couple of minutes." Nathan stretched, trying to soothe the strange aches in his back and legs. He walked over to the old metal ice chest and pulled out a bottle of water. "I'm dying of thirst today. Like I can't get enough water in my system."

"Water purifies the body and spirit." Eve peeked up from a large tattered book titled *Bulfinch's Mythology* that she had forced Marty to purchase her at the old shack of a used bookstore near the market. She sat at the edge of the cabin's porch in a flattering ruffled blue sundress. Her chestnut hair hung off her shoulder as she absentmindedly drew in the dirt with her toes. "Flesh knows what it needs. The spirit less so."

"What?" Nathan scratched his head. "That almost made sense in

147

crazy sort of way."

"She's right in a fashion," Papo said, tipping his hat to Eve. "Purified water is considered an element and can have special properties. Jesus was baptized in the Jordan River near Qasr al-Yahud after all. 'Baptize' is the English form of a Greek word which means 'to immerse': to place something into something else. Water has long symbolized a border between states, between life and death. When you immerse yourself in water, you are symbolically dying and then reborn in your faith. Drink and let yourself be reborn if you must."

"Really? That makes an actual difference?" Nathan groaned and gulped down more water. He wiped his face and shook his head. "I'm never going to learn all of this. I feel like I've been dropped in the middle of some strange planet and I don't know any of the rules or the customs."

"You're doing just fine, Nate. Some of it will come with experience." Papo pointed at the bottles with polite and quiet determination, unwilling to let Nathan delay the practice any further. "Try again."

"If I'm doing fine, why haven't you taken me to the Highway West yet?" Nathan sat down next to Eve defiantly and stared at Papo, daring him to tell him the truth. "I'm not ready. I won't be any time soon."

"That's not a walk in the country, boy." Papo smiled, showing a great deal of his white teeth almost as a warning, like a dog brandishing his fangs. He opened the ice chest and pulled out a beer and held it to his head. Sighing loudly to show his appreciation for the cold sensation, he popped off the cap and took several swallows. "When you're ready, I'm going to start helping you along the path to katabasis."

"What's that?"

"Here's how this works. I have to teach you to tap into your magic, make you feel a connection to the universe. Once that's done, you have to take a step into this new world. These days, the arm-chair scholars call it the hero's journey into the underworld. The ancient Greeks called it katabasis. Your father named it the Highway West." Papo took a sip of his beer and then offered the rest to Nathan. "You must be brave and cross the threshold to emerge from the cocoon of childhood."

"Isn't that just a myth?" Nathan scoffed with a sour face and waved away the beer. "Stories like that have been around since cavemen and fire right?"

"Nathan, I believe that myths are stories told to teach truth about life," Papo explained.

"So then why not just tell me the story? Why do I have to actually do all of this crap?" Nathan asked.

"Rituals are just a way to step inside of a myth, to make us connected to the story. Have you taken communion?"

Grandma Loni had insisted that Nathan attend church twice a month. He had always felt so empty inside of a church without even knowing why. It was always a house, but never a home like Papa Ray had always said. "Since I was thirteen."

"During the Last Supper, Jesus broke bread with his disciplines

149

and told them to remember him this way in the future. Why?" Papo held up the bottle and offered it to Nathan as though he were passing him the Holy Grail. "Drink of this wine and it will be my blood. Eat of this bread and it becomes my body. What purpose did it serve?"

Nathan tilted his head, very confused. "You believe in Jesus? Doesn't all of this magic stuff invalidate the bible?"

"Transmuting water into wine is certainly something that I would consider magical. Not to mention casting demons from a man into a pig." Papo laughed joyfully. Somehow it made the lecture a little easier to swallow. "But then I've been known to enjoy a fine wine on occasion. Don't change the subject. Think about the reason for the ritual. What purpose does it serve for those that follow Jesus?"

"You're talking about Transubstantiation, aren't you? Grandma Loni believes that with all her heart. That doesn't happen literally, does it?" Nathan leaned close and stage-whispered as though somehow, hundreds of miles away, his grandmother might hear him. "I haven't been eating Jesus, right? I mean at this point everything seems possible."

"Millions of people believe just that. It's an act of faith. A ritual that reminds everyone of the Last Supper and the sacrifice of a great man. A man that gave of his body and soul for others." Papo wrapped his arm around Nathan. It made him a bit uncomfortable. He wasn't used to such easy affection between friends. "And, when you follow in the very same steps that so many others undertook in times past undertaken, you become part of something greater than yourself. You honor that tradition by becoming part of it. That will give you strength in the times that come."

"Did my dad do this ritual?"

"They were young, lost, and mad with the power of their youth. Your father and your uncle only had each other when they started on the Highway West. Knowing nothing of the universe, they blindly went forth unprepared for the darkness that awaited them," Papo said very sadly. "It led them into trouble before they were ready. They were not inoculated against what lay before them and by the time they confronted the New Flesh, it was too late. The damage to their souls had already been done. Choices had been made."

"What was my father like?" Nathan asked. It had been the question weighing on his mind over a thousand sleepless nights. "Honestly."

Papo nodded as though he had been expecting this question. "Your father was a good man and a friend. He loved effortlessly, was kind to strangers, and faced the world with a pubescent sense of humor. He was also an angry man. Injustice, however slight, burned him, almost consumed him."

"Why did he give it up? Why did he allow his magic to be bound?" Nathan asked.

"The universe is both sacred and profane; beautiful and hideous, light and shadow, just and monstrous - a complex study of contrasts and paradoxes. Bill was not ready for the brutality of this life where we must navigate between those poles of existence. Their journey took them to dark places and they were not prepared. It tainted everything that came after and then the magic no longer came easy to Bill. The shadows won."

"Why give up magic, Papo? Why give up on it all?"

"Magic comes from life, and just like everything else that comes from life there are hard rules. Different methods can be combined to create hundreds of different orders of magic. Alchemy, the subtle art of transmutation. Tantric, the breath of life and healing. Thaumaturgy, blood magic and voodoo. Theurgy, white magic performed with the aid of spirits and tulapas. An infinite number of combinations, but there are only three ways to power magic."

"What does that have to do with my dad?"

"I'm getting to that, Nate. A strong soul, a mystic, can access spiritual energy called Chi. We gather that through our deeds, mediation, willpower. It takes practice and effort and a certain level of purity. This homeopathic source is based on the assumption that like produces like. We are the culmination of our actions."

"That's what you and Marty are teaching me right? This is the whole point of me trying to shatter those bottles."

"Exactly. Bill had great potential, like you, but you have something he lacked."

Nathan tried to imagine something he could possess that his father didn't. It seemed impossible. "I don't understand."

"You have known sorrow and darkness, Nathan Carver. I watched you withstand it as an abandoned child on that farm, as the spirits of the land called to you. You trembled with fear against the ancient enemies and yet you fought for your life and your soul. Some actions we take cannot be undone. It damages our souls. You will do as you have done your entire life. Endure."

"And this journey hurt him?" Nathan asked. "That's why he wanted to return to a normal life."

A dark shadow seemed to pass over Papo's face, exercising any hint of a smile from his face. "There were five of us bound in a circle of fellowship. We were going to change the world."

"What happened?"

"We were crushed upon the rock of our own arrogance. We thought that we could change the entire world overnight. We flew too high, too soon and our dreams were shattered. In our hubris, we failed to understand the nature of our gifts."

"I don't understand."

"Magic is generated from life. We find it in the little moments every day. A child's laughter, the touch of a lover, the embrace of a friend. It can change a soul forever, heal the flesh, and nurture the best possible future."

"I have to admit that sounds pretty good right about now, Papo."

Papo's scowl deepened. "Magic is also the omega, chaos, hatred. The darkness at the end that burns us all. How magic is used is almost as important as why it is used. The very act changes you."

"You said there were other power sources for magic. What are they? Why not use one of the other sources of magic?"

"Invocation requires that you call upon higher powers to aid your magic. Some of those higher powers are very dangerous and it weakens the Great Barrier. You have to give them faith and adoration for their help. You, in essence, trade the stuff of dreams for power.

Never a good bargain." Papo shook his head with disgust. "Transference requires that you take power from other places or sacrifices. You give something for something."

"You mean killing people, don't you?" Nathan asked horrified.

"Or taking energy from the land. There is power in a place. A life that can be drained. Stolen."

"Papo, isn't that bad for the land?"

"It makes it barren. Tales speak of the Sahara as a paradise before a sorcerer drained it of life. Your father was damaged in such a way that he found it difficult to recover that balance. He protected the world by surrendering himself to it."

"And you want to protect me from the burnout? Learn from the mistakes you guys made." Nathan thought about it. "You think showing me this darkness now will help me later."

"You will be confident in your power. You will feel the urge to right wrongs and set order to the universe."

"You're afraid that I'll go after the New Flesh, aren't you?"

"I fear that you will confront Cenotaph before you have come into your power and that he will consume you," Papo said, his words dripping with worry and concern. "He will tap into that which is natural to you and he'll have enough energy to shatter the Great Barrier and bring darkness to the world."

Nathan cleared his throat. "I should avoid him then."

"You will feel compelled to best him in time."

"Why?"

"That is not a story for me to tell. You'll learn at the right time and the right place." Papo pointed again to the bottles. "And such will never come unless you complete this lesson."

"Good point." Nathan held up his hands in defeat. "I can't seem to control this chi energy you guys keep talking about."

"Your fear holds you still."

"That's not it at all," Eve argued.

Silently, they both turned to look at her. Eve continued to read, ignoring them. Papo bowed dramatically. "Perhaps you can clarify o' mistress of the arts."

Eve sighed and closed her book. She pointed to Nathan and then the bottles. "He doesn't accept your symbology. You are training him to be you. It doesn't feel right to his heart and thus won't ever work for him."

"I have had many students in the last fifty years, girl," Papo protested.

Nathan tilted his head. "How old are you? You don't look like you've aged a day since that photo of you and my dad was taken."

"That's not important right now." It was clear that Eve's suggestion had stirred something inside of his brain. Papo pointed Nathan to the row of bottles. "How would you imagine that you could break that glass?"

"It's not like I can just do this." Nathan absentmindedly bent his fingers into an imitation of a gun and pointed it at the bottles. He felt the heat rise once more until a wave of blue eldritch energy erupted from his hand towards the bottle and when it struck shattered into hundreds of melted shards. Bottle after bottle exploded each time he imagined pulling the trigger. "Holy crap!"

Papo eyed Eve suspiciously and then turned to Nathan, placing his hand on his shoulders in a fatherly way. "It'll do, Nate. I'll line a new row and we'll start again until it feels completely natural."

Nathan spent the next couple of hours shattering bottles, crushing cans, and eventually blasting logs to splinters. The summer heat was oppressive, but Nathan felt his spirits lift just a little with each bottle shattered. By the time the sun started to set, Marty had cooked a feast of hamburgers and kielbasa sausages and prepared a variety of condiments. They ate together laughing and telling old stories of the road.

Papo waited until the meal was over and then turned to them. "Nathan is ready."

"Son of a bitch! He just started being able to control the energy. Are you sure?" Marty asked.

"The journey will increase his focus and his skills." Papo turned to Nathan. "His passion and his control will come. His innocence and courage shall not fail him."

"Maybe you could explain the ritual to me and I could make my own decision?" Nathan looked from Papo to Marty. "Isn't this what this whole trip is about? A choice? Specifically my choice in all of this?"

"Very well. This is a story known only to a few." Papo paused and glanced over at Eve. Nathan wondered why Papo seemed to distrust her so much. "This world, as you know has been protected by the Great Barrier for thousands of years. It surrounds us and protects us from the Old Ones that wait in the emptiness in the void. This world was once a great nexus. A place of power. Much of that energy now powers the Great Barrier and that has an effect upon us all."

"How so?" Nathan asked.

"The Great Barrier is not merely a shield. It is a living place. A universe we call the Dreamlands. A mystic place where that energy is transformed by our dreams. You see, it isn't merely the power that protects us, it is our dreams, our souls," Papo explained.

"And that's why places of worship and power help power the Great Barrier?" Nathan asked.

"Exactly. The dreams that inspire and lift us protect us and help us build a better future."

"This is why rituals are so important. It reminds us that we are part of the story," Marty explained. "It ties us in with the stuff of dreams all around us and recharges our soul."

"The universe is made of stories," Nathan muttered, recalling his uncle's words. "Go on."

"There have been champions in every age. People touched with the gift that create and define the time. Heroes. You have been called to a higher purpose and now you have to test yourself. You have to journey to the underworld to seek out the other. To understand what lies beyond you're perceptions," Papo said in a very excited tone.

"I don't have to die, do I?"

"Nothing like that. There are thin spots in the world where we can access the Dreamlands. You and I are going to try to sneak through to take a spiritual walkabout. We're going to remind ourselves that we are part of the story and seek if we can face the monsters," Marty said.

"This is where you said I could meet my dad, isn't it?" Nathan asked.

"This place where the thin spot is located is where you and I left his ashes, Nate." Marty lifted his drink in a silent toast to his dead brother. "I promised you we'd return there when you were old enough."

"Can I go?" Eve asked.

"Alas, you cannot. It is too dangerous for you to go into the Dreamlands." Papo stared into her eyes as though he were searching for evidence of some spark of malice. "You are a hollow. Flesh without spirit. It would be too easy for something to possess you there and escape that realm."

Eve pouted. "But I think I could learn about myself if I go."

"I have given some thought to your needs, Eve." Papo folded his arms, resolute. "There is a spring in Oregon where we might find the answers to your problems."

"The one near the Synchronicity Café?" Marty asked, horrified.

"It is the next step in the journey for her and you, Martin," Papo said.

"I don't understand, what's so bad about that?"

"That is where your Uncle Marty faced the beast and then blinked. And it is where the Carver family has a debt to pay," Papo answered.

"A debt?"

Papo nodded knowingly. "There is a boy there that needs your help, but only when you know who you are and why you fight the darkness."

Marty pulled out a cigarette and started coughing horribly before he had a chance to light it. That horrible wet-sounding cough almost stopped Nathan's heart. "I was hoping to delay that a bit."

"The demons of our soul must be met sooner rather than later."

"Will you come with us?" Eve asked.

"I will. You and I shall take a journey together while the boys pay their family debt," Papo explained.

"When do we do this ritual?" Nathan asked.

"In the morning."

# Chapter Nine: The Highway West

The trail spiraled down the hillside between towering sequoias, moss-covered boulders, and the faint trickle of a shallow brook that pooled into a narrow pond. The woods vibrated with life from the gentle concert of the brightly feathered orioles, the curious squirrels scrambling up the trees, or the sluggish frogs languidly swimming around them. Each step brought them further into the wild, away from the popular campgrounds and civilization, as the scenery changed from brown and green to the expansive crescent meadow fields of lush greens and golden yellow that shimmered in the sunlight. The field continued all the way to the Great Western divide of the mountains.

Nathan soaked in the environment. It was like a living dream in the daylight hours. Had he been here before? Everything felt sacred and somehow familiar. Scents of the wild were surprisingly invigorating like swimming in a pool of liquid caffeine. He had to admit that Marty had been more than right about the healing power of this place. The last few months had been tiring, like he had been a car with all of the accessories running at once and now he felt like everything was running at full capacity.

They had walked for almost three hours when Marty called for a break. He passed around the canteens. "Drink just a little. Too much and you'll get sick."

"Just admit it!" Nathan complained wryly. "We're lost and you guys have no idea where we are, do you?

"The place we're looking for isn't on any maps." Marty flashed a grin. "That's kind of the point of finding this place."

Nathan eyed both of them suspiciously. "If we know where the cave is, then why have we passed that stream three times so far?"

"Know that finding this place isn't as easy as dropping by the local Pit-Stop. This cave is a place of magic and will. It will allow us to discover the entrance at the proper time." Papo smiled knowingly. "Until then, it can alter our perceptions or fade into the background. We must prove our worth to find it."

"But you've been here before, right?" Nathan asked.

"Twice. Once with your old man when we needed a place to hide," Marty revealed. "A second time with you."

"That's where we scattered Dad's ashes." Nathan tried to remember that day, but only bits remained. The rest was faded, lost in time. "I don't remember the cave."

"It is no surprise, Nathan. You were young and the potency of the cave is immense," Papo explained. "One of the thin spots in the world is contained within those walls. It would have seemed as a dream to you."

"We have to be close by, don't we?" Nathan felt the energies of the valley and the sweet magic of life all around him. If he was ever to decide to create a magical place, this would certainly be it. "Can't you feel it?"

Marty shook his head. "I'm usually pretty good at dowsing magic, Nate. I'm just not feeling it."

Eve leaned her head back and enjoyed the sunlight. She had been following quietly for several hours, but finally spoke. "Nathan should try to find the cave."

"It's not as easy as it looks," Marty complained.

"Perhaps for a time, to allow you to rest if nothing else," Papo suggested.

"You can do this, Nathan." Eve smiled, shaking her head wildly, and twirled in a circle. "Feel all of it around you. Life birthing life. That is the real magic of this place. Try it."

He shrugged his shoulders and tried to do as Eve suggested. Nathan had been able to feel the creature that lived under the Snake River. If it was true that he was destined to find this place, maybe it wouldn't hide as well from him? One foot followed the other unconsciously as Nathan walked along the base of the hills and walls weaving around the massive trunks. "Huh?"

Marty shook his head with equal bits of pride and credulity. "Son of a bitch!"

Eve smiled knowingly. "You found it, Nathan."

The entrance to the cave was hidden by a colossal sequoia tree that was so large it blocked the sun in the sky. The entrance was really little more than a large hole; a tear in the wall of the mountain. "It doesn't look like much," Nathan observed.

"Magic rarely does." Papo pulled the leather pouch from his belt, opened it, and produced two sticks of pink gum. "I have prepared a spiritual facilitator to help you cross over."

"What is it?" Nathan asked, horrified.

"This stick of gum has been dosed with a dimethyltryptamine variant," Papo offered a stick to both Nathan and Marty. "It is a naturally occurring hallucinogenic that has been used for thousands of years by Shamans to help souls through a time of crisis."

Nathan looked at the stick of gum as though it was a rattlesnake. "Is that like acid? Isn't that dangerous?"

"A tool can be dangerous and still serve a purpose." Papo's face was resolute like a fierce gargoyle. "This will help you process what you see quicker. Had we months to train, I could teach you the proper meditations."

"Psychologists prescribe drugs to patients to help them heal. It's not anything different." Marty accepted the stick of gum and unwrapped it. "I know you aren't comfortable with this sort of thing because of your mother."

"I don't want to get addicted. Hell, the idea of being like her has kept me up at nights, Marty. You know that."

Eve wrapped her long arms around Nathan from behind and pulled him close in an awkward hug. "You are a brave soul. A hero has to face that which he fears the most before going to the underworld. You can do this."

Marty popped the gum into his mouth and flicked on the flashlight. He turned and nodded to Nathan. "OK, kid, this is our stop. You coming or not?"

"Let's get this over with." He slowly put the gum into his mouth and started to chew. Nathan leaned back slightly so he could look at Eve's face and said with an amused smile, "You'll have to let me go."

She did as asked, but pouted and stamped her foot. "I wish to go as well. I could help you there. I know it!"

Papo grabbed her by the shoulder as though to restrain her and shook his head. "This is for the two of them. We will guard them. Besides, that is a holy place where the walls are thin. You are most vulnerable there."

Nathan couldn't help but laugh at Eve's sour expression. She could have sucked a dozen lemons and still couldn't have had a less pleasant expression. He turned to face her and then gently brushed a rogue strand hair out of her eyes. "Besides, we'll need you to guide us back if we get lost. Papo promised to watch over you."

"Remember that everything there represents a thought. And don't walk alone in the desert," Eve warned.

"Yes. That is correct." Papo seemed to tighten his grip on her shoulders. With each nugget of information that Eve dropped, his eyes narrowed with worry. He nodded towards Nathan as though to punctuate Eve's concern. "Seek the answers to the questions you've never asked."

"You ready, Nate?"

"No," Nathan admitted. "But that's never stopped me before. Why start now?"

They stepped through the hole into a dark universe of glittering crystal-lined walls, wickedly sharp-looking stalagmites made it look as though they were in the mouth of a great and terrible leviathan. The beam of light from Marty's flashlight shattered through hundreds of violet crystals, creating a faint cage of shimmering light and fading colors. The air around him felt expansive, as though he was at the center of infinity and yet he shivered as though trapped in his mother's closet on the farm. The flow and ebb of the power tingled as his eyes vibrated. The stuff of dreams and hope washed over him. This was a place where anything wondrous might happen. Marty offered his hand. "The steps are difficult. Take my hand. I'll lead you."

Nathan accepted the offer. There was comfort in the touch and bond of family. "Where are we going?"

"I'm dowsing for the thin spot. The place we can step through to the Dreamlands."

Just when his eyes had adjusted to the dark, blinding sunlight struck him. Did they go back outside? When his sight returned, he saw that the greens and brown of the Sequoia National park had been replaced by the browns and whites of the vast open desert. There was a strange sensation as though he had dived off a cliff, but that his stomach and heart were yanked into the stratosphere.

The terror of the desert; it's vast emptiness that can only been hidden by the curvature of the earth. Nathan stared out at the golden-white shifting sands marked only by the gentle wind, and pondered if each grain of sand was a single thought or dream. He shivered under the steel-gray sky that had the fuzzy feel of a television turned to a dead channel. The sun was an orb in the sky that burned cold.

He took a step and only then realized that he was standing on concrete. The long winding cracked road twisted and turned into the shimmering horizon. Despite the cold, Nathan was sweating profusely. The horizon waved in and out of focus. "This is the Highway West, kid."

"Isn't the metaphor getting a bit thick here?"

"I don't think this place has a real name." Marty laughed a bit. "Bill and I called it the Land of the Lost."

"Wasn't that an old Saturday morning T.V. show with really bad special effects?" Nathan asked, sarcastically.

Marty laughed. "The name seemed to fit. That was a gift Bill had. There was a writer that said something like 'to name a thing was to kill it.' There's a reason that names were important in the old stories. Names are concepts of power, of domination."

"So why that name?"

"Bill had a theory that this is a place where ideas and dreams go to die."

"This is the graveyard of dreams? Really? What's the point of it all? What are we supposed to do on a desert highway?" Nathan asked. "What kind of vision quest is this?"

"It is what we make of it." Marty gestured to the wide space. "Make something of it."

"There's nothing out there but sand and we're supposed to stay on the road, right?" The old highway stretched out before him. Nathan pointed to the horizon. "Then, I take it we walk."

"Unless you know how to fly."

Nathan blinked, not quite certain if Marty was serious or not. "Let's try walking for now."

They walked the Highway West in determined silence. It was no longer time for questions or amusing quips. Step by step, they moved forward in a place where time held no dominion or sway. There was no monster to slay; no enemy to defeat. There was only the road and the determination to not stop; to never to fall to the side in surrender. They walked until their feet ached and pulsed and blisters began to form under their toes. Slowly, with every inch forward, the worries and fears melted until there was only the thought of another step; to move that much further along the journey. Despite the chill, Nathan's limbs felt warm and strong now that there was a defined rhythm. Without a word, they drew strength from each other; lost in the delirium of the forced march.

Sweat stung his eyes. Nathan glanced up at the sun irritated that it seemed to alternate between freezing them and burning them. Just as he felt acclimated to one climate, the desert shifted seemingly to solely make it that much more difficult for him.

Marty shook his head. "It wasn't like this before."

It was the first thing said in hours or days. Nathan wasn't sure which. "Yeah? You wouldn't tell me what happened to you."

"That's because really I'm not that sure." Marty sighed and struggled to keep his breath. It was clear that the grueling walk was starting to get to him. "I only know who we met. Only, it wasn't who we met."

"Marty! Fess up already!"

"Ok, but you won't believe me," he replied solemnly. "Jim Morrison."

Nathan stopped walking and scowled at his uncle. "Jim Morrison! You met Jim Morrison here?"

Marty twitched a bit. His face was red with exertion, and yet clammy as though he had just been soaked in a rainstorm. "Kind of.

We met Jim Morrison, but it wasn't him. Morrison had died years before."

"So you met someone that looked like Jim Morrison? Or a tulpa?"

"No, it was him. In every real sense that I know. It was also something else." Marty stepped to the edge of the highway almost dipping his toe into the desert sand. "Do you know why we have to stay on the road? There are more than dead dreams and lost ideas out there. If you look closely enough and make no sounds, you'll see movement out there. Something vast and unknowable swims through the sand like a shark. Bigger than a man or a mere beast."

"Maybe that's why we're here," Nathan suggested. "To talk to those creatures.

"Bill had a theory about them and Morrison. You know the graphs you find in the paper? The ones that tell you the economy is going up or the housing market is going down?" Marty's voice cracked and his breathing became much more labored. "Those graphs are representations that the common folk can understand. The real data, the real numbers, are so huge that we couldn't understand it if we took a year to add everything by hand."

"And you think what you saw was something like that? A representation of something larger?" Nathan asked.

"It was a mask made to interact with us on our level. Imagine that! A creature so epic and brilliant that we couldn't have understood it unfiltered. Our lives changed that day."

"What happened?"

Marty smiled in a poor attempt to put him at ease. "I can't explain it exactly. We talked. And afterwards, I knew that I'd never be like you and that was OK. I felt happy."

"I wish we could let them know we were here somehow."

"They know we're here, Nate. They'll come to us when they're good and ready."

"How did you travel last time? You didn't walk the entire way did you?"

Marty felt his vest for his missing package of cigarettes and coughed nasty, green phlegm pocked with specks of red onto the road. He wiped his mouth and did his best to pretend that he wasn't dying. "Bill summoned forth the tulpa of the van. It had been our dream so naturally there was an echo here, but that's not your dream."

"Yeah, but maybe I have something else." He thought of his jealous dreams of the rich kids in school driving fancy and restored cars. Nathan had never wanted a new car with computers that spoke to him. Knowing that his grandparents struggled sometimes to even put food on the table, Nathan had never even admitted aloud the dream that always held his heart. "Like that!"

A sleek black Camaro sparkled in the sunlight. Its classic shape reminded Nathan of a panther. Marty sighed with relief and grinned. "Bitchin camaro! 75?"

"Yeah. I've always wanted a car like that. Uncle Wayne had one that he restored and then sold when his kids went to college," he said shyly. "I know it's pompous and loud. We could never afford it on the ranch, but I always thought someday I'd have a car like this."

"Your dream car, if you will," Marty said with a great deal of pride in his voice. "It didn't occur to me that you'd have a dream car. You've never seemed interested. I know it might seem silly here and now but I feel like we have actually something in common."

"Will it work?" Nathan wondered.

"Only if you have the will."

They climbed into the Camaro with Nathan taking the driver's seat. "Wow, the keys are in the ignition."

"Of course, the keys are in the ignition. It's your dream car."

"What now?" Nathan asked.

"Drive."

Nathan grinned and turned the ignition. The engine roared deafening them. He turned the wheel, shifted into gear and slammed his foot on the accelerator. A loud whine echoed around them as the Camaro burned the proverbial rubber. They quickly picked up speed on the desert highway and chased the horizon. It felt magical being behind the wheel as though this car was built only for him on this road. With a bit of reflection, he supposed that might actually be the case.

"How's she handle?" Marty asked.

There was only one answer. "Like a dream. So what now?"

"We're not using real-world logic now. We're well past that. You are a hero descending into the underworld and tradition states that the challenges always come in threes." Marty explained. "The first test was endurance. You didn't just talk the talk. You literally walked it. And then you showed mastery of the realm. You endured the wastelands and summoned forth a tulpa from your private dreams. I consider that a win."

"What's the third challenge?"

"Not a clue," Marty admitted. "Don't worry about it, Nate. We won't have to look for it. It'll find us soon enough."

The outlines of structures appeared on the horizon signaling that they were near the edge of the desert. They passed through a strange maze crafted from monstrous circuit boards and telephone wires. The denizens of the realm were faceless creatures attired in perfect suits that ignored them whenever possible and shuffled to and from their business.

Marty shook his head with disgust. "This must be Cubeland. I've heard about it, but I didn't imagine that it was horrible. Dreams of listless office drones that can't escape work even in their dreams."

They drove through many different realms while Marty played tour-guide. Vast cities of ebony and stone monoliths. A lonely realm of cinder and ash named Charn. The wild city of walking cats named Ulthar. A house made entirely of words in a strange land of a billion snakes known only as Ouroboros. Slowly, the landscape shifted to a more familiar setting.

Endless rows of orange trees stretched out to infinity with a sweet, familiar citrus scent. The Camaro passed by farmhouse after farmhouse and Nathan found himself searching for the ranch. Everything was familiar, but he couldn't quite place any of the environments around him. "Is this the Sanger?"

Marty laughed bitterly. "Better. It's the dream of small-town America. The heartland."

A lone figure walked along the side of the Highway West. Nathan slowed as soon as he noticed that it was a man sticking out his thumb, clearly hoping for a ride. "You see it?"

"You sure that's a good idea?" Marty asked.

"A wise man once told me that he knew what it was like to be lost and alone on the road, so he always picked up hitchhikers when he could." Nathan flashed the familiar shit-eating grin back at his uncle for a change. He slowed the Camaro down to pull up next to the hitchhiker. "And like Papa Ray once said, the sun will shine even on a dog's ass on occasion!"

Marty rolled down the window and waved the hitchhiker over. Nathan had halfway expected Morrison, Elvis, or the boogieman, but instead discovered a tired old man wearing a tattered army green coat that had clearly seen better decades. He had a white beard like Santa that failed to cover the lines of sorrow on his face.

"You need a ride?" Marty asked.

The old man in green peered through the window. "Maybe. Who do you work for?"

Nathan looked over at Marty seeking an answer, but he simply shrugged his shoulders. "Don't really have a job at the moment. I'm just on a trip before college."

"What about him?" he asked, pointing at Marty.

"I don't think he's had a job in twenty years. He's my uncle. My name is Nathan." He pointed over at his uncle and tried to smile to show that he was comfortable. "This is Martin."

The old man scowled at Marty. "Martin? Seems I once met a boy by that name in another life. Got himself into a lot of trouble with his brother."

Marty blushed. "That might have been me."

The old man walked around the front of the Camero and tapped on the window until Nathan rolled it down. He poked Nathan with his gnarled finger. It felt like it went right through his chest and straight to his heart. "You're Bill's son! Why isn't he here?"

He shrugged almost to apologize. "He died when I was five. Marty's here to guide me on my journey; whatever that means,"

"Is he now?" He grimaced at the both of them. He was missing some of his teeth; the rest of them were black and rotten. "Either your uncle has grown up a bit, or he has other motives. Either way, I could use a ride. You can call me Joe. Some of the kids call me Stanky Wanky Joe."

Nathan opened the side door of Camaro, pulled his seat to allow Joe to climb into the backseat, and immediately regretted it. Joe's alliterative nickname suited him quite well. He smelled of curdled milk, rotted apples, and sweat. "Where have you been, old man?" Marty asked.

"The usual. Going to and fro, as I am want to do," the old man in green replied.

"So you aren't supposed to guide me, or something?" Nathan asked. He pushed the seat back into position and slid into the driver's seat. "We're kind of lost, in case you can't tell."

"Guide you? Do I look like Jimeney Cricket? The world ain't nothing but free will. If only old Pinocchio has realized that sooner.

Might have gotten to be a real boy. That what you want? To be a real boy?"

Nathan groaned. Marty and Stanky Wanky Joe both laughed like they were sharing a private joke. "I don't like being jerked around."

"No one's jerking you around, Nate. You just aren't asking the right questions," Marty explained.

"How about you tell me who you really are?"

"I told you the name I liked to be called. If that's not good enough, ya'll can drop me off here and I'll walk the rest of the way," Joe retorted.

Martin looked a bit worried, which caught Nathan off guard. Was this man dangerous? "That's good enough for now. I just don't understand. Marty told me this was a trip to learn about the world."

Joe coughed. It was the sound of a dying man; Marty's ghost of Christmas future in the flesh. "You think you aren't learning, kid?"

"I guess I am. I just don't understand what I'm supposed to be doing. Marty can't or won't tell me what I'm supposed to do here, except to talk to you."

Stanky Wanky Joe glanced at Marty. It was as though he was trying to peer into his heart. "You want my advice, kid?"

"That would be a lot of help."

The old man in green smiled through the rear-view mirror, flashing his blackened, rotten teeth. "It's all a con. Don't buy into it. Find yourself a good woman with a fat ass. Settle down and have babies. Enjoy the sunshine and the snow. Experience the small joys of life. Ignore your uncle and that sweet bit of candy you're traveling around with."

"But what about the magic?"

Joe laughed. It was bitter and cold and drenched with regret. "Magic is part of everyday life. Any fool knows that. Everything worth knowing and doing can be found in the simple life. Everything else is a sham."

"I can't believe that!"

"You think I got these wrinkles by living a good and happy life?" He poked Nathan in the shoulder and it burned. "I walked roads of eternal night to seek out the answers to magic and the universe."

"That doesn't sound so bad."

"To sense the magic is a gift. To have the potential is the worst blessing of all. To master it, you have to work hard, boy. You have to study and meditate. Surrender everything else that you will ever be. That requires discipline and willpower. It means sacrifice."

"It obviously didn't do you a lot of good."

He laughed again. This time it was an angry laugh. "You think I'm here because I don't have a choice? Ha! I used to shit in a gold crapper. I had everything money or magic could arrange!"

"What happened?"

"There comes a time, boy, when you have everything you want. You have power over life and death. You've been to the moon, danced with angels, and walked every corner of the world. There comes a time when you begin to lose interest in collecting, cataloging, and processing. I did it all, but for the wrong reasons and so in the end I came here."

"What's the right reason?" Nathan asked.

"If I knew that, I wouldn't be here."

"Why did we start off in the desert? What is that place? Where am I supposed to go?" Nathan asked.

"That land is the realm of shattered dreams and broken ideas that never were." Joe's voice turned soft, filled with longing. "Once I heard a song by John Lennon and Paul McCartney. It was beautiful and poignant while being tragic and uplifting."

Nathan thought of Phoebe and smiled. "What song was it?"

"A song that never was. It was a song they would have written if John had lived. This place is full of ideas that were killed before their time. If you travel long enough, you might see all manner of creation's bastard children."

"Why are you here?" Nathan asked, confused.

"I feel at peace here. This is a land of second chances. Among the shattered dreams, I ponder what went wrong and see if I can do better next time," Joe explained.

"Next time? If this is the land of second chances does that mean at some point you'll get to live your life all over again?"

Stanky Wanky Joe smiled his rotten-toothed grin. "I think you might just get it kid."

Nathan had to let himself wrap his mind around the idea of living his life a second time. If he was here and this was the Land of the Lost or the place of second chances then it might just be possible. He had to pinch himself to make sure that he wasn't just dreaming. "How long have you been here?"

Joe muttered a moment and scratched his head. "Shit, I can't recall. It's been a long time. The real question is why are you here?"

He glanced over at Marty. "Well, Marty tricked me into coming with him on this road trip. He used the money left by my Dad to force me to take a look. I wouldn't have believed him otherwise. I wouldn't have come with him."

Stanky Wanky Joe nodded. "And now that you've looked, you feel the craving. You want more."

"Didn't you?"

"I never wanted anything more in my life. But, your father did. That's why he walked away from magic, although a part of him always regretted it."

Nathan gritted his teeth. Sometimes, he hated being compared to his father. "It didn't help him any. He died a grocery store clerk."

"Did he? I think he left a lot behind. His choice doesn't matter. You have a lot of potential. You can squander it like I did, refuse it like your father, or do something worthwhile. Maybe that's what the world is looking for these days? Someone to restart the circle."

"What's the circle?"

"A fellowship of those with the gift. Magic can inspire others to great deeds. Myrddin Wyllt inspired a retired roman solider to gather his men over a round table. Their deeds imbued the spirit of the age with hope and stories of courage and honor." Joe coughed once more; Marty offered him tissue to spit into. "Names and details changed over the centuries. Time corrupted Myrddin into Merlin, but the inspiration continued. Maybe that's what the world needs now. That's

177

why she came to you."

"You mean Eve. Do you know who she is?"

"I know what she is. I knew the star from which she came. She found you for a reason, but such things are never kind or pleasant to mere mortals. Let the cup pass you by. Return home."

"I don't think I can," Nathan admitted.

"Then you don't need me at all." There was a grim satisfaction in the old man's voice. "Sounds like you already know what to do."

"What about me?" Marty asked.

Stanky Wanky Joe scoffed. "You didn't listen last time."

"I wasn't ready," Marty protested. "I promise I will this time."

"You don't have the gift, Martin. You never did. Don't try to be Bill or even Nathan. Use what you have." The old man poked Marty fiercely. "You gave up the talents that were yours and never sought the wisdom available to you. You are blind. You've never realized that, but you will soon."

"What do I do?"

"You have demons that have chased you during your whole life. Be a man. Stand or fall. Face your worst fear. When the world is black, return to the beginning. Lose yourself to find what you seek. In the valley of the blind, the one-eyed man is king."

"What the hell does that mean?" Nathan grumbled.

"What do you think I am? I'm not the clue store! I'm here to scare you off running home to Mama." Joe cackled. "Don't think I did my job too well, did I?"

"You're the third test?"

"Not many would have picked up a man with a face like this. Shows you're kind and worth the effort everyone is pouring into you. Keep at it, kid. You'll be there before you know it." Joe clamped Marty's shoulder. "There's even hope for a sorry son of bitch like you, Martin."

"If you say so, sir."

"There! There! That's my stop!" A bus station appeared on the horizon. It was a lonely, filthy building littered with garbage and broken machinery and toys. A motley collection of men, women, and anthropomorphic animals waited in line for shiny metal buses. Nathan pulled over and let out Joe. The old man chuckled and capped him on the back. "Never forget what you felt that night your Momma left you in the grape fields and you'll do alright, kid."

Nathan searched for the words to say, but couldn't think of anything profound. "Uh, thanks."

They left Stanky Wanky Joe playing poker with a monstrous-looking bulldog on a bus bench. It was a scene that belonged only in a nightmare or a velvet painting. Many miles passed in silence as they considered what they had learned and the sunlight began to fade on the horizon. "We're going back, aren't we?"

"I think we both learned what we needed. We have to face the world sometime," Marty answered.

"What did he tell you last time?"

"Quit smoking."

Buildings, pyramids, and orange groves gave way back to the open desert. "When do we know we're back where we started?"

Marty shook his head. "We're not going there. You have one person to speak with first."

"Who?"

His uncle folded his arms. "You'll see. Trust me this journey isn't over yet."

Many miles passed on the Highway West through endless desert and open sky. The feel of the road vibrating through the Camaro slowly lulled him into a hypnotic state where his muscle memory kept his hands on the wheel and beyond the thought of drive. He felt the flow of the dreams and the infinite ocean of sands that melded with the human consciousness. He wondered what it might feel like to walk the sands off the path.

Marty tapped his shoulder; gently at first and then with more resolve. He was yelling at him. "Brake! Brake!"

Nathan blinked forcing him out of a daze. A figure walked confidently towards them on the Highway West straddling the white dotted line. Nathan slowed the Camero to a stop. It was a man walking towards them. "Who is that?"

"Go talk to him. You'll find out everything you need to know," Marty answered grimly.

Nathan opened the door and looked at the strange man coming towards him with kind green eyes, a familiar nose with a particular bump, and blond shaggy hair. He knew this face better than his own through countless hours of study and memorization. He looked over at Marty. "Is that who I think it is? Is it a dream? It is really him?"

"Or maybe the best of both. Consider it a reward. A reflection of what was and could be again.   A way to say good-bye."

"Won't you come?" Nathan asked.

"This is your moment.  Take it."

Nathan stood upon the Highway West and looked into the reflection of his father's face.  He cried freely and embraced him.  They shared a lifetime of love in a single moment.

# Chapter Ten: The Devil Haunts a Hungry Man

Nathan Carver sat on the porch with a worn notebook in his lap and a chewed-on pen in his hand, trying to remember all of the details. The orioles and blue jays battled via a sweet song that shifted into a shared duet over the spectacular summer morning. The blackbirds watched silently. Sunlight glimmered through the leaves and the trees, illuminating the entire field with a haze that made everything feel like a dream. Eve waved from the tire swing that Marty had made a couple weeks ago. "Nathan, come push me!"

He smiled and slipped the pen into the spiral binding of the notebook to do as she asked. Her hair followed her like a cape on each downward arc of the swing. "You don't have to spend all of your time on that thing. There will be other swings."

"But this is our swing. The first swing we've shared."

A month felt like an absurdly short amount of time to turn a cabin into a home. Papa Ray always told him that a home was a place where you loved, not just lived. "It will still be the first swing we've ever shared. We'll just have more memories."

"I have so few of them. Makes me want to horde all of them," Eve explained.

Nathan added a little extra weight to his push and sent Eve so high that she paused for a brief moment at the apex of the swing. "That just cheats you out of seeing the possibilities of tomorrow."

Eve didn't respond right away. She leaned back into the swing and let her hair dangle freely. "I can see why so many people like to hang from trees. It gives perspective."

"Yeah? How so? Never really thought about it."

"Well that Christ god that Papo always talks about was hung upon wood to gain wisdom." She threw her body into the swing, pushing farther and higher. "He saved the world."

"I'm not sure that's the lesson to be taken from that." Nathan shook his head. "Or maybe it is. I've never felt the faith others seem to have so easily. I kind of envy those with faith. Papo seems so happy."

"Do you think we're safe in the trees?" Eve asked.

Something clearly was bothering her. "Safe? Safe from what?"

Eve stuck out her feet, dragging them along the ground, until she stopped. She looked around to make sure no one was watching them. "The Bandersnatch."

"Bandersnatch?" Why did that name sound so familiar? It sounded like a nonsense word. "Is that a real creature?"

Her voice cracked with terror. "It moves swiftly, faster than the wind, with a thousand eyes stolen from weeping children. Spawned from the dark time before the lights in the night sky and it is doomed to be forever ravenous."

"Did you dream about it?" Nathan asked, confused.

Eve nodded, her hands quaking. "I did after reading about it."

What sort of books was Marty letting her buy? "Where did you read about it?"

"A book of poems by Lewis Carroll."

"Wait? Are you taking about the Jabberwock? Snicker-snack?" Nathan asked. She nodded timidly. "That's just a story made up with nonsense words to amuse children. Besides, we're protected here. It can't get you."

"It won't come for me, Nathan. In time, you'll go to it." She wiped her nose on her sleeve. Tears welled in her eyes. "You'll kill it."

"That's not so bad, is it? Killing the monster?"

She turned away from him. "You won't be the same that you are now. You can't be and take on that much power and pain."

"Do you remember anything about the time before?" Nathan asked, hopeful.

"I was trapped in a dark, empty place. A prison." Her brow furrowed as she struggled to find the right words. "All of the colors were drained."

"And then what happened?"

"A methuselah came to me with a young voice; an ancient trapped in the body of a boy almost a man. He showed me how to access the light." She shook her head. "I remember being chased and then waking in the hospital."

"Sounds like someone helped you escape." Nathan hugged her close. "That's good, Eve! Another clue!"

A loud bellow from Marty cut off Eve's response. "Son of a bitch!"

Nathan gestured to the cabin. "We should go check on them."

They left the swing and quickly ran to the cabin. Nathan opened the door to discover Marty sitting on his ass in the middle of the floor with his back to the wall. Papo knelt next to him examining his leg. "You guys OK in here?"

Marty shook his head. "I slipped on the floor."

Papo lifted his friend's leg for a moment and gently released it. "Clearly the Carver family was not destined to be dancers."

Nathan looked around the cracked wooden walls that had sheltered them only a short time and the memories brought a smile to his lips. "Maybe we should stay a few more days. I'm still trying to process everything."

"I'm running on the clock, Nate." He clearly wanted to stay. Nathan had the feeling that this cabin had become a second home for his uncle as well. Marty coughed for a few moments, spitting out atrocious mucous. "I have a responsibility to see this through to the end. Have some demons to fight and windmills to tilt against."

"You guys figure out what Joe really was?" Nathan asked.

Papo shook his head. "It was the same entity that Martin and Bill faced decades before. Curious that he referred to Eve as though you were meant to find her."

"I told you that I should have been there." She folded her arms resolute. "I could have helped."

"Joe did say that she was important," Nathan observed. "So we should make sure to keep her around."

"If that is the case, we should ward her against possession as best that we can," Papo declared. His eyes were narrow. Clearly he didn't trust Eve, but supported Nathan's decision. "I can cleanse her body via a baptism and then inscribe a protection circle over her heart. The circle shall have to be permanent."

"A tattoo? That seems kind of harsh," Nathan protested.

"It's the only way to keep Eve safe for the duration. It has to be permanent." Marty looked over to Eve. "That going to be OK?"

"Will it hurt?" Eve asked timidly. "I've never felt real pain before."

Marty rolled up his sleeves and showed off the many glyphs and runes tattooed upon his arms. He pointed at tattoos of the Seal of Solomon and the Mark of Behemoth; two pointed stars encased in a circle of protection. "These two hurt like the devil. Pain fades and that's sometimes the price for beauty. Or safety in this case."

"I'll be right there." The thought of Eve suffering turned Nathan's stomach sick. He smiled, trying to get her to join him. "I might get my own tattoo."

"The blessing will take several days to complete. I'm calling in a favor from an old friend to help with the casting. You and Marty are needed elsewhere during that time," Papo explained.

"Can't it wait?" Nathan looked at the terrified Eve. "She's more comfortable around us."

"Bobby Johnson has been a good friend to me and mine; that includes your father. He taught us both how to survive out here and now he needs our help." Marty coughed and wiped his mouth. "I don't want to go back there any more than you do."

"We must answer this call. Mr. Borri wouldn't have contacted me if this wasn't a grave matter," Papo stated grimly. "We made a sacred promise to protect the families of our fellowship should any of us pass on. Eve must be protected or I would be there as well. She would be vulnerable to the forces in that land."

"It's OK, Nathan. Papo will help me." Eve smiled and laughed. "I've never been baptized before."

"Thankfully, our destinations are very close. My friend Anton shall be meeting Eve and I at the Devil's Punchbowl; a local tide pool with great energies." Papo nodded to Marty and Nathan. "The two of you shall progress to the Synchronicity Café. By the time you have completed what needs to be done, we should be ready for you. I give you my word that I shall protect your charge with my life."

Papa Ray once told him that logical arguments from those you love were the worst because it was that much more difficult to resent them for making you face a difficult truth. "Let's just get the van packed."

Working together they managed to make short work of the load. The only difficulty proved to be Eve's budding new book collection. "I need them!"

"You can't take all of them. We have four people crammed in there," Marty argued. "We're going to be cramped as it is with just the basics."

"I've never owned anything before." Eve looked at the three boxes filled beyond capacity with books and her eyes almost teared. "They teach me so much. Just looking at them comforts me."

Papo blinked and watched in silence. Nathan wondered why he always seemed so surprised when Eve acted just a bit human. He laughed at her struggle, but fully understood how she felt. Thankfully, his room was still waiting for him at the ranch. "Eve, we can't pack around all of these books. Tell you what, why don't we pack them and mail them back home. My home. And then, they'll be safe."

"But I won't be able to read them."

"You won't have a chance. There will be new books," Nathan promised.

Her mood brightened. "New books?"

"In Portland, there's a bookstore the size of a warehouse," Marty said with a smile.

"How can there be that many books?" Eve asked with delight.

She surrendered the boxes to Marty. "OK. Can I take one with me?"

"Just one!"

She plucked a thick, well-worn purple edition of *Zen and the Art of Motorcycle Maintenance*. Marty sighed, imagining the questions that would come from that one in the future. Eve gingerly took Nathan's hand and tugged him away from the van. "Do we have time for one more walk?"

Nathan looked to Marty for an answer. "I was going to cook the last of the chicken to use up the last of the food. A quick walk won't break us," Marty said with a lecherous smile and a sly wink. "Twenty minutes enough?"

"For a walk, yes!" Nathan glared at his uncle and then turned to Eve. "Anywhere you want."

"I want to see the yellow-star thistle. Beautiful, but sharp thorns! Like Marty's spicy chicken."

He followed Eve silently as she joyfully led Nathan through the trees into a field of golden-petal flowers. "This place felt safe. I don't know that I've ever felt safe before."

"You'll be safe with us," Nathan promised.

"Little is safe in this world. All of you worry constantly." She sighed and released his hand. "That's the point, isn't it? Struggling and clawing your way to a bit of happiness."

"I don't really know what the point of it all is. You might ask Papo that one." He laughed nervous. "I'm just trying to figure out that stuff myself."

"That's why I'm here."

"Did you get your memory back? Do you remember your real name?" Nathan asked.

"I remember truths, not details."

"The man we talked to in the Dreamlands said that you were important. That you picked us. Is that true?"

"I've learned so much from you and Marty. I have found purpose here with you. As to a reason..." She shrugged her shoulders and looked to the sky as though the answer might fall from it. "I did learn a new song, though it vexes me horribly."

"How so?" Nathan asked, noting the change of topics, but going with it anyway. He learned that sometimes the best way to get Eve to talk was to avoid restricting the flow of the conversation. "What about the song bothers you?"

"The chords are easy to learn. I enjoy playing them, but I don't understand the meaning of the words." She blinked and he wasn't quite certain if she was serious or trying to draw a laugh. It was refreshing to see the passion in her eyes either way. "If his friend was a bullfrog, how did he have so much wine? And if his friend was only a metaphorical bullfrog, how come he never understood a single word he said? And if that is so, then why were they friends?"

"Not every song has a meaning you can define. Just like the Jabberwocky poem. Sometimes we just create images that touch our hearts without even knowing why." He shook his head frustrated. "I wish I knew the secret. That's what I wanted to do before all of this started. I wanted to write and touch people."

"The distance between you and others weighs on you." She touched his chest roughly near his heart. "You can let that go out into the world. Let it leave you."

"You think I haven't tried?" His face flushed with anger. "You think I like being afraid? Trapped on a farm I can never leave?"

She flinched away from him. "I didn't mean to hurt you."

Nathan sighed. "It's just not easy for me. I let it go a little at a time. Day after day. Sorry, it's just a little raw since I saw my dad in the Dreamlands."

"He must have loved you greatly to manifest there as a shade." She sighed a bit. "I wish I knew my father. Or at the least remembered him."

"He did love me. I never really knew that before. I mean really know it." He tried to put the feelings into words and utterly failed. "We didn't have long to talk. He only had time to say nine words."

"What did he say?"

190

He shook his head. "I'm not ready to talk about it yet. Can we talk about something else?"

Eve flashed a crooked smile that showed off her beautiful uneven teeth. She leaned forward and batted her large expressive green eyes. "Am I pretty?"

He blinked, surprised. "What?"

The smile dropped into a pout. "Am I pretty? Men always tell women that they are pretty in books. Especially when they spend a lot of time together around flowers."

"You know those are just stories right?" He saw the flash of hurt in her eyes and felt horrible. "Not that you aren't beautiful, but you do understand that world doesn't work that way, don't you? There's no Bandersnatch."

"I'm beautiful?" She smiled once more and he found it more than appealing, even sexy. "Would you kiss me? I've never been kissed. Or at least I don't remember being kissed so it's the same thing, right?"

It was a conundrum he had been dreading for a while now, but couldn't resist. He felt like a sailor at sea that could see the blackened clouds in the distance and knew that the danger would come, but had no power to stop it. "You don't have your memory. I feel like I'd be taking advantage."

Her eyebrows lowered and her eyes narrowed. "Do you have a girlfriend?"

He thought of Phoebe and their last night together. "Not anymore. We broke up months ago. We even said good-bye the night I left home."

"Do you still have feelings for her?" Eve asked.

He wasn't sure where this was going, but the metaphorical clouds had already enveloped him and the best he could do was ride out the storm. "You always have feelings for the people you love. Even if you get angry with them or you have to part."

"What if you don't remember them?" she asked timidly. "Does all that you were die when you can't remember it? If you don't remember something, did it ever really happen?"

The real big questions were like lightning strikes; you can't hide from them, they strike from nowhere, and sometimes you simply had to endure them. "Love never dies; it sleeps sometimes. If you have family out there, we'll find them. I promise."

"What if they don't like me? And they left me out in the woods like Snow White? What if I was supposed to die on the road? Or from the vampires?" Eve asked.

He rubbed her shoulder gently. "Then you have a new family. Marty. Me. Hell, I think even Papo is starting to come around about you."

"He's just worried that I'm a danger to you," she said quietly. She quivered with fear. "He might be right. It might be better for all of you to leave me on the side of the road."

He cupped her chin with his finger and gently pulled her face skyward towards him. Eve shifted her weight to her toes and reached for him. They leaned together like a flower unrolling towards the sun and kissed. One kiss quickly led to another. She had no practical experience, but certainly she made up for it with enthusiasm and passion. Nathan would have been content to stand there with her the rest of the day until the sounds of flapping wings and occasional squawking surrounded them.

He looked up to see the contingent of blackbirds watching them and blushed. It was a bit vague to him if Papo could literally see through their eyes, but it wasn't a risk he was willing to take at the moment. "We should get back."

"I can see why there are so many good books about kissing," she whispered into his ear. "I want to experience that again."

He scratched his head and laughed uneasy. "I think I can make arrangements for that."

When they returned to the cabin, Marty greeted them with a warm smile, pointedly ignoring Papo's sour expression. Eve sat down at the table nonplussed, very excited by the last meal at the cabin. Nathan ate in silence wondering if he had just made a mistake.

*       *       *       *

The scenery passed by the window in a series of colors; dark green changed to yellow and brightened to orange. A sweet breeze that smelled of leaves and rain blew through the old brown 1977 Dodge Tradesman. Martin Carver lounged in the passenger seat with his snakeskin boots resting on the cracked dashboard. A Pall Mall cigarette twisted in his mouth while he cradled an old Gibson guitar in his lap like a baby. He plucked at the strings intently trying to perfect the melody.

Nathan was at the wheel trying to enjoy the scenery. Neither of them had spoken since they had left Papo and Eve at the Devil's Punchbowl. It had been a long time since he had seen the ocean, but that was not to be on this trip. "Seriously? You've been trying that same chord for fifty miles."

"Someone's a little cranky that their favorite girl isn't along for the trip." Martin took a long drag off the last of his cigarette and then flicked the stub out the window. He coughed. It was deep, nasty, wet cough powerful enough that he put his feet down to the floorboard and doubled over. When his throat finally cleared he continued their conversation, pretending that nothing had happened. "The lessons of Sir Jimmy are long and difficult, but worthwhile. Some folks believe that the precise musical note can literally melt a pair of panties."

Nathan nervously placed his hair back behind his ears. "Some things just don't get better with age, old man. Don't you think it's about time you settled down? Live a little healthier?"

Martin pulled the pack of Pall Malls from his flannel shirt pocket. He lit another cigarette and continued his playing. "I have time enough to get the job done. Still have some traveling to do. What's this gonna do, kill me quicker? Besides, who else is gonna teach you?"

The young man scoffed. He excelled at whatever he put his mind to do, but he had nothing to work towards. How could he learn something when he didn't even understand what was expected of him? "I don't see how visiting the Belhaven Museum of freaky jars filled with dead babies and the world's largest set of chest drawers is gonna teach me magic."

"The world's full of magic, Nate. Just need to know how to look at it. That's the whole point of the Highway West." His uncle shifted chords playing a slow-beat blues melody. "It's a spiritual walkabout. See how the world looks and what signs you get from it."

Nathan's expression soured. "Why Oregon? Seems a bit weird to drive all the way across the country just to see a graveyard."

The old man shook his head. "There's history here. Family history. Many a generation of Carvers have been buried in these lands all the way back to before this was a state along the Oregon Trail. Our family braved the ocean to escape persecution and make a new start. Our blood was spilled in the Appalachian mountains for the American Revolution. We horribily murdered our kin during the Civil War and then when that was over they headed out west. When your daddy and I did this trip, we started here."

Nathan looked out at the desolate wasteland of dirt and yellow grass. "Why?"

"The water in this land is special. A nexus. Our blood is tied here." Marty played another chord. "Your great-granddaddy left only because of the Depression."

"And?"

"Your daddy found proof that we weren't the only ones with the gift," Marty explained.

"It's genetic?"

"And some around these parts keep to the old ways. They can help us." Marty stopped

playing and placed the guitar behind his
seat. "Turn left up here. You'll miss it if
you don't pay attention."

"Don't want to miss the biggest ball of
string in the world," Nathan scoffed.

"We're stopping to help an old friend."
Marty scolded his nephew and muttered under
his breath. "And taste the best barbequed
pig in all creation."


The dusty van rolled into the gravel parking lot and stopped
among the old pickups and diesel engine hauling trucks. Nathan
turned off the engine and glanced up at the large flickering sign for the
Synchronicity Café. Martin tilted his head and grinned. "Listen."

Sweet piano tones wafted on the wind with a hint of barbeque.
The melody sounded like a bastard fusion of jazz, blues, and funk.
"Someone has talent. Never heard a song like that."

"That, my boy, is the skill of one Bobby Johnson. One of my best
friends in the entire world." He winked at his nephew. "He helped
your daddy learn a bit in his day and saved our lives."

"Another magician?"

Marty nodded sincerely. "He beat ol' Scratch with his guitar.
Saved my life."

"Seriously?

Martin shrugged innocently. "You'll have to figure that part out
for yourself."

Walking into the Synchronicity Café felt like entering a dream. It had the feel of a classic greasy spoon from a movie decades ago. Old photographs and album covers adorned the walls. Most of the midday customers were finishing their meals while taking in the music. Martin pointed at one of the old Polaroid pictures. Nathan was amazed. His father, Marty, and another tall man were lounging in this very café smoking cigarettes. "That's Dad! And that guy, I have a picture of him."

"That's why we're here." Martin casually walked towards the giant, ancient piano. "They still let a fool like you play in here!"

A pair of wide, gentle brown eyes peeked out from behind the piano. A boy with a tightly cropped afro poked his head further to the side. He was tall and thin, but Nathan didn't think he was any older than twelve. "Ma!"

Nathan tugged on his uncle's arm dragging him back. "I think you have the wrong kid."

A tall, curvy woman with bright eyes and a scowl emerged from the kitchen wearing a stained apron. She stared fiercely at them for a moment, then her face suddenly softened. "Marty Carver? Is that you?"

The old man grinned. "Guilty. Betsy Johnson, the years have been kind to you."

"They have not been as kind to you." Nathan suppressed a laugh. She looked over at him. "Is this your son?"

Marty grimaced and shook his head. "Bill's son. My nephew Nathan Carver. I'm taking him on his vision quest to learn the trade."

"Then you didn't get my letter?" Betsy asked, concerned.

Martin smiled, uneasy. "I move around a lot."

"Mailed it two weeks back to California. Junior here's been hearing the music." Nathan noted the stress in her voice. It was the same tone as when Grandma Loni worried that he was about to do something foolish. "Scared something fierce. Come to my office in the back. Can't have anyone hearing this."

She led them past the kitchen into a small office crammed to the brim with papers, files, and boxes. Betsy practically collapsed on the old office chair. The boy curiously watched Martin and Nathan. "He hears the songs of the wild. Doesn't know how to make them stop. I'm too afraid to take him to the church. You know what happened last time."

"What about Bobby?" Martin asked confused. He glanced around the office. "He should be able to take care of this. He did the first time."

The boy's face looked crestfallen. "Daddy died three years ago."

"It was a robbery. Can you believe a fool would want to rob this place?" Betsy asked.

Nathan believed it. His hands shook with the memory of his own father. He knelt beside Bobby Jr. "I heard voices too, when I was about your age."

The boy stared into Nathan's eyes. "They keep me up at night. Asking me to do things. You understand, don't you?"

"The spirits liked to play around me when I was a boy. Most folks can't hear them." Nathan remembered the strange green eyes that haunted him in his dreams as a child. "I thought I was crazy until Marty told me the truth."

"Did you stop them?"

Nathan looked to Martin for an answer. "For a while, son. You have some of your daddy in you. Nothing to be ashamed of. Proud blood. Problem is that your blood comes with abilities you aren't ready to handle."

"What do we need to do?" Betsy asked.

Martin tried not to look at Nathan, but the guilt shined through. "We have to bind his powers until he becomes a man. That will make the spirits and tulpas leave him alone."

"Will that work?" Betsy asked skeptical.

"It did for me." Nathan laughed just a bit. He hadn't put it all together until this moment and patted Martin on the back. "Thought it was all nonsense I made up as a kid. Some of it started to leak through as I got older and eventually it all came back to me."

"In the old days, his daddy would have been able to raise him and teach him slowly." Martin shook his head sadly. Is that what it is like to get older? To see your friends die each in their own turn? "We do the best we can."

"Will this make Scratch leave my dreams alone?" Bobby Junior asked timidly.

Martin shook his head wistfully. "Not by itself. Scratch is a lot more powerful in scale than an average spirit or tulpa. Nate and I will have to handle him personally. We can do that tonight. Run it just like last time."

Betsy sniffed, worried. "Bobby told me you failed last time and he had to save your sorry behind."

Martin raised an eyebrow, looking very confident. "To be fair, I was a wee boy just off the farm back then. I've improved a bit and seen my fair share of the world."

"Who'll teach Bobby then? We can't just push off the problem until later without having a plan." Betsy strained to keep from crying. "I worry for him. What will happen to him?"

"I don't know that I'll be able to by then." Martin had never before admitted before to anyone else that his health wasn't the best. "I'm not as young as I used to be."

"I'll do it." Martin and Betsy blinked with surprise. "I mean it won't be for eight or so years right? I should be good enough by then to teach him."

"That's a lot Nathan." Betsy shook her head. "I wouldn't ask, except I don't know what else to do."

"You sure you want to do this, kid?" Martin asked. "This is a sacred sort of promise. You can't quit after this. You have to see it to the end."

"Dad would want me to help his friend. Besides, we owe them, right? His daddy saved your lives."

Martin tapped his Pall Mall's plastic case and slipped one absent-mindedly into his mouth. Betsy snatched it before he could go for his lighter. "Don't you dare smoke around my boy!"

Junior grinned. Nathan joined him. Martin nodded obediently. "Yes, Ma'am."

Betsy turned to her son. "Take these two out to the good table. I'm going to cook them the best meal of their lives."

Nathan's stomach rumbled in response. "It'd be appreciated, Mrs. Johnson."

She smiled like a pleased mother. It melted Nathan's heart. "Call me Betsy. You're helping my boy. Ain't nothing too good for you."

Junior led them to a comfortable booth in the back of the café. Nathan looked at the menu. Martin smirked and shook his head. "Don't bother."

"How will I know what I want?"

"Momma will bring you what you want," Junior said with a knowing grin.

"Junior, can you leave us to talk a bit?" Martin asked. Bobby frowned but returned to the piano and started playing once more. This time the mood was very somber.

"Who is Scratch? That can't be the Devil, right?" Nathan leaned closer with a fervent whisper. "The Great Barrier prevents the big monsters from coming through. If it were to have happened, we'd hear about it."

Martin shook his head. "It's not one of the big boys. Just a tulpa. A very, very old tulpa."

He was almost too afraid to ask. "How old?"

"Thousands of years. Back to the dawn of it all."

"How did it get here? Is this an Indian spirit?"

"Nope. It came from Africa via slaves. Started off as a psychopomp named Legba." Martin drank a bit of his water and continued. "From the Greek word psychopompos meaning guide of the soul. They help escort the newly dead to the afterlife."

Nathan couldn't help but look up at the pictures on the wall and imagine his father eating here. This place and these friendships had been important to him. It was almost like getting to know his father in person. "Why would this guy want Bobby Junior?"

"Ol' Scratch is a test. He has a love of music and stories told around the campfire." Marty coughed a bit, but was too excited to let it slow him down. "You go to him when you want to face the beast and see if you have it."

"It?"

"The ability to tame the wild. To let it inside you, but not become you." He gestured to the photos of old musicians and dusty album covers. "All of these people beat Ol' Scratch in their time and became better for it."

"That how you learned to play so well?" Nathan asked.

"Nope. I learned that later." His uncle shrugged his shoulders and his voice dropped with equal parts of defeat and shame. "I tried to beat him, but couldn't. Bobby and your daddy had to save me."

Nathan thought about the various tools available to them. "And what can we do to stop him? Binding spell? The Dybbuk Box?"

"Scratch is way too powerful to be contained." Marty finished off his coffee and leaned back into the booth. "And, to be honest, I'm pretty sure he is smarter than both of us put together."

"Then what?"

Marty flashed a wry, defiant grin that could have rattled the devil.

"I have to challenge him to a rematch. I have to beat him."

*    *    *    *

The old Tradesman rode in the center of a swirling dust cloud as it rolled over the old country road. The sun illuminated the juniper trees around them, giving them the illusion of glimmering as they passed. Pebbles sprayed the undercarriage of the van, causing loud metallic echoes to ping inside of the cabin. Shocks absorbed most of the rattling, but Nathan still had to hold onto the side strap to keep centered. "We could slow down."

Marty grinned a bit, but kept his hands steady on the wheel. "Only way to keep my courage up is to ride straight ahead, Nate."

"Some of us plan to live beyond the summer. Can you slow down?"

"Look at the bright side. We're in the middle of nowhere. If we crash, we won't have to worry about the cops or my insurance rates going up." Marty quipped.

"If only it would finally rain," Nathan complained.

"Think it will?"

"I can smell it." Thunder echoed in the distance signaling the start of a storm. Rain poured down upon them washing away the dirt and the grime. "I didn't do that."

The clouds darkened the sky, but the sun still shone brightly. "The devil's beating his wife."

Nathan titled his head, confused. "What?"

"Not literally, of course. That's what Grandma Loni always called a storm like this."

"I must have missed that one since there's been a drought in the last few years."

The rain dissipated just enough to turn into a beautiful rainbow that seemed to end ahead of them. "I've never seen a rainbow actually end before. Usually, it's just the arc."

Marty grunted and leaned forward to make certain he had a good view of the road. "Just be glad it's not March or we'd be dealing with leprechauns."

"Seriously? Leprechauns? Kiss me, I'm Irish. You're after me Lucky Charms, Leprechauns?"

His uncle's only answer was a wink and a laugh. Nathan turned on the radio to discover the last chorus of *Sympathy for the Devil* warbling through the speakers. He quickly turned it off. "That's a little on the nose. You going to finally tell me where we're going?"

"The Devil's Tramping Ground."

"Where's that?"

"Down in Eugene." Martin kept his eyes on the road. "Thirty miles off."

Nathan scratched his head. "I thought we had to find a crossroads. Isn't there one closer?"

"A crossroads might get his attention, but we want to give him a good punch in the nose. For that, we need a nexus. The closest nexus is the Devil's Tramping Ground," Marty explained.

"And that is?"

"A burned spot in the outlands that's never recovered. Oldest legend in the area says that this is the very place the devil himself can rise from the depths of fiery hell and come to earth." Marty kept the Tradesman moving at a steady pace along the dirt road. It was actually a bit easier with the rain keeping the dust down. "The devil walks in circles plotting his mischief."

Nathan snapped his fingers, figuring it out. "It's a thin spot in the Great Barrier."

"Exactly."

"Why is everything named after the Devil? The Devil's Washbowl. The Devil's Stomping Grounds. The Devil's Steps. Why's everything gotta be named after the Devil?"

"We've accepted it in our bones that the world sometimes sucks. Evil exists, maybe not always in a tangible way, but we can always feel it." Marty tapped his head. "We can suffer a great travesty, but the little indignities overwhelm us. We die from a thousand cuts. It helps to rail against the devil. Reminds us that there are bigger things in the world."

"And what about Scratch?" Nathan asked.

"Popular stories changed it over time. That's his power. He gains juice from the legends, even the ones where he loses. And tonight, the devil is gonna get his due."

By the time they reached their destination, the rain had dried to a faint mist, clouding the sky above them into an eerie summer fog. The burnt circle didn't seem that menacing to Nathan until he stepped closer to it. It was a black spot in the ground surrounded by a dirt field and luscious pine trees. He shined his flashlight onto the ground. Everything around the circle was dead. How was that possible? He stepped closer and felt the emptiness in his bones. The vastness of the universe seemed open and should he misstep he would fall.

Nathan looked back to discover Martin lighting a cigarette. His old guitar was strapped around his neck. "Don't you think you should stop that?"

"I'm about to play against the beast, kid." Marty tapped his chest over his heart. "My lungs just need to get through this last song. After that, everything else is gravy."

A rush of chilly wind blew past them. The pungent scent of sulfur filled the air. A thin, elderly man in an antiquated black suit appeared in the circle, then tipped his hat quite graciously. He stepped out of the stomping grounds and grinned wildly. "Martin Carver! Been a real long time since I've seen you. A real long time."

Marty nodded respectfully. "Scratch, we've come about Bobby Junior."

"What about Bobby Junior?" Scratch flashed his white teeth with a smile that seemed more menace than mirth. He had no worry or concern on his face and might as well been at the market picking up groceries. "That boy's blood is mine. Same as his daddy. Their blood is my blood."

"He's not ready." Nathan instantly regretted speaking, but it was already too late. "I mean he's just a boy. Give him time to grow up. Why pick the fruit before its ripe?"

Scratch sniffed towards Nathan and then winked at Martin. "Is this Bill's boy? Nathan Carver. I remember you. Did you come to see me? I can smell the talent on you from here."

"He's not here for you. I am." Martin growled. He puffed out his chest and tapped his guitar. "I'm ready to beat you."

"Beat me? Beat me?" The beast howled with laughter. "Why would I play you? You're washed up. A never-was. Nathan on the other hand, has potential."

Nathan shook his head. "I don't play. Not yet. But I'm learning."

"Then, I don't see where we have a challenge. You have nothing I want, Martin Carver." Scratch laughed and laughed. "Why would I give up my claim when you have nothing to wager against."

"My soul."

"Your soul!" Scratch's face turned sour like he had just smelled an insidious fart. He shook his head with a trace of disgust. "Who said I'd want your nasty old soul? No good to anyone anyhow. Now Nathan has a lot of life to give. His soul might be worth a risk or two."

"No!" Marty screamed. His face turned red and his hands balled into fists. "Don't even look at him. I don't know how, but I'll make you regret it. Don't underestimate the levels I'll sink to get you."

"That's the best thing about you, Martin Carver. None of us underestimate your ability to wallow in the muck." Scratch laughed yet again. "You play at being on the side of angels, but in the end you'll come home. The prodigal son always does. Looking forward to the fall."

"Won't happen. I regret some of my choices, but they're mine,"

Marty said defiantly. "I'll atone for them or not, but either way I'll do my ever-loving best to put my boot to your ass."

Scratch wagged his bony finger at Marty. "Ah, shit, son. I thought you were gonna make this a real challenge. First rule of the game. Don't let the devil get your goat. Never let'em see ya sweat."

"You can't have Nathan."

Scratch reached into his vest pocket and produced an old-fashioned golden pocket watch with the symbol of Saint Christopher engraved upon it. "Seems to me that's up to him. He's a man now and that means making the hard decisions. You want him to save the world, but not risk his soul. You don't fight a war without diving into the muck."

"Marty, this is for Bobby. Let me talk to him." Nathan took a step towards Scratch. "You want my life? Why?"

"Don't want you dead, Nathan Carver. That would upset all manner of spooks and I don't want to rock the boat. Besides, you have a lot of suffering and sorrow in your days before the end. It would be like stopping a symphony in the second movement." The beast tipped his hat and bowed. "What I want is simple. Just a taste. A year. You're young after all. You can spare it. Your daddy did and he turned out just fine."

His eyes narrowed suspiciously. Losing a year off his life didn't quite seem so bad, but what if that was what happened to his father? "And if we win, you'll leave Bobby Junior alone?" Nathan asked.

"Don't do it, Nate!" Marty tried to pull Nathan away from the beast. "That's how he hooks your soul. He tricks you into taking a risk."

Scratch shrugged wryly. "He'll come to me in time. They all do. The ones that seek greatness, that is. You should know this Martin. Isn't that why you and Bill sought me out the first time?"

What was it that Grandma Loni told him? *Get out there and do some good in the world.* "You'll leave Bobby alone until he comes to you. Deal?"

"You understand that I am a sentimental sort. A traditionalist despite all of my talk." A contract in the shape of an old scroll flashed into Scratch's hand with a flourish of flame and brimstone. "You'll sign in blood of course."

"We'll need to read it."

Scratch held his belly and laughed. "As you should. Always read the fine print. You never know what you might be agreeing to."

Nathan and Martin read and reread the scroll several times. They looked for any loophole or possible misinterpretation. The agreement was there clearly printed in red on slightly yellowed parchment, which Nathan really hoped wasn't human skin. "Looks like he's not going to try to cheat us."

"Why would I?" Scratch asked, holding up a mystical old-fashioned pen with sharp edges. "There's no way I'm going to lose. Why bother with chump change, when you've already won the jackpot?"

"You seem to be fairly confident, Scratch," Marty observed.

"That's the thing of it. I've done this a long, long time. Took many a man's soul. Got to be real good at reading a man and knowing when he's ready to face the beast. You've always run away, Martin Carver. Never faced the music, pardon the pun. Why would you start now?"

"I'm playing for that boy and my family." Marty stabbed his palm with the pen and then inked his signature. "Son of a bitch! That hurt!"

"And I have faith in Marty." Nathan took the pen and followed suit. "You'd think there'd be a better way of doing this."

Scratch nodded sympathetically. "Tisk! Tisk! If you can't stand a little pain, then you shouldn't play games of souls."

The beast knelt down to the dirt and the muck. He drew a guitar in the dirt with his big bony finger, reached down and pulled a fine-looking Fender Stratocaster from the blackened earth. He grinned like a shark, showing all of his teeth.

As Scratch began to play, lightning flashed in the sky. Each chord had the power and force of thunder from a galloping horse and the screeching wail of a horny demon. The wind blew through the trees accompanying the song and the guitar's licks seemed to be accompanied by a chorus of dark angels. His song had the fire of Hell and the lament of the lost. Nathan stepped back in the face of the song of the beast. He had never imagined that damnation could sound quite so epic and for a brief moment he wanted to surrender to it all with a primal scream and watch the whole world burn to ashes. When finished, Scratch tipped his hat and waited.

It had been the most brilliant song Nathan had ever heard. He nodded to his uncle, silently wishing him the best. Could he really beat

Scratch?

Martin took a last drag off the cigarette and then flicked it at the Devil's Stomping Grounds. He winked at the beast and started to play a riff from Jimmy Page. Ol' Scratch recognized the tune and grinned as though the contest had already been lost to him. Marty shifted chords to a song that Nathan had never heard before.

It was equal parts joy and sorrow; a raging celebration of life and the pitfalls of the world, life, and love. Nathan remembered stolen kisses late at night, endless summer days with friends with no place to go and all of the time in the world, and dreams of a bright tomorrow. He found it difficult to believe that Marty could produce such beautiful haunting music. It was as though his uncle had managed to store all of the pain and love he had ever experienced and expended that energy into this single song.

And in the end, to the amazement of everyone there, Martin Carver beat Ol' Scratch. Scratch threw his hat to the ground. He disappeared with a flare of flames. Nathan ran to his uncle. "How did you do it?"

"I thought of rain during spring. Fishing with your daddy. Mom's fried catfish. My first kiss. That last stop at that museum. I thought of everything I love and the notes just came to me. Love always tames the beast."

# Chapter Eleven: Streetlight People

The city of Portland is a study of diverse contrasts; a mixture of new century steel-grey towering architecture punctuated by old world brownstones surrounded by a circle of bridges, highways, and rivers. She was a thriving city with the heart of a small town and the low self-confidence of a third-world city. The cutting edge of the cultural zeitgeist of the decade had been captured like a genie in a bottle in the millions of tons of steel and brick that formed the City of Roses. New music blared on every corner from musicians and bars hoping to be the next rising star on the map. Vendors hawked everything from cigarettes in tin-plated mobile homes to the latest indie comics in stores of glass and plaster.

People of every stereotype and social stature walked the streets openly together from punks with shaved green hair, homeless in tattered jackets, bright-eyed hippies, sharply dressed yuppies, tragically sad emos with dark circles painted around their eyes, and any other modern variety of youth. Those that craved a nostalgic return to their childhood wandered the streets at all hours mingling, in a fashion Nathan had never witnessed in California. There were just some neighborhoods you avoided there no matter what social class you imagined that you belonged to.

The mid-day sun shined a little too bright for Nathan as he stumbled out of the Acropolis. It had been mostly dark inside, except for the neon track-lights that surrounded the mirrors on stage, and the quick transition to the sunlight blinded him. After shielding his eyes, the colors of the city slowly sharpened into focus. "I feel lightheaded."

"That's the air they pump in there." Marty winked very satisfied. "Higher oxygen-count to keep you drinking and spending money."

"Well, it seemed to work. How much did you blow in there?" Nathan asked.

"Hey, I didn't spend more than my stripper budget allowed." Marty folded his arms defensively.

"It just felt awkward."

"That's an art as old as Ishtar. Sacred goddesses living at the temple. Tantric energy created between man and woman." Marty sighed, very happy. "Besides, I strongly believe in supporting single mothers."

"At least the steak was damn good." Nathan rubbed his belly. "And we managed to sit down for a while. You've dragged me all over this city. Let's see. We talked to that ghost Nina in the Shanghai tunnels, visited the creepy dark spot in the White Eagle Tavern, and then walked around the Villa Saint Rose School for Girls looking for a tulpa that didn't exist and almost got arrested."

"By the way, I was very impressed with that glamour," Marty said with sincerity. "I don't know that I could have fooled that cop. He had a strong mind."

"Let's not make it a habit, OK? Speaking of which, I had a thought about the money you've been throwing around. You don't have to keep hold of an object once you glamour it, do you? You could turn a five-dollar bill into a fifty and no one would notice until hours after you left." Nathan cleared his throat. "There isn't anything you want to tell me is there?"

Marty waved away Nathan's concern. "Took you long enough to figure out that trick. It was the first thing I did when I learned the art. Back in the day, your daddy and I tricked our way around this country before we realized the cost." He snapped his fingers. "Everything has a cost. There's no free lunch in this universe. Magic is about what you do. Doesn't matter if you intended to have a bit of fun, it all comes back to you when you least expect it. Stealing is stealing."

"And sneaking into bars and strip clubs underage? What does that do?"

"There's a difference between morality and legality. A lot of what we do isn't strictly legal in a lot of places." He clapped his nephew on the back and laughed. "Doesn't make it wrong. Doesn't make it right, either. You'll have to learn the difference and do the best you can."

"So why couldn't we go pick up Eve and Papo? Why'd we have to go ghost hunting?" Nathan asked.

Marty flashed the wry grin that he used on occasion to puppy-dog his way out of trouble. Nathan felt the urge to check his wallet. "Truth is that I wanted to spend a couple of days with you. Just the two of us." He shrugged his shoulders. "And the purification ritual wouldn't have been too exciting to watch, believe me."

"I've never seen one."

"You will soon enough I expect." Marty waved to the watchful flock of blackbirds that surrounded them. "The little bastards can be damn creepy, but he's close."

"How can you tell?"

"They get happier. Dance around a bit. Look at them." The blackbirds cawed eagerly and flapped their wings wildly. "Some of them are too smart. I think they can actually understand us."

"Maybe you shouldn't call them bastards then," Nathan suggested. The leader of the blackbirds seemed to nod and then crooked his head to stare menacingly at Marty. "Just saying..."

He mock-saluted the flock and grinned. "Sorry guys. Didn't mean to insult your parentage."

"Are you drunk already? It's barely past noon." Nathan checked his phone for the time. "OK, it's almost three. Time really does have no meaning in there, does it?"

"Kid, for you only the very best." He stumbled just a bit. "I must be getting old. Time was I'd still be mostly sober after that piddy round of drinking. Yeah, you should drive us back to the motel. We might just beat them there."

A warm smile graced Nathan's face. "You're not shitting me, are ya?"

"Never tease a man about the object of his affections." Marty drunkenly wagged his finger at his nephew. "It only leads to violent ass kickings and, on occasion, being stripped naked, handcuffed to your van, and run through a car wash. Not a pleasant experience, I assure you."

"Clearly that is a story that the world demands be told." Nathan ducked under Marty's arm and allowed him to lean against him. "I am supposed to be soaking up all of that wisdom like a sponge."

"Two things." He held up two fingers to punctuate his point and

215

quite possibly keep count. "One, there is indeed a mighty and terrible story about the night before your father married. Truly worthy of songs and epic poems."

Nathan nodded with enthusiasm. "I'd love to hear it."

"And two, I'm under a strict geis to never reveal said story under pain of death. A blood oath between brothers. The story's never to be spoken of again."

"I'm sure he wouldn't mind so much if he told me. It'd mean a lot," Nathan cajoled.

"Listen, I'm pretty sure that if I broke this promise that he'd rise from his ashes, solidify into one pissed-off zombie, and then stick his undead foot six inches up my ass." Marty laughed madly. "And then, he gets mean. Bill liked a righteous fight."

"Well, just in case, let's protect your ass and get you back to the hotel and maybe have some coffee."

Marty was quite the handful getting into the van. It took several tries, and in the end, Nathan slid open the side door, pushed him into the back, and dusted off his hands. "I beat the devil, son! Show some respect!"

Three days in Portland left Nathan with a vague sense of where things where located in general, but the number of one-way streets and bridges still confused him. Thankfully, the charitably so-called motel was located nearby the Acropolis for what Marty jokingly referred to as easy access. Nathan tried not to think too much about it since he had to sleep in those sheets. The old brown Tradesman parked in front of the rack-shamble motel. Nathan ran around to the side and opened the door just in time to dodge Marty's experiment in projectile vomiting a foul-smelling mixture of alcohol, cheap steak, and green mucus. "That's nasty!"

Marty gasped for air and coughed a vile imitation of a death rattle. "Can't take the booze as much anymore, kid."

A familiar booming baritone voice laughed. "You're an old man, Martin! You have to be careful about what you eat!"

Nathan turned to see Papo and Eve waiting for them at a table at the nearby coffee shop. "I could use some help here."

"Nathan!" Eve ran across the hot pavement in her flip-flops. Her white dress blew wildly in the breeze. She ignored Marty and half-hugged, half-tackled Nathan, not caring that she stood in bits of the vomit. "I missed you."

He kissed her cheek and then blushed a bit realizing that Papo and Marty were staring with fat, knowing-grins. "I missed you. Did the ritual go well?"

"It did," Papo answered for Eve. He helped Marty stand from the van and then stumble a few feet towards their room. "Much better than expected, but there is time enough for that. Our journey was long."

They quickly settled into the motel. It was a dingy room like a million other such rooms and used only as a respite between journeys. Papo plopped Marty down upon the king-sized bed and he sighed with great pleasure. Nathan brought him a cold glass of water, which he denied for a bit until sheer peer pressure encouraged him to drink half of it. "Just celebrating! I beat old Scratch!"

"Congratulations! You faced down the beast. A great weight must have been lifted." Papo tapped his temple for a moment. "Just as the entity that called itself Stanky Wanky Joe said?"

"Good point! Looks like you did good, old man!" Nathan ruffled the drunk man's head.

"Hey! The room spins enough right now." Marty shook his head and coughed another round of vomit into the garbage can. This time was less bloody, but no less disgusting. "This hero needs a nap."

"And I require a bit of meditation. The ritual required a great deal of will and I am severely exhausted." Papo rolled Marty to his side, and sat on the other half of his bed, and slipped off his massive boots. Nathan did the same for Marty. "Perhaps the two of you should purchase supplies and enjoy the sunlight."

Nathan raised an eyebrow. Papo never suggested that he and Eve spend time alone together. In fact, he usually did everything within his power to separate them. What happened to change his mind? "Are you sure?"

"You two shall be quite safe together while the sun shines." Papo leaned back on the bed and folded his hand under his head. "However, you must return before dark!"

"You know the golden rule, kid." Marty's words slurred, but his tone and his intent was deadly serious. "We don't split up after dark."

"I did promise a certain pretty girl that I'd take her to a special bookstore," Nathan said.

Eve's eyes opened wide, very excited. She bit down on a hopeful smile. "Am I that pretty girl?"

"Well, to be fair, he did also promise me that we would go to the bookstore, but I require some sleep at the moment," Papo interjected playfully.

Eve leaned forward, very concerned about something she noted on Nathan's t-shirt. She carefully plucked a speck of golden glitter and held it up to his face. "What strange thing is this?"

Marty started a dreadful combination of laughing, coughing, and dry heaving. Nathan quickly shuffled her out the door before he had to explain the Acropolis. The sun gleamed off her hair as they walked through the parking lot. A light summer breeze tumbled scraps of dried fast food wrappers between the scraping seagulls and blackbirds. Eve shyly held his hand. The world could have ended that moment Nathan decided and still he'd find a reason for a little joy.

*　　*　　*　　*

The old van pulled to a stop just outside a large brick building that encompassed an entire city block. During the last trip, Marty circled the block four times before he found a suitable parking spot. Somehow, they found perfect rock star parking on the very first pass right under the gigantic sign that read *Powell's Books*. "You must be good luck, Eve."

She blinked innocently. "I can be. If the purpose is true."

He leaned over and planted a gentle kiss. "No purpose is ever more true than impressing a pretty girl."

Once they passed through the front door, Eve emitted a high-pitched squeal that Nathan had imagined only came from excited squirrels or horny bunnies. She walked dazed through the maze of stacks and books. "I never imagined that there were so many books in the entire world."

"Marty said you were only allowed to buy three." He sighed trying to keep up with her. "Three!"

Eve wandered through the stacks finding each row of books more fascinating than the last. She joyfully jumped from fiction to mythology to history to biography and he found her energy infectious. Nathan had already looked through the stacks for several hours, but he found each nook and cranny new through her eyes. He followed her loosely, occasionally finding a volume or two of interest, until he lost track of her completely.

Worried, he searched the stacks and then finally sought out the coffee shop where he found her sipping orange juice and reading a large red tome. She peeked up from the pages and smiled, holding up a small brown bag. "Nathan! I bought cookies and juice."

"Where'd you get the money?" Nathan asked.

"Papo gave me emergency money on the way here. In case we were separated," Eve explained.

"Was it an emergency to buy this book?" He grinned a bit and then tilted the book to read the cover. The letters were familiar, but not quite the standard Roman alphabet. The author listed on the cover was Vladimir Nabokov. It sounded oddly familiar like he should know it. Was this book in Russian? "Do you understand this?"

Eve nodded absentmindedly. "This man feels a great deal. It

burns his words."

"What is it?"

"The title is Zashchita Luzhina. In English, the Luzhina Defense. It is about a man obsessed with a game called chess. He fails to complete a tactic and then finds that he is empty inside." She turned the page, keeping her eyes locked on the words. "I think it hurts to love something so much and to lose to it."

Nathan found it difficult to keep his mouth closed. "You can read Russian?"

"I can read any language. Any that I've seen so far." She smiled. "Is that unusual?"

"I've never met anyone that was a perfect polygot. Brilliant and beautiful." He blushed a bit as though he had said too much. "We've been here a couple of hours. You ready for food?"

"I didn't even realize that I was hungry." She felt her stomach. "Eating still seems so strange. Can we try something new? Something Marty won't let us eat."

"There's a wonderful teriyaki chicken place around the corner." He wrapped his arm inside of hers. "Allow me to escort you, my lady."

They ate quickly between bits of fevered conversation and laughter. Afterwards, they walked along the park and explored Portland. "I think this is the best day of my life," she said sweetly. "That I remember."

"I enjoyed it too."

"Will we kiss again?" Eve asked slyly.

"I'd like that." He leaned down to kiss her, surprised by the passion.

She tasted of eternal sunshine and strawberries. He had never kissed a girl that devoted quite so much of herself into the kiss. Nathan almost felt the beating of her heart in her lips and tongue. "I want more."

"More?" Nathan coughed and glanced around the sidewalk. "I don't think we can do that."

"Why not?"

Nathan waved at the sidewalk, the side-street, and the people passing by. "I think we'd get arrested."

"I want to know you. I want to feel my body sing like it describes in the books." Eve kissed him again and pulled him close. "I want to feel alive."

"Eve, you still don't remember who you were before we found you." It was very difficult to pull away from her. He wanted so much to hug her. "And if Papo is right about you, then you were made, not born. And maybe not that long ago. You look my age, maybe a bit older, but you could be very young. It feels wrong."

She grunted, frustrated, and tried to pull him closer. "But I want you. My skin itches to be with you. If there was something wrong with it, then why are there hundreds of books that describe the moment?"

"Maybe you don't know what you want and you feel lost."

Eve looked at his serious face and giggled. "Silly, I'm much, much smarter than you are."

"Of that," Nathan said with a smile. "I have no doubt."

"Help me then. I need to feel close to you. Even a little."

"A little couldn't hurt, but we only have the one room," Nathan protested. He imagined Marty and Papo jeering at them from across the room. "I think we should wait for the right moment."

"I told you I was smarter than you." She shook her head with mock sadness and pointed wryly to the van. Her breath was hot against his ear, sending a wave of goose bumps down his face and neck. His hands trembled for the want of touching her. "Isn't there a tradition about making out in cars?"

Marty had long ago prepped the old dusty brown Tradesman van for such situations. Curtains were quickly pulled closed for privacy and darkness. Nathan unrolled the sleeping bags and layered the cushions to provide comfortable bedding and told himself that they would take things very slow.

Her hair smelled of flowers and sweet apples. How was it that her skin felt so good next to his? Each kiss, each caress was cherished and savored like a fine meal. She pushed him away playfully and laughed. With a crooked grin, she tore at his shirt until he finally relented and pulled it over his head. Biting her lower lip with a naked expression of desire, Eve slowly unbuttoned her blouse and then pulled it open revealing her pert breasts and the newly scarred tattoo of a sigil over her heart. "Did it hurt?" Nathan asked.

"Delightfully so." She shivered and pulled him close and bit him on the neck. "I had no idea that flesh had so many intense sensations."

Hands tenderly explored flesh. Naked skin pressed against skin unto an aching ecstasy. "We should stop soon."

"Why?" Eye asked, her eyes very hungry. "I want you."

"I didn't exactly come into this prepared."

She felt along the edge of his pant near his crotch. "I think you are ready."

He laughed. "No. I didn't bring a condom. I didn't expect anything like this."

Eve nodded quietly and stared at him thoughtfully a moment. "Marty bought condoms last time we went to the store."

"How do you know that?"

She smiled knowingly and kissed him. "Do you really care this moment?"

"No, but Marty's not here at the moment," Nathan observed. "For which I'm glad, but we don't know where he put them."

She raised an eyebrow and reached behind Nathan to flip open one of the compartments. Eve promptly fished out a bright red condom box and a crinkled magazine with a tall, partially nude curvy woman with enormous man-made breasts. "Marty seems very fond of this magazine in particular."

"You should put that back," Nathan said, trying not to think too much about what Marty did with the magazine. He laughed nervously, not entirely sure why. "At least the magazine. How did you know about that compartment?"

"I was very curious about this van." Eve kissed his neck and placed her hand on his chest. "And really, is that what you wish to discuss at this moment?"

Nathan laughed and pulled her close to him. "You really are smarter than I am."

*    *    *    *

It was a peaceful sleep of the sort that he could not have previously imagined. Nathan was exhausted, yet completely satisfied, and more than anything else in the world he wanted to hold tight to that feeling. A slight movement jarred his head. "Sleep. I'm just looking for my bag," Eve whispered.

"You planning on reading? Now?" Nathan asked, amused.

"I'm hungry."

"We just ate a little while ago."

"I want those cookies."

"Can I have one?" Nathan asked.

Eve rooted around the floor until she found the bag and brought it over to their nest of blankets, sleeping bags, and pillows. She wrapped his arm around her and popped a cookie into his mouth. He took a bite and the taste turned sour in his mouth. Raisins! "What time is it?"

"I don't carry a watch."

"Where are my jeans?" He stood and felt the wet prophylactic against his leg. Nathan smacked his head, remembering that he was still wearing his condom. Shit! He carefully pulled it off his penis, stashed in an old fast food paper bag, and promised himself that he would throw it away before Marty found it. Eve found his jeans in the clothing pile and handed them to him. Nathan pulled out his phone and checked the time. He peeked out through the curtain to see darkness and suddenly remembered Papo's warning. "Crap! Marty will shit himself."

They scrambled to dress. Nathan sniffed his shirt and knew that Papo and Marty would be able to smell sex on them. It couldn't have been dark for very long, hopefully it wouldn't cause too many problems. Eve watched him, amused, and laughed when he stumbled trying to slip on his shoes. "They'll understand. Neither of them is a stranger to love."

"Or kicking my ass for not being back before dark." Nathan helped Eve slip on her dress and then quickly slid back the curtain, and hopped into the driver's seat. "I'd rather not test it either way."

Summer evening traffic was heavy for this part of Portland. They seemed to hit every possible red light. It felt like an hour had passed before they pulled into the parking lot of the motel. Marty and Papo were pacing outside. He could see their angry, panicked faces through the windshield. As soon as they slid to a complete stop, Marty ran up to them and banged on the window. "What the hell were you thinking Nate!"

He opened the door meekly, knowing he was in the wrong. "We lost track of time."

"Jesus, you two smell of fuck!" Marty groaned. "You risked your lives for a bit of ass that you could have had back here where we could protect you!"

"We should argue on the road until we reach Olympia," Papo declared. "This place is no longer safe."

A low, throaty feminine voice cut off their conversation. "Brother, you ain't wrong." Nathan tried to warn them. He tried to open the door, but Agony moved with blinding speed and pushed him forward, wedging him against the door. She grinned wickedly at Nathan, showing off her perfect fangs while she twisted Marty's arm behind his back. "Marty, it's been a long, long time. I'm going to enjoy this."

Papo extended his arms, holding his hands in a protective mystical gesture against the vampire. His hands crackled dangerously with flickering blue eldritch energy, but his attention was divided between concern for Marty and anger towards Agony.

It was at that moment, when Papo was weakest, that Acrimony leapt forward from the shadows. His jaws opened wide like a fierce shark and bit into Papo's shoulder. Jagged teeth burrowed deep into his flesh; cutting through muscle, bones, and arteries. Blood splattered like water from a lawn sprinkler as he screamed. Acrimony continued like a shark, biting and biting, every move sliding forward like a machine. The crackling energy faded and he jerked trying to pry his way loose.

The passenger's door opened suddenly. Eve screamed as a tall thin man with braided brown hair and potent hazel eyes wrapped his hands around her torso and neck and quickly jerked her out of the van. "I am Zeal." He had several blood runes painted on his face and grinned with the fanged ferociousness of a victorious predator. "And I have waited for many generations to hold another avatar in the flesh."

Nathan extended his arm and aimed like he had been trained. The energy built quickly in his hands, fueled from his primal fear and savage anger. He blasted the stranger. Flesh and muscle peeled back from the vampire's arm. Zeal shook his head and held up his skeletal hand as though to examine it. "Flesh is transitory, boy. You will come to understand."

The high pitched shattering of glass filled the van. Powerful hands reached through the window and wrapped a hood around Nathan's head. Blind, he tried to summon forth the energy to fight, but suffered a number of blows to the stomach and the kidneys. He was thrown on to the street and then bound with a metal chain.

He tried to fight, but his opponent was too strong. Nathan was dragged back into the hotel room. Marty's voice was nearby. Nathan sighed, with relief knowing that he was alive. "We don't need to fight," Marty pleaded. "We can make a deal!"

Agony laughed playfully. It was a cold, hollow sound devoid of joy. "We already have a deal, sweet Martin, and it's time to pay up."

Eve's soft sobbing could be heard only faintly. Whatever their plan, they clearly wanted her alive. Zeal spoke to her in hushed whispers that Nathan couldn't understand at first, but Eve's reply was clear. "Don't kill him. I won't fight if you don't kill him."

Zeal laughed. "Then we have a proper understanding between us. I was once a spirit, a dream given form. The Norse called me Freyr. One god to another. Nathan shall live if you cooperate."

The sloppy sound of slobbering biting and chewing assailed Nathan's ears. It had the flavor of rending and tearing mixed with the brutal tenderizing of a steak with powerful chomping sound constantly repeated like a car misfiring. It finally stopped and then Acrimony cleared his throat. "Hmm... nothing better than Cuban man-meat. It's very sweet."

Nathan tried to think of a way to talk his way out of this. "You said I was going to be one of you, right?" Nathan asked. "Sign me up. Agony can bite me. I'll join you now."

The scent of meat and flesh and blood permeated everything. Nathan vomited in his mouth and swallowed it, not wanting to give them the satisfaction. Acrimony's voice was very close now. "Now, now, Nathan. I see you wiggling your little boy bottom at me, but it isn't your time. And frankly, that's simply not fair to o' Uncle Acrimony."

"I'll give myself to you. I'll be your Sorrow. Just let the others go," Nathan pleaded.

Gentle fingers caressed his shoulders and neck. He instinctively knew it was Agony; or at the least prayed that it wasn't Acrimony. "We can't take you just yet, but we appreciate the offer."

"Why not? Take me and leave the rest."

The New Flesh laughed as one. It was Zeal that finally answered. "You have so much more to lose."

"What are you going to do to us?" Marty asked.

"She who was a spirit shall come with us. Cenotaph will pay almost anything for her, though it has been written in the Book of the Flesh that it shall benefit him not," Zeal explained. His voice was hypnotizing; a perfect combination of an authoritative lover, best friend, and wise shaman combined. "Until then, there is so much we can learn from her."

"Why bother then? Why not leave her with us?" Nathan asked.

"It is in your nature to chase her down and rescue her," Zeal revealed. "You cannot be part of the Flesh until you have suffered, and become that which we need."

"She's innocent. She doesn't know any better," Nathan protested.

"She knows more of time and space than anyone here," Acrimony answered. "She is a spirit made flesh. Beyond good and evil. Beyond all of this. A dream given form."

Nathan tried to struggle against his bonds. It felt like some form of chain was tightening upon him. The fire was there, he felt it burn under his skin. Somehow he couldn't quite concentrate enough to summon forth the magic. "You don't need Cenotaph. We can learn from her together."

Agony cackled. "Perhaps in another life. Alas, Marty has a debt to pay. Don't you, sweetie?"

"I brought the box with us. We can make a trade."

"Martin, I'm disappointed. You promised a little girl one pair of eyes. We're under a magical geis to enforce said contract. Can't complete our plans until we're out from under the deal. You wouldn't want to be a welcher, would you?" Acrimony asked.

"Please! No!" Marty cried.

"Hold him still. Cenotaph requires that he lives. I wouldn't want to slip and lose control of my blade," Zeal ordered. Nathan struggled, trying to burst free. He could hear the horrible sounds of a struggle.

"I promise that this will hurt you much more than it hurts me, but you will live."

The room was deathly quiet, like a graveyard, with only the sound of a burning flame breaking the silence. Then, the smooth flash of a knife and the horrifying scream of a man enduring searing pain. Every fiber of his being ached with empathy for his uncle. How could a man scream so and still live?

And then there was blessed silence, only the sound of labored breathing filled the room. "There! There! Don't scratch at the sockets, you'll cause an infection. I've crafted a special poultice for those bandages. The nerve endings have been cauterized and if you receive proper medical attention, you'll live."

"You need him to live. You said so. You have to get him help," Nathan pleaded.

"He'll be out for a time. I am not without mercy, Nathan Carver. Friends of yours are on the way," Zeal said magnanimously. The New Flesh chuckled at that one. "McCreedy will know how to treat him."

"I don't know any McCreedy. We need to go to a hospital."

"We took the liberty to call him. He has an arrangement with Cenotaph. He understands how things are." Agony brushed his cheek with her finger. "You could learn a lot from a man like him."

"What about Papo?"

Acrimony cackled and then repeated the words in a mocking tone. "What about Papo?"

"Is he OK?"

"I found him to far more than OK. He was simply delectable."

Acrimony sucked the blood and bits of flesh from his fingers. "I'll miss him, but frankly if I knew how sweet his meat was, I would have killed him years ago."

Somehow, he forgot how to breathe. It was as though his chest had frozen from pure fright. His hands shook. It was impossible to imagine a world without his friend. "Why did you have to kill Papo?" Nathan screamed, struggling against the restraints. He wanted nothing more than to burn them all, but try as he might he couldn't summon the fire. The mere effort drained his strength, but he raged against it. "You didn't have to kill him!"

"Have to kill him?" Acrimony asked. "I had the privilege of personally escorting his rotten soul to Hell. I suppose that's a matter of perspective."

Acrimony pulled off the hood. Nathan blinked, trying to focus on the environment, but everything was spinning and bile rose from his throat into his mouth. He tried to move, to protect his friends, but he was bound by a silver chain to a chair at the hotel room. Marty lay still on the bed tied to the metal posts. His head was wrapped with blood stained bandages. Clearly, the vampires had tortured him, but at least his chest still moved shallowly.

Zeal held Eve close bound in silk rope with a Cheshire grin. Her eyes were red-shot and there was a large bruise on her cheek. Nathan tried to stir, but lacked the strength. "Why?"

"You burned my flesh." Zeal snapped, raising his skeletal hand in the air and then pointed to the body on the ground. "Papo wasn't protected as part of any agreement and it seemed a suitable punishment. The Laughing Man had his last jest."

Nathan turned over to see the remains of Papo. Their attack had been brutal, with hundreds of savage bites gouging his flesh; only the face locked in an expression of horror and pain remained unmolested. The words choked in his mouth.

"We shall leave you now Carver family to stew in your own important lesson in this life. Always leave your audience laughing." Acrimony clicked his teeth, barely able to contain his malicious laughter. The rest of the New Flesh awaited his joke with great anticipation. "What did one psychic say to the other?"

Nathan didn't have an answer. He couldn't think well enough to speak words. He tried to look away from the pale body of Papo or the sheer look of terror in his bloodshot, open, dead eyes. Marty writhed on the ground, reeling from Zeal's none-too-gentle administrations and bleeding from the black sockets that once held his eyes. The sound still haunted Nathan. How could anyone scream like that and still live? Eve cried softly, muffled by the gag, held closely by Zeal. Nathan tried to get her attention but the blood and the trauma stunned her.

"Listen, I'll be needing an answer from you promptly." Acrimony wagged his gloved finger. "That wouldn't be polite. Zeal insists we can't kill you, but I can take a bite out of you."

Nathan looked up at the brutal shark teeth dripping with blood and flesh, and avoided thinking too much about what that horrid maw had done to Papo and what it might do to him. "I don't know."

"I know how you're doing, friend, but what about me?"

# Chapter Twelve: The Strength of Street Knowledge

The scent of freshly-cut wet meat hung heavy in the air. Papa Ray always took one or two of the family's herd to the slaughter house in the early days of winter. It was to ensure that the family claimed the best cut of the beef before the cold weather burned off the majority of the fat. The first time Nathan Carver watched a cow that he had raised from a calf effortlessly slaughtered by a hammer, he quietly vomited in his mouth. Papa Ray kindly pretended not to notice.

The slam of cheap plywood against plaster triggered a panicked sigh of relief. Was this a sick Acrimony mind-fuck? Did they really leave them alone? He dared to hope just that the New Flesh left enough open his eyes and search the cheap motel.

Dripping blood slowly trickled down the faded off-white walls creating an intricate design that mirrored a fresh Pollock painting. Did the New Flesh really just leave them here? Nathan rolled to his side, flinching in severe pain. Several of his ribs had been cracked at the least, his jaw felt numb, and there was a low pounding on the back of his head; all of which were easy to explain as a result of the beating he had endured.

The dull, burning ache around his chest and arms were a mystery. When he was thirteen, he had fallen into a patch of poison ivy and for several weeks had severe itching around his arms and legs. It felt like someone had lit a match and then pressed it against his flesh. Was he

234

allergic to the chains? His skin felt raw under the dull shine of the silver metal. The chains were much smaller than he had expected blinded by the hood, but they dug into his flesh like talons. They weighed heavy upon him and they seemed to bore into his skin. What was this metal? He leaned closer, examining the individual links to discover runes. The chain was magical, and that was how they trapped him!

How long had it been since he passed out? Surely the police should have arrived by now. He edged closer to the wall. If he could leverage himself, he might be able to stand and check on Marty. It took a bit of effort and ignoring the searing pain in his cracked ribs, but he managed to brace himself against the wall and force himself to stand.

Marty's head rested in a pool of dried blood on the bed. His upper head was wrapped in gauze and bandages that barely hid the bruises. "Jesus. What did they do to you?" And then he remembered what his uncle had said he owed and tried not to think about how the New Flesh recovered the eyes. "Marty, you alive in there?"

His uncle's only response was a low moan. Marty turned on his side and coughed until he spat out blood and mucus. "Only in my dreams, kid. You OK?"

"I'm caught in chains. Can't break them. I tried using my magic."

"What do they look like?" Marty asked. The mention of the word look brought a moment of silence. "I'm Stevie Wonder for the duration. I'm going to need you to be my eyes. What do your chains look like?"

"Silver with tiny runes."

"Son of a bitch! A Prometheus chain. Damn. Cenotaph must have given it to them." He coughed once more and then touched his face where the blood-soaked bandages covered his eyes. "It binds your powers and makes you mortal. So you can suffer."

"How do I get it off?" Nathan struggled against the chains, trying to slip out of them. "Acrimony said we'd have friends stopping by soon to help us. The idea of Acrimony's help doesn't fill my heart with joy."

"Do you see a lock?"

Nathan tried to feel around for a lock. His hands were starting to feel numb. "I can't see it, but I think I can feel it on my back."

"Alright come over here." Marty pulled himself up by the headboard out of the sticky, dried pool of blood. Nathan did as requested and Marty blindly reached forward to feel the chains until he found a small, bone-shaped lock. "Here's the little bastard. A dead lock. Shit, this is gonna be a challenge. Too bad they took Papo with Eve."

His voice cracked with each word. "They didn't take Papo," Nathan said quietly.

Marty shook his head, numbly, refusing to believe it. "Son of a bitch!" He took a deep breath. "OK, Nate, I'm going to ask you to do something you're not gonna want to do."

"Anything to help get us out of here."

"You might not say that once we're done." Marty coughed once more. "Papo always carried with him two things. Important objects of magical power."

"You want me to touch the body!" Nathan couldn't help but glance at Papo's corpse. There were multiple jagged wounds as though a rabid pack of dogs had torn him to shreds. There were bits of flesh and bone and skin scattered all over the room. Papo's sad face was caught in the middle of a scream frozen for eternity. It turned his stomach. "I can't."

His uncle kept his voice calm. "Around his neck, on a leather strap, Papo always wore an old rusty skeleton key. You need to get that key; assuming the New Flesh didn't grab it. It can unlock anything."

"I'd have to touch him." The thought was certainly not pleasant. Nathan nearly choked at the idea. "He was murdered, Marty. Right in front of us!"

"Nate, Papo wouldn't mind. More than anything he'd want us to survive," Marty said, and then added under his breath. "And later kill those bastards."

It was an awkward position. Nathan's arms were bound behind his back, so he had to squat in front of the body. That's how he had to think of it. The body. Not Papo. Not his murdered friend. It was just an object existing in space. It felt cold and moist like he was dipping his hands in ground beef that he had just pulled from the refrigerator. He found the neck and then fumbled around. Large chucks of the flesh had been shredded and mutilated, but the leather strap remained. He tugged on it a couple of times until the leather snapped. "Got it."

"Bring it over here."

Nathan walked to the other side of the bed and turned his back towards his uncle, pushed his hands out as far as he could until Marty blindly fumbled onto them and grabbed the key. It took a few moments, but Marty groped along the chain until he found the lock, inserted the key and finally the lock snapped open. The chains dropped to the ground with a clang.

Nathan ran to the bathroom and then dropped to his knees and then vomited into the toilet until his throat was raw and his lungs ached from the lack of oxygen. "You OK in there, kid?" Marty asked. "I kind of need some help here."

He lifted his head out of the toilet bowl and answered his uncle. "Yeah, give me a second." He washed his face in the sink, wiped his mouth, and returned to his uncle who was sitting quietly in shock. "You feeling OK?"

Marty opened his mouth to speak, but his lips were trembling. "I need some water, kid."

Feeling like an ass, Nathan rushed to the sink and brought his uncle water and used a warm washcloth to wipe some of the blood from his face. "I'm surprised there's not cops or an ambulance; some sign of help. We had to have been heard."

Marty gulped down the water and then wiped his mouth. "Nah. Cenotaph cast some sort of befuddle spell over the area. It made Papo's birds get lost. We couldn't find the door to the motel. Made us a bit crazy."

"That's how they snuck up on us. I didn't see them. And I

looked."

Marty stumbled to the little nightstand next to the bed and groped for the drawer. He fished around a bit and grinned when he procured the last of his cigarettes and a lighter. Popping one into his mouth, he lit it in one single smooth motion and then grinned.

"Think that's a good idea?"

He took another drag off the cigarette, savoring it to the last bit. "Nate, I'm pretty sure I lost the deposit on this place and I can only die so fast."

Nathan didn't really have a response. "You're taking this pretty well."

Marty laughed hollowly. His hands shook, but Nathan could see that his uncle struggled to keep it together. "I'm pretty sure I shit myself kid." Nathan didn't have a response. "Hey, you get a crazy vampire cutting out your eyes and see if you have purely white undies."

"How are you alive? You lost a lot of blood and it's not really sanitary." Nathan examined Marty's head. The blood wound smelled foul. "What did they do to you?"

"Zeal knows his hoodoo. They had to keep me alive for the transfer to work. If I'm not living, the eyes lose their potency when they do the transplant. He used a bit of poultice and an IV tainted with vampire blood."

"Are you a vampire?"

Marty scoffed. "Have to be alive for the ritual. They used the strength of their blood to keep me alive and heal my sockets. Won't last."

"Do we take you to a hospital?" Nathan asked. How would they explain the missing eyes? "We have to do something."

"That would cause a lot of questions and I don't know that they could really help me. I don't have a lot of friends locally. Only one that could make a difference is in Olympia. That's about two hours north, but a straight shot. How's the van?"

Nathan had heard several large clangs when the New Flesh left and he feared the worst. He peeked out the window and saw that the old van had clearly seen better days. There were dozens of dents and flat tires. "We're not going anywhere in the van for a while." He remembered the last thing Acrimony had said to him. "Crap! Acrimony said that he called someone to help us."

"That could mean that he actually called someone to help us or someone that will want to skin us alive and chew on our bones. Did he say it with any amount of malicious whimsy?" Marty asked.

"Kind of hard to say. He said the name McCreedy, I think."

Rolling like thunder, the distant roar of powered engines could be heard. It grew louder like the rising tide during a storm. "This might sound really weird right now, but I think they actually wanted us to live," Marty said. "OK, this is really important. Look on Papo's right hand. If you can find it."

"There's not much left." Nathan didn't want to touch Papo again if he could help it. "What am I looking for?"

"You know that bone charm he used to wear? The one that used to jingle? Look for it. Hurry before the rest of them get here. It can save your life later."

Nathan scrambled on the floor, searching through the wet, bloody muck and shredded clothing and skin until he found it and shoved it in his pocket. He listened to the roar of motorcycles, Nathan guessed that there might be dozens of them, pull into the parking lot. He peered outside just in time to see a large tow truck park next to the van. Dozens of hardcore-looking bikers clad in leather vests started forming a perimeter around the motel. Was it an invasion? "It's a biker gang."

"That could be good or bad at this point. Look at their colors. Is there a name? Any symbols?"

Nathan peered through the blinds and tried to catch a glimpse of their backs. "Gold letters against a field of blue with weird looking lilies."

"Fleur de lys. French lilies used in coat of arms. Only one gang I know of uses old-timey coat of arms in their tags. Thanes." Marty tilted his head up as though he were looking up. "And thank you at least for that. Make sure you put that key and the charm in your pockets and don't show them to anyone."

"Right." Nathan did as he was told. "So they're friendly, but not totally trustworthy."

Marty didn't have time to answer before a large bulky man with a greying pompadour slowly slid out of the tow truck. He had the easy weight of authority and when he twirled his finger in the air to suggest a circular motion, the bikers quickly formed around him with the speed and discipline of a military unit. "Martin! You in there?"

"Son of a bitch! That's McCreedy! The old behemoth himself

came to collect my sorry ass." Nathan helped Marty to the door. They opened it just a sliver. "I'd say that it's good to see ya, but you know how it is."

"Christ on a crutch!" McCreedy had the face of an aging fighter that had seen more than his share of brawls, with the size to win most of them. There was a wicked scar on his left cheek. "I told you not to make deals with the devil, Martin! They always bite you in the ass in the end."

There was something familiar about his face. Nathan tried to place it for several moments until it clicked. "I've seen you in a picture with my dad." McCreedy was the large protective man in the background, only a few years older, but with more battle scars. Why had Marty brought him on this journey? Was it to meet everyone in that picture? Did that have some hidden meaning? His uncle might be blind, but Nathan suspected that he was more in the dark than the man that just had his eyes cut from him. "You were his friend."

"Shit! Martin, you brought Nathan into this? Do you ever use the sense that God gave you?! Only the curvature of the earth could have prevented you from seeing this!" McCreedy bellowed.

Marty stumbled back a bit and reached out to Nathan to stabilize himself. Whatever anesthesia Zeal had applied to him was starting to fade and the pain appeared to be manifesting in killer migraines. "Clearly not."

"Marty, sit down, please." Nathan led him over to an old ratty chair and helped his uncle plop down. He moaned with a bit of relief. "Rest a bit. We'll take it from here."

McCreedy put his hands on his waist and looked at Papo's corpse with sad disgust. He didn't bother to hide the anger in his eyes. "Christ, those bastards fucked you guys up real good! Damn, Papo didn't deserve to go out like that."

"What are we going to do? What about the police?" Nathan asked, almost frantic. "Sorry if I'm asking too many questions, but I've never seen a friend murdered before."

McCreedy nodded grimly. "Portland police are owned by the vampires. There won't be a report. No patrols stopping by. No justice for the dead." He shook his head angrily and looked out the window. "Cenotaph made sure there wouldn't be any witnesses. My boys will clean up the mess. If we're lucky, no mundanes will even know anything happened."

"Is that right? Shouldn't people be warned?"

The old biker poked Nathan in the chest. "You think I want to be digging up brains of murdered friends out of shitty shag carpet?"

"No. I just don't understand why. Why cover their tracks for them?" Nathan asked.

"We don't have laws or armies to protect us when we're alone in the night. All we have are agreements; treaties that limit the damage any one side will do." He yanked the soaked comforter off the mattress and respectfully covered Papo. "People just don't want to know. Forcing that knowledge on them now will just cause more deaths. We have to wait until we have the upper hand."

"How does that help?" Nathan asked.

"More and more people are starting to be born with the natural talent, just like you," McCreedy explained. "We don't know why. Maybe it's part of some cosmic cycle. Someday there'll be a revolution and things will change."

"Nate's kind of had a bad day," Marty muttered sardonically between moans. "Don't think it's time to get into that right now."

McCreedy grunted his agreement. "My boys will take care of the mess. We'll jack your van to the truck, take you to the garage, and do what we can for you."

"What about Papo?" Nathan asked.

"We're going to have to bring the body with us." McCreedy brushed his meaty hand through his greying pompadour. His words turned soft, but with an edge of sorrow. "If we leave him, they'll plant him in a potter's field where the hobos will piss on his grave. He might have been a son of bitch, but no friend of mine is going out that way."

The Thanes worked quickly as a team; they hitched the van onto the old tow truck, started cleaning inside of the hotel room, and did a quick triage check of their wounds. With the exception of the burning rash and monstrous headache, Nathan came through the fight without too many wounds. Once McCreedy let him move around, Nathan checked inside of the van to verify that the New Flesh had indeed taken the Dybbuk Box. The compartment had been broken into and smashed; Eve must have been forced to locate it for them. Determined to make his uncle comfortable, he searched through the torn piles for clean blankets and a change of clothing for Marty. Once inside, he helped his uncle wash most of the blood and grime and shit from his body and get dressed. His snake boots were too hard to slip onto his feet so Marty wore two pairs of thick wool socks.

By the time they were ready; the Thanes had wrapped Papo's body in plastic and covered him with an old rug that had been brought just for that purpose. Nathan wondered at how practiced this crew was at this. Did they spend their time covering up for vampires? Or worse, were they murderers? It hardly seemed like the time to ask when they were at the Thanes' mercy. McCreedy placed an old metallic flask in Marty's hand. "That should dull the pain and kill a couple of brain cells while we're at it."

"I don't have that many to spare, but what the hell?" Marty took several long gulps. "Well, your booze is still top shelf."

"So are my roofies." McCreedy wrapped his arm under Marty and gestured for Nathan to do the same. "You need to sleep for a bit. I'll take care of you and the kid until you wake."

"Son of a bitch!" His words were already slurring. He snorted, already losing control of his muscles. "Really? Needed me to pass out that badly? Nathan, it'll be up to you to protect the family honor and more importantly my hiney. Remember, they're Scottish. They invented the kilt because sheep can hear a zipper go down at a hundred paces!"

Nathan helped steady Marty, wrapped him in a blanket, and led him to the truck. "Was that really necessary?"

"You ever been stabbed? It hurts like a mother-fucker. He's being brave for you. Marty needs to sleep and let whatever they did to him heal a bit." They gently placed Marty inside of the truck and closed the door, ensuring that he had a comfortable place to lay his head. By then, he was already snoring loudly with his sweaty head leaning against the glass. "My wife Sarah knows a bit about medical care. She said to keep him sleeping."

"Fair enough." Nathan offered his hand, trying to remember what Papo had told him. "Nice to meet you, Mr. McCreedy."

"Call me, McCreedy. Everyone else does." He held up a hand and turned to the bikers. "Switowski, make sure this gets cleaned up and the right palms get greased. We're going to start ahead."

The giant Latino biker with long greasy dark hair and inquisitive brown eyes nodded. He had a sleeve of tattoos down his arms featuring symbols of death and the reaper. Switowski turned to leave paused a moment and then added. "You need a ride along?"

"Two should be fine, just in case. Be careful with the body. That guy saved my ass once upon a time," McCreedy ordered. "And he hung from the tree. He didn't wear the colors, but he was once one of us."

Nathan wasn't entire sure what McCreedy meant, but the tall man nodded with respect. "Sure thing, boss. I'll make sure everything gets done." Switowski stomped out of the hotel room with his thick perfectly black riding boots.

"Alright, Nathan. We have two hours of ground to cover going the speed limit. Let's make this happen."

\*       \*       \*       \*

They crossed the Willamette River in the old tow truck. Nathan sat silently in the backseat watching the blend of green and metal as they left Portland. The city had a personality, with a grace and quiet dignity to it that he had loved, but now it would forever be tainted with Papo's murder. McCreedy stuffed a stogie in his mouth. "Three things we need to get straight here and now, Nathan, before we make it back to the garage. One, your uncle is a strong son of a bitch. He'll make it through this."

"I hope so," Nathan agreed quietly.

"Two, none of this is your fault. Your uncle signed up for this fight. He knew the risks."

Nathan shook his head. "I let my dick do all my thinking for me. Marty's blind. Papo's dead. Who knows what the New Flesh is gonna do to Eve?"

"You think you're the first man that let a pretty face screw you around? Ha! Story of my life." McCreedy took a long, quiet drag off his stogie. "Besides, we know what the New Flesh is gonna do; turn her in to Cenotaph for the reward."

"How do you know that?" Nathan asked suspiciously.

"They passed along the message through me to send on to Cenotaph. Wanted to make certain he got it right away. The Thanes work as neutral messengers as part of the treaty."

"What treaty? I thought you were one of my dad's friends, but you work for the bad guys?" Nathan asked.

"I wasn't aware that it wasn't possible to do both when the world demands it," McCreedy snarked gruffly. "The world's not perfect,

Nathan. I don't think I have to tell you that. Sometimes you have to swallow a shit sandwich and smile while you're doing it."

"I get that. I really do." Nathan shook his head. "I don't understand why you'd take their messages."

"Right now we're officially a biker club that mostly stays in within the law. Sure, we occasionally run weed and deal in pussy, but that's mostly for show," McCreedy explained. "We've been around since the old country. Guardians. Protectors of the land. Thegns, once upon a time, until Shakespeare caught ahold of us with that damned Scottish play."

"You mean MacBeth? What does that have to do with anything?" Nathan asked.

"Don't say that name! Next, you'll be putting the sheeny curse on me!" McCreedy made a strange gesture with his hand putting it to his mouth. "That Limey bastard twisted things around. Took the legend and made it a curse. We're waiting until the end of days."

That just sounded wrong to Nathan. Was this some sort of cult? "End of what?"

"One day magic will flood the land and the Great Barrier will fall. On that day, the real monsters return. The Old Ones wake. And then on that day, the whole human race gets one hell of a prison fuck unless there's a revolution. If we're very lucky, that night we fight back."

"The Thanes?" Nathan asked credulously. "You guys are gonna save the world?"

"Sure as shit ain't gonna be anyone else," McCreedy answered with a bit of pride. "Until then we keep the peace. Keep most of the fighting quiet. Hope as many people as possible clue into what's happen out there on the big day."

"Isn't there some sort of authority that can help? Police?" Nathan asked.

"Beh! Closest thing is something called the Omega Watch. Offshoot of the Pinkertons! Selfish bastards just try to seal away everything special and magical about the world. A poet once said to live outside the law you have to be an honest man. That's what we are. Honest men that live outside the law and so we do what we can." McCreedy took a long puff off his stogie and beamed with pride. "We keep the creeps at bay so most humans live ignorant if they wish. Those that get involved do so at their own risk. Some stay in the light. Others get drowned in the darkness, but it's their choice."

Nathan thought about it. "That's what this whole thing is about. Choice. Guess I can't fault that. I just feel so useless. They kicked my ass. I couldn't do anything about it."

McCreedy growled. "Tough shit! You can either cry about it or get meaner. You get smarter and tougher. You got an ass kicking, you get up as soon as you can and deliver one right back."

"Yeah. I managed to bust down on Zeal though. Don't know that he'll ever heal that arm." Nathan looked over at Marty and resisted the urge to check him again. "How am I gonna get her back?"

"The girl?" McCreedy asked. "Don't you know she's not a human? Cenotaph has had everyone searching high and low for her."

Nathan shook his head. "She has a good heart."

"You don't know that. She's a mask made of flesh. A translation from a higher power to an avatar. She's beyond the scope of our understanding of the universe." McCreedy shook his head sadly. "We just don't know."

"I know. I felt her when I was inside her." He blushed a bit, thinking about what he just said. "I felt hope and love."

"If you say so, Nathan." McCreedy laughed a bit. "You sure you're not just feeling with your pecker? That sort of thing has gotten many a good man in trouble over the years. Won't be the first or last, I'm afraid."

"I get it. I really do, but what if I'm right? What if she is important somehow and Cenotaph has her." Nathan closed his eyes and tried to remember the warning she gave him. "Besides, I think maybe this was supposed to happen. We went on a vision quest and talked to a spirit or a tulpa named Joe. He said Marty would beat his demon and then beat the darkness in him. And he did. Beat the demon. Literally. And what's darker than being blind? He can do this. He has more guts than anyone I know."

"Marty Carver?" McCreedy resisted the urge to laugh. "Lil brother always following Bill. The only one of the circle to crap out on the tree."

He thought back to the conversation with Eve on the swing. "What tree? I've never heard about a tree?" Nathan asked.

"You were supposed to stop by my place after Portland. Marty should have explained it to you." McCreedy sighed. "Twenty years ago, we found an ash tree blessed with ripe magic, in Olympia of all places. We heard a legend that it sprang from a splinter of Yggdrasil."

"I've heard that name before." Nathan tried to remember what story he had read it from. "Where's it from?"

"It's called the World Tree in Norse mythology. Odin wanted to learn the secrets of magic. Such things were believed to be the providence of women who knew the secret of life. He mastered the secrets of the runes and more by hanging upon the tree for nine days. Some say that was the source of all of his wisdom and foresight."

"But why hang yourself from a tree? What can you possibly get from it?" Nathan asked, a bit disgusted.

"Heh! That's what Martin said," McCreedy observed. "Why suffer without a concrete benefit? The truth is that there's something in our blood, our very souls, that compels us to hang men from trees. It appears over and over again in every mythology. The dying god of the field, the Hanged Man in Tarot, Odin, shamanic suspension practices of the Mandan people, and even the ritual crucifixion of Jesus. Our souls innately know that someone who survives such an ordeal is stronger and understands the world in a way no other can."

He couldn't believe he was considering this. "Did it help you?" Nathan asked quietly.

"That experience helped me understand my place in the world. Afterwards, I knew with every fiber of my being how I could make a difference. It helped your father understand what was important to him. Gave us both the strength to endure the bad and be noble during the good times. And, through the suffering, I mastered the Art."

"And Marty refused to even try?"

They passed over a thin metal bridge that looked like it was

251

designed to protect a train crossing the river. "Listen, don't take this the wrong way. Marty is a runner. He always runs from that which really scares him. Ran away from his chance with the World Tree. Ran away from the real world when he couldn't hack it as a mystic. Ran away at his one chance at love. Don't have a lot of time for pussies this in world. Metaphorical ones anyway. I love the ladies, you understand."

Nathan stared out the window as they passed a large metallic refinery decorated with Christmas-style lights. The fields of yellow grass and dirt slowly transmuted into pine forests of green and brown. He couldn't think of Marty that way. "Maybe twenty years ago. He came back and faced everything with me. Man's lost his eyes and still ready to take on the world. That's a man that put his nuts on the table and tells the world to pull out its measuring tape."

"Let's see how he does when he wakes," McCreedy said without much hope.

"Yeah, I can't imagine what it would be like blind," Nathan muttered. "And sick."

"Sick? What's wrong with him?"

"Lung cancer."

McCreedy pulled the cigar out of his mouth and flung it from the truck. "Christ on a crutch! I didn't know."

"He wanted a last chance for redemption. And I'm going to do what I can to make sure he gets that chance," Nathan declared.

"Sounds like he really made an impression on you."

"I would have laughed at you a couple of weeks ago if you said that. Now? Shit, he's like that crazy older brother that occasionally sneaks you beer, but fights with you every step of the way." Nathan glanced over at Marty. "Think your wife can help him?"

"Sarah's a natural-born healer. Brings all manner of dogs, birds, and every other creature in creation to the house to fix up. She has the gift, that connection to the universe like your Dad did. Been trained by a dozen pagan circles. Knows all manner of secrets. So she's better than a sharp stick to the eye," McCreedy's voice softened a bit every time his wife was mentioned. It felt weird that the mean-looking biker could speak so lovingly. "If she can help, she will."

They rode in silence, listening to the hum of the engine and the tires over the road and gravel. The tow truck passed under a bridge leading to the state capital building of Washington. It was built in a classic republican architecture and lit with spotlights like a museum set piece glowing against the black of night. The highway expanded into several lanes and traffic almost disappeared until finally they turned off exit 7a into a suburban paradise that Nathan hadn't expected.

After several turns down a confusing series of one-way streets, McCreedy pulled into a large, rickety, blue three-door mechanic's garage. Several mechanics wearing Thane colors were working on a variety of vehicles and moving about like ants building a colony. The old biker turned to Nathan. "Oh yeah, I forgot point three. If you tell my wife I was smoking, I will punch you in the cock."

A tall, plump woman with greyish blond hair and striking blue eyes impatiently paced outside. The breeze blew the edges of her long summer dress until it almost blosomed like a flower. She waved at them. Nathan turned to McCreedy. "Yeah, I understand. Promise."

Nathan, McCreedy, and a few of the mechanics helped carry Marty back to the old house behind the shop. It was the sort of building that would never appear in a fashionable magazine, but it was obviously well loved judging by the orderly state of repairs and the immaculate lawn. The lady led them quickly to a guest room where there was a comfortable bed already prepared. "I forgot my manners. My name is Sarah. Welcome to our home."

"Thank you. I'm Nathan in case you didn't know." It seemed proper to express gratitude. He looked about the room and noted rock posters, a computer, and clothing and wondered who lived here? It looked as though it was someone his age. "Is there anything you can do to help?"

"Goddess willing. I'm going to try to examine him." Sarah brought in a silver tray and set it down on the nightstand. It carried a number of ceramic bowls and containers filled with a strange, bubbling liquids. She smiled and Nathan felt better, just a little. "You should leave us for now. I promise to do what I can."

McCreedy clasped his arm. "Follow me. We have a spot on the couch just for ya."

He followed, but gestured back to the room. "I hope we didn't put you out."

McCreedy shook his head. "That's my boy's room. He's overseas fighting in the army."

It felt strange being reminded of the war. He had forgotten there were mundane problems and entirely ordinary ways to live and die. He hadn't thought of Doug Houston in weeks. How long would it be before he was on the front lines and possibly dying in a land not his own? McCreedy led him to the living room where there was a blanket on the couch with matching pillows. "It's not much, but it ain't the street and it's better than a poke in the eye with a stick."

Somehow that old expression just wasn't funny anymore. Nathan nodded grimly, slipped off his sneakers, and lay down on the couch. Despite the brief nap he had caught in the van with Eve, he was very tired. He thought he would have trouble sleeping with all of the worry.

That night he dreamed of raisins falling from the sky.

# Chapter Thirteen: This Thing That Builds Our Dreams

A tiny tickle along his ear dragged him from deep slumber like a net trolling the water. The savory smell of bacon combined with that itch brought him back from his sweet dreams of the road. A quick painful flick on his ear brought him to full alert status, with his eyes jerking open wide awake. "Wake up, kid."

"Marty?" He jolted upright to discover Marty sitting next to him, grinning weakly. His head was wrapped with clean bandages with cotton protecting his eye sockets. His skin was pale, but there was still life there. "You're alive!"

"Bah! It'll take more than a pack of insane vampires ripping out my eyes to kill me." Marty chuckled briefly. "Although, I admit not much more, mind you."

"Yeah, you really are doing OK?" Nathan quickly wrapped his arms around Marty squeezing him with a lot more emotion than he intended. "I thought we might have lost you."

"I know." He coughed a bit and patted Nathan's back. "I know, kid. It's not the end of the world. Not yet. Mrs. McCreedy made eggs and bacon. Clearly, she is paying off karma at an acerbated rate to be married to this old bastard."

"You shut your mouth in there or no bacon!" McCreedy bellowed.

"Michael!" Sarah admonished, very shocked. "These are our guests."

He helped Marty into the kitchen and they sat around the breakfast nook while Sarah dished out a wonderful-smelling feast of eggs, bacon, potatoes, and buttered toast with homemade jam. Marty shoveled in several bites quickly. "I swear to god this breakfast is worth coming back from the dead."

Nathan almost choked on his eggs. "I'm sorry I didn't make it back in time. I got distracted. Eve..." He looked over at Sarah and blushed like a school girl. "It was crazy."

"Kid, I got drunk. I thought since I beat the beast, I was immortal. I'm old enough to know better, but still dumbass enough not to care." Marty smirked with a proper amount of chagrin and finished his toast. He patted his shirt, feeling for his cigarettes. "I just wanted to celebrate and I knew this was dangerous territory. I knew the Fangs controlled Portland, but I thought we could do anything."

Sarah clicked her tongue with disapproval. "Martin! Even with the vampire blood and the slice of the Indunian Apple healing your body, you shouldn't be smoking! Not in your condition!" She placed her hand on her husband's shoulder and beamed proudly. "Besides you should be setting a better example for Nathan! Michael quit smoking and drinking six months ago."

McCreedy snuck a glance over to Nathan and it might have been his imagination that McCreedy raised the back of his hand as though to remind Nathan of a certain promise. Marty laughed then immediately regretted it. "I'm certain that McCreedy is a fountain of virtue and a shining example to all." He stifled a chuckle, coughed, and then blushed a bit. "Sorry, the vampire blood has me tittering on the edge of euphoria. It's a wicked high."

"Don't get cute, Marty. You wouldn't see it coming now." McCreedy's words were harsh, but his tone was kind. "Not that you could really fight before. Hell, this could be an improvement.

Sarah coughed, stopping the conversation. "Michael, I need help in the bedroom."

"I bet you do," Marty muttered under his breath.

"Let's let them talk." Sarah walked past Marty and lightly cuffed him in the back of head. "There's no need to be crude, Martin."

She led the large man out of the kitchen and Marty nodded with appreciation. "She's a smart lady. Too bad she fell in love with that son of a bitch! Everyone has their flaws."

Nathan drank a bit more of his juice and sighed. "What are we going to do?"

"Right now I feel pretty good between Sarah's medicine and the vampire blood. She said my nerve endings were still alive, which explains why it itches so badly in my sockets. The vampire blood is keeping it alive. When the blood's out of my system, it'll all die."

"How long does that take?"

"Could be months by the time it's all done. But that's not important." Marty waved away discussion about his health. "What we need to discuss is you and Eve. Are you ready to let Cenotaph have her?"

"Hell no."

"Cenotaph is a full-fledged, hard pipe-hitting mother fucker. No mercy. Brilliant. Devious. And completely ready and prepared to fry us both." Marty tapped his finger on the table to catch his nephew's attention. "I need to know if you've got the grit in your eye and fire in your balls! If we make a run at Cenotaph, we could both die and I need to know if you think Eve is worth it."

"There's something beautiful and wise about her. I'd hate to leave her behind with anyone, much less an evil wizard." He bit his lip and then continued the thought. "Even if we didn't...well you know."

"Well, Nate, looks like she got you good where it counts." He laughed graciously with a bit of good-natured envy. "I didn't have the guts to make the move when I had a chance for my lady."

"I screwed up." It was that simple and Nathan knew it. "If I hadn't been out too late, we could have left Portland."

"Nothing that could be helped. Papo explained everything while you were out," Marty revealed. "It was Kismet. Fate."

"How so?"

"We knew that Eve was a spirit; or maybe some sort of tulpa that was caught and wrapped in real flesh. The truth is that she's a lot more than we imagined." It was difficult to read his expression with the bandages covering his upper face. "There are giant bits of all of our collective consciousness that float freely in the Dreamlands. Somehow elements of hope found each other and jelled into a single form. That pretty little girl is the zeitgeist of our age; the spirit of the potential of magic. Everything I've fought for and believed in my entire life is represented by her."

"But she's just a girl. Someone sweet who made me laugh."

"She knows every language in the world, but lacks basic

knowledge. She's not just a hollow," Marty revealed. "She is Buddha mashed with Prometheus to give us the spark we forgot."

"Why does Cenotaph want her?" Nathan asked.

"She is the harbinger of the coming age. If she becomes Cenotaph's prisoner and he manages to change her, then the age of darkness comes at last," Marty explained.

"She'll change him before she bends." Nathan shook his head with biting frustration. "I'm more afraid of what he'll do to her."

"Eve will fight his influence at first. But given enough time, he'll change her, steal everything about her worthwhile, bind her power, and hollow her inside out," Marty said quietly. "He has infinite time and resources to probe every weakness until she will become his."

"What can we do?"

"We fight them. Find her."

"We didn't do too well against the New Flesh," Nathan observed.

"We were stupid and caught with our pants down. Pun intended. If you are ready to see this through, then we'll take the next step before we figure out our next move."

"What's that?"

"We put Papo in the ground and pay him the proper respect due to a man."

*　　*　　*　　*

Marty Carver strummed on his old guitar playing the somber melody of Amazing Grace under a giant ash tree in the middle of a field of yellow grass and solitary boulders. It felt wrong to bury their friend in this place, but both Marty and McCreedy had insisted that this was the place more than anywhere else in the world that Papo had wanted to be laid to rest. The mere sight of the tree turned Nathan's stomach. It felt wrong somehow, like it was an abomination with dozens of twisted branches gnarled and bent like an old witch's broken fingers. There was something magical about this place, and it scared the shit out of Nathan. Hundreds of blackbirds chose this moment to nest under the protection of the branches of the ash tree. They watched the proceedings quite closely with only a few mournful caws to announce their presence.

The Thanes dug a proper grave a few feet from the trunk of the ash tree, but still under the canopy of the leaves. McCreedy had cut an epitaph in the large stone that would serve as a headstone. *"Here lies a brother to all men."*

A somber, but sweet voice started to sing. Nathan looked over at Sarah McCreedy. She had a good voice, with little training, but a great deal of emotion that mixed perfectly with the words and meaning of the song. It was no surprise that he started to cry. Did Papo die in a state of grace? Were his sins forgiven? Did he find the redemption for which he searched? What did it mean?

Tears clouded his eyes. He tried to remember the last time he cried so openly. One by one the Thanes paid their respect to a man they barely knew, but were forged into brothers by virtue of having hung upon the Ash tree. What was it that they had learned from the experience? Could it have changed them that much?

Once the song was complete, McCreedy stepped forward and poured a fifth of whiskey into the open grave. It splashed onto a red pinewood coffin. Familiar words were read from the bible, but Nathan couldn't focus on their meaning. Marty stood silently, holding the guitar, his face pointed to the ground. Was it possible to cry without eyes?

"Do you have something you want to say?" McCreedy asked.

How do you find the words to describe the life of a man? "I knew him only a short time, but he was my friend and he showed me a world of magic. I'll miss him."

The Thanes drew pistols, much to Nathan's surprise, and quietly cocked them. Each of them fired three shots into the air and then quickly holstered their weapons under their belts. At the last, Marty stepped forward. "Our friend now walks in lands hitherto undreamt of by mortal men. He always said that death was just the end of one story and the beginning of another. I believe that with all of my heart. Our friend isn't in that coffin. That's just his shell, his former cage. Flesh fades leaving only the bones." His voice cracked with grief. "I hope that he is there waiting for me when I pass beyond. Very likely, he will have already drank all of the beer and run off all of the women, even the ones he has no intention of sleeping with. But, at that moment, I will hug my friend knowing that love and friendship truly are forever."

With everything said, two of the bikers took their shovels and began to push dirt into the grave. McCreedy wrapped his arm around his wife and kissed her gently on the cheek. Nathan remembered the bone charm in his pocket and slipped his hand through it. The agitated caws of the blackbirds changed into human-like whispers.

He tilted his head to hear them better. The crows and the ravens spoke a low guttural language that sounded like a demonic bastardization of Latin and German. "Can you hear that?"

"What?" Marty asked.

"The blackbirds are speaking to each other in some sort of language." Nathan tried to discern the words, but it was too foreign. "I hear words, but don't understand them."

"You put on the charm, didn't you?" Marty shook his head. "I thought we were going to wait."

"It felt right to do it here and now." Nathan looked up at the birds surprised to meet their gaze. It seemed as though they were trying to communicate. "They miss him."

"Maybe trusting your instinct is a good idea. Mine certainly haven't been picture perfect." Marty reached blindly for his nephew until his hand rested comfortably on Nathan's shoulder. "The language you are hearing is the secret language of crows and ravens spoken only in the shadows. Papo used it to communicate with them."

"I can feel them." Nathan felt pangs of sadness and anger all about him. Their caged emotions pecked at his heart. All of them together were oppressive and overwhelming. "They want revenge."

"As they should. The blackbirds have the heart of the wild, but no soul. They loved Papo. As he loved them. He could see through their eyes and let them know his will." He coughed just a bit and then

263

continued. "They watched you all your life in one form or another and thus their love of Papo , in a small part, to you."

"They need to grieve and a task to complete. A way to help Papo." Nathan reached out to them with his mind. The charm on his wrist seemed work like a giant projector allowing him to project his own thoughts into the flock. He thought of Acrimony and the rest of the New Flesh, locking their images in his mind. Once he was certain that the flock understood that these images were of Papo's murderers, he concentrated on one single word. "Find."

With a single shriek made of a hundred voices, the flock took flight and dissipated into the horizon. "What did you tell them?" Marty asked.

Nathan kept his eyes on the flock. "I told them to seek out the New Flesh to find them no matter where they hide."

"We can't worry about them right now. Cenotaph has Eve," Marty argued. "They have the patience of a spider. They can afford to wait until the stars are right."

"Eve told me about a book she was reading. Can't remember the name of it, but it was about a champion chess player that couldn't believe that the other guy beat his defense. He spent the rest of his life replaying that game." Nathan squeezed Marty's shoulder. "You've taken me thus far. It's time you lean on me."

"What do you mean?"

"I can't beat Cenotaph or the New Flesh," Nathan admitted.

"You can't give up, Nate. You have the gift," Marty protested.

"I'm not giving up. I'm looking in the mirror and not flinching."

264

Nathan glanced up at the tree and swallowed. "I can't beat them. Not like I am now. I have to change. Eve knew that. She tried to warn me back at the cabin. I have the talent. I know this now. I think I even understand how to access it, but I'm still inexperienced. I'm not a monster and I don't want to be. But, I need to face death, not just tip my toe in the water. I need to hang from the tree."

"What? Now?" Marty asked. "That's insane. We need to come up with a plan. Some way to trick them."

"You can't cheat death. Sooner or later, we're all cut down. That's their strength. Our fear of death is our weakness," Nathan explained. "I froze during the fight. I knew an instant before the fight that they were there and I didn't react because of fear. I need to prove to myself that I can beat them. I have to face the tree."

"McCreedy told you I wouldn't do it, didn't he?"

"He might have shared a few details," Nathan answered vaguely. "That's not important."

"It is important. We're men, not gods. The divine has a way of burning off everything else until there's nothing left. You want to know why Bill gave up this world? He didn't want to be the Buddha. He wanted to live as a man. Are you ready to give that up?" Marty asked.

"For her. I don't know why she picked us to protect her, but she did," Nathan said with a great deal of passion. "Out of everyone in the world, she picked us."

"She didn't tell you?"

"Tell me what?"

"She didn't come to this world for our help. She came to protect you," Marty explained.

"What? How do you figure?"

"Papo figured it out during the cleansing ritual. She spied you across the Dreamlands when you were a boy. That quiet night when your mother abandoned you on the farm." Marty paused for a moment as though still trying to process what he had been told. "She felt your suffering across the Great Barrier and tried to make contact. Papo told me that you heard her whispers and even saw a glimpse of her form. But she couldn't reach across, not all the way."

Nathan thought back to that night. He had always imagined that it had been a monster scratching at his window. "That was Eve?"

"No. Not exactly. It was a tulpa born from our dreams, our hopes. It felt for you. For once it cared more about the wonders of the universe or the edge of what was possible. It loved you, but it couldn't reach out to you fully across the Great Barrier. So when Cenotaph was experimenting on creating a hollow, the tulpa allowed him to make use of her essence, not fully understanding what magic he stamped into that flesh until she escaped him."

"How did Papo discover this?"

"Anton Morgan had some of the clues from the signs of the blessing. Papo remembered the spirit from that night you were abandoned. He saw it through the birds, but never understood where it was from or what might have happened to it. Eve remembered a little. She only remembered the boy, but hadn't consciously connected you to that boy."

"She became flesh for me? Because she felt for me?" Nathan asked.

"She was meant to be the inspiration for an entire generation of mystics, but she felt a connection to you." Marty shook his head. "She wanted you to know that the universe didn't hate you."

Nathan nodded his head, resolute. "That just proves everything I've been saying. She gave up the universe for me to come down to this shithole of a planet. I have to save her and this is the only way."

Marty involuntarily shivered. "I'll do it with you."

"No. You just took a big one for the team." Nathan shook his head. "Mrs. McCreedy barely let you come to the funeral."

"No time like the present. No rest for the wicked." Marty grinned like a madman. "And believe me I see better now than ever before. I have about a month before I come down from this high. After that, I don't know that I'll ever be any good to anyone again. Don't take this away from me, Nathan."

Nathan considered his plan for a few moments. "I have a job for you."

"You have a job for me?" Marty asked credulously.

"You've done a good job showing me the ropes, Marty. I never could have imagined such a world, but we need to try something new."

"Something new? You think you can come up with something new?" Marty laughed.

"Me? Hell no. I'm just fumbling in the dark," Nathan admitted. "The thing is that Eve is smarter than all of us put together. I think she knew all of this would happen."

"If she knew all of this would happen, then why wouldn't she stop it?"

"If I knew that, I'd be as smart as she is." Nathan admitted, nervous. "The thing is that I can't help but think about what Eve showed me yesterday. She made a point to show me a book about a chess player that lost a match and then spent the rest of his life regretting it. I wish I could remember the name of it. The plot involved this player losing everything because he wouldn't accept that his tactic didn't work. He blamed everyone and everything, but his inability to change."

"And that applies to us how?" Marty asked.

"This isn't something we can charm our way through and I can't do it alone. This time you have to lean on me."

There was a silent pause. Marty's lip trembled. "If I didn't know better, I could have sworn that I was talking to Bill. What job do you need me to do?"

"I need you to find out everything you can about the Bandersnatch while I hang from the Ash tree. Dig up any weaknesses."

He pulled on his nephew's arm with a strength born of fear. "Why would you want that? Those things are quick and deadly. They are the most devastating predators this ecosystem can withstand -- vile star-spawn from the death of an older universe or so the legend goes."

Nathan flashed his best imitation shit-eating grin. He knew that Marty couldn't see it, but just the act added a bit of confidence. "That's for the future. Can you do it?"

"I'll make it happen. Promise."

He clapped his uncle on the shoulder. "Good. We'll want to hit things running when I recover."

\*　　\*　　\*　　\*

Nathan watched as McCreedy ordered his men to fish out special hooks made of bone from a locked metal toolbox in his truck. The points appeared to be wickedly sharp and at the thought that they would soon pierce his flesh, Nathan discovered that his knees were shivering despite his best effort to still them. The muscles in his throat and stomach reflexively tensed and he bit down the urge to try to vomit his fear away.

Marty leaned close, facing away from the McCreedys. "You don't have to do this." He clapped Nathan on the shoulder. "There is always another way."

Sarah coughed. "Martin, you should be resting in bed."

"I'm not leaving Nate to this alone," Marty whined.

"Marty, I'll be fine." Nathan forced a smile. "I need to start this now before I lose my nerve and she won't quit on this."

He led Marty to Sarah McCreedy's car and helped him inside. "I'll take care of him, Nathan."

"Thank you, Mrs. McCreedy."

"It won't be easy for him once the vampire blood is out of his system." She shook her head sadly. "The nerve endings will die. It will already be very painful so I'm afraid to cauterize them until then."

"Don't do it."

"Why?" she asked, horrified. "That pain will be unbearable."

"I have an idea about that. Mr. McCreedy told me you had special healing magic. Is that true?"

"Yes, but I can't just regenerate his eyes. That would be impossible, Nathan."

"That won't be an issue. Can you implant eyes if you have a donor?" Nathan asked.

"You aren't going to kill someone, are you?" Sarah asked horrified.

Nathan shook his head. "No. I'm going to kill a monster that kills children."

Sarah narrowed her eyes, not quite understanding. "It is possible, but I've never done it before. I would have to get help and even if it worked, I couldn't promise that he would see like he did before."

"All I can do is ask you to try. Please?" Nathan pleaded.

She smiled as though she were a proud mother. "I will. Your father would have been so proud."

Her words sparked a resurgence of his courage. "I aim to do us all proud."

Nathan watched Sarah McCreedy's car drive away on the dirt road. McCreedy strode over to him, holding a large knife. The Thanes had quickly spread out a protection circle made of stones and salt. "You sure you want to do this right now, Nathan? We just put Papo in the ground."

"Eve doesn't have the time to wait. Neither does Marty. I know what I need to do. Papo will understand." Nathan looked over to the gravestone. "And if there's any sort of luck in this crazy world, he'll be there for me."

"Strip off your shirt." McCreedy started sharpening the bone hooks. "This is going to hurt like the devil. You'll hang for two or three days until your skin and muscles tear. I'll have one man stand guard here twenty-four hours. He'll be available to give you water once a day or call me if there is an emergency. Otherwise, he won't interrupt the ritual until you ask to be taken down."

"How long before I know if it works?" Nathan asked.

McCreedy laughed. "When you figure out your shit, you'll know it. Like a fucking thunderbolt to the forehead."

"Anything else I need to know?"

"Yeah, you won't be able to control your bladder for three days. You won't be able to help pissing and shitting yourself. Don't try, you'll hurt yourself," McCreedy advised.

Two of the bikers brought forth a lamb to McCreedy. It bleated nervously as though it sensed what was coming. Nathan followed them to the shadow of the ash tree. McCreedy had been busy preparing for the ritual. There was an assortment of knives and a wooden bowl filled with ashes.

"What's that for?" Nathan asked, gesturing to the knives.

"There is always a sacrifice, Nathan." McCreedy lifted up the lamb's head and then gestured to its throat. "You are the one taking this ride so you have to pay the bill."

Nathan nodded. Papa Ray taught him how to kill with mercy. He selected one of the knives that McCreedy had laid out for him and quickly slit the lamb's throat. McCreedy washed his hands in the warm blood and then rubbed ash over his hands. "We leave this man in the shadow of the World Tree to suffer for the future."

Thanes around them started to chant in a strange mixture of German, Norwegian, and Latin. McCreedy organized the men by waving his hands as though he were conducting a ceremony. Switowski stepped forward with a large coil of rope and threw it up over one of the largest branches of the tree and prepared rigging. McCreedy maneuvered Nathan under the largest branch. "Believe me, Nathan, this is gonna hurt you a lot more than it hurts me."

He flinched briefly as McCreedy lifted the hooks. Nathan tried to control his breathing as he didn't want be a coward in front of McCreedy. Nathan wiped the sweat from his eyes and turned his back toward his friend. "Do it!"

McCreedy grunted an acknowledgement and then gripped Nathan's shoulders. The sharp pain throbbed down his back, and buckled his legs. The hooks looped under the skin in his back under the shoulder blades; the agony paralyzed him and the only thing he could do was scream helplessly.

Switowski and Wolf groaned as they pulled the rig hoisting Nathan into the air under the protective canopy of the higher branches. His feet dangled strangely while his arms and legs felt limp while he swayed. How was this educational in any way? The only thing that he could think of was the searing pain that riveted every bit of his body. It started as an intense white-hot agony and slowly dulled into a manageable ache that merely watered his eyes. The only thing he could think of to say was his uncle's favorite phrase. "Son of a bitch!"

The first day was the most difficult. Boredom was the worst enemy of a man in pain. The empty fields, open sky, and the wind provided no entertainment; there was nothing but the pain to meditate upon. It seared and burned, but it was something that could be diminished. It was mere flesh and his spirit was more than that. Was that the point? To teach him to ignore the needs of the flesh?

The pain helped him step into a trance where time and consciousness stretched into an eternity. Each second felt longer than an hour. He had only the light in the sky to judge the passing of time as his very blood tingled. His consciousness felt free and unfettered. The world passed him by. He only knew his flesh and that he was the master of the pain he suffered.

"Remember that history is really just His Story. The story of our past." The familiar voice brought him out of the haze. Was that really his old history instructor? "Eyes up front, Mr. Carver. I'm not just speaking for my own benefit."

"Mr. Barrett?" Nathan blinked, trying to focus his eyes. "Is that you?"

The teacher's face sharply came into focus. Mr. Barrett stared up at Nathan over his glasses. "Looks like you are having a bit of your own story at the moment, Mr. Carver. What have you learned?"

"Is this real?"

"It is as real as you need it to be, Mr. Carver." He shook his head. "You can ask better questions than that. Now, what have you learned from this experience?"

"Hanging from a tree hurts like hell!"

"Do I need to stump you?" Mr. Barrett wagged his stump towards him.

"No, sir."

"You needed me and so I am here. Nothing more needs to be said on that account. You came to this tree for knowledge." Mr. Barrett adjusted his tie with his left hand. "Ask."

"How did you lose your hand?" Nathan asked.

"You could ask anything in the world and that's what you want to know about?" the teacher asked, confused. "Why?"

"You dealt with a loss and made a good life for yourself. I want to know how."

Mr. Barrett chuckled. "The truth is that I lost it in a car accident. Mrs. Barrett isn't the best driver. When we moved school districts we decided not to tell anyone. The mystery kept you knuckleheads interested in class."

"Yeah, I guess that makes sense. You wouldn't believe the stories."

"Believe them? I started most of them." Mr. Barrett held up his stump. "This symbolized every war fought and every tragedy the world has had to endure since Cain smashed Abel's head with a rock. This is not to say, of course, I wouldn't have rather kept the hand. Much like Wild Bill, we all have to play what we're dealt with."

Mr. Barrett took a step back and slowly his face tightened and became younger. His thin head of greying hair flushed out into a curly mop of dark brown hair. His sweater vest, shirt, and tie melted into a light greyish green camo jacket. With a single salute, Nathan knew that it was no longer his teacher. "Doug! Is that you?"

The solider slung his rifle over his back. "What was the last thing I told you?"

Nathan groaned. "Don't be a dumbass."

"How well would you say you followed that advice?" Doug asked playfully.

"Hard to say, but I found a girl." Despite the pain, thinking of Eve made him smile. "I think I love her."

"Then why are you hanging here?" Doug sniffed a bit closer. "I'm getting a whiff of dumbassery here."

He coughed. "I shit my pants a while back."

"You love her this much?" Doug asked.

"Yeah."

"Then play it straight. Don't let anything get in your way." Doug grinned. "Nathan Carver admitting that he's in love. I never thought I'd live to see the day."

He wasn't sure if this was real or not, but he needed to know the truth. "Are you OK in Afghanistan?"

"I doubt there's anyone worth knowing that's OK during a war." Doug tilted his head down so that a shadow passed over his face. "Killing changes you. You lose something."

"I don't think I have a choice, Doug."

"We rarely do in these situations. Remember when we tipped Mrs. Higgins?" Doug asked. Nathan laughed, it tore the flesh on his back and ached. "I ran away. You covered for me. That was the bravest thing I ever saw when I was a kid."

"Grandma Loni knew the truth," Nathan admitted.

Doug scratched his chin. "How about that? She never said."

"She figured that you were such a good friend to me when I needed it that she could let that one slide."

"Good lady. You were lucky, Nathan."

Luck was never something Nathan considered that he had in abundance. "That's kind of hard to swallow right now."

"You have greatness in you. That's why I'm here." Doug chuckled. "I'm supposed to remind you that we're both men and soldiers now."

"Says who?"

The soldier shook his head. "He's next in the lineup. Can't spoil the surprise."

"Will you try to be careful?" Nathan asked.

"I could ask the same of you. I can smell it on you."

"Smell what?"

"The dumbassery. You plan to do something epically stupid, don't you?" Doug asked.

"Of an epic nature that is sure to be legend everywhere."

"Good for you. Sometimes you are too smart for your own good." Doug turned away from the tree and looked back over his shoulder. "Keep your head down and remember that with a bit of heart and luck anything is possible. Oh yeah, and remember to name your first kid after me."

"What?" Nathan shook his head finding it impossible to locate his friend. Did he disappear? "Doug?"

The words carried on the wind like a ghost. "Just remember..."

"Doug?" Silence. He was alone once more. His vision blurred from the rain. The wind washed dust, leaves, and grit against his face. "Are you there?

"I always did wonder about the two of you." It was a soft, feminine voice that would forever be linked in his memory to sweet kisses under the summer sky, endless nights when anything seemed possible, and the hope that love really did exist outside of the movies. "I read somewhere that you never completely fall out of love with someone. Do you think that's true?"

Nathan blinked, trying to wipe away the crude and years from his eyes. "Phoebe?"

"You never forget your first love." She looked up at Nathan and smiled encouragingly. "I know I never will."

"You were right."

Phoebe laughed. "How so?"

"I already miss home," Nathan admitted. "I never thought I'd say that."

"Sometimes you have to leave home to really find it."

"I'm sorry, Phoebe."

"Because you fell in love? Thats never something to apologize over. We had our time together in the sun. You knew I had another year of school and I deserved that time, those memories." She laughed once more. "You were always so serious. How do you know I don't have a boyfriend now?"

Nathan felt an odd pang of jealousy. "Do you?"

Phoebe spun in a circle; her dress lifted like a flower unfolding. "Does it matter? We loved each other for a time. It gave us strength; helped us grow."

"Did I do the right thing?"

There was no answer except for the empty roar of the wind and the songs of the blackbirds. They whispered words of encouragement and lamented that they had not yet found their prey. He found strength in their simple determination and glory in their beauty. A baritone voice brought him back from the edge of unconsciousness. "I see that you've met my friends."

Nathan shook his head, trying to wake. He rubbed his eyes and searched the field to find Papo standing under the Ash tree with his hands on his waist, grinning like the cat that just sacrificed one of his nine lives. "Is that really you?"

"I have looked after you the whole of your life," Papo stated enthusiastically. "Did you really think I would stop now?"

Tears welled in his eyes. His heart vibrated so much that Nathan thought that it might burst from his chest. "I'm sorry."

"For what, Nathan?"

"I got you killed, Papo. I came back late." The guilt crushed him. "You died because I couldn't keep it in my pants."

Papo shook his head. "There were many factors that contributed to my death. I didn't trust you enough to give you the complete truth. I fed it to you piecemeal, thinking to allow you time to digest it. I was, as they say, hoisted by my own petard."

"That doesn't excuse my screw-ups."

"No. It doesn't. But I love you and thus I must forgive you. You understood this as a boy. Do you remember what you told your grandfather?" Papo asked. Nathan shook his head wearily. It might have been the pain, but he had no idea what Papo was talking about. "You said something wise to him on the day that he took you from your mother. 'You have to forgive the ones you love no matter how terrible they treat you.'"

"I don't think that's true anymore." Years of resenting his mother burned Nathan's heart. "Some things you just can't forgive."

"Perhaps that is true. It is definitely as true as we wish to make it." Blackbirds landed upon Papo's shoulders and whispered secrets. He laughed righteously. "However, such a burden can weaken you for the fight ahead."

"I don't understand."

"You can't be the man you need to be as long as your heart is divided and chained to the past. You can't escape yourself on the Ash tree." Papo raised his hands as though to embrace Nathan. "You can't escape the true terror of knowing yourself on that tree. Any other time you can look away from the thousand cuts made to your soul and ignore them. You have a choice here and now."

"What choice?"

"You can empty yourself of your sorrow. Deny the New Flesh that which would make them whole," Papo explained. "If you are to cause the change this world needs, you need to be very brave here and now."

"What do I need to do?"

"There is one more ghost waiting for you." Papo pointed to the hill on the horizon where a lone figure waited. "You must face that which you've always feared to face."

"Does that mean that everyone I've spoken with is dead?" Nathan asked, terrified for Doug.

"All flesh is but a shadow for the soul, Nathan. Death is just another shadow. The real question is simple. Will you see her?"

Nathan knew who awaited him on that hill. "No. She has no right to be here."

Papo nodded sadly. "If that is what you wish."

"I don't have a choice, do I?"

"Choice is all that we have, Nathan."

"I don't want to see her. Not after what she did."

"The Buddha said that desire is the cause of all suffering. What you desire is for her to suffer as you have. Sorrow is a selfish emotion that comforts only yourself and yet always cripples you in the end."

"Bring her."

Papo's body splintered into a thousand crows and ravens and took flight. The sky blackened with their presence, and the hills echoed with their song. Gentle rain fell. The Ash tree protected him mostly from the elements, but drops of refreshing water dripped through the leaves.

Nathan kept his eyes upon the hill, watching as the lone figure moved closer. Lightning flashed in the distance. Her form slowly became distinct as she moved closer. It seemingly took hours for her to transgress down the hill and reach the protection of the Ash tree. She was pale, much more than he remembered, with a thin, malnourished frame. He greeted her with a simple word. "Mother."

Her lip trembled. "I've missed you so much."

"You could have found me anytime," he said coldly.

"I didn't know how to face you after what I did." Her voice drooped with shame. "I thought about you every day."

"It wouldn't have mattered to me." Nathan hadn't realized it until that moment. "It would have made me so happy."

"I couldn't let you see me like I was. I wanted to be better."

"You couldn't come because of pride?" Nathan asked credulously. "Really?"

"A boy deserves to have a mother he is proud of."

"A boy deserves to have a mother."

"You hate me."

"Maybe a small part of me. The part that doesn't understand," Nathan said quietly.

"I didn't realize how badly the drugs had hold of me until it was too late. They burn in your mind until there's nothing left, even love of a son." She sobbed, and he felt the potent hatred building in his head. "I couldn't control myself."

"You made a choice. Now you have to live with the consequences."

"I can't do it if you hate me. I can't change if you can't forgive me," she pleaded.

"I don't hate you. I hate that you're sick. I hate what that sickness did to me." Much to his surprise, the words were true. "I hate that I'll never get to know you."

"If I know that you would be waiting for me, I could change," she said quietly.

"In the end, we're all alone. If you want to change, you have to change yourself." The anvil of the lesson seemed clear now. He hated her for her weakness that he imagined reflected in himself. "If nothing else, you helped me see things about myself. Thank you."

"Then you forgive me?" she asked.

That was the question in his mind. Do you forgive someone that is sick? Do you forgive a mother that can't live up to the name? But then, didn't his family fail his mother as well. Didn't Marty admit that he ignored the signs? He thought of those lonely nights on the farm and the pain that he carried around with him since then. He had never felt worthy of friendship or affection and always feared that his friends would leave him. Did he want to always be trapped in that single moment? Would he let it define him forever? "Yes. I forgive you."

She smiled through the tears. "I have always loved you, son."

"I love you too, Mom," he said as she dissolved into the mist.

Time passed slowly on the Ash tree. He teetered on the edge of consciousness; straddling between dreams and pain. Flashes of an unrealized reality poked at the edges of his mind. Did he hear children singing? Their soft voices were so filled with hope that it lifted his spirits. Was this a sign?

He dreamt of an empty concrete fountain in the middle of the city of tomorrow. There were dozens of Promethean chains binding it and trapping its power. It had cracks along the foundation, but it still had possibility. All it needed was water. Was this a sign for the future? What sort of metaphor was this?

Rain fell from the sky and refreshed his body, but the pain and the hunger never fully quit gnawing at his skin. A painful tear along his back woke him. He opened his eyes to see a vision of a gigantic monster of shadow with a thousand eyes. It hid in a long tunnel waiting and creeping. It gnashed its teeth and smelled of the sweat of children. Finally, the flesh snapped and ripped. His skin broke and he fell to the ground. Two days and nights had passed and now that he was free from the hooks, he was free of the prison of physical limitations. Reborn, like the sun, Nathan stumbled to his knees rubbing his bare chest. Offering of the flesh was a way to offer the physical body in exchange for spiritual life.

Switowski helped him get to his feet. "You alright man?"

"I know what to do now. I'm not afraid."

*     *     *     *

Sarah brought Nathan a steaming bowl of chicken noodle soup to drink while she stitched the wounds on his back closed. He winced from the pain, but the soup was so tasty that he managed to gulp it down without choking. McCreedy poured black coffee from an old metal kettle into several cups and passed it around the kitchen nook. Marty accepted his cup gracefully and took a sip. "Did you find what you needed, Nate?"

Nathan ignored the question. "I saw a monster with a lot of eyes. A killer of children."

McCreedy grimaced. "The Bandersnatch. Nasty little bugger. We have it trapped in the murder tunnel. Can't kill it, but it can't hurt anyone."

"Nathan, I think I know what you are planning and it isn't worth risking your life. Not your life," Marty interjected. "I bet against the house and lost. I've accepted that."

"What's this murder tunnel?" Nathan asked, ignoring his uncle.

"There's a tunnel under the city, near downtown where there were a couple of murders. The blood sanctified the tunnel and we trapped the beast there with a containment ritual." McCreedy's face showed a great deal of fear, which surprised Nathan. "We lost three men and we were lucky to have had so few losses. This monster is nigh-unkillable."

"Why is this so important to do now?" Sarah asked.

"I figured out what Eve was trying to tell me. This thing has a bunch of eyes. Human eyes. Stolen from children." Nathan swallowed the rest of his soup. "I'm going to kill this thing and if we're lucky Sarah can use some of those eyes to replace Marty's."

"Too dangerous, kid."

"We're going to face Cenotaph and I need to be blooded before then. I have to know I can do this. Besides, that ward can't hold forever can it?"

McCreedy shook his head. "We're doing our best, but Nathan's right. The ward will eventually come down when we least expect it. That said, killing that thing is going to be a major undertaking. It will take incredible power to kill it. The last time one was killed was way back in 1870 and that was done with a sword allegedly blessed by Saint Michael."

"I can do it. The vision said so. And I need Marty for the final battle."

McCreedy grunted. "You look like you can take on the world, Nathan."

"I can and will. One monster at a time. Take me there."

"Don't you want to rest?" Sarah asked.

"There's no rest for the wicked."

*    *    *    *

The downtown square of Olympia was the bastard child of an ethereal dream of a small town and the quiet trendy little sister of Seattle. They circled a city square of immaculately trimmed green grass surrounded by the usual tropes of a small town mixed with a hip afterthought. An old-fashioned barber shop was nestled between a tattoo parlor and a used bookstore. It was the quiet sort of place where he could imagine himself settling down one day and starting a family. Nathan shook his head. Where did that thought come from?

The noon sun shined overhead and many pedestrians went about their business in local shops. It was going to be a pleasant summer day custom built for families and picnics. McCreedy lead him through the town to their destination. Nathan had imagined a frightening gothic dungeon hidden away from mortal men, but instead discovered an innocuous concrete drainage tunnel that opened in the shadow of the Capital Building. This was the so-called Murder Tunnel? It was somehow disappointing, not quite the epic battlefield that Nathan had imagined while hanging upon the tree, and yet, there was a subtle hint of sickness in this place. There were dozens of gang tags and murals of pain and suffering around the walls. McCreedy grunted and gestured to the tunnel. "It's weakest during the day, but you can't surprise it. You can't trick it."

Nathan nodded like a gunslinger while he strapped the gladius to his side. He felt like he was about to walk into the O.K. Corral, guns blazing. "Not planning on either."

"You sure you don't want to wait a few days and recover, Nate?" A wash of concern and a bit of pity played over the old biker's face. "That beast's not going anywhere. Sarah's coven trapped it there going on twenty years ago. A strong ward on each end of the tunnel contains it in that prison of iron and steel. It took damn near two dozen men and women to put that cork in that bottle. Lost a lot of friends along the way. They sacrificed their blood to keep the kids safe. You sure you can do this?"

"Marty doesn't have the time." Nathan shook his head. "The vampire blood will be out of his system soon and those nerve endings will die, then none of this will matter."

McCreedy slipped a stogie in his mouth and nodded. "Marty wouldn't want you to throw away your life. Or risk the kids if that thing gets out. Neither would your old man."

The thought of this monster escaping had occurred to Nathan

more than once. Somehow, he knew this was the right choice; the only choice for a future where everyone survived. "I need him for the run on Cenotaph. I need everything in place for this to work."

"What exactly did you see on the tree?"

Nathan laughed. How do you describe a vision that changes your life? "I saw that I need to do this alone."

"I respect that. There's a fire in your eyes." The old biker clapped his back. "We'll do what we can to back you up, Nate."

"Just keep your men at the edges of the tunnel and make sure no one else enters."

He stepped into the shadows and the tunnel. It stank of filth and sweat. Broken glass and trash crunched underneath his boots. Shadows moved near the center of the tunnel. Nathan pulled out his father's lighter and flicked it. The small flame produced an enormous bubble of light that illuminated most of the surrounding area revealing two men in dirty clothing huddled together passing around a bottle wrapped in a brown paper bag. They flinched from the light, holding their arms over their faces.

Nathan pulled out a twenty-dollar bill from his pocket and flicked it near them. "Gentlemen, I have some business here. Why don't you go get some food?"

They exchanged looks that seemed to wonder what sort of business he might have in a place like this, but grabbed the cash and quickly left. Nathan waited until he could no longer hear their footprints, then raised his hands and willed the fire to come forth. Azure eldritch flames erupted from both hands and circled them in a protective globe of power. The entire tunnel lit under reflective light that moved and shimmered like water.

A single shadow moved. It flickered briefly, then was deathly still as the grave. "You have something I need. You can feel it. You know I'm here for you."

It grew quickly, absorbing the remainder of the shadows and darkness in the tunnel, and quickly slithered towards him. The monstrous, amorphous beast had a thousand angry eyes. It opened its maw to rage against the light. It was covered with thousands of serrated bone coils that protected soft, moist flesh. He felt the ravenous hunger from this beast. It had lived thousands of years and had been denied solid flesh far too long and forced to live upon the sorrow and despair of rancid transients. The scent of a man of mystical power whet its appetite beyond reason.

Roaring, it leapt to coil itself around Nathan. The monster wrapped itself around his arms and chest to choke the life from him. It squeezed, and the bone shards pierced his flesh and brought forth pain he had never before known. The monster extended its form slowly and enveloped Nathan's legs, his arms, and eventually his head. The pressure upon his eyes, nose, and mouth was horrendous as the Bandersnatch tried to force itself into Nathan's mind.

Fear was its dominion and that which it eternally craved. A stray memory from childhood inspired a wicked assault with needles. The pain of that flu shot had never escaped the back of his mind, a moment of betrayal and surprise. The Bandersnatch tried many forms to trigger that primal fear that would give it strength and the power to escape this thrice-cursed trap.

Clutching onto Nathan and slowly feeding. It shifted into many shapes trying to find the exact one that would break him: *a black widow spider with the feared red dot on its abdomen; thousands of gelatinous cockroaches burrowing into his skin; barbed wire entangling his neck and squeezing; enclosing walls of wood, a coffin entering the earth forever.*

Each form brought a brief flicker of ancient fear, but it quickly died. It staggered his body, but not his will. He rubbed his father's lighter as though it was a meditation stone and called forth the fire.

Nathan concentrated like Papo had taught him and summoned forth the eldritch azure flame from his very soul erupted from his body, burning away the monster's flesh, until his face was free once more. He gasped for air. "Marty said that you'd try to take advantage of my fears. I figured it out on the tree. Monsters don't scare me. Pain doesn't make my knees wobble. Not like you need it. You need the primal fear that comes from my soul." His face twisted to a snarl. "I had my worst fear come to life on the farm. That's not a fear you can reproduce. You can't abandon me!"

The azure-tinged flame continued to sear the monster's flesh. Nathan's realization brought forth strength and intensity that doubled the potency of the blast. Heat reflected off the metal and concrete of the tunnel, boiling and transmuting the skin of the Bandersnatch into ash and sulfur. It recoiled, screaming, trying to stamp out the flame.

Furious, it slammed side to side against the concrete, bringing Nathan with it. His head and back cracked against the unrelenting walls, forcing all of the air in his lungs out with a yelp. He slid to the ground, forcing his eyes open against the field of white that coalesced around his field of vision.

Nathan drew his gladius, forced himself to his feet, and began to chop and slice into the creature. The flames protected him and allowed him to move closer without getting trapped by the tentacles. The Bandersnatch was difficult to corner as it moved quickly like a rabbit, but Nathan walled off the escape routes one by one with flaming pillars. Once it was backed into an intersection without an exit, the flame finally caught up to the monster and began to burn it while Nathan hacked and hacked until one of its heads was severed.

Skewering it with the gladius, he lifted it over his shoulder like a backpack. Nathan walked out of the murder tunnel slowly, making certain that no remains of the Bandersnatch lived, then he tossed the smoking head onto the ground before McCreedy. Each step brought a spasm of agony down his back and his legs, but he was alive and the monster was dead.

He jerked his thumb over his shoulder. "The rest is burning inside. There's bound to be two eyes there that Sarah can use."

# Chapter Fourteen: All My Pictures Fade to Black and White

Nathan Carver sipped his root beer on the McCreedy front porch with his feet up against the rail. Every muscle in his body ached as though each had been stretched out by a rolling pin and smashed back together at the last moment. He listened to the mechanics bang their machinery and occasionally swear at each other. The sweet air of summer air mixed with occasional taints of oil and garbage. Sarah and her coven had been with Marty for several hours since Nathan returned with the head of the Bandersnatch. Every passing moment gave him time to create dozens of worst-case scenarios. It was times like this that he understood why Marty still smoked.

McCreedy opened a beer and sat next to Nathan, groaning like an old man all the way to the floor. "If anything can be done, Sarah and her coven will make it happen. They might smell like patchouli, but they managed to put up wards that held a Bandersnatch for almost a twenty years."

"I'm not worried. I know he'll pull through. He's strong." Nathan took a long drink, trying to collect his words. "I'm less certain about Eve."

"You really do love her, don't you?"

"I think she was made for me to love." Nathan thought back to the image of his mother. "Almost like an apology from the universe for all of the shit we're put through."

"Shit son, that's all you had to say. How can we help?"

"You serious?" Nathan asked. "Are you willing to risk the treaty? Won't that screw the Thanes?"

"I wouldn't have met Sarah, much less married her, without your father." McCreedy toasted the sky with his bottle. "We did a lot of good together and if I can help you, then I figure I owe it to the universe."

"I appreciate that," Nathan said earnestly. "Marty and I have to face Cenotaph alone, but there's plenty of work to be done afterwards. I have a couple of ideas on how to change things."

Sarah McCreedy opened the front door, cutting off the conversation. Her normally pale cheeks flushed with success. "I have good news."

"Don't keep us waiting, baby." McCreedy hugged his wife. "Sounds like you pulled off a miracle."

"We contacted some friends in Seattle and managed to get a sliver of a golden apple from the VuTente clan. Between that, the vampire blood, and the eye donated from the Bandersnatch, we managed one successful transplant." Sarah smiled proudly. "The left socket was too damaged for an operation, but we sealed off the nerve endings."

"Only one eye?" Nathan asked.

"But he can see. That's not too bad of a bargain," McCreedy countered. "In the valley of the blind, the one-eyed man is king."

"If it works."

"It works," Sarah revealed. "Normally, he'd be out for several hours, but with the magicks involved, he just woke a few minutes ago.

The apple slice practically healed his entire body right away."

How far did that magic go? Did it cure his cancer? "Can I see him?"

Sarah McCreedy nodded serenely. "The coven is already gone. He's resting in the bedroom now. He asked about you."

Nathan hugged her tightly and quickly rushed to the bedroom to find his uncle resting with his back on the headboard of the bed. Marty blinked his new greyish-blue eye. "What do you think, kid? I think my eye reminds me a little of Frank Sinatra. You can call me old Blue Eye."

"I was so afraid for you."

"You did it, kid. You killed the Bandersnatch." Marty shook his head, trying not to cry with worry. "Hard to believe that my own flesh and blood killed such a thing. I knew you had the potential, but to see it realized. Hell, I'm impressed just seeing again."

"I hate to ask this, Marty, but how long do you need for recovery?" He offered his uncle the glass of water that had been waiting for him on the dresser. "The New Flesh must have surrendered Eve to Cenotaph by now."

Marty waved away the glass of water and laughed. He pulled up one sleeve and flexed his bicep like a wrestler. "I feel strangely good right now. Maybe it's something that Sarah put me on after the surgery? I feel like I could fight a bear."

He shrugged. "She said something about a golden apple."

"What?" Marty's eye flashed with anger and his lips trembled with rage. "Why would you let her do that?"

"Woah! I have no idea what that is." Nathan put his hand on Marty's shoulder. "Calm down."

"Sarah? Are you there?" Marty called out.

She poked her head through the door as though she had been expecting this. McCreedy followed quietly. "Yes, Martin."

"You fed me a golden apple, Sarah?"

"A small slice, but yes." Sarah knelt beside him on the bed. "We were convinced that it was necessary to trick the optical nerves to accept the foreign eye since it was corrupted by demon blood."

"Where did you get it?" Marty asked quietly.

"I think you know that already, Martin." Sarah remained calm and resolute. "It was the only way."

"Don't you know what this will cost her?" Marty sighed and his entire body looked crestfallen. "Does she know?"

"She was willing to pay the price so that you would live," Sarah stated.

"I don't understand. What's going on? Who are you talking about?" Nathan asked.

"A friend of ours had the means to heal Martin." Sarah smiled. "She was quite willing to do so even though Martin left her."

This was the woman that McCreedy had told him about; the one that Marty had been too afraid to love. "Who is this friend? Did my Dad know her? How can she help?" Nathan asked.

"Sarah, can I talk to Nathan a moment?"

"You boys behave yourselves now." She checked Marty's temperature and then left.

"Her name is Loxi Collins. Bill and I met her twenty years ago. She's a half-demon raised by her human father, and we fell in love." He swallowed uncomfortably. "She can look at someone and know what's wrong with them and tell you their most vulnerable points."

Nathan tilted his head very confused. "How does one become a half-demon? That seems a bit odd. Didn't you say that the Great Barrier keeps the demons out?"

Marty shrugged. "There are a lot of theories. Some of them would surprise you. How familiar are you with the Bible?"

"I went to Sunday School twice a month for eight years," Nathan said. "How does that apply?"

"Have you ever read the Book of Enoch?"

"I don't think that's in any book of the bible I've ever read."

Marty chuckled a bit. "It's not likely to be. You've read the story of Jesus answering the scholars' questions in the temple at the age of twelve, but have you read the story of Jesus making little birds out of mud, bringing them to life and watching them fly away?"

Nathan smirked a bit. "That one I missed."

"People sometimes mistake the Bible for being an authorized book of God. It's really a collection of stories authorized by the church. A long time ago, a group of church elders called the Council of Trent picked the best of the lot and bound them together," Marty explained. "It doesn't mean that the Bible isn't worth knowing or reading, but it's an interpretation by that council of the best of the materials.

Nathan thought about that a moment. "That's what college literature professors do. They pick the best material and canonize it for the curriculum. That's why school kids read *Catcher in the Rye*, but not *Fear and Loathing in Las Vegas*."

Marty nodded. "Exactly. One of those lost books is called the Book of Enoch. This book describes angels falling in love with mortal women and taking them as wives." Marty closed his eye and continued. "And when the angels, the sons of heaven, beheld them, they became enamored of them, saying to each other, Come, let us select for ourselves wives from the progeny of men, and let us beget children."

"Wow! That's not something they teach you about in Sunday School."

Marty opened his eye. "That's one translation. And it's suspected that's where the demons that live on earth originate from. There are a lot of bloodlines from that time period. Hell, I expect that the VuTente don't even know where they come from. And when one of those demons has a kid with a regular human you get a half-demon. Calling them demons is the current vogue. They used to be called the Divine and the Greek called them gods. Hard to say what really happened."

"So there aren't full demons running around, are there?"

"It's said that true demons live in the void somewhere beyond the Great Barrier and they wait for their chance to come back to the Earth," he replied.

"Cheery."

"The VuTente clan takes their power from a special tree. Every female member of the clan is given just one apple. Each apple represents their immortality," Marty said, continuing the story. "Loxi wanted to share her apple with me to cure the cancer, but if she did it would have taken some of my humanity away."

"Wait? Does that mean you're cured of the cancer?" Nathan asked.

"No. Sarah didn't feed me but a sliver. I'd have to eat the whole apple, but if I did, I'd rob her of a thousand years," Marty revealed. "My life's not worth that. Not for the woman I love."

"Who knew that Martin Carver could get so weepy over a girl?" Nathan asked. They shared a good laugh over it. He had almost given up the idea that their luck might turn. "Seriously, are we going to start synching our menstrual cycles now?"

"Too late!" They laughed until their bodies ached. "Son of a bitch! That hurts. So what now?"

"Tonight we rest as best we can. Tomorrow, Seattle."

\*     \*     \*     \*

Nathan spent the rest of the afternoon napping on the couch until the smell of tangy chicken filled the house. He rolled over, managed to stand, and find his way to the kitchen. Much to his surprise, Sarah McCreedy sat sipping tea in the kitchen nook next to her husband. He looked over to the stove to find Marty cooking a large skillet of chicken with sliced green bell peppers and diced sweet onions. "Shit, did I miss the Apocalypse?" Nathan asked. "I thought Martin Carver only cooked on the open grill."

"Times are a changing." Marty added a dash of pepper to the mix. "I wanted to thank the McCreedy's for their hospitality and I remembered a dish I had when I was in love and just had to eat it."

"What is it?"

"Spicy fajitas. The best night of my life was eating these under the stars with a pretty girl," Marty said wistfully. "I hope one day you have a night just like it."

"I did."

"Then no matter what, I consider this trip a win." Marty dished out portions of the fajitas onto unwrapped flour tortillas and rolled them into perfect burritos. "That's what this trip was supposed to be about. No agendas. Just magical nights of wonder."

"I think you delivered on everything you promised," Nathan stated.

"Speaking of which, there is the little matter of your bill for the van," McCreedy interjected uncomfortably.

"Michael!"

"I have to pay the guys for their work, Sarah," McCreedy said defensively. "Some of them put in a lot of overtime for the modifications Nathan requested."

"We can pay." Marty winced thinking about the cost. "It might eat up the rest of the budget. But we can do it. The Carver family pays our debts."

"Don't worry about it, Marty. I think the sale of the Bandersnatch bones will more than cover it. Right?" Nathan asked, eyeing McCreedy.

The old biker nodded his head enthusiastically. "I think you underestimate the rarity of what you killed. You could buy a fleet of vans and still vacation for the next ten years on the dough from the sale of the bones and the ash."

Nathan scratched his head. "Is it dangerous? Can it be used to harm anyone?"

"It is mostly of value for medical purposes if you know the secrets," Sarah McCreedy explained.

"Do you have a buyer?"

"Listen, I only know one guy that has enough extra scratch to buy the whole lot and not cheat us." McCreedy wiped his hand through his thinning grey hair nervously. "Thing is that he is hard to get ahold of unless you have special juice. We can't get to him without making a stink."

"Remington Borri." Marty delivered the plate of burritos to the table and sat down next to Nathan. "I should have known it would come down to him in the end. That little bastard always has his fingers in every pie."

"My dad's lawyer?" Nathan asked. "What he got to do with all of this?"

"Borri isn't just a simple lawyer. He's a master alchemist and a whole lot more. Cenotaph might run Seattle, but Borri's sway can't be denied. He's the keeper of the law," Marty explained. "He was the one who brokered the deal where I sold my eyes. Borri is tough, but he'll be fair, and we need to see him anyway. If we take a sample and have some solid numbers for him we could see a good profit and it might earn us a favor from him."

"Of which, we will split with the Thanes." Nathan turned to McCreedy. "You guys can use some good luck and we'll need time to prepare for the future."

"What happens when we kill Cenotaph? Does Borri take over?" Nathan asked.

"I don't know that you can fully kill Cenotaph. His flesh is mortal still, barely kept alive by dark magic, but his soul is bound to this place," McCreedy explained.

"He's a shadow kept alive only by his will," Marty added.

Nathan shrugged. "But if we kill him, then what happens? Does Borri take over?"

"I suspect the bad guys will start a shooting war over the throne unless someone takes it," Marty mused.

"We need to figure out a way to keep civilians out of danger," Nathan declared.

"We don't even have a plan just yet. You sound just like Bill," Marty said with an encouraging smile.

Nathan learned forward and grinned like he had just beaten the devil. "Wait until you guys hear my plan. I'm a little sketchy about the details, but I think I have a good start. No one has ever tried something like this."

*    *    *    *

The Tradesman had not looked so shiny and new in many, many

years. Marty stood before the van with a teary eye. The Thanes had repaired all of the mechanical damage to the axle, replaced the old rusted rims with bright new chrome models that spun and replaced the old motor with a rebuilt supercharged eight-cylinder engine. That alone would have made Marty happy, but the Thanes went above and beyond the call of duty. They fixed every bump, scratch, and dent in the body and repainted the van a sleek black with flame racing stripes that ran from the center of the hood down the sides. He walked along the side examining the wondrous craftsmanship. "That is the most beautiful thing I've ever seen."

"They made a slight modification inside as well," Nathan muttered under his breath.

Marty opened the driver's side door and was aghast at the changes to the dashboard. "What the hell is this?"

Nathan climbed into the van from the passenger's side. "I asked them to add a docking port for my phone. We don't have to just listen to your cassette tapes."

"Jesus, did you tattoo my ass too, while I was out?"

"That's next time. I'm thinking a lovely butterfly." He flashed his best imitation-Marty grin at his uncle. "You said this would be my van someday, right?"

"It just feels wrong like I just got finger-banged by God." Marty rubbed the wooden paneling of the dashboard and examined the docking port. "Wait, this is a sign of you moving-in for good, isn't it?"

"Let's not buy wedding patterns yet." Nathan locked his phone into the dashboard. "But you are not driving just yet. I'm ready to die for love if need be, but not because you only have one eye."

"Alright, only until I get used to this." Marty tapped his empty eye socket. McCreedy had bought him a leather eye-patch and it took every ounce of control Nathan possessed not to start on the pirate jokes. "Shit, this is gonna take a spell to get used to, but it's better than the alternative."

They exchanged positions in the van and Nathan locked his seat belt. Marty rolled down his window and stuck his elbow out attempting to get comfortable on the passenger's side. Nathan adjusted the mirror and then started the motor. It roared like a lion. "This could be the final run of our trip. We're about to storm the fucking gates of Cenotaph."

"Yeah buddy, this is gonna be a righteous ride! I think this calls for our secret weapon. I've been waiting more than twenty years to try it out." Marty dug through his tape box until he found a special one wrapped in plastic marked *Bill's Battle Music*. "If we're going to go out in a blaze of glory, I think we need the proper sendoff. And I think somewhere up there, he'd appreciate it.

Nathan unwrapped the plastic around the box and slipped the cassette into the deck. The first few bars of *Highway to Hell* by AC / DC raged through the new speakers. "Somehow that seems very appropriate."

He shifted the van into reverse and pulled out onto the street. McCreedy waved from his office in the garage as they passed. Marty flipped a solid salute to the Thanes until the garage grew smaller and smaller in the back window. They listened to the sounds of classic rock as they drove onto the ramp to I-5 towards the Emerald City.

It was a short trip; less than two hours even with the traffic near Tacoma. A good portion of that time they were stuck in a bumper-to-bumper jam just outside of a large domed arena that appeared to be designed to mimic an erect breast complete with an additional circle for areola and a flag for a nipple. "I'm not sure what that smell is, but I think something is punishing us."

"That's just the Tacoma Aroma. Or sometimes justifiably referred to as *Tacoma's Revenge.*"

Several casinos with giant flashing animated billboards advertising recent bookings slowly crawled past on the other side. Marty pointed to the largest casino. "Hey, Styx is playing! If we live past this, we should see them on the way out."

"If we do live, I'm just not thinking I'm going to want to celebrate with a rousing rendition of *Domo Arigato, Mr. Roboto.* There are some trials a man just can't face."

Pine trees lined both sides of I-5 as they progressed towards Seattle. Were they going the right way? Nathan checked the signs once more to verify he wasn't driving off to the woods. A sprawling mall appeared on the right-hand side through the trees which showed that they weren't lost yet. The highway rose over dozens of small suburban houses and valleys until they rode around the crest of a small hill overlooking Boeing Field. He was amazed to see workers crawling around half a dozen large jetliners; the flash white color of the welding torches and sparks made it difficult to look away.

Traffic once again started to flow freely. On the left, they passed

West Seattle and hundreds of giant cargo containers stacked up along the Port of Seattle by towering metal cranes painted orange. Marty pointed out the mustard-colored Rainer Brewery, the International District Clock Tower and the street lamp dragons that marked the borders of the International District. On the right, there was a colossal adobe structure constructed on a hill that overlooked downtown Seattle like the menacing lair of a mad scientist.

The city of Seattle cradled around the Puget Sound with towering, glittering buildings of glass and steel stacked next to colossal brick buildings. She was a glorious city that had both the promise of tomorrow as represented the beautiful Space Needle as well as the failures of yesterday in the slums along the waterfront and the tent cities constructed between the freeway ramps and overpasses. An eerie graffiti depicting a tall thin skeletal black man dressed in a hoodie pointing a gnarled finger at the city. Dozens of sail boats and ferries dotted the clear blue water while pedestrians carried about their business on the streets. Somehow, he expected Seattle to be larger from the reputation, but still he felt a strange sort of awe like he touched a legend.

"Skip the downtown exits. Take the University District exit."

"Why? Isn't Borri on the wharf?" Nathan asked, as they passed the downtown exits.

Marty gritted his teeth. "I have one bit of business first at Apropos."

"Apropos?" Nathan asked.

His uncle grinned shyly. "That's the name of her coffee shop.

Loxi's a barista. With any luck, her café is still open."

The highway passed through the edge of downtown like a river of concrete raised to the heavens far above the city streets. It felt like flying, navigating through the buildings of dark glass and lights. Nathan turned down the radio and smirked. "So this dreaded VuTente half-demon is a coffee barista?"

The stretch of road dipped down into a concrete tunnel that passed under a section of the city. The skyscraper ahead seemed to grow to biblical proportions until it swept over them like a tidal wave. "What else is a temptation demon going to do for a living in Seattle?" Marty asked wryly.

It was afternoon by the time they reached the University District and the Saturday shopping traffic had slowed to a leisurely walk. There were dozens of pierced, scruffy-looking teenagers with a variety of hair colors unknown in nature, dressed in baggy clothing wandering the streets. They were chatting, hanging around, and generally enjoying the summer day. Apropos was on the corner of University and 55th. This area was named after the University of Washington campus and the university's presence could be felt in the used music stores, the Husky clothing shop, five teriyaki chicken restaurants, a tattoo parlor, a comic book store, and a dozen coffee bars. There were several empty lots and closed-down businesses.

"Where are we going?" Nathan asked after they had circled the same block four times.

"I'm looking for a place to park," Marty replied, irritated.

"There's a lot right there."

"That's a pay lot."

"We're going to have to pay more in gas circling the building if we don't stop soon," Nathan replied.

"There's a spot ahead to the right." Marty pointed fervently. "Right there!"

"No, there's not. There's a SUV there," Nathan complained.

The SUV started and turned on its turn signal. Nathan slowed down and waved the driver through. Nathan quickly took the freshly vacant spot, parked the van, and turned off the engine. Nathan and Marty glanced at each other for a brief moment. "How did you know that?"

"I don't have a clue, kid."

They walked around the corner to the main street of the University District, known as the Ave. The building was made of brick and had an old cherished feel about it. Marty pushed open the main doors and beckoned Nathan to go before him.

The atmosphere of Apropos was lively. There was a stage in the front corner where someone was reading poetry from an open microphone. A few people watched the performer with fervent interest. In the other corner, near the entrance, there was a row of laptop computers that patrons were quickly typing upon while sipping coffee. A little bit further back there were a few steps that led to a slightly raised area that looked like it would be a great location for an in-depth conversation. Local artwork was displayed on the exposed brick of the wall between the computers and the conversation area.

Many of the café tables were filled with people. It didn't seem unusual at first, but on a second glance, Nathan was surprised by how many of the customers had a strange vibe. Most of them were sitting side by side with regular people drinking coffee and reading books or working on laptops.

The front and side of the building had windows that allowed for an easy view of the bustling avenue and a mellow side street. Where the windows ended there was a wooden coffee bar and pastry display. Nathan took a deep breath; the coffee and teas smelled enticing. The woman behind the counter was clearly the master of this domain. Seeing them, she smiled and wiped her hands on her brown apron. "Martin Carver!"

Nathan glanced over at her and saw her hair was a beautiful mixture of black and purple dreadlocks. What struck him the most odd that she looked very young. Marty said that he had known her for over twenty years, yet she didn't look like she was much older than Nathan. He caught himself staring at her in awe and quickly looked away at one of the advertisements for a local band.

"Loxi Collins! You are as beautiful as ever!" His words were earnest and it was rare for Nathan to hear such honest unshielded emotion in his uncle's voice. Marty gave her a wink and spread his arms. "You up for a big hug?"

"Of course I'm up for it Marty!" She came out from behind the bar, wiped her hands on her apron, and gave Marty a big hug. She squeezed her eyes tight, apparently fighting back tears. She rubbed her face on his neck like a cat. "I wasn't sure if you would come and find me afterwards. I know I broke my promise."

"After what you gave up, how could I stay away?" He wrapped his arms around it and for a moment the regret and pain washed away from his face. Marty had never seemed so young. "I couldn't ask you to do it."

"Your eye is blue now. I suppose I can get used to it." She touched his face near the eye-patch and sniffed. "Did it hurt?"

He wrapped his hand around hers and brought it to his lips. "The only thing that's ever hurt more was when I left you."

Nathan snorted. They looked at him derisively. "Sorry." He shrugged his shoulders. "I just couldn't help myself there. That was quite the line."

"He's right, you old goat! And I let you get me caught up in it." Loxi smiled and shared in the laughter. She smacked Marty on the chest and turned to Nathan. "Wait! Is this Bill's son? Here in Seattle?"

"We need your help, Loxi." Marty sighed, wincing as he spoke the words. "Again."

"Sounds like we should talk privately," Loxi said earnestly. "Follow me."

She took them into the private back area. A flight of stairs led up to another door. That was the moment when Nathan first noticed her eyes. They were purple in color with slit pupils like a cat. "Ooh, your abilities will be strong, Nathan. Go ahead and come in."

The room was very inviting with a bright red couch, light-colored hardwood floors. Nathan imagined that it was trying to flirt for their attention. Loxi invited them to sit down.

Once Nathan sat, he sensed the emotions in the room intensify and then slowly began to fade. It was almost as though he could hear someone trying to whisper to him, someone trying to get him to release his inhibitions. By the time Loxi spoke, the feelings and the whispers were muted, but still there was a subtle undercurrent. "I know you wouldn't come here unless it was important. How can I help you guys?"

"We need information." Marty winked, but somehow with the eye-patch it just wasn't as amusing as before. "I've been out of touch with Seattle politics for a few years. I was hoping for a run down on the local factions."

"Not much has changed since you were here last, Marty." Loxi started counting off on her fingers. "The Omega Watch never returned after Cenotaph ran them out of their tower. The Zhongstan still run the docks and West Seattle. They own a house in Rat City."

"Zhongstan? What the hell is that?" Nathan asked.

"They're a mean bad-ass voodoo vampire gang that doesn't take shit from anyone. Refugees from New Orleans after Katrina." Marty turned to Loxi and then nodded for her to continue. "What else?"

"There's been a pretty subtle power struggle between Borri and Cenotaph for years." Her eyes dilated with fear just saying his name. "Cenotaph had the edge on personal power with all of those pacts he's made over the years. It feels like parts of this city just belong to him. That's because he takes power from the Heart of the City."

"What's that?" Nathan asked.

"If a city captures enough of its people's imagination, it can have a second life in the Dreamlands. The Heart of the City is a tulpa avatar that has limited control over the dreams of the city." Marty explained. He turned to Loxi and raised an eyebrow. "How did Cenotaph get control over Chief Seathle?"

"Avatars change over time to reflect the city or die, Marty. You know that," Loxi answered. "Cenotaph managed to split the Heart into two pieces that represented the two fundamental aspects of Seattle."

"What are they?" Nathan asked.

"The Blue Lady is the personification of hope. She is the protector of children and dreams." Loxi smiled a bit when talking about her. "She disappeared a few years back. The children still tell stories of her and sometimes, very rarely, her presence can be felt."

"And the other one?" Nathan asked.

"Mr. Bang is just what you might imagine. They say he is little more than a walking skeleton with his skin stretched tightly over his body. They also say that he can kill you by pointing at you." She shivered just thinking about it. "He is the despair on the face of every street kid in the night."

"Cenotaph somehow made a deal with Mr. Bang and shut out the Blue Lady. Sounds like we should make a new friend." Marty tapped his chin for a few moments, thinking. "How come Cenotaph hasn't completely taken over?"

Loxi grinned widely. "Thankfully, Borri has an ace in the hole. Mrs. Aithne is his best customer and very fond of him."

"And she is who?" Nathan asked, feeling a bit lost.

"Mrs. Aithne is a dragon." Marty held up his hands as though to say 'yeah I know how crazy this sounds'. "One of the last real dragons that walks this earth from the time before the Great Barrier was erected."

"You mean thousands of years ago? And her name is Mrs. Aithne?" Nathan asked. He scratched his head trying to remember where he had heard that name before. "Do we know her?"

Marty shook his head. "We're not that high-class, Nate." He extended his arm around Loxi and rubbed her shoulder suggestively. "Thankfully, we know of one lovely lady that is friends with her."

"Marty! I fix her refrigerator sometimes. I can't get her to fight for us," Loxi protested. "Besides, her age is catching-up with her. I don't think she is in fighting form."

"We don't need her to fight," Marty promised. "Just need her support with Borri. You said it yourself that he respects her."

"I can try."

"Have you heard anything at all about a girl being brought into town for Cenotaph?" Nathan asked. The hope hung on his face like sunshine trying to burst forth on a cloudy day. "Maybe by the New Flesh?"

The mere mention of the New Flesh brought a shiver to Loxi. "They blew into town about three nights ago. Acrimony killed a couple of the Zhongstan. I heard that they made an appearance in the Underground towards the Portal."

"Then, they met with Cenotaph," Marty said, thinking about the implications of this new bit of information. "We need to meet with

Borri discreetly. Can you help?"

"You're going to make a run at Cenotaph?" Loxi clearly was shocked by the idea. The mere mention of his name caused her to look about the room, searching for his face in the shadows. "Do you know the number of investments he has from higher powers? I doubt his soul is more than a glimmer in the eye. How do you think you'll beat him?"

"I'm just going along for support." Marty pointed to Nathan. "That's where the kid comes in. You've read his power levels. With the right plan at the right time, we think he can TKO the bastard."

"That's suicide!" Loxi protested. "The power Cenotaph has available to him is unthinkable."

"The New Flesh brought someone to him. A girl," Marty explained. "We can't leave her with him. It would be bad for the entire world."

"And even if that weren't the case, I love her." It was the first time that Nathan spoke the words and it felt right--as though he had finally spoken an ageless truth. "She's beautiful inside and out."

"What?" Loxi blinked surprised. She slow craned her neck to look directly into Marty's eye. "You guys are doing this for love? Martin Carver, should I check to see if gravity still works?"

"Eve might be the avatar of magic fallen to flesh and might be the key to building a better future." Marty muttered. Nathan noted that his uncle did not bother to correct her on the other assumption.

"What?" She held her hands on her hips, very angry. "I think you boys need to explain everything to me right now."

Once Marty and Nathan were done explaining the events of their trip, her face turned white and her cat eyes flashed with sadness. "McCreedy didn't tell me that Papo died. Or that Nathan killed a Bandersnatch! But this isn't a story. Cenotaph will kill the both of you and consume everything that Nathan is."

Nathan shrugged. "The universe is made of stories; or so a wise man once told me."

She laughed and then looked sideways at Marty with suspicion. "That's the first thing I said to Martin almost twenty years ago."

"That explains a lot, actually," Nathan admitted.

Loxi blinked. "I know this is a lot to ask and you don't have a lot of time to prepare, but can you give me a few minutes alone with your uncle? We have something to discuss. Between the two of us."

He shrugged his shoulders. Nathan could imagine what subject they were going to discuss and it was better to get it out in the open now rather than later. "Sure, do you have someplace I can wait?"

"I'll have my staff make you a late lunch on the house." Loxi picked up her phone and quickly dialed. She waited a moment and then talked into the phone. "Chazz, I'm sending down a handsome blond. Treat him like family. What? No! Treat him like a really good customer. Sit him in the leather room and make him comfortable. Best seat in the house."

Afterward, he descended the stairs and bumped into a tall handsome man, not much older than Nathan, with a mop of unruly curly black hair, bright eyes, and a chiseled jaw. He looked as though he belonged on the wall of a thirteen year-old girl. "I'm Chazz." He

313

smiled as though to apologize. "You must be Nathan."

He offered his hand. When they shook, Nathan was surprised by the cool temperature of the man's hand. "Loxi said you'd make a late lunch."

"Sure thing, boss." He wrapped his arm around Nathan's and pulled him uncomfortably close. "Let's get you to a good seat first."

Chazz led down the stairs and through the main seating area into a quiet back room modestly decorated with Monet prints and comfortable-looking thick plush leather chairs. The only other occupant of the room was a pleasantly smiling old woman wearing a black old-fashioned tea gown with a lace bustle and a marvelous bonnet with a large red bow. She was blissfully staring at an open plastic case that proudly presented rows after rows of buttons. "Why, hello there! There are rarely other customers in the back. I'm told that it is stuffy and too warm. This must be a special occasion."

He swallowed uncomfortably. His many years of living with Grandma Loni had trained him to avoid the living room when her friends were over and planning a crafting event. "I'm getting a late lunch while my uncle talks to Ms. Collins."

"That's very nice." She pulled the plastic case towards Nathan and gestured excitedly towards the various slots. "Would you like to see my buttons?"

Dozens of excuses ran through his brain. He imagined faking a leg cramp and then limping out to the main area. The bright happiness in her eyes killed any thoughts of escape. How would he feel if Grandma Loni were alone and ignored? "Sure."

She pointed out several strange buttons and detailed their history for Nathan until she stopped at a tiny bone button that looked very old and fragile. "This button was made from ivory in the late 1800s. My husband brought it back from the war while he was in London."

"My grandfather was in London during the war." If Grandma Loni was here at this moment, she would have stabbed him with a fork for forgetting his manners. "I forgot to introduce myself. My name is Nathan Carver."

She blinked pleasantly as though she had been given a rare surprise. "Are you by chance related to Raymond Carver?"

"That's my grandfather! How did you know?" Nathan asked suspiciously.

"Please forgive my lapse in manners. I'm called Mrs. Aithne. My husband George served with a Raymond Carver." She smiled slyly, as though she were holding an amusing secret. "What amazing synchronicity it is that we found each other, isn't it?"

Suddenly, Nathan remembered where he had heard the name Aithne before and his throat and mouth turned dry. Was this really a dragon? If she was a dragon, why did her husband fight in a human war? "Yeah. Strange that."

"I wish I had a photograph to show you. He was such a handsome man." She sighed wistfully, just like Grandma Loni might have if Papa Ray died. "There was a terrible fire a few years ago and I lost all of my photographs."

He imagined Grandma Loni alone without even the memories of a photograph to warm her final nights. "I might be able to help you on that account."

Her eyes blinked with hope. "How?"

"I did a project for Papa Ray a couple of months ago. Scanned a lot of old photos. There's a couple of his old unit." Nathan smiled a bit, hoping that he didn't offend her. "I can't promise anything, but I think I remember the name Aithne on the back of one of them."

"Can I see the photographs?" she asked eagerly.

"Well, they are back in California."

She sighed, dejectedly. "I understand."

"But, there's no reason we couldn't look them up on a computer," Nathan suggested. "My files should still be there and then you can have your own copies printed locally. If we could borrow one, I could get you set up right now."

"This is possible?" Mrs. Aithne asked. Her eyes flashed with power. She rang a little bell. "Chester!"

Chazz rushed into the backroom. Nathan tilted his head. "Chester?"

"Mrs. Aithne, I really do prefer to be called Chazz now." He flinched at the sight of her impatient eyes. "Of course, I'm always glad to be of service an august customers such as yourself."

"We will need a computer." She nodded to Nathan. "This young gentleman will be able to tell you everything he needs. I should prefer that this be done sooner rather than later."

The man formerly known as Chester left with an alacrity that Nathan had rarely witnessed before. Mrs. Aithne turned to Nathan. "You are a kind soul and this is rare in this terrible age. Most young men would have ignored me completely." She added a wink. "Especially if they are so completely and thoroughly bored with the subject matter. Your grandparents raised you right."

"Thank you." He hated the idea of offending her, but he had difficulty imagining this woman as a dragon. "Do you mind if I ask you a question?"

"I am indeed a dragon," Mrs. Aithne answered his unspoken question as though she had read his mind. Her eyes flashed wildly and Nathan supposed that it might be possible. "These days I keep strictly to a human form in honor of my dead husband."

"What's it like being a dragon?"

"We wandered the stars seeking undiscovered worlds of sensation and wisdom. I remember floating cities of light and gleaming rivers of darkness and mystery." She sighed wistfully. "This world was a nexus then. A crossroads of energy and power connected to the universe and so it was natural that my brothers and I eventually came to this land."

She was a living record of history and Nathan couldn't help himself. "What was the world like then?"

"It was savage and beautiful. Your people were little more than hunters then, trying to escape the notice of angry gods and beings beyond your understanding." Mrs. Aithne paused a moment, trying to recall days of long ago. "And then something wondrous happened. The Great Barrier arose from the very essence of your dreams to protect the world. It kept the Old Ones confined to the last remains of the dead universe and allowed your people time to build, to learn.

Those of us that were trapped here made this world our own."

Chazz returned with a laptop, knelt, and placed it before them. Nathan quickly accessed the internet and his fileshare folder. Dozens of black and white photographs popped up on the monitor. Images of young men in uniform bonded by trials of the spirit and blood smiled at them. Nathan pointed to Papa Ray as a young man. "That's my grandfather."

She smiled and moved his hand over a handsome man with pale skin, freckles, and red hair. "That's my George."

He copied the files to a separate folder so that she could access it later and then wrote down the appropriate information. "I'll make sure to give this information to Loxi so she can print you copies of these photos."

The dragon stared at the screen and cried, apparently happily, that she had the image of her husband again. "You would think I couldn't forget the face, but this form ages you. Soon I will be gone and join him."

"You must have really loved him."

"I met him on a warm summer day in London. The bombing raids had continued night and day for almost a month before, but then and there it all paused." She smiled, warmed by the memory. "He and his friends were handing out chocolate bars to the children boarding trains to leave London. Children have always been a weakness of mine. I saw the kindness in his eyes and I knew that I wanted him. And amidst the horror and the terror, we fell in love. I knew the price, but I simply didn't care. I've never regretted it."

"What price?" Nathan asked.

"To be immortal is to be untouchable; to live as you will. To love is to become part of the world. That's why I spend the time I have left with children. I teach music and encourage them to sing."

"You teach kids to sing? Human kids?"

"To use your voice is a great gift. We all have a song to sing, even if not exceptionally well." She smiled softly, lost in the haze of the past. "Your grandfather had a lovely voice. My dear George, well, he sang with great enthusiasm. And I loved him for it."

"I've never really thought too much about it, I guess. I've always wanted to learn to play."

"The challenge of immortality is not living forever, but to know how to spend a lovely afternoon." She patted him on the knees. "I think you're starting to know a bit about that, aren't you?"

He blinked and thought about the children singing in his vision. Was it a consequence or synchronicity? McCreedy had warned him that some learned a great deal hanging upon the tree. Did the Ash tree give him a glimpse of the future? "Do you know why we're here?"

Mrs. Aithne smiled serenely. "Loxi filled me in on some of the details. I made arrangements for us to speak. You're here to fight for your love and the world."

"Can you help us?"

She shook her head sadly. "It is not my place to fight the battle against Cenotaph for you. I have my own charges that I must protect and my own difficulties to endure."

"Mrs. Aithne, I have to be the one to fight him. I know that." Nathan smiled slyly, as though he had the upper hand for once. "However, there is one thing you can do to help all of us. I have the beginning of a plan. Would you like to hear it?"

*    *    *    *

Marty and Loxi slowly descended down the stairs with mutual contented faces, as though they were cats that had raided an entire store's worth of canaries and clearly had returned as the victors. Nathan noted with a bit of pride that there was a bit of a smear on his uncle's neck that matched Loxi's lipstick. After the last couple of nights, Nathan figured that the old man deserved a bit of happiness. Marty grinned, slightly uneasy, like he had been school boy caught with a hickey. "Loxi agreed to help with your plan, Nate."

Mrs. Aithne looked up from the laptop with an approving look. "Excellent! I just finished telling Nathan a charming, but a tad bawdy tale of Raymond singing in a small tavern outside of London."

"The word blackmail will be used often in the future in regards to this story," Nathan added. He gestured to the kindly old woman. "Speaking of help, Mrs. Aithne agreed to help."

Loxi shook her head. "Mrs. Aithne hasn't been feeling well. A fight with Cenotaph would kill her."

"I don't need to fight physically to help, Loxi." Mrs. Aithne shared a knowing look with Nathan. "The plan is sound and unto my dying breath I shall always be glad to help someone on a quest for love."

Marty's eye opened wide, clearly impressed. "What now then?"

Nathan grinned as though he had been waiting for someone to ask that very question all day. "Now it's time to see the wizard."

"Technically, he's an alchemist," Marty corrected him.

"Man, I don't step on your lines." Nathan bumped shoulders with his uncle. "Either way, we should see him now."

"I shall be at the appointed place when you need me, Nathan." Mrs. Aithne extended her hand and Nathan helped the dragon to her feet. "I have my own preparations to complete before this evening."

"Good, then we have time for a special side trip." Marty rubbed his hands together, very excited. "Nathan, if you wouldn't mind driving?"

"Marty, you going somewhere else now?" Loxi asked suspiciously.

"This might be my last day on this world. I have two stops I want to make while we have a bit of light. It's kind of karmic law." He leaned over to kiss. "You should come with us."

"I'll be just fine, Loxi." The dragon waved Loxi off. "Enjoy the quiet moments when they come. They may never come again."

# Chapter Fifteen: A Magic Man

Capitol Hill was the trendy neighborhood of the young filthy rich and the slightly filthier poor. The streets were lined with coffeehouses, taverns, and churches along with fleabag motels nestled between foreclosed high-priced McMansions of dubious taste. The crowds were denser than in the University District with a hipper attitude and savoir-faire demeanor.

Nathan found a parking lot near the Egyptian Theatre, in a former Masonic Lodge that had been converted into an Art Cinema House. Marty pointed to something in the distance. "It's over there. Across the street!"

He followed Marty across the street to a bronze statue of a passionate man playing the guitar as though his very soul counted on it. Remembering the battle against Scratch, Nathan figured that both of them might owe the dead rock star a special thanks. Marty held his hand to his head in salute. "It's time to pay respect to Saint Jimi."

"This is why we came?" Nathan asked. "To see a statue of Jimi Hendrix?"

"When going into battle, it is always a good idea to get the blessing of the Saints." Marty knelt before the statue for a moment and then lifted his head. "Thank you, Jimi. I finally beat him."

There was a pregnant pause, as though the statue might answer. Nathan helped Marty to his feet and smiled. "I saw him play the Monterey Pop Festival in '67. He was a handsome man," Loxi said cheerfully.

322

Nathan was dying to ask Loxi how old she was, but was trying to be polite. Once Marty had his moment, they piled back into the van and headed downtown towards the Space Needle. The Craftsman weaved in and out of traffic towards the heart of the city until it passed the famous flickering Elephant Carwash neon sign and turned towards Convention Center Park. The large saucer grew wider as they drove closer to the grey metal tripod base tower and found parking right outside of the park near an enormous steel ferris wheel. "What the hell is that?" Nathan asked, pointing a colossal building that seemed to have been made piecemeal out of dozens of broken metal pieces of a variety of colors and welded together to form the vague shape of a guitar. "It hurts my eyes just gazing at it."

"Son of a bitch!" Marty muttered, looking out the window. "I was hoping my new eye would make it look better somehow."

"It's the 'Experience Music Project'. It's one of the biggest museums in the world for music of all kinds, including rock and roll." Loxi explained.

"Maybe it's better on the inside," Nathan suggested hopefully.

"It's actually quite nice," Loxi added with a smile. "I think you would like the guitar exhibit."

Marty folded his arms like a five-year old. "It looks like someone painted a dog turd." He shook his head, not able to stand looking at the building any longer. "Let's just go."

Farmer's Market was the next destination. It was easier to find, but parking took a minor miracle. Marty insisted that they find street parking and refused to let Nathan use one of the parking lots. "Look you cheap old bastard, just pay for a parking lot!" Loxi exclaimed. Nathan snickered.

"Five dollars for one hour is highway robbery!" Marty complained. "They should have the honor to put on a mask and draw a gun on me for the sheer entertainment value."

After parking, Loxi led them to the cement steps leading down to the Farmer's Market. Nathan thought it looked like a bomb shelter, but there were dozens of vendors hawking fresh food, flowers, and strange and delightful crafts. It was a busy day with a bustling crowd and he had to walk around two vendors flinging fish for the crowd. "This is the Underground?"

"This is one of the entrances to the Underground." Loxi waved for them to follow her. "There's a befuddle spell cast near the entrance so Mundanes can't wander inside."

They descended to the lower levels, passing by a street kid playing guitar with an open case and a hungry-looking kitten. Marty subtly dropped a twenty dollar bill into the mix pretending that it had been an accident. Nathan smirked, not wanting to point out that the old man had argued for almost an hour about paying for parking, but was willing to slip some cash to a street musician.

Loxi led them to a side corridor that people seemed to completely ignore. Nathan watched as he seemed to fade from the crowd's perception. The sweet tingle of magic and power tickled the back of his neck. Marty pulled out a cigarette and prepared to light it. Loxi stopped him and gestured to the warning sign on the entrance. The sign carried the same message in half a dozen languages, some of them inhuman. *Smoking is banned in this establishment. Violators will be hung by their entrails.*

"I suppose I should quit anyway," Marty replied.

"How does something like this get built without people knowing about it?"

"Actually, many people do know about it. They even offer Underground Tours. The tours were started up by a wizard named Spiedel. Of course, the tours only visit sealed off sections of the Underground. It works out quite well. Humans think that they've seen the underground and don't poke around at the more mystical locations."

"What makes it special?"

"Well, it's not really that special. Many cities have undergrounds: Paris, Rome, Constantinople." They descended three flights of creaky old stairs. "It's just that it is easier for the supernatural set to conduct their business without prying eyes and gaping mouths."

Near the bottom of the stairs, they heard the soft murmur of a crowd of muffled voices and random pieces of conversations. At the base of the stairs, there was a set of double steel doors. Loxi pushed them open and beckoned them to enter the Underground. The Underground was narrow and cramped; every inch was occupied or used. The air was a bit musty, but everything else was surprisingly clean. There were apothecaries, demonic looking vendors peddling magical charms, fish restaurants, and bookbinding shops. There were dozens of strange humanoids in a variety of different colors and bizarre clothing.

"Who are all of these people?" Nathan asked.

Loxi gestured to the large thoroughfare. "Some are of the last remains of dying breeds from races that walked this world before the Great Barrier, like the dragonkin. Others are creatures born from darkness such as vampires. A few are humans like yourself that have learned to see beyond the Befuddlement Charm. They hide themselves so they can live quietly."

A tall gaunt figure wearing a long sea-green cloak with a hood stopped in front of them. He peeled back the hood to reveal a scaly face with bulbous fish eyes and a savage looking dorsal fin. He pulled long webbed claws from his pockets and bowed gracefully to Loxi. His voice was deep and gravely. "Salutations, Ms. Collins?"

Loxi remained smiling, but Nathan felt a subtle shift in her friend's demeanor and her hazel eyes narrowed. "Triton, these are my friends Nathan and Marty Carver."

Nathan shyly offered his hand, uncertain what else to do. "Pleased to meet you!"

Triton carefully took the hand, sniffed it, and then shook it. The claw was three times the size of his slender hand, but he was careful to treat it lightly. Nathan felt like he was holding a wiggling fish that might eat bite him. "Please to meet you, Mr. Carver."

"What is this? A demonic swap-meet. How could all of these be built without anyone noticing?" Nathan asked.

"As resident tour guide, I think I should answer that one. At the turn of the nineteenth century, Seattle was a fairly large city for the northwest, but we lacked some of the basic advantages that some cities had." Loxi pointed at the curved walls. "One of the problems was that Seattle was built on a tidal plan with really poor drainage. Which basically meant that every time the tide came in toilets would flood. Not a good place to do your business."

"How does that translate into an underground city?" Nathan asked.

"In 1889, there was a horrible fire. It burned most of the city to the ground. It was terrible. There was a violent struggle for control among the supernatural gangs," Loxi continued. "It looked like we were all going to go to hell in a hand basket, but then Cenotaph and Borri appeared and created the current peace."

"No wonder he controls the city," Nathan muttered.

"At that time, there were few cities on the west coast that had ready made tunnels for those that shun the day light or wanted to keep away from the humans. Not all of the human half breeds are beautiful like myself and can pass for human," Loxi said, winking.

Neither Nathan nor Marty were inclined or even dared to disagree with her. The strange looking fish humanoid shuffling past them carrying a wooden barrel punctuated her point. Most of the crowd was vaguely human, but many of these were obviously more than human. Loxi led them to the entrance to *Ye Old Curiosity's Shoppe* and then gestured for them to enter. "I have to speak with my mother about your plans. I'll be here when you are ready to leave."

"Is that the same shop as on Fisherman's Wharf?" Marty asked. "The tourist trap where they sell fake plastic heads?

Loxi shrugged as though to say what can I tell you? "This is the special shopper's section. Above the artifacts are faked. I believe you will find it interesting."

Ye Old Curiosity Shoppe reminded Nathan of a subway tunnel that had been transformed into a used bookstore with countless stacks and shelves arranged haphazardly. He tried to absorb it all, but every spare inch of room was crammed with artifacts of interest and various knickknacks from all over the world. They found everything from enchanted glasses, talking skulls, and dancing stone gargoyles. He held up a bizarre curved crystal decanter that seemed to hum at his touch and almost dropped it when a voice surprised him from behind. "That is boiled essence of knotweed and burdock. It can be used to cure certain unnatural poisons that certain creatures of the night are known to polish their fangs with."

He flinched with surprise. He had not seen the thin, frail man with delicate features until he spoke. Marty stepped between them quickly. "Hello, Mr. Borri."

"Mr. Carver, I'm quite surprised that you would return after missing your deadline." The youthful looking man cleaned his glasses on his sleeve. "Are you here to resolve your debts?"

His uncle pointed to the eye-patch. "This doesn't count?"

"An argument could be made that I was supposed to extract said eyes and that a third-party vendor had to collect the debt by force." He adjusted his glasses and studied Nathan for a moment with his large hazel eyes. There was a sense of familiarity in his face that he couldn't quite place. "I suppose in the interest of a good future relationship that I can wave the penalty clauses you agreed to in the contract."

"Mr. Borri, this is my nephew Nathan Carver." Marty gestured to Nathan. "I brought him in to settle his account."

A brief flicker of amusement flashed across Remington Borri's face. It was a predatory, hawkish expression. "Indeed, I had heard through my contacts that Mr. Carver was in Seattle. It is a pleasure to meet you, Nathan Carver. I've heard ever so much about you. Please follow me."

They exchanged worried glances, but not really having a choice, Marty and Nathan followed him into an elaborately decorated office. Borri sat at his oversized oak desk and began searching through a drawer. "I shall be with you in just a moment. I was just looking at the file this morning just in case."

Curious, Nathan glanced around the office looking at the various photographs. Some of them were very old. One of them was labeled Great Seattle Fire, 1889. The photograph depicted several men searching through a burned out landscape. One of the men looked suspiciously like Borri.

"Yes, I am in that photograph, Mr. Carver," Borri said, without looking up from his drawer. Startled, Nathan looked away. "No, it is okay for you to look at my photographs. I have displayed them, after all."

"How can you be in that photograph? Wait, are you an immortal?" Nathan asked.

"There are many different paths to immortality, young man. Each with their own price."

"How old are you?"

"That is a very long story, Mr. Carver. I am the third eldest resident of this city. Perhaps I shall share it with you in time." Borri rummaged through his files a moment until he produced a large legal folder and flipped it open. He scanned the page with his finger until he found the exact spot he was looking for and then laid it out on the table for Nathan to read. "As you can see in your file, your father and uncle managed to provide for you quite well. And they made the exceptionally wise decision to leave myself as the custodian of said funds, which I invested brilliantly."

Nathan and Marty looked at the figure quoted on the page and their eyes became as wide as saucers. The number was a lot bigger than Marty had previously suggested. "Is that number right?" Nathan asked.

Borri sighed as though he were being put upon. "Indeed said number is correct. Witness the miracle of compounded interest over twenty years! Have you decided what you want to do with this inheritance? I understand college is in your future plans."

Nathan swallowed. "I do want to go to college, but not right now. I'm learning a lot on the road. I don't have to decide what to do with all of it right now, do I?"

"Not at all, Mr. Carver." Borri nodded with approval. "In fact, it might be a wise choice all-together to wait until you have locked down your future plans."

"You have the power to issue payments and move the money around? I'm not really sure how this works?" Nathan asked.

"I have power of attorney in this affair until you revoke it," Borri explained. "As your uncle can no doubt recall, I was paid a modest sum at the start of this endeavor."

Nathan grinned. This is something he had wanted to do ever since he first discovered the possibility of an inheritance. "I want to pay off the mortgage on my grandparent's ranch. Free and clear. Can you do that?"

Borri scribbled a few notes on his pad. "It will take some research. I presume you would like this done without the permission of your grandparents?"

"You know me so well." Nathan eyed Borri suspiciously. "How did you know?"

"Mr. Carver, I have toppled empires with but a few words and key financial investments, I have loved and lost a thousand times, and conquered the subtle art of Alchemy such that I have mastery over life itself. I am a professional and understand how these transactions work."

"Fair enough." Nathan swallowed. Did he really think he would be able to trick this immortal? How many times had others tried and failed. "I trust you to handle it. And if I need access to the rest of the funds, I should contact you?"

"Indeed, I should be quite happy to continue to serve as executor for as long as you require it." Borri took a couple more notes and then looked up from the desk. "Was there anything else you needed, Mr. Carver?"

Nathan put his hand on Marty's shoulder and shot him a look that read I got this. He turned to Borri. "I have a couple of questions, if you don't mind?"

"I do not object to questions," the Alchemist reported. "But I cannot guarantee answers, Mr. Carver."

"I think you have these answers, Mr. Borri." Nathan leaned closer and flashed his best shit eating grin. "Can you tell me how a homunculus is made?"

Borri blinked. It wasn't much, just the faint molecule of surprise, but it was enough to let Nathan know he was on the right track. "That is a difficult alchemical formula to complete. Only a few have mastered such a thing on a large scale so as to be useful. Why would you ask such a thing?"

"I wanted to narrow down the suspects, but you just did that for me." Nathan winked at his very confused uncle. "You might be immortal Mr. Borri, but you should never play poker."

Marty pulled Nathan's arm. "Nate, it's not a good idea to antagonize him. We need him."

"We do need him. And he needs us. Don't you get it, Marty? Mr. Borri has been pulling our strings all along." Nathan turned to Borri. "Isn't that right?"

"How did you know, Mr. Carver?"

"I knew that someone was helping Eve. She couldn't have escaped on her own. It was someone smart enough to fool Cenotaph and powerful enough to get away with it." Nathan smiled wryly. "And I knew as soon as I saw you that it had to be you."

"How?" Marty asked.

"Imagine Mr. Borri with longer hair and pale skin."

"Son of a bitch!" Marty snapped his fingers. "You made the homunculus out of your own blood and helped that spirit merge with it! There was a problem with the transmutation process and that's why Eve doesn't have a human soul."

"A human soul is earned, gentleman. I helped her spirit transmute into flesh based on my template. Eve will grow one in time," Borri explained. "If she is allowed to live by Cenotaph."

"She's made of your flesh. You have to help us save her," Nathan argued.

"I am not permitted to strike directly against Cenotaph," Borri stated coldly. "We have a mutual geis that was designed to keep the peace in Seattle. It is why we had to use third-parties to resolve our differences."

"Let me see if I figured out the timeline. You helped Eve come to this world and she escaped." Marty tapped his head finally getting it. "Cenotaph sent the New Flesh after her and you sent your own dupes to find her. Us. Used some sort of karmic spell to make sure that we'd come across her."

"That's why he contracted you for that deal with the Dibbuk Box for Cenotaph," Nathan added. "It was misdirection."

Borri folded his hands on his lap and nodded. "Continue."

"You set me up. You knew I couldn't return the box and that I'd be going to Nathan for his trip." Marty groaned. "I can't believe I let you con me."

"Cenotaph captured Eve once in California and you freed her and gave her the clues to lead us back to you," Nathan said, catching onto Mary's train of thought. He thought about all of the people they had met on the journey and realized that Borri was behind it all. "You helped Papo find us. You were the one that gave him the message about Bobby Johnson. And you told Eve about the Bandersnatch. She put that idea into my head. Why?"

"I loved her," Borri said simply and then pointed at Nathan. "She was born out of a jar to be my wife, but she already loved another. I wanted her to be happy."

"Why would you bother with it? Can't you find a wife out there in the real world?" Marty asked.

"I have had many wives in my lifetime." Borri's eyes turned cold, but his voice was tainted with sadness no matter how hard he tried to maintain his composure. "Josephine died young. Heart failure while I was on a business trip. Heather I met when I was the older man and she the young woman. Slowly, year after year, she fell to the revenges of time and could not stand the look at me when she appeared to be my elder. Emelina died from the plague in Florence. I lost a son not half a mile from this very spot. I could continue to list each and every stab into my heart, but I believe my point is made."

"You wanted someone that could live forever." The thought troubled Nathan more than he wanted to admit. "You wanted an immortal."

"And now I fear that it is too late." Sorrow and regret cracked Borri's voice. "Eve as you named her is lost to us forever"

"I don't believe that. Not after everything that's happened.

Everything we've fought for in the last couple of weeks. Please help us," Nathan pleaded. "You must have loved her. I can see it in your eyes. No matter how hard you try to hide it. Everyone says that you're the smartest person around. You managed to get us this far. You have to know something."

Borri shook his head. "Do you not believe that had I power to do so, that I would not finish this? You have no idea of the power Cenotaph welds. Know this, Cenotaph is the oldest creature that was once a mortal man that still walks the earth. His power is inconceivable."

"Aren't you exaggerating this a bit, Mr. Borri?" Marty asked, shrugging his shoulders. "The story is that he's just another wizard that thinks he's a god."

"Cenotaph is merely an alias he assumed a few centuries ago for the sake of anonymity. His real name is a curse. A name reviled through the ages. J--." Borri tried to finish the sentence, but his throat began to constrict as though an invisible hand slowly choked the life from him. His face turned beet red as he struggled to breathe. It lasted several seconds as Nathan and Marty quickly moved to help him. He pushed them back shaking his head as he gasped for air. "It seems the geis is a bit strict on direct information."

"I hate to press this, but this is about Eve. You can't strike against Cenotaph, but you can answer questions right as long as it doesn't directly pertain to Cenotaph right?" Nathan asked.

"I can answer theoretical questions." Borri raised an eyebrow, almost as though he was considering if he could dare to hope. "If you are less clear as to why you wish to ask such questions, it might be easier."

He scratched his head. So they could ask questions as long as it wasn't obvious how they were going to use the information against Cenotaph. "How could we find the Blue Lady?"

Borri spoke carefully as though attempting to skirt the very edge of the agreement. "She is lost to the wild. Her portal to this realm has been closed. Only an Oracle can find her now."

"That means the Freemont Troll, Nate. I know how to contact it." Marty clasped his nephew's shoulder. "Where is her portal and how do we open it?"

"Her power springs from the Prefontaine fountain. The waters have dried as the hope of tomorrow left the city," Borri answered. "Return that which was lost and the Blue Lady can return."

The final piece of the puzzle unlocked in Nathan's mind. He strived to keep from smiling. It was better to keep the whole plan hidden from Borri until the right moment. "Is she imprisoned?"

"Yes."

"Where can I find her? How can I free her?" Nathan asked. Borri shook his head. Nathan considered the puzzle. Clearly, the Blue Lady prison was connected to Cenotaph. This information was new, but totally unexpected. "How could one find a tupla?"

"A tulpa is part of those that brought it to life," Borri explained. "Find those from which it sprang and they can lead you to that which you seek."

"How can I fight Cenotaph one on one?" Nathan asked. Borri

shook his head. He had to change the phrasing of the question to not include Cenotaph. Hypothetical questions could be answered without violating the geis. "How can one mystic fight another mystic without interference?"

"The path by which Hector was slain by Achilles. The ancient challenge of blood to the death. Monomachia." Borri scratched his nose as though signaling Nathan and then added. "Those that follow the old ways must obey this tradition least they lose respect from their patrons and their investments and invocation pacts no longer work."

"How can I find Cenotaph?" Again, Borri shook his head. Nathan thought about it and realized that there was no way to gain this information without it being for an attack on the wizard. "OK, I have a different question. You have mastered life and alchemy. Can you cure Marty's cancer?"

"Kid, I'm not important right now," his uncle protested.

Borri ignored him. "Yes. It is a difficult process and requires a rare ingredient."

"The bones of a Bandersnatch, right?" Nathan said finishing the sentence. You need it for your own immortality serum, don't you?"

"You seem to have a good grasp of the situation, Mr. Carver. I can prepare enough of my elixir for my own purposes and share enough to cure Martin's cancer." Borri nodded approvingly like a teacher proud of a promising student. "You have done better than I could have expected based on your familial relations,"

Marty let the insult pass. "Wait, you can cure my cancer? You never told me about this before!"

"Such an arrangement was simply not possible before, Marty. However, now the possibility exists."

Nathan fished out the paper McCreedy had given him from his pocket and passed it over to Borri. "Here's the deal. This is how much of the bones we managed to salvage from the corpse. We will supply you enough to generate the cure for Marty and the rest will be sold to you at a good price. Half of the proceeds will go to McCreedy to pay his men. The rest will be funneled into a special project that you will assist with using your unique skills. Agreed?"

"Does this project involve assaulting Cenotaph in any fashion?"

"Not at all." Nathan flashed his best shit-eating grin. "You'll be providing a service to the community and you might even gain a tax benefit."

Borri calculated the volume of the bones in his head while tapping his fingers on the wooden desk. His nose twitched with interest. "A very equitable arrangement, I admit. However, I feel that I must confess that such a cure is not easily made. It shall take months for the formula to germinate properly. And of course, there are certain requirements for the cure to work."

"Such as?" Marty asked. Nathan could see hope in his eyes for the first time in a long time. "I'll do whatever it takes."

"For the treatment to be fully effective, the body must be purified of toxicants, stimulants, and opiates," Borri explained. "You're mind and body must be made ready to allow the alchemical properties to heal you."

"What about the vampire blood?" Nathan asked.

"I can only estimate, but it should only take a month or less for it to flush through his system." Borri shook his head with a surprising expression of pity. "At present it dulls the pain of the injuries you have suffered. However, as the taint fades from your system, your nerve endings shall start to die and others will reconnect. You will experience a great deal of pain."

"And I won't be able to take anything for it, if I want the cure to work, will I?" Marty asked.

"That is the price of the cure. I wish it were otherwise, Martin."

Nathan sighed. He didn't look forward to his uncle's suffering, but it was much better than death. "Doesn't look like we have much of a choice; I think we have a deal."

"I have an additional stipulation for my own protection. I think that you will understand." Borri cleaned his glasses on his shirt. "This project that you wish me to assist you with cannot directly harm Cenotaph. Should this be agreeable, then I should be prepared to act on your behalf shortly."

"Are you sure you know what you're doing, kid?" Marty asked.

Nathan shook Borri's hand in agreement. "Trust me. Cenotaph will never see this coming."

# *Chapter Sixteen: Empty Places*

The yellow moon dilated through the haze of smog emerging slightly red over the Seattle skyline as Nathan Carver stepped outside of the Pit Stop. With a large plastic cup baring the standard of a football star filled with chopped ice and root beer in one hand and a pack of gum in the other, he sauntered over to the old 1977 Craftsman enjoying the refreshing night air. The sounds of the city were starting to quiet for lull of sleep in the early hours of twilight before dawn.

He tried to imagine working in a place like this night after night numb to the world as time crept past. His father had given up the magic of the night for the flickering halogen lights of convenience store commerce. He did it for the love of his family and the dream of a better tomorrow for his son. Nathan glanced over his shoulder at the bright sign welcoming customers twenty-four hours a day. "Thanks, Dad. I think I get it now."

Opening the driver's door, Nathan tossed the gum to his uncle. The packet of gum bounced on his hand and dropped into his lap. Marty's depth perception was getting a bit better for the one eye missing, but he still wasn't ready to drive. "Thanks, Nate. I picked a hella of a day to quit smoking again."

"You beat the Beast." Nathan grinned knowingly. "You can do anything now."

Marty nodded and cradled his old guitar like it was a security blanket. "And I'm ruggedly handsome. You forgot that part."

Freemont was a quiet neighborhood of Seattle across the Puget

340

Sound that was mostly known to outsiders as an artist community. In a city obsessed with the future, Freemont had always been content to enjoy the moment. The vibe was quieter, relaxed. There were more coffee shops than bars, which were always referred to as Pubs. "Think it will be quiet enough to see the Troll now?"

"It couldn't hurt. Last call was about an hour or so ago. I think as long as we watch out for hobos, we should be just fine."

"Let's do this then and with any luck, we'll live to regret it." Nathan drove a couple of blocks north and then turned into a sleepy residential community. He parked the van under a large highway overpass with dozens of concrete columns and parked in a dimly open area. Several artful spray-can graffiti depictions of the notorious Mr. Bang seemed to point menacingly directly at them from every angle. "That just touches me in all the wrong places."

Dozens of men wandered the shadows looking for a dry place to rest for the night in makeshift tents of dirty plastic and then parked the van on a quiet residential street. He parked the van and pulled out a small bundled blanket from under his seat. "This neighborhood's gone right in the crapper," Marty muttered.

Half of the lights in the neighborhood were out. The air was misty, almost ready to rain. "Still a lot of people out and about. I hope Borri was right about that Befuddlement Spell around the Troll."

"Nate, I'm not sure I can do this."

"Do you mean the Troll?" Nathan asked credulously. "We've faced far more horrifying things than this and that's just this week. And Borri said he was mostly friendly if we pay the proper tribute."

"I've met him once before. If you show enough reverence, he likes answering questions. That's what he does. Birds gotta fly, ya know? Just do it like we practiced and we'll be fine." Marty swallowed uncomfortably and popped another stick of gum into his mouth. "I'm just not so sure about the next part. The plan is utter genius, but I've never done anything like it before. Not in the light. Not in front of a crowd of sober people."

Nathan laughed. "You beat old Scratch! A literal duel with the closest thing to the devil that walks this world! I think you'll do just fine." They opened the side door and started moving several boxes to a secure spot under the bridge before the ginormous stone and plaster statue of a large bearded troll reaching out of the rock to snatch old Volkswagen Bug. Was the troll winking at him or was that a reflection off the hubcap eye? "I really hope they aren't screwing with me. . ."

They knelt down to the concrete and cleared a spot and then unrolled a dirty blanket in front of the statue and unloaded several items from the van and placed them around it. Nathan sat down Indian-style in the center and accepted the old paper bag that his uncle handed to him. One by one Nathan pulled out the items needed for the summoning ritual; scented candle, a grey tail-feather from an owl, and a small wooden bowl. Marty bowed, gestured to his nephew and took a step back. "The rest is up to you, kid."

Nathan raised his father's lighter and flicked it a couple of times until it produced a mighty flame. A gust of frozen bits of rain and wind raged through the underpass as though the city had been holding back and conserving it's strength until that moment to strike causing the flame the flicker until he protected it with his other hand. "Great Spirit of the Mountain, I've come seeking an oracle. I'm a lost soul seeking guidance."

He held the quill of the grey feather in the flame of the candle until it caught fire and then dropped it into the bowl. As the flame consumed the feather, Nathan pulled out his pocket knife and sliced across the palm of his hand. It hurt like hell, but he knew that would pass. He allowed the blood to drip from his palm onto the flame, extinguishing it.

As the smoke rose from the bowl, he felt a small tremor. Waves of heat emanated from the lifeless stone. The eyes on the Troll blinked as though waking from a nap. Mystically animated, the Troll released its grip upon the old Volkswagen and stretched. It spoke in a low rocky voice. "Where is the tribute for the Spirit of the Mountain?"

Marty pulled over the large cardboard box between Nathan and the troll. Nathan reached into the box and produced a metal pick in one hand and a sizable dark rainbow colored limestone rock in the other. Taking a deep breath, he plunged the pick into the rock several times until it split to reveal a hollow core filled with purple Amherst and multicolored quartz crystals. "First, we bring you a geode in honor of the strength of the mountain."

The troll reached over and carefully plucked the stone with its thumb and forefinger as though it were delicate and examined it closely. "From the land of the three rivers. The Spirit of the Mountain approves."

Marty dragged the old metal ice chest to the front and stepped back quickly not wanting to be within the troll's reach for any longer than required. Nathan suppressed the urge to laugh and continued. "We have brought you meat of deer and lamb."

"It has been many nights since I have tasted flesh." Nathan wondered what sort of flesh it normally ate and shivered. The troll lifted the ice chest and poured the packages of fresh meat into its mouth and slowly ground them to paste and swallowed, grunting with pure pleasure. It wiped its mouth and snorted. "Where is my drink?"

Nathan and Marty slowly lift the keg of imported beer towards the troll. Eager, with its fingers twitching, it snatched the metal cask from their hands and began to drink. They watched in amazement as it gulped swallow after swallow like a machine. "At least we now know trolls don't need to breathe," Marty muttered with a bit of awe and jealousy in his voice.

With a mighty belch of such a foul stench it almost made Nathan gag, the troll was satisfied. "Three questions are owed. Three questions may be asked. What secrets do you desire from the Spirit of the Mountain, Scion of the Last Light?"

Nathan's jaw tightened. That was a new title and not a pleasant one. What did it mean? Should he waste one of his questions to ask? "I seek the true name of the wizard known as Cenotaph."

"Shrouded is his name. To call forth his true name is to invite his presence." The Troll's face twisted with what Nathan imagined was fear. "Answer I can, but it shall come with the price of summoning forth his attention. Do you seek to face him now?"

"No. I think that's not the smartest thing in the world right now.

Thank you for the warning, Spirit of the Mountain." Who was this wizard that his very name invoked such fear? Nathan felt certain that he didn't want to keep the Troll waiting and so proceeded with the next question. He'd have to solve that mystery later. "I seek a way to free the Blue Lady from the wizard known as Cenotaph so that she might return to her place. I am told his place of power is hidden. How might I find the Blue Lady and then free her?"

The Freemont Troll laughed in a booming voice. "Ho! Ho! You think to trick me by placing many questions in one. I have sat on this rock for many an age helping those that come in respect."

"I come with great respect and reverence," Nathan said putting his hands together as a way of showing supplication. "Answer as you feel is proper."

"Hmmm. . ." The troll narrowed his eyes and scratched his chin as though examining Nathan. Exercised from the boulder, the creature was so tall that it almost had to stoop to avoid banging its head on the overpass. "Very well. The Blue Lady is trapped in the realm of Cenotaph in a city of bones at the edge of the Dreamlands where the Great Barrier is thinnest. She is bound to a circle of his blood and has no power while her portal is empty. Shatter the circle and she will be free."

That wasn't the wealth of information that Nathan had hoped for, but he didn't give up hope. "And so how do I find her?"

"I was getting to that!" the Troll roared. Nathan flinched properly as Marty had instructed. He didn't need much motivation to follow the advice. "A tulpa though mighty in reverence is bound to that which they symbolize. Mystics with the sight can follow such a connection through this world and any other, but Cenotaph has locked the path."

Nathan grinned over at Marty and tapped his chest. His uncle nodded getting his reference to Papo's Skeleton Key. What should he ask for this next question? Certainly Eve would also be in the same place as the Blue Lady? How many mystically hidden safe houses could the wizard reasonably possess? Should he waste a question to be certain? His plan had a lot of assumptions built into it. Despite the help from Borri, McCreedy, and Mrs. Aithne, Nathan wasn't certain that they could pull it off by tomorrow morning. Would Cenotaph fall for the trick? And then suddenly the answer, or more specifically, the right question occurred to him. "Will my plan tomorrow succeed?"

"Ho! Ho! Clever boy!" the Troll grumbled. There was a pause of silence. The wind rustling through garbage was the only sound. "The answer is yes. If you are willing to pay the price."

That was not the answer he was looking for. "What price?"

"Three questions were owed. Three were answered." The Troll laughed again. "The peace of the stone calls to me."

"I need your help!" Nathan pleaded.

The troll had already started to slink back into the rock and the boulder. "Try again in the new year when I am less stonish."

Nathan sighed at the troll once again returned to stone and plaster and grabbed the old Volkswagen once more. Marty walked over looking very proud. "Hey, you did so much better than Bill and I did back in the day. We wasted two of our questions."

"Really? What did you guys ask?"

A shadow fell over the statue as the lights began to dim suddenly. A faint moaning surrounded them killing any sort of jovial reply. The denizens of the tent city started to rise and all at once they turned towards them. Marty held up his hands and called out to them. "Sorry guys, but we're out of the beer and meat."

They staggered forward like broken puppets on loose strings avoiding the light. Nathan flicked on his lighter, waved his hand over the flame, and willed forth energy from the fire. A strobe burst shot into the sky like a rocket briefly illuminating the area. Decayed faces spitting black bile leered from the shadows while broken bodies shambled towards them.

"Son of a bitch!"

He held the energy tightly around his body like he had been taught. Nathan felt ready for this fight. "What are those? Zombies?" Can I fry them?"

Marty shook his head horrified. "They're broken men with shattered souls possessed by Mr. Bang! Look at their pallor! Shit, I think they are still alive in there! I think Cenotaph heard us and he's pissed!"

"What's the black stuff coming out of their mouth?"

"I'm afraid to even think about it," Marty admitted. "Better not let them bite you."

"No shit." Nathan felt the magic pulse through his hands. "Any other bright ideas?"

"Run!"

The broken men had already shambled between themselves and the Craftsman. Marty pulled out his pistol, but aimed it down towards the street. "We should make a run for it, kid. Come back for the van later."

Nathan extended his hands and concentrated on the air and the wind around them. He had a plan, but it would take fine control. Concentrating on the air and molecules around his hands, he tried to imagine himself pushing all of them to the ground at once and then the thought of the fire slipped into his head unwanted. Surging blue blasts of eldritch flames encircled his hands supercharging the very air around him with heat. Waves of energy cooked the air around him creating violent pressure around them transforming into blasts of concentrated concussion blasts sending the broken men to the ground.

"When did you learn to do that?" Marty asked.

"Just now. Run!"

It took several moments for the broken men to recover and push themselves up from the wet street. By then, Nathan had already climbed into the driver's seat, started the van, and started down the street. Marty watched from the rear-view mirror as the men slowly dispersed. "That was too close."

"Think he learned too much?" Nathan asked worried.

"I think your plan will be hard for him to predict, kid. It's not in his nature to understand that angle." Marty absentmindedly reached for his cigarettes. Realizing what he was doing, he frowned and then switched gears and found another stick of gum. "I'm worried about how much control he has over this Mr. Bang character."

Nathan pointed to a spray-painted rendition of the tulpa on a wall they were passing. "How could this city lose so much hope? Without the Blue Lady, it's like they gave up or something."

"Tomorrow is the start of a new day for us and Seattle." Marty playfully punched his shoulder. "And I can't think of anyone else that I'd rather face down the end with than you Nate."

"I'm not going to see Styx with you." He resisted the urge to smile. "End of the world or not, I have my standards."

"What? After that heart-felt speech? I could have won an Oscar!" Marty popped another piece of gum into his mouth absentmindedly. "Seriously? How did you come up with this plan?"

"I saw bits of it on the tree. I saw the pieces and then I did the smartest thing I could think of," Nathan answered grinning. "I asked Mrs. Aithne for advice."

*　　*　　*　　*

The morning sun glittered as it reflected off the black glass of the skyscrapers. The morning crowd frantically went about their business like ants on a feeding frenzy. Traffic slowed to the point that the streets were an informal parking lot. Nathan waited at a stop light for two cycles before advancing a block. He noted with some small satisfaction that the flow of the sidewalk movement tended to move towards their destination. They parked in a pay garage near Pioneer Square that appeared to be the bow of a mighty ship sticking out of the black concrete sea.

Marty unlocked the back hatch and pulled out the old green duffle bags and his cracked black guitar case. "This is not me doubting you. I just wanted to do one last smoke test before we start. You sure about all of this, kid? This is going to change everything."

"Am I certain? No. This could be a colossal fuckup on a scale that the gods themselves will weep." Nathan slid one of the straps over his neck and lifted the bag. "But then a wise person once told me that the universe is made of stories and if we're going to go out fighting, we should make it as epic as possible."

"I'm worried about your plan. It takes years of mediation to build up the concentration to control that sort of power." Marty swallowed, clearly worried. "What if you burn out? Cenotaph won't surrender."

"That's my advantage in this situation. Cenotaph is fighting for power. His ego won't let him stand down. I'm fighting for love. And either every song in the history of the world is wrong or that's the greatest power there is."

"Isn't it a bit soon to be using that word?" Marty asked. He found it amusing that his uncle seemed equally worried about the use of a single word as fighting a dark wizard. "I've loved a lot of women in my time. It didn't always last."

"You can't love expecting it to have an expiration date, Marty." He laughed a bit self-conscious. "Maybe it won't last. That doesn't mean we can let her rot."

"Nate, I've never been more proud of you than I am right now. Win or lose, stand or fall, after today we'll be legends. What else can men want from this world?"

They hauled the equipment up a very steep hill passing by Pioneer Square Park and the bronze bust of Chief Seathle. Several police cars rushed by with their lights flashing as they crossed the street past the old adobe buildings with scowling gargoyles and a surprisingly sparkling famous Smith Tower. He looked up at the glass pyramid at the top of the tower and for the first time a white light shining through to the sky. Was this as a result of their actions? Were they actually making a difference? He made a note to ask Marty about the Smith Tower later; if they survived the day.

The crowd of the day pushed past them. Nathan caught himself flinching at the site of several homeless on the corners holding signs. He hated the revulsion and worry, but resolved to press forward. Crowds congealed on the sidewalk and spilled out into the street. "Looks like Borri kept to his end of the deal."

An entire section of the city had been closed to traffic. Third Avenue from Cherry to Jefferson Street was blocked by black and yellow barricades staffed by police officers. A small stage had been erected near the park under a brightly colored banner that read *Blue Lady Society for Hope*. Dozens of volunteers wearing the Thane colors dished out food, water, and sodas. Marty poked Nathan in the ribs and then pointed at the infamous Bloodbath McCreedy enthralling a circle of children making animal balloons. "Oh yeah, that's an image that's never going to go away."

Nathan snapped a picture with his phone and raised an eyebrow. "There will be t-shirts. And quite possibly mugs and doilies."

"You are a devious person and I hope to never be on your bad side. Ever." Marty dropped the duffle bag. His face was red from exertion. "I'm getting too old for this shit."

"If this were a movie that would be the last thing you ever said."

"Nah, I've already decided my final words," Marty explained. "Long time ago in fact."

"Care to share them?"

"Only at the right time, kid." He pointed over to a crowd of children. "Look at that!"

Mrs. Aithne pranced about in a circle clad in a glorious blue Victorian dress complete with a fanciful blue wig and a sparkling wand with a rare verve from one of her age. The hope was that if she sparked enough imagination as the mascot of the Blue Lady, it might fuel an unconscious faith in the tulpa. The dragon played her role to perfection and for a moment Nathan forgot that she wasn't human, except for where it counted the most. A number of parents brought over their children to meet this wondrous lady and take pictures. Loxi followed her friend carefully and managed the children's chorus. She was the first to spot them and the wave of relief was clearly visible on her face. "We were worried you weren't going to make it!"

"Traffic is crazy!"

"I can't believe Borri made all of this happen in just a couple of days," Nathan muttered. The scope of the project seemed that much larger in when he looked at it. They had shut down this part of the city and the entire block. It must have taken a massive amount of cash and political favors from Borri to make this happen in such a short time. Clearly he was highly motivated. "The cost must have been enormous to make all of this happen."

Loxi rolled her eyes. "I just bumped into him. He said it was a tax right-off. Somehow the creepy little bastard's gonna make a profit on all of this!"

"If it helps the city, then does it really matter?" Marty hugged her tightly and kissed her on the lips like there was no tomorrow. "Looks like we're doing some good here aside from our selfish alterior motivations."

"And, you guys might have even managed to pull that stick out of his ass." Loxi pointed to a wooden booth near the stage decorated with purple fabric and strange colorful banners. It was manned by the notoriously publicity shy Remington Borri wearing a tuxedo and a bright red fez. "He seems to almost be enjoying himself."

Nathan asked a couple of the Thanes to pack their gear behind the stage while he walked amongst the people. It felt as though a swath of people from every neighborhood in Seattle walked amongst the booths and donate money to feed the homeless. A short line formed at the edge of the park to a make-shift kitchen where Sarah McCreedy ladled chili and delicious cornbread. It felt weird to see his plan so fully realized. He glanced over at Marty and Loxi having an animated discussion with the children's choir and laughed. It was a scene he never could have imagined in a hundred years.

The dried, empty Prefontaine Fountain marked a border in the city between the new steel buildings of the new century and the classy old brick buildings that had once been the pride of Seattle. Nathan walked to the edge of the fountain a bit underwhelmed at the size of the pool.

He knelt down to touch one of the turtle statues and stared closely at the fountain. It took some effort, but slowly the Promethean Chains came into his view. Much effort would be required to shatter the bonds of these chains, but he hoped that the day's efforts were having an effect. Hope was ever the enemy of despair and today they needed as much hope as possible.

He returned to the park pleased that the sky was filled with blackbirds and other avian friends and temporary allies. Natural enemies perched side by side sharing in the fight for this one single day. Nathan opened his heart and reached out to them through Papo's Bone Charm. The flock bustled with excitement. They watched the entire neighborhood from a bird's eye view and seeking out any possible danger, threat, or occasional snack. Despite his worries that Cenotaph might attack them openly, the day seemed clear of threats. Sharing his intentions with the entire flock, he opened his mind to their reply. Their conclave of thoughts became a cacophony of cries until a single response had been agreed upon.

"Thanks, guys!" he replied looking up at the birds.

Marty waved him over from the fountain. "I think we're as ready as we'll ever be on this short of notice."

Nathan grinned. Everything was coming down to this moment and he felt great. "Let's get this party started."

Mrs. Aithne led Marty and the choir onto the stage and tapped the microphone capturing the attention of the crowd. "Welcome all of you. Some of you know me from my charity work. My name is Mrs. Aithne. I am not a native to this city, but I have lived here a long time.

I moved here with my husband George after the war." The mention of her husband's name cracked her voice. She wiped her eyes with a handkerchief and then continued. "There was a time in this city when we looked after each other. We had a sense of community and while this day has a bit of whimsy to it, we wanted to bring a message to the good people of Seattle. It is time to bring it back. We want to live in a world of hope. The Blue Lady Society for Hope wants us all to remember that earlier time and give. Let us feed and clothe our brothers and sisters and remember a world of community."

The crowd applauded and that was the signal for Marty to play. It was a sweet song and then the children began to sing an old song that he remembered from his earliest nights.

*Soft the drowsy hours are creeping*
*Hill and vale in slumber steeping*
*I my loving vigil keeping*
*All through the night.*

It was an old Welsh song that Papa Ray used to sing when he couldn't sleep. Did Marty pick this song? His uncle played along smiling and remembering the often forgotten good times of his childhood. Nathan tipped an imaginary hat to his uncle and struggled to remember its name. There was something pure about the voice of a child singing that injected joy to the heart. Marty smiled and nodded to Nathan.

The crowded started joining in and Nathan could feel the hearts swell of emotions. People were starting to remember a sense of community. The distances between souls didn't seem that great. He felt the swell of emotions swirl around him as men and women remembered the fragile hope of a child looking out into tomorrow. It was working. The web of despair that Mr. Bang had somehow managed to cast over the entire city was beginning to fade, if only for a night.

After several songs, and the force of the hope energized him to the point that the tips of his fingers buzzed, Nathan decided it was time for the next stage of the plan. He waited until Marty was too distracted with the performance and returned to the fountain with the two duffle bags. The Promethean chains started to crack under the wave after wave of good cheer and faith. He imagined the very notes of the songs slowly disintegrating the metal chains. Deciding that now was the time to act, Nathan felt along the bottom of the fountain searching for a keyhole and found it near the center under a loose slab of concrete that seemed to move because he willed it.

A familiar warm voice surprised him. "You weren't planning on leaving without me?"

Nathan flinched slightly and looked up at his very disapproving uncle. How did he get there so fast? It must have taken longer than he thought to find the keyhole. "I was just checking the portal entrance."

"You were going to leave me, weren't you?" Marty folded his arms angry. "After everything we've been through. Together."

"Marty, I have to fight him alone." He shook his head trying to put the feeling into words. "I saw it all on the tree. I saw how it all fits. And it only will work if I face him alone."

"And you will. But I am going with you to the end. I made a promise to you and your father." Marty shot him a pleading look. "Don't make me a liar."

"Wouldn't think of it. It's you and me until the end of the world." He tossed one of the duffle bags to his uncle. "I think the chains are weak enough."

"Can you open it?"

"Let's find out."

Nathan pulled out the skeleton key under his t-shirt and untied the leather strap around his neck. He tried it in the hole. Slowly the mechanism clicked and the portal began to open. He hopped out of the fountain afraid that the very ground would dissolve out from under him. Concrete bricks one by one folded back onto each other revealing an empty black abyss. He looked about worried that someone might see them, but the Befuddlement Ward was still in proper effect and the children's choir still held the crowd's rapt attention.

According to Mrs. Aithne, he had only a few moments to find the thin silver cord that would lead him to the Blue Lady. It glimmered almost like a soul. Nathan wrapped a blue silk ribbon around it and attached it to his belt. He felt the buzz of the crowd through the ribbon like plugging into a nuclear power plant; a resonance of positive vibrations and goodwill. The rush of adrenaline beat through his body and his eyes pulsed with energy.

Marty stepped back, a little awed. "Kid, you look like you could go ten rounds with the devil himself. You ready for this?"

He didn't answer right away. The blackness felt so vast and intimidating. "Thank you for being here."

They locked arms and jumped into the abyss.

*      *      *      *

The open blue sky, empty and vast, oppressively stretched over them. They stood in the desert upon the Highway West dwarfed by the city of bone and flesh that seemed to absorb the horizon and reach ever higher into the sky. This was the realm of the discarded possible and the never-was realized in one last place in the universe. Nathan felt the pull of the soul-thread towards the tainted white necropolis.

He was very glad that Mrs. Aithne had suggested the ribbon to tether him to it as the vastness of the Dreamlands would have made it forever lost to him. It ground him to hope represented by the Blue Lady and channeled all of that essence into his flesh and soul. A small part of his mind still heard the children singing in this desolate land; a kernel of light to fight the darkness.

Marty dropped the duffle bag and armed himself with a gladius strapped to his side, pistols in his belt, and cradled a wicked looking shotgun.

"Think you brought enough dynamite there, Butch?" Nathan asked.

The old man popped a wad of gum into his mouth. "Some of us

don't have superpowers, kid. We have to kick ass the old fashioned way."

The dream of the sun blazed overhead as they walked towards the horizon. Thousands of blackbirds filled the sky blacking it with furious clouds as they cawed with a fierce anger. Nathan shielded his eyes with his hand and looked up thankful that so many of his feathered friends had joined them. "It worked!"

"They tagged along with our souls, Nate." Marty shook his head, stunned. "I didn't think it would work. A little bit of Papo must have survived inside of them."

The thought of their fallen friend cheered his heart considerably. It felt good to be reminded of why they were fighting. "I hope so. It feels right that he'd be here fighting the good fight."

As they walked closer, the distinct features of the city of bones sharpened into domes of stretched flesh upon towers of bone and cartilage that had been built with arcane and unnatural angles unknown to men. It stank of despair and rot and hurt. Their eyes ached merely to gaze upon the necropolis. It was as though they were gazing into a black sun and their eyes froze and cracked with despair. What manner of beast could live and thrive there? What horror forged Cenotaph to erect a monument to living death?

Slowly, creatures painfully emerged from the bones; birthed from the flesh and the despair. Cries of anguish carried forth pleas from the damned. They were the hidden secret of every murder. Every hideous deed ever done in the dark and never brought to the light lived in their corrupted essences. Nathan instinctively knew what they faced. "Can you feel it? Those are the souls of the damned?"

"We're in the region of the Dreamlands that boarders Hell." Marty gripped his shotgun tightly. "How can Cenotaph call upon the souls of Hell?"

A legion of the damned souls marched upon them. Malevolent hate shimmered in their black eye-sockets. Each step, every reach of their claws, was a desperate struggle to claim the warmth of flesh and to consume the purity of their souls. "Nate, this shit just got real!"

Nathan looked up at the sky once more and asked for their help. He had learned the secrets of the avian. It was the last lesson that Papo had taught him and it applied equally to humans. All birds dream that they are the eagles of the sky. Upon his signal, they attacked.

The damned dead and the souls of the blackbirds fought bitterly without mercy or quarter. Countless waves of the brave blackbirds dove into the fray. They pecked and clawed the damned scions of Hell. Damned flesh and feathered souls scattered about haphazardly upon the dusty desert floor.

One by one the blackbirds exploded in the sky. Nathan felt the loss of each soul as a pang in his heart. They were losing the advantage quickly. He raised his arms and used the anger and the pain to summon forth eldritch energies and blasted at the coming horde of the damned. Swaths of the damned were exploded back to Hell. The legion of the damned charged ahead in a giant crescent arc, attempting to flank them on both sides.

The sheer volume of the legion coming wave after wave allowed small groups of them to cross the line of fire and dodge the murder of crows. Those that managed to get close were mowed down by Marty and his shotgun. Despite his best efforts, several managed to get close enough to claw and bite their flesh. Each successful attack distracted Nathan just enough that the legion was allowed to move that much closer.

Nathan learned to moderate his attacks least he faint for exertion. He brought forth great strikes of lighting from the sky and animated the sand and the muck to pull the dead back into the earth.

The damned did not tire nor fear for their safety. What did those that dwelled in Hell have to fear? Nathan waved his arm and a mighty quake created a deep gulf around them. They did not stop. Crawling and shambling into the black abyss until they filled in the hole and their very bones and flesh made a bridge. They were forced to pay for every inch of their advance with their blood and sweat.

The birds slowly one by one fell to the claws and the maws of the dead until there were no more. Nathan felt their death cries all around him like a thousand cuts to his flesh. His spirit waned, but he tried to press on.

"Gah! Everything smells like overcooked bacon!" Marty grumbled, reloading the shotgun.

"Now you've done it!" Nathan warned. The energy swelled in his heart. The anger refueled him and forced him to continue. "You just ruined Sarah McCreedy's bacon! I owe you one!"

He raised his hand and allowed his heart to completely open to the soul-thread. A distant song from a land so far removed Hell built to a crescendo of hope and cheer. His knew instinctively that soon his advantage would fade and what greater weapon was there against Hell except hope?

Fire rained down from the sky devastating the landscape. Flesh and bone and bile melted in the infernal maelstrom. Marty watched the destruction from the safety of the glittering blue energy dome protecting them. His jaw dropped with horror as the complete and absolute devastation cleansed the desert.

Once the bombardment ceased, Nathan lowered the shield. He was breathing hard and his face flushed with exertion. Marty opened his duffle bag and handed him a bottle of water. He unscrewed the lid and slowly swallowed some of it. "Think we got them?"

Marty shook his head and pointed. More and more of the damned crawled forth from the city of bones. It showed no sign of slowing or stopping. "Another wave is coming!"

Nathan waited until the last possible moment, when he had proved that he was a valid threat to Cenotaph and had reached the threshold of the city of bones, but had not wasted his energy in the battle. "Monomachia!" The dead stopped silent and furious. "As in the days of old, I issue the call of Monomachia as did Achilles when he slew Hector!"

The city of the dead laughed. "Nonsense! You are but a child. What do you know of the old ways?"

Nathan smiled ferally. He had expected this and put on his best fight face. "And you are afraid! Your time has passed and you fear me. I wonder how those you serve in Hell will take it if you reject this offer freely made."

"I cannot die, fool!"

"I can destroy your form. Isn't that true?"

The voice of the city boomed. "What are your terms?"

"I wish the freedom of the Blue Lady and the one known as Eve," Nathan declared.

"And should you lose?" Cenotaph asked.

"You can feed from my soul."

"Nathan! Marty cried.

"This is the only way to tempt him. I know what I'm doing!"

Cenotaph emerged from the darkness of the white necropolis cloaked in a robe of sundered skin pocked with the screaming faces of the damned. He wheezed with every step; an ancient man with burned flesh that fell from him like leaves in fall. His eyes were black pools empty of emotion save despair surrendered by dark circles of flesh as though he had not slept soundly for many years. His fingers were gnarled and broken, but moved quickly as he dragged them through the last whips of his white hair. "How does the phrase go? Ah yes, allow me to introduce myself."

He had not imagined that his enemy would be an old man barely able to stand. How could this creature that stood before him be a threat? Was this what he was afraid of for so long? "I know who you are, Cenotaph."

"Do you now? Not yet I think. You were brave to face my Legion of Betrayers. The most foul and damned souls in all of Hell. My single reward for this miserable excuse for a life." Cenotaph nodded with respect to Nathan. It was a surprising human quality. "I would not kill you this day. You have been used by those that you have trusted the most and I know how that feels."

This Nathan did not expect. What was Cenotaph's game? Was he subtly trying to trick him? And yet, none of this story made any sense. Why would someone this powerful need Eve? Was Marty keeping yet another secret? "How have I been used?"

"You were placed on this path." Cenotaph gestured vaguely to Marty in a dismissive fashion. "Manipulated by your Uncle to right old wrongs and salve his conscious. Everything that shall happen this day stems from his actions."

He shook his head defiantly. "This is between you and me. You arranged for the New Flesh to kidnap Eve."

"And Eve did not change your perspective. She did not open your mind to new possibilities?" Cenotaph smiled with rotten teeth and split lips. "You know nothing of the true nature of all of this. And what they want from you."

"You want to talk? Tell me your real name and then I'll listen," Nathan declared defiantly. "Otherwise, let's get to the fight. You're trying to burn me out."

"You've already lost your connection to the Prefontaine Fountain, Nathan Carver. The blue ribbon has been cut. That was very clever by the way." He gestured up and down his body and laughed hollowly. "Likewise, the investment pacts that have kept me young and fresh have been halted for duration. A rare moment of weakness, I assure you. The harmonic resonances of your little plot and your challenge caused my links to be severed however temporary."

Cenotaph rubbed his belly proudly and then added. "Had I not just consumed Tenochtitlan trapped by you in the Dybbuk Box, I might have died ever so briefly and we would not have been able to have this conversation."

"He's stalling, Nate!" Marty warned. "Trying to recover from the mojo you laid down on him."

Nathan nodded. "Tell me who you are now! Or this conversation ends now."

"Do you know the meaning of the word cenotaph? It is an empty tomb. An empty place you place the dead until you are ready to bury them. A suitable nom de plume, I thought, for my unique circumstance." The decrepit old man sighed and then nodded as though talking to a disruptive child. "There is a very old story about Hell. It is said that there are nine circles. The ninth circle is the very center of Hell surrounded by the Titans of old where there is lake of frozen fire called Cocytus that burns eternally. This is where the greatest traitors of all time are kept. My throne of ice and tears awaits me there should I ever be allowed to embrace death."

"My God!" Marty cried. "Nathan, I think we need to rethink this. I know who this is."

Nathan ignored his uncle. This was a game of nerves and he wasn't going to be the one that blinked first. "Who are you?" Nathan asked Cenotaph. "I want to hear it from you."

"A loyal follower that was once hatefully used so that his master could apotheosis." Cenotaph's words were bitterly cold. Nathan almost felt sorry for this man suffering for some weight of pain that clearly broke his soul. "And for that service I was forever forbidden to die."

"How can that be?" Nathan asked. "Even the immortals can be killed. Borri said so."

"I hanged myself once just after I performed by final service. I was dead for almost a day before my soul was brought back into this shell. I endured heartless agony as I scraped across the shoals and reefs of eternity tearing my soul to shreds. I must suffer and walk the Earth until the end of time when the Great Barrier falls and Hell comes to Earth. My story is told often. My deeds recounted at every corner of the world. I am the cause of the Resurrection for it could not have happened without the betrayal." Cenotaph turned to Marty. "You know who I am. The name cursed for generation upon generation. Say it."

Two words were spoken. Nathan's jaw tightened as soon as they were spoken. Words he never expected. "Judas Iscariot."

"And have I not suffered for more than two thousand years?" the eternally dying man asked. "I must be allowed to die. That is why I need Eve. She knows the secret of pleasing Death within her mind."

"I won't let you hurt her," Nathan stated coldly. "I don't care why you want her."

"Don't you see? She must surrender it to me. That's my punishment. I am being used again." His eyes were crazed. Mad after thousands of years of torment. "Forced to commit another great act of evil. I must do this for peace. That is part of the great design of the universe."

"And then the Great Barrier falls, right?" Nathan asked. "You want to put your selfish desires ahead of the entire world. Damn everything just to get relief! No. You made your choice. You'll have to live with your choice."

"It is my purpose to shatter the Great Barrier, but now it seems that I have no choice but to live with it for now. Perhaps after I have consumed your soul I'll have the power to break her." Cenotaph bowed slightly offering his enemy one last gesture of respect. Nathan felt the waves of power and despair wafting off the creature once known as Judas. "Very well then."

"Remember that you won't be able to invoke any of the higher powers in this, Cenotaph!" Marty warned.

The dark wizard laughed. "I have walked this world and many others for a very long time. I hardly need them to handle a whelp of a boy unprepared for such a battle. I shall have no need of any pacts to deal with one such as you."

Cenotaph raised his hands and a bolt of crackling black and purple energy blasted down toward Nathan. He barely was able to raise a sparkling blue shield to repel the attack. "You should have waited, boy. You might have had a chance in a few years."

The flames raged inside of him. Nathan screamed letting the fury erupt around them trapping Cenotaph in a cyclone of fire and agony. It seared his flesh until the wizard cried out in a powerful voice. "Stop!"

Nathan blinked, surprised that the rest of his body had frozen. He couldn't talk or even concentrate enough to summon forth an additional blast. His lips trembled and his jaw locked horribly as though a giant invisible hand reached through his skin and locked his throat.

"Curious to know how I have bested you before the fight even started?" Cenotaph pulled forth a small glass tube from his belt and held it up to the light. "It was sloppy of you to allow the New Flesh to capture your essence. One of the oldest ways of magic is powered via the principal of like is attracted to like. Sympathetic magic. Never surrender your essence."

How could Cenotaph have captured his essence? The New Flesh never collected anything from him. Because Cenotaph willed it, he could now speak, but only with great pain. Tears welled in his eyes as the pressure built in his eyes until they bled. "Don't understand."

"You copulated with the creature you named Eve. You spent your essence and left it in the garbage where anyone could find it." Cenotaph laughed and squeezed the tube. The dried flakes of Nathan's sperm mixed in with a gel solution washed over the wizard's hand and he squeezed. "The New Flesh rather enjoyed their bonus for delivering you onto me."

His heart stopped. It was as though an unbending invisible vice squeezed through his chest and clenched on his heart. His eyes budged fighting the whiteout as he began to slip into unconsciousness. Nathan wanted to apologize to Eve and Marty for being such a failure. And then the strangest sound he had ever heard rang in his ears. It was laughter.

Marty was laughing like an insane monkey on a drunken bender chattering away. "I can't believe it!"

"Do not think that your life shall be spared Martin Carver!" Somehow the grip lightened and Nathan was able to breathe again. "You will be next!"

"Doesn't matter!" Marty struggled to catch his breath. He had been laughing so hard that tears dripped from his eyes. "It's almost worth it."

"You find this amusing? Silence!" Cenotaph demanded. "You belong to me, Martin Carver. All betrayers do."

"We might die here today, but we'll be heroes. Our story will live on forever in legend." Marty laughed again, this time dropping to his knees. "You get to be the wizard that touched Nathan's man-spunk."

"What?" the wizard bellowed. Nathan felt the grip on him slip. Cenotaph's concentration must have been slipping. "You dare!"

"You heard me. Everyone will know that you won by touching his essence. Your name will be a joke forever."

It was a moment of doubt; a seed of surrender and that was all Nathan Carver needed. He summoned forth the fire of his soul and blasted the wizard. His power could not be denied and the bottle shattered; the essence was lost.

Released from the hold, Nathan struggled to stand. Marty stepped back. He might be willing to throw in a few comments, but he knew that if he acted physically, the law of monomachia would be shattered and they would have to deal with a fully powered Cenotaph with all of his invocation pacts. Win or lose, he knew that his nephew had to win this fight on his own. By the time Cenotaph was able to fire another volley of attacks, he had recovered enough to raise his shields.

Cenotaph flicked open his fingers and cast a multitude of bone shards. They penetrated the energy barrier that Nathan erected and then burst into a swarm of devastating skeletal wasps that bit and tore at his skin and flesh. He screamed and tried to swat them with his hands, but that only cut and shred the flesh from his bones staggering him to his knees.

Nathan summoned for snakes made of the very desert to swallow whole the beasts. They twined around his body to protect him and consume the horde. Cenotaph continued to release wave after wave of black lightning hammering against his shield until it faded into blue glitter that dropped to the ground like coins dropped into a fountain for a wish that would never come.

Black razor-thorned whips shot out of Cenotaph's fingers scourging Nathan's arms and back. The sand snakes bit into the tendrils forcing both to dissolve into dirt and sand. His back shivered from the poison and his hands shook.

What was it that Marty had said about magic? There were only three means to power it. The very act of the monomachia removed any threat of invocations from a higher power. Marty helped him eliminate the threat of the sympathy magic. Now they battled only with skill and their will. How much energy could a creature of despair build through mediation? Papo had warned him of the danger of burning through his reserves.

Cenotaph was thousands of years old, but did he have the strength of will. The old man's face drooped with exertion. His body suffered the ravages of time without magic to regenerate it continually. The only key to victory was to endure until Cenotaph started to burn.

The dark wizard wove spell after spell upon him. Incantations of fire and ice singed his flesh, only the will and his energy renewed his body. Nathan concentrated on everything he loved in the world for strength.

*Papa Ray reading to him as a boy in his deep baritone voice that would always mean comfort and strength. The gentle touch of Grandma Loni cradling him during a sweaty night suffering through a horrid bout of chicken pox. Watching movies late at night with Doug. Midnight walks with Phoebe. Long drives with Marty talking about the universe, the stories, and every story in-between. His first kiss with Eve and the taste of strawberries. There were so many that had given him strength; the McCreedys, Loxi, Mrs. Aithne, and then at the last poor Papo.*

He waited and watched his opponent using the memories and love of his friends and family as his last shield until the moment that Cenotaph began to stagger and his breathing turned labored and shallow. And then Nathan Carver stood before Cenotaph; his strength renewed and vital while he watched his foe burn from exhaustion and the magic took over his veins and his heart.

Nathan's hands burst with the savage white eldritch flame powered with the memories of his lost friends and the love of his family. It felt different; a profound purity in this place of the profane at the edge of Hell and the refuge of the lost and the damned.

"How is it possible that you still stand?" Cenotaph demanded.

He stepped forward, every movement sent shivers of pain in his limbs and his eyes glazed into a milky white. He no longer felt his face and his words slurred, but he had the strength to say one word. "Love."

The fire of his soul sprang forth from every limb, every orifice into an avenging blinding phoenix that dove straight into the already decrepit and burned flesh of Cenotaph. He had withstood the terror of the ages and his eternal curse, but the purity of Nathan's love was a threat his tainted soul could not withstand. The horror of that which had been denied to him proved too much and his puny soul fled the shell leaving it to crumble to dust and ashes.

The city of bones mirrored the body of its foul master. The domes of flesh burned disintegrating to ash. A mighty earthquake shook the remaining city into ruin and collapse leaving only two figures in the ruins. He ran to Eve and instantly shattered the blood binding that bound her to that spot. They kissed though it pained Nathan. He hugged her tightly promising her to never let her go.

The shimmering essence of the tupla the Blue Lady appeared to them and granted them her blessing healing his tangled and bloody flesh. Her hair was blue and curly with flowers growing in her hair. Her skin was a soft aqua as though she had been painted. "The waters of the Prefontane Fountain shall flow again. Hope will return to Seattle."

Marty hugged all of them. "Did we win? Is it over?"

"The battle rages onward unto every generation. Cenotaph will return once more. You shall not be able to stop him with monomachia again. He shall be leery of the power inside of your hearts." The Blue Lady kissed Marty on the cheek. "But on this day a great battle was won."

"I remember, Nathan." Eve kissed him once more. "I remember why I came here and I still love you."

"I love you."

"But there's a secret I must tell."

"I already know that you met me as a kid." Nathan squeezed very hard. "It only made me love you even more."

Tears welled in her eyes. "No. I came here to prepare the world. Within a generation the Great Barrier will fall. You will lead humanity to prepare for the new age."

# Chapter Seventeen: Lay Your Weary Head to Rest

Nathan Carver hated stepping into water if he was unsure of the footing. It stemmed from a camping trip with Papa Ray long, long ago. The fear remained hidden in the back of his mind, but the bright light of the summer day stifled it. The dark cold waters that washed along Alki Beach hid a thin strand of sand and rock buffering along the Puget Sound. Colorful kites flapped overhead as seagulls fought each other for the scraps of bread offered to them by the beachgoers in relaxing chairs. He squeezed Eve's hand trying to dump his worry in the pleasure moment, but couldn't help but look over his shoulder watching for monsters. She stood on the tips of her toes and kissed him once more. "You look lost."

"It all just weighs down on me." He had felt this way ever since they had returned from the Dreamlands. "We're talking about the end of the world. No more concerts, summer dances, school, stories, songs, families. Everything that's ever been or ever could be. . .gone."

"Silly, silly boy. That's not going to happen tomorrow. We have time enough ahead to look to the future." She tugged at his arm dragging him deeper into the chilling water. "Look at everything you've done. You saved me from Cenotaph. Released the Blue Lady to spread hope to the hopeless. Restored your uncle's sight and found a cure for his cancer. That's a good enough start for any legend."

Nathan tried to laugh, but it caught his throat, almost choking him.

"I'm not a legend."

"Not yet. Legends start off as a story. All of us made a little difference. You, me, Marty, Papo, Loxi, all of us really. Those stories will touch others and they will make their own stories and a legend will grow as it is needed."

"History is just a way of saying His Story," Nathan said recalling the favorite phrase of his favorite teacher. "The story of all of us."

"One story leads to the next. You saved me, but you helped others. Mrs. Aithne remembered why she loved humanity. My father remembered why he wanted to live. All of us in turn freed the Blue Lady and she spreads hope. That hope will fuel more change and more choices." She smiled widely and her eyes sparkled in the light. "You went out into the world and did some good. We all did."

"You really do remember everything, don't you? What you were? The secrets of the universe?" Nathan asked gingerly. It was awkward holding a woman that might as well be a goddess. "All that meaning of life stuff?"

Eve shook her head. "Morality has a price. The gift of life is the veil of death. I know my purpose. I know what I was. I had to give up eternity for the flesh."

"Is Cenotaph really who he claimed to be?" Nathan asked. "Is that even possible? What does that mean?"

"He was a man once. Just like you. He made a terrible choice and betrayed his best friend. The man he loved most in the world." Her voice turned sad, but even then Nathan detected a hint of hope. "It's a terrible burden to have your very name become a curse."

The philosophical implications swirled around in his mind like a maelstrom. "Is it true? Was he Judas? The actual Judas?"

"That name was his at the beginning of his story, but he is not merely that name any longer. Each step he took was another choice. Our choices change us in subtle ways until we renew ourselves."

"He said that it was his destiny to bring down the Great Barrier. Is that true?" Nathan asked.

"Destiny is a human concept." Eve twirled in a circle, splashing around. "Everything we do touches the universe, each other. That's the point of it all, isn't it?"

"I don't know that I can make a difference, Eve. It's all too much. The New Flesh is still out there waiting for me to crack. Cenotaph will return eventually, won't he? I don't think I can fix all of this. Not alone."

She laughed once more. "Silly! You aren't supposed to fix everything. That would make you a god! You are the Last Scion of the Light. It will fall to you to find those willing and able to fight in the last night before the fall of the Great Barrier."

"Why?" Nathan asked. "Why me?"

Eve hid her face with her hair. "I brought you into this."

"How?"

"The task was given unto me to select one that could gather the others. I searched the world and found a young boy left alone on a farm; abandoned by his mother and aching for love. I knew then and there that you would always understand the purpose of a community. You'd always feel the loss of a connection and understand the power of brotherhood."

Nathan scoffed. "I'm no hero. I only got this far because of the friends I've made along the way."

"Silly." She splashed a wave of water at him drenching his shirt and face. "That's the whole point. You build a new community and reforged old bonds. Look over there! You started something that will grow."

He saw a spot along the beach where Sarah McCreedy rubbed lotion on her husband on a thick blanket. It amused him to see the old tattooed man enjoying the sunlight next to his wife sharing a rare smile. Loxi listened attentively as Marty serenaded her on his old guitar. Mrs. Aithne rested at a nearby table under a large canopy umbrella playing chess with Remington Borri. "What am I supposed to see?"

"A community." She pulled him close. "This is how it all gets started. A new circle to fight the darkness."

He pulled her close. "Are you sure, you can't come back with us now?"

"I can't. Not now. I was selfish before," Eve admitted. "And I must contain that."

"You've given me everything. I never imagined on that farm that I'd have such adventures. How can you say that?" Nathan asked.

"I felt for you. I wanted to hug you across the dimensions. Cradle you to my flesh. I envied your will and soul. It was why I allowed them to capture my essence in a cage of flesh and bones."

"That wasn't part of the plan?"

"I was supposed to inspire you; not fall in love. You almost died. I should stay with Father for a few weeks to learn his secrets and ensure that he keeps his word to Marty." Eve leaned up and kissed him. "Besides, I do not know if I am ready to meet Grandma Loni. Marty makes her sound quite frightening."

"Borri isn't your father. He's more like your creator. Or blood donor." Nathan scowled remembering that Borri had intended her body to serve as his wife. "And besides, he always keeps his deals."

"We need him in the light. He was a good man once; burning to change the world for the better in a time of darkness until the world crushed his soul. You know what is at risk. He needs to be part of the community."

"I know. I just wish you were coming with me," Nathan said pouting. "I don't like the idea of you staying with him. Who knows what the city will be like when they realize Cenotaph is gone?"

"Loxi said that I could stay with her. I should be perfectly safe between Mrs. Aithne and my new father. We'll meet up with you as soon as we're able."

"The summer has passed by really quickly." Nathan sighed thinking about driving home. "I do owe it to them to explain why I'm not going to school."

"There are many miles ahead of both of us. You won't forget me? Or find another pretty girl?"

"Never!"

Eve giggled. "Never is a long time. I'd understand if you wanted to find a human girl. A real one."

"Lady, you are a real human girl.  The Blue Lady said so."

\*    \*    \*    \*

The blinking yellow hazard lights shone through the raging storm. It was the middle of badlands between Oregon and California and a red corvette was haphazardly parked along on the side of the road in the black of night. Jagged claw-like scratches marked its sides. Bits of scattered tire littered the road. Through the cracked windshield, they could see a man clutching his head fighting to remain awake.

The 1977 Craftsman skid to a stop and parked in gof the road. Two men left the van ready to help. One was an older man with a mustache and an eye-patch. His name was Marty Carver. "Rest easy. Try not to move."

The other was a younger man with blond hair and a wicked smile. He walked to the driver's window and knocked. "My name is Nathan Carver. This is my uncle Marty. We're out here in the world to do some good. We can help you."

Nathan decided that if this was his destiny, it wasn't a bad life at all.

# About the Writer

**Jason Andrew** lives in Seattle, Washington with his wife Lisa. By day, he works as a mild-mannered technical writer. By night, he writes stories of the fantastic and occasionally fights crime. As a child, Jason spent his Saturdays watching the Creature Feature classics and furiously scribbling down stories. His first short story, written at age six, titled "The Wolfman Eats Perry Mason" was severely rejected. It also caused his Grandmother to watch him very closely for a few years.

His short fiction has appeared in markets such as *A Mytho Grimmly: A Lovecraftian Fairy Tale Anthology* (Wanderer's Haven Publications)), *Frontier Cthulhu: Ancient Horrors in the New World* (Chaosium), and *Atomic Cthulhu: Tales of Mythos Horror in the 1950s Coins of Chaos* (Chaosium). In 2011, his story "Moonlight in Scarlet" received an honorable mention in Ellen Datlow's List for Best Horror of the Year.

In addition, Jason has written for a number of role-playing games. His most recent projects include *Mind's Eye Theatre: Vampire the Masquerade* (By Night Studios), *Shadowrun: Data Trails* (Catalyst Game Labs), and *Rites of the Blood* (Onyx Path Publishing). He currently holds the position of Developer for the Mind's Eye Theatre line published through **By Night Studios.** Check out his website at http://www.jasonbandrew.com

# About Simian Publishing

**Simian Publishing** is a small press company devoted to primal dark fantasy and horror fiction. We're interested in seeing how the old gods, monsters, and Jungian archetypes work in the modern world. We want fiction that touches our souls.

With Print on Demand technology, Simian Publishing is able to take chances on a story or novel that might never see the light of day through a mainstream publisher. Currently, we looking for more direct distributors, but for now you can find our products on a variety of online stores.

www.simianpublishing.org